FROSTHAMMER
DWARVES OF NAGDOR

AETHEAON CHRONICLES
BOOK THREE

LEONARD D. HILLEY II

 Formatted with Vellum

FROSTHAMMER: THE DWARVES OF NAGDOR
AETHEAON CHRONICLES: BOOK THREE

LEONARD D. HILLEY II

AETHEAON MAP

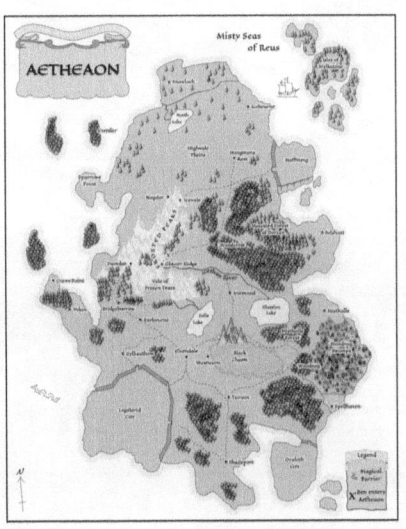

FROSTED PEAKS MAP

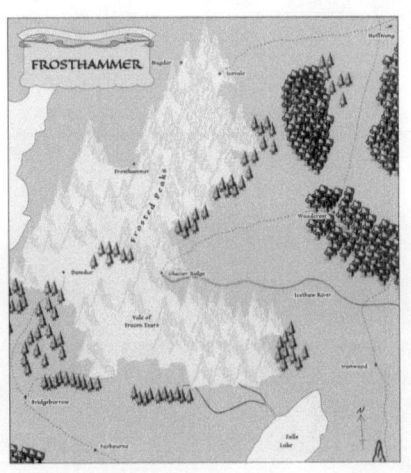

ONE

oldair—Nagdor's newly appointed Dwarven King—marched through the dungeon halls beneath Hoffnung's Castle, escorted by Drucis and Dwiskter. Their chainmail tunics clinked in riveting waves against their steel plate-legs. Their hair was tied in long braids down their backs.

Reading Boldair's emotions was difficult, despite his narrowed brow and hardened face. His eyes indicated the internal, stormy struggles his weary mind endured. Neither Dwiskter nor Drucis offered any words as they strode down the hallway, but occasionally, they gave brief side glances to Boldair. During times like these, silence offered more assurance than words.

Their heavy steel armor and boots rattled and echoed their unified purpose in equally timed steps. Since they weren't in a hostile environment, their helms were with their mounts in the Royal Stables.

Near the steel prison gate, two Hoffnung guards stood at attention with their swords sheathed. Their heavy, long shields were propped against the wall. When they noticed the three Dwarves marching their direction, their eyes widened, and they grabbed their shields.

After recognition set in, the guard to the right of the gate set his shield against the wall again. He took a heavy key ring from his belt and unlocked the door.

"Welcome, King Boldair," the guard said. "Queen Taube sent word of your arrival earlier today."

The guard swung the gate open. He took a torch from a barrel of viscous pitch and touched it to the flaming sconce. The torch ignited with a quick engulfing swoosh, and hissed momentarily before curls of black smoke rose.

Boldair faced Dwiskter and Drucis. "You two wait here."

"Are you certain?" Dwiskter asked with a frustrated frown.

"Aye," Boldair replied. "I won't be long."

Dwiskter and Drucis exhaled heavily but didn't relax. Their massive hands rested on the hilts of their weapons. Their eyes stared into Boldair's. Without words, the new king recognized their devotion. Should events somehow go awry, the prison gate wouldn't prevent them from rushing to his aid. Not that Boldair expected any true danger. His weaponless father was enclosed *inside* a cell, after all. The Hoffnung's guards were no threat, being close allies. However, entering any prison offered unforeseen dangers, because no prisoner could be trusted, especially not his own father and Nagdor's former king, Ulthor.

Boldair shook his head with disappointment. How horrible to have a father he couldn't trust.

Ulthor, now dethroned, might still have loyalists determined to free and return him to his former throne. Even the worst vagabond rulers had ardent followers who were blinded to their transgressions. Some dwarves in Nagdor might've believed Ulthor's constant condescending insults about Boldair. They might view Boldair too weak to rule Nagdor successfully. And if so, those dwarves were his greatest threat and camouflaged enemies that held an advantage since he didn't know who they were.

"This way." The guard pointed to the right.

The dungeon prison in this castle was, by far, more *comfortable* than any prison Boldair had seen in other kingdoms. Some prisons he remembered from the *other* side of the bars. Such was the price of a drunken, boastful dwarf whose tales of vast treasures ignited the jealousy of lesser treasure hunters who angrily called his honesty into question. Nothing angered a dwarf more than accusations of dishonesty. Boldair's temper flared whenever tavern patrons attacked his veracity. He seldom lost a tavern brawl, but at times, the guards in major cities subdued and arrested him. Not for a crime, but for his own safety. The following morning, he awoke in a lightless acrid cell filled with mold and uncertain sticky, greenish-brown wastes he never dared examine closer.

Boldair winced and choked back his nausea.

Sconces blazed soft dancing fires outside each prison door. No cries of anguish echoed, so none of the prisoners were being tortured. None ever were in Hoffnung. Such was contrary to Queen Taube's nature but not necessarily unbecoming in a Dwarven prison.

No rats scurried along the corridor. Strangely, the prison lacked the acrid odor of the sewers or the gagging aroma of decaying flesh, which were common traits in other kingdoms' prisons.

No barred sections interrupted the thick, rock walls on either side of the hall. The dim passageway seemed to go a quarter mile or more at an underground depth dwarves found suitable for habitation. The heavy, wooden cell doors were spaced every ten feet along the walls, but not directly across from one another to prevent prisoners from making eye contact with a prisoner across the hall.

Boldair recalled the miserable prison cell where Taniesse had imprisoned and threatened to incinerate him for stealing her treasure. Luckily, the dragon had a change of heart, spared him, and hired him to lead a battalion into battle. They regarded one another as friends, and for a new king, having a dragon for a friend was a great asset.

The wrinkles around his eyes creased, a half grin spread on his face, but faded with his next breath. From having been a prisoner shackled beside a crisp, decaying corpse to becoming Nagdor's next king, Boldair found the switch of fate more than unusual and somewhat satisfying. He'd witnessed a lot of odd things in his life. Not once did he ever consider visiting his father, the former King of Nagdor, inside a prison cell.

In many ways, months earlier, he half expected the tables might've turned the opposite direction. Except, Ulthor's uncontrollable, selfish greed caused him to deceive the dwarves of Nagdor and the surrounding Dwarven kingdoms. His father's deceit was something Boldair never anticipated. He found it difficult to believe even after receiving valid proof. His father was the last soul Boldair would've ever thought to possess a traitorous demeanor.

The guard led Boldair past a dozen cells before finally stopping outside a door. "Sire, should I open the door so you can speak face-to-face with your father?"

Boldair pursed his lips slightly. His eyes narrowed beneath thick, bushy eyebrows. He ran a hand through his long beard and slowly shook his head. In his gruff, authoritative voice, he said, "No. Speaking through the window grate is plenty."

"As you wish," the guard said. The guard spoke several Elven words. A glow-stone inside Ulthor's cell lightened the prison room. A moment later, the guard turned on his heels and marched to the gate.

Boldair rose slightly on his toes and looked through the barred opening. Ulthor stood in a long-sleeved, aged, sweat-soiled undershirt and pants. He was stripped of his armor, his weapons, jeweled rings and necklace, and worst of all, his crown, which now belonged to Boldair. By all measures, Ulthor was no more than any filthy peasant prisoner in the neighboring cells. Had his name been unknown, most wouldn't have thought him a former king.

Ulthor's gray hair was untied and frazzled. His dark-skin was abnormal and ashen like a corpse. The knots in his long beard had loosened and looked more like frayed rope than hair. The strength his gray eyes once possessed was absent. His eyes held the hopeless gaze of an aged soul near the threshold of death. His weakened resolve was progressing, but Ulthor wasn't a dwarf to readily admit his defeat.

His father's thick knuckles were bruised and bloodied from repeatedly punching the solid prison walls to diminish his anger. At least Boldair speculated that's what caused the injuries. It wasn't so Ulthor could escape. Even with the best blacksmithing hammer, these rock walls could withstand hours of the hard strikes without cracking or allowing a flick of the rock to chip.

The stones were carved from sea deposits composed of petrified layers of seashells and oyster shells. The stone was not only capable of resisting the blasting sticks dwarves used to open new underground tunnels, it could withstand the harshest cannon fire from the best

Dwarven cannons. The only weak points were the cell doors inside the dungeon halls. It was highly unlikely the outer prison walls could ever be breached.

Boldair stared at his father a bit too long and pricked his father's awareness. Ulthor turned toward Boldair with a fury that'd send Hellhounds scurrying to the Lava Pits in mere seconds. In spite of his father's indignant stare, Boldair didn't flinch. Instead, his eyes narrowed with an unleashed inner fury of his own.

TWO

"Come to gloat, have ya, ol' son of mine?" Ulthor peered through the barred, square window and gritted his teeth. Anger creased Ulthor's brow. A slight craziness loomed in his tired eyes. His wild eyes indicated he had slept little, if any, since his incarceration.

The shock of how far his father had fallen within several days weighed on Boldair. All the zeal and power the former king displayed before the Battle of Hoffnung was buried beneath his wallowing self-pity and loathing. Had Boldair passed this version of Ulthor on the street, Boldair wouldn't have recognized his father. He would've assumed Ulthor was a beggar.

"No, father," Boldair replied in a near whisper. "What's to gloat over?"

"Have you already forsaken the crown?"

"No."

"Then where is it? Why aren't you wearing it?" Ulthor asked.

"It's in a safe place."

Ulthor eyed Boldair with great suspicion. "Have the guard open the door. Or don't ya 'ave the courage to stand face-to-face with me? Bah! Figures. You've always proven yourself a coward."

"I've no fear of you," Boldair replied softly. "Or your mocking words."

"Because I've no weapons?"

"I've *never* feared you. I once held respect for you, but dat has faded."

"Then have the guard open the door, if you possess no fear."

Boldair stood firm, unflinching. His hardened, angry stare bore into his father's eyes. "I came to say me good-byes, father. Nothin' more."

"You're looking forward to your father's hanging, eh?" Ulthor said with a sudden, fiery glare. In two steps, he stood at the prison door. His hands tightened around the window's steel bars. He hoisted himself slightly until his face was in full view. For a moment, Ulthor's desperate eyes glanced at the Boldair's sheathed axe before returning a look of disdain at his son.

Boldair held his father's furious gaze without fear or faltering backwards as he might've done a few years earlier. Boldair had suffered several swift backhands from his father during heated arguments. Boldair never sought or considered retaliation since Ulthor was not only his father, he was the Nagdor's king.

Boldair rested his hands on the hilt of his heavy axe. His jaw tightened, but he said nothing. His anger faded and he looked at his father like he might a stranger.

Ulthor sneered. "A worthless son once under my rule now possesses my throne. Ah, ya shall boast well, adding fury to your drunken bard tales. The taverns are where you belong. Not on *my* throne."

"I've never desired the throne."

"Bah! You've waited a long time to find a way to *steal* it. Owning the city's wealth legitimately as king is a quicker reward than your gambles to find hidden, lost treasures. You never proved your valor on the battlefield. Not to me."

"No?" Boldair said. He pointed a thick stubby finger to the Dragon Skull pendant riveted to his steel collar. "You see this? Lady Dawn honored me, Dwiskter, and Drucis as Knights of the Dragon Skull Order because I led them and my troops through Hoffnung's gates. I fought the Vyking horde, alongside every other warrior, to regain the throne for Lady Dawn."

"Bah! *Any* dwarf could storm a city without fear when aided by three dragons. Even a halfling or sprite could defeat a city with dragons. But those dragons won't be there to protect Nagdor's throne should any outside forces attack my kingdom."

Boldair grinned. "It's not *your* kingdom. Your actions dethroned ya, remember? Your execution's an unavoidable consequence. The blame falls on you. No one else. You're a traitor to Hoffnung and betrayed an allied king. Most likely, *your* lust for gold's the reason Erik's dead."

"A trait you've inherited, you ungrateful scamp. You think robbing the dead isn't unscrupulous?"

"At least I didn't cost a king his life," Boldair said gruffly.

"It's interesting you favor the Dragon Skull pendant over wearing the crown, or did ya sell it for gold?"

Boldair's eyes narrowed. "Dat's enough with your insults."

Ulthor chuckled. "Well, you'll have the satisfying glory in seeing ya father hang in the gallows."

"Bah, I won't be watching," Boldair replied.

Ulthor's eyebrows rose. His wearied, bloodshot eyes widened with despair. Ulthor never sought pity. Did his father actually expect Boldair to hold sorrow after his father's treacherous actions?

"What were ya hoping for?" Although Boldair's face was stern, his eyes glistened tears in the flickering sconce light. "All me life I've held you in the highest esteem, father. Even when you belittled and taunted me. After you degraded my reputation with Nagdor's council, I still viewed you as a king with great valor and thought I'd never be near your equal. A braver heart I'd never known. My judgment was in error. You 'ave no valor. You're a traitor, a liar, and a scallion. No king could fall any lower than you."

"You dare judge your father?" Ulthor's face tightened with bitterness. Spittle flew from his mouth, sagged at the edges of his mouth, and coated his wiry beard.

"I didn't until the truth emerged," Boldair replied. "As king, I've the power to judge you openly."

"Taniesse cannot be trusted," Ulthor said. "If you believe she's innocent in all dat's transpired, you've been deceived."

"She and her two sisters fought to reclaim Hoffnung's throne for

Lady Dawn. You deserted Hoffnung's former king. I cannot trust ya, ever again."

"I fought the Vykings, too!" Ulthor gripped the barred window tightly. "I brought my best troops, or 'ave ya forgotten already?"

"I didn't forget, but your betrayal outweighs every good deed you've ever done. Every time someone mentions your name, I'll be reminded of who you really are."

Ulthor spat on the floor. "Bah! Ya think yourself sanctimonious now, do ya? What? 'Cause you led a small battalion into war after years of refusing to carry a battle axe to prove yourself worthy of being a Nagdor warrior? You think yourself better than those who served and sacrificed their lives in my armies for a hundred years?"

"I might not've been in your armies, but I've proven myself. Even had I followed your every detailed command to the utmost perfection, I'd have never been worthy of your acceptance or praise. You've held contempt for me my entire life. Perhaps you be more angry dat I've become something you've not? An *honest* king?"

Ulthor's eyes narrowed and darkened like obsidian. The flickering sconce reflected on the moist sheen of his eyes. The flames seemed a part of his internal, raging fury boiling to the surface. His reddened face glowed like metal inside a hot forge. If Ulthor was a mechanical pressure gauge, he'd have exploded. "Says the dwarf dat robbed the great dragons' treasuries of Aetheaon and the dead! Which, by all accounts, is treasonous to Queen Taube."

"Taniesse has settled the issue with me. The grievance was between she and I! No one else. Not Hoffnung. Not *you* nor any dwarf, elf, or human! She and I." Boldair's lips snarled. "One cannot be a thief by taking treasure from the dead. They've no use for gold."

"But she and her sisters were *not* dead!" A sly grin spread on Ulthor's face.

"Aye, tis true, but you told me a barrel of lies about her demise, didn't you? You convinced Nagdor into believing your lies. Some probably still believe. But not much longer."

Ulthor shook his head but didn't respond with words.

Boldair said, "When Taniesse revealed herself, I offered her treasure, and dat of her sisters, back without question."

"Did ya now?" Ulthor said. "Or was it the threat of her scorching breath dat persuaded you the most?"

Boldair huffed. "Have you knowledge of any dwarf dat's ever survived the fiery breath of a dragon?"

Ulthor roared with a belly laugh. "Aye! Yes! A coward through and through. Not something you can say about me though. I fought her. I stood boot to boot against—"

"Dragons don't wear boots," Boldair said.

"You know what I mean!" Ulthor said. Clenching his hands into tight fists, his moment of laughter ceased and his boiling anger resumed. "I risked my life and fought to strike a deathblow!"

"She meant no threat to you," Boldair replied. "Not until after you attacked her. She was on dat mountain peak looking for King Erik, as *you* should've been. But you feared she'd discover your true reason for being there. *Dat's* why you tried to slay her."

"Still—"

Boldair shook his head. "No, she could've killed ya after wind-blasting you unconscious. She could've fried your body and let the snowfall bury ya. Instead, she spared you."

"No matter." Ulthor released the bars and turned from the door. "There's no escaping me death now."

"Death comes for us all," Boldair said. "Regardless if one is a peasant or a king, Death comes. It's how we're remembered *after* our demise dat counts da most."

"Aye," Ulthor sighed. He glanced away from Boldair. "'Tis true, son. Perhaps you hold more wisdom than I ever credited you."

"Aye, father, dat's true as well. No treasure hunter survives this long without quick wits."

Ulthor looked at his feet. His shoulders slumped. "I've failed as a king, and worse yet, I've failed ya as a father."

"Too late for apologies," Boldair said with an even glare. He sighed and turned to walk away. "I've said what I came to say."

Boldair stepped away from the prison door.

THREE

"Wait, son." Ulthor's stern whisper weighted with grief.

Boldair faced the cell.

Ulthor gripped the window bars. "Our battalion's escorting you to Nagdor?"

"No," Boldair said. "Dwiskter, Forboud, and Drucis accompany me."

"That's it? No warriors?"

"It's enough."

"No." Ulthor shook his head. "Where's our battalion?"

"I sent them ahead with King Staggnuns and King Thorgum."

Uneasiness settled over Ulthor. Fear widened his eyes. "It's a long journey to Nagdor and not like before. You're the king. Don't you understand the dangers an unprotected king faces? Never journey without an army? Any fool understands '*a King's ransom*'. Should a tyrant take you hostage, he'll demand wagons filled with gold for your safe return. Don't risk the gold and silver coffers of Nagdor due to your foolishness."

Boldair frowned and grunted. "You value the loss of Nagdor's treasuries more than your son's? I've spent years scouring Aetheaon, ancient dungeons, and abandoned dragon lairs, often by myself. Finding treasure isn't a risk-free pastime."

"Dat was *before* you were king," Ulthor said with a tightly knitted brow.

Boldair shrugged his thick shoulders. "Besides, Forboud's always watched me back whenever he assisted me. More so, now dat I'm king."

Ulthor sighed and looked away. "Forboud was the one I'd 'ave chosen to take the throne."

"Why?"

Ulthor smote his chest with a solid fist before pointing a stern finger at Boldair. "I trained him. I've seen him in the heat of battle."

"'ave you now? Where was he during the Battle for Hoffnung? He wasn't amongst us, nor was he knighted into the Dragon Skull Order like I."

Ulthor stood silent for several moments. "No matter. Staggnuns and Thorgum had no right placing you on my throne. They've their own kingdoms to rule."

"Your crimes gave them little choice."

"Bah! I've never stuck me nose in their affairs. They've no—"

"What's done's done, father. Their choosing me was no doing of me own. They acted on behalf of the Northern Dwarven Alliance's bylaws. So, they had all authority based on circumstances."

Ulthor sighed. "Forboud's always been more worthy. Dat is, until he began scouring Aetheaon with ya to find treasures. *Dat's* when he disappointed me the most."

Boldair's eyes narrowed. "He's never spoken an ill word about you."

"He didn't need to say anything."

"What do you mean? You'd disown your sons because we've chosen to walk different paths than you'd hoped?"

Ulthor's broad nose scrunched. Bitterness coated his words like poison dripped from a Rusktin bat's fangs. With maddened eyes, he stared at Boldair. "Sometimes actions speak louder than words."

Boldair stood in silence while studying his bitter father. Delirium was overtaking Ulthor. "Indeed. Words of truth, father. Your actions put you here. You've disgraced even your father—my grandfather—The Mighty Thorseg, by your betrayal. If rocks could weep, a new river would rush beneath Nagdor, but even dat won't cleanse the filth you've brought upon us."

Redness flushed Ulthor's ashen face. His pale bloodshot eyes narrowed, and his jaw trembled.

"I pity what awaits you after death, for it cannot be good." Boldair lowered his gaze, turned, and walked away.

"Wait, son!" Ulthor cried. His thick hands wrapped around the bars. The desperation in his voice equaled the panic in his eyes. "Don't leave yet! I've more to tell you!"

"I'm done listening," Boldair said in a gruff whisper. He waved a stern dismissal without glancing back.

"Don't be a blasted fool! It's more than *your* life you risk! The Kingdom of Nagdor is at stake. You must listen! The war isn't over!"

"Aye, father it is! And we won!" Boldair took fierce steps.

"Not *dat* war! Another one stirs, it's in the making, and it'll be a great war unlike anything Aetheaon has witnessed!"

"More lies, father?"

"No lies."

"You're delusional."

"Turn around and listen to me, you blasted fool!"

Boldair's jaw tightened. He marched to the gate where the two Hoffnung guards stood. He refused to reply, even though Ulthor kept shouting and pleading.

"You've no knowledge of how to rule Nagdor, Boldair! Don't be a fool. The council won't serve ya! Keep Forboud at your side for guidance. I've failed ya as a father and disgraced our alliance, but don't you fail our kingdom! The Dredgemen never left Snowloch. Their city's farther underground. Much deeper than our own."

Boldair paused his stride at the last statement before shrugging off the comment. His fuming father loved a heated argument, and being confined inside the small prison cell didn't allow Ulthor any physical means to burn off his rage and frustration. Of course, his father could be telling the truth, but he might've said the words to capture Boldair's attention, in the hope to lure Boldair to the cell to continue arguing.

Boldair flicked his gaze to the guard. The guard unlocked the door and swung it open. The guard acknowledged Boldair and glanced toward Ulthor's cell. Ulthor bellowed.

"Does he prattle like dat often?" Boldair asked.

The guard, hearing Ulthor's tirade, shook his head. "No."

"If he continues, thrash him. He'll calm down. He's not so brave without an axe and shield. But unarmed, it'd still take the two of you and possibly a few more. Ya can't do dat to a king, but a *former* King who's lost his glory—dat be a different tale. You've my permission." Boldair gave a quick wink.

A slight smile tugged at the guard's lips, but he kept his composure in check. "Sire, I'm certain that's not necessary."

"Ah, ya never know." Boldair shrugged.

The guard secured the gate and stood at attention once more.

FOUR

oldair glanced at Drucis and Dwiskter. He ignored his father's bombastic, insulting shouts, as though Ulthor didn't exist.

Was his father telling the truth about the Dredgemen and their deep underground dwelling at Snowloch, or was it a pitiful attempt to further postpone Boldair's coronation?

Boldair curiously wanted to know, but he resisted. He was tired, hungry, and needed stout.

Boldair sighed. "Ah, now. We're a long way from home. Tis best we journey to Nagdor."

They nodded.

Forboud approached the gate where the dwarves stood. "What's our father shouting about, Boldair?"

"Utter nonsense," Boldair said in a low tone. He tapped the side of his head with a firm finger. "Father's deranged. *Dat*, he is. More so than ever. He doesn't take too well to confined quarters."

"Perhaps I should speak with him?" Forboud turned to the gate.

Boldair shook his head and grabbed the ruby-encrusted bracer covering his brother's left wrist. "No."

Forboud scoffed. "He's rambling endlessly down the hall. What did you say to him? What'd he tell you?"

"Just his usual spiel about how unworthy I am for the throne and how worthless I've always been."

Both Drucis and Dwiskter cocked a brow and faced Boldair. Their anger was instant.

"He didn't!" Drucis said.

"Aye, he did," Boldair said.

"I don't doubt you, brother," Forboud said. "Father's held no secrets about his feelings for you."

"Ulthor should speak," Dwiskter said, chuckling. "Tis *he* who stands on the wrong side of the cell door."

Forboud cast an angered gaze at Dwiskter. "Yet, he *was* our king. Hold some respect instead of mockery."

Dwiskter turned to Forboud with his hand on the heel of his heavy axe. "*Was.* He's no longer king. His treason outweighs any good he ever did. Your brother's da king now. Ulthor deserves less respect than being spat on. No sense insulting spit. Ulthor's the reason King Erik's dead, lest you so easily forget. I rang the alarm bell in Hoffnung when the Vykings stormed and invaded the docks. I took up arms to help Lady Dawn reclaim the throne. I willingly risked *my* life to save a kingdom to which I was an outsider. I'd do it all again. I serve your brother, Boldair, as the rightful king. Where are *your* loyalties? With your father or your brother?"

Forboud met Dwiskter's fierce gaze. Dwiskter's hand tightened on the axe heel. Forboud huffed and looked away.

Down the long corridor, Ulthor shouted obscenities. Within a few seconds, his voice lowered in defeat or perhaps he fell asleep. Nothing was worse than a disgraced king stripped of his rule and former glory, especially for a dwarf.

Dwiskter pulled his axe partially free of its sheath. "Well? Ya never answered."

Forboud stepped away from Dwiskter, eyed the locked gate with the Hoffnung guards, and he faced Boldair. "Brother, I'd never question your authority as king nor protest your seat on the throne, but father's *never* behaved in such a maddened behavior. Surely, he discussed more—"

Boldair's lips tightened. His eyes narrowed. "What was said between the *former* king and Nagdor's *new* king has nothing to do with ya."

Forboud read the anger in his brother's eyes. Boldair's bluntness cut quick. Forboud lowered his gaze. "Aye, brother."

"Now, let's waste no more time in Hoffnung," Boldair said with an optimistic tone.

"And leave father?" Forboud asked. "Are we not staying for his execution?"

"Stay, brother, if dat be your wish. You're entitled to do so, but I've no want to view his last moments. It'd make no less the bad memories of his ill-treatment of me," Boldair said firmly. He turned to Drucis and Dwiskter. "Time to fill our bellies with hearty stew and tankards of stout before we journey home."

"Now you're talking!" Drucis said. "I'm all for dat. But it best be something powerful enough to coil my beard hairs tighter."

Boldair laughed and placed his hand on Drucis' left pauldron. "In a few days time, I'll buy you a drink dat'll make ya think your insides are boiling lava."

"Bah! Nothing's *dat* good!" Drucis howled before offering a sly grin. Eagerness set in his eyes and drool hung at the edges of his mouth.

Boldair didn't offer the slightest smile. He held a dead serious stare the other dwarves recognized. Whenever Boldair boasted of a new treasure discovery, his eyes gleamed. Although Boldair embellished his treasure hunting events, he never lied about the loot. He might lie about *how* he obtained it, or exaggerate the obstacles he overcame to retrieve it, but he never lied about the quantity or quality of the gems or gold he had found.

"Oh?" Drucis said. His broad grin shrank. He wiped drool from his mouth with the back of his hand. "Such a drink exists?"

"Aye, it does," Boldair said. "The harshest drink I've ever swallowed. Its kick will drop ya to the ground. When you fade into the blurry darkness of its stupor, it kicks ya again."

"Sounds like good stuff!" Dwiskter grinned and combed his red beard with his hand.

Remembering the heat of the drink, Boldair cleared his throat and tears burned his eyes. "Ah, it's the most powerful drink I've had.

Thought I'd die. I swore I'd never drink it again. But these past few days, I've craved it."

"Ya got me curiosity," Drucis said. "Where's the tavern dat sells this?"

"*Not* a tavern. It's a small vendor camp on the winding Meadwyrm Pass," Boldair replied.

"Odd way to serve brew," Dwiskter said.

"Meadwyrm Pass?" Drucis said. "Dat's well *out of the way* to Nagdor."

The four dwarves stopped at another locked gateway and waited for a guard to unlock it. They turned to the right and ascended a short set of rock steps and faced another locked gate, which opened to the final ascending spiral stairs.

"I've a feeling we could've been at the camp for as long as it's taking us to get out of Hoffnung's prison," Drucis said.

Boldair chuckled. "Aye, tis a long ways down and back again. But perhaps the cleanest prison I've ever seen."

"True," Dwiskter said. "Peasants should 'ave it so good."

"At least your father's in a comfortable place," Drucis said.

Forboud frowned. "He's still going to be put to death."

"Traitors usually are," Dwiskter said evenly.

"He's a traitor to whom?" Forboud asked angrily. "He's king. A king serves no other king or he's no king at all."

Dwiskter turned sharply, clutched Forboud's throat with his thick hand, and hefted the prince off the floor and pressed him against the wall. Anger narrowed Dwiskter's eyes and leveled heated hatred at Forboud. "Your father *was* king. While I agree no king bows before another, one dat betrays another to gain wealth isn't fit for *any* throne. Your father's a traitor."

Forboud used both hands in an attempt to pry Dwiskter's viselike grip off his throat but couldn't. He gasped, and his face reddened.

"Dwiskter." Boldair shook his head. "Release him."

Dwiskter opened his hand and Forboud landed on his feet. Forboud rubbed his throat. Boldair stepped between Dwiskter and Forboud and stared intently into his brother's eyes.

"Do ya wish to travel to Nagdor with us?" Boldair asked. "Or are your loyalties to father too strong to accept me as your new king?"

Forboud took a deep breath and cleared his throat. "Aye, my loyalties are to you, brother. It's—too difficult to fully accept father as a traitor. Where's the proof?"

"The words came from his own mouth," Boldair said. "On the battlefield. What more proof is needed?"

Hurt saddened Forboud's eyes.

"Aye," Drucis said, "I was there when he spoke them."

Forboud's shoulders slumped. Glancing at the floor, he shook his head.

"It's hard to accept, brother. I genuinely wish it weren't true. Such disappointment cuts to the heart," Boldair said. "But our kingdom must redeem itself for what he's done. Understand, I never requested the crown. King Staggnuns and King Thorgum gave it to me."

"What gives them the right to dictate such an order?" Forboud asked.

"They've every right. Our kingdoms are joined with theirs in the Northern Dwarven Alliance. Whenever one kingdom suffers attack, the other two join the battle to defend the city. As kings, they're bound to hold one another accountable for derisive actions."

"Should we not hold a public hearing for father?"

"He *admitted* his guilt," Boldair said.

Forboud swallowed hard. "You'd have held him guilty regardless. The animosity between you and he are too great, which makes you bias."

Boldair gently placed his hands on Forboud's shoulders and stared into his brother's eyes. "Look, father'd rather have had you crowned king instead of me, but *dat's* not what the alliance decided. For whatever reason, they've placed me on the throne, even though I've never desired to reign. If it's too much for you to 'ave your brother reign over you, perhaps you should stay for father's execution. Afterwards, Damdur or Icevale might accept you into city."

Forboud frowned. A tear trickled down his cheek into his beard. "You're exiling me?"

Boldair smiled and shook his head. "Not at all, brother. But you've a decision to make. One not to be taken lightly."

"I'd like to speak to father," Forboud said.

"Aye," Boldair said with a nod. He removed his hands from Forboud's shoulders. "You've made your decision then."

Forboud's brows rose in confusion. "I 'ave? What decision did I make?"

"To stay behind and find a new home," Boldair said.

"I never said such a thing!"

"You don't 'ave to. Since father wants you on the throne, he'll do everything in his power to convince you to take it. You're my brother. I know you quite well. You covet the crown."

"Dat's not true," Forboud said, shaking his head. "What crime is it for me to talk to him, especially since he's to be executed? I can't talk to him *after* he's dead."

Boldair smiled evenly. "You were given a choice to make. You've made it."

Forboud shook his head. "No, if dat be the choice, I won't speak to him. I'll follow you to Nagdor. I hold no grudge against you. I vow to serve you without any malice. But you never had the bond with father like I 'ave."

Boldair looked at Dwiskter and Drucis and nodded. "'Tis true. Perhaps this is why Staggnuns and Thorgum chose me to assume the throne. If you remain behind to speak to him, you're not welcome in Nagdor."

"You don't trust me?"

"I don't trust his influence over you," Boldair replied. "Especially not in his current state of mind."

"Then tell me what he said before I arrived? It had to be more than him wanting me on the throne instead of you."

"He prattled about random nonsense, Forboud. Nothing more. Perhaps he's edged closer to senility than what we realized. He might've been bewitched or poisoned. Whatever the case, his mind's no longer rational."

Forboud rubbed his bearded chin. "His mind wanders from time to time. Dat always concerned me. I assumed he was preoccupied with his thoughts."

"Murder derails a mind," Boldair said.

"We don't know he murdered King Erik," Forboud said.

"He did *nothing* to rescue Erik," Drucis said. "And dat's essentially the same thing."

"What's your choice?" Boldair asked.

"I travel to Nagdor with you."

Boldair smiled. "Good to hear, brother."

"What other choice did you leave me?"

"Come." Boldair motioned up the spiral stairs.

"Ah, blast it all to Hell!" Drucis said with a gruff growl. "*More stairs!*"

"You think they'd might consider building a lift to the prisons, eh?" Dwiskter said with a sly grin. "For you?"

"Bah! They never took a dwarf's short legs into consideration with these endless stairs." Drucis cocked a brow and shook a stubby finger.

"Why should they?" Boldair asked. "They're human. Ever notice dat we never build high ceilings in our tunnels for *their* convenience and comfort?"

Dwiskter howled with laughter. "Aye, tis true! Never seen a human brave our mining tunnels and emerge *without* a bruised forehead."

Drucis laughed. He glanced at Forboud. Forboud wasn't amused by their conversation. In the light of the burning sconce, he appeared rather sickly. "You okay, Forboud? You look a bit under the weather. Maybe Hoffnung's high altitude is making ya lightheaded?"

Forboud grumbled.

"Oh, let 'em be," Dwiskter said. "It's not often he's ventured to the heights of Hoffnung's cliffs. He certainly didn't to fight the Vykings."

"He's a lot on his mind," Drucis said.

"Yes," Forboud said in a harsh whisper. "But nothing you'd understand."

"You're still young," Dwiskter said. "Wisdom increases with age. Whether you believe me or not, I understand you being torn inside concerning your father and Nagdor's transition. But the change will strengthen the city."

"I think more could be done," Forboud replied.

"For father?" Boldair asked with a shrewd stare.

Forboud didn't make eye contact. "Aye."

"When crimes go unpunished," Boldair said, "chaos goes unchecked. Greater problems emerge."

"I understand, brother, but it doesn't make it any easier."

"No," Boldair said softly. "It doesn't."

They reached a door at the top of the spiral stairs that opened to the east ramparts overlooking Hoffnung Bay.

"Oh, praise be!" Drucis placed his hands on his knees and leaned forward. "Level land, at last."

FIVE

Boldair stood outside the door. Drucis and Dwiskter stepped into the courtyards and admired the towers of Hoffnung's Castle.

When Forboud stepped through the door, Boldair placed a hand on his brother's arm. "Come, let's speak privately."

Forboud wiped sweat from his brow and nodded. "Aye."

Boldair walked with Forboud to the edge of the wall near the lifts. They stood overlooking the bay. Few ships remained in the harbor. The charred ruins of several Vyking ships bobbed near the docks.

"So you'd already noticed father's mind was slipping?" Boldair asked.

"Aye, from time to time."

"Did you notice anything else unusual about him?"

"Like what?"

"His complexion."

Forboud frowned and shook his head. "What about it?"

"Like me, he's dark-skinned. But today his skin's ashen white. Has he been sick?" Boldair asked.

Forboud shook his head.

Boldair rubbed his bearded chin. "Hmm."

"What?"

"Don't rightly know," Boldair said. "He and I 'ave always kept a wall wedged between us. Seldom 'ave we seen eye-to-eye, but he seemed out of sorts more so than normal."

"In what way?"

Boldair squinted. He folded his hands together and rested his elbows on the rock wall. His eyes wandered from ship to ship, and then he watched the workers on the docks. "He seemed—given to a fear dat everyone was out to get 'em."

"Would you not, given his current situation?"

"I'm not referring to his imprisonment."

"Then what?"

"Ah, his mind's in disarray, thinking a Great War's coming," Boldair said.

Forboud's eyes widened. "He said dat?"

"Aye, he did. You believe 'em?"

Forboud rubbed his bearded chin. "It's not the first time he's mentioned such."

"Then you know what we're dealing with? The details?"

"No, I don't," Forboud replied. "He's never said more. But, each time it's slipped from his lips, it's been when he studied the land maps bordering Nagdor. Whenever I've asked what he meant, he shrugged off my question and changed the subject. He's never told me more."

"Never?"

Forboud shook his head.

"He insisted dat you remain by my side and aid me with your council since I was appointed king."

"Dat brother, I can do."

"But given dat he's never told you more about this war, you think his mind has a few cogs loose? We've no true evidence."

"Perhaps." Forboud sighed. "What should we do?"

Boldair shrugged. "The only thing we can."

"And dat be?"

"We return to Nagdor."

"Like dat?" Forboud asked. "Leave him to his death?"

"Nothing more we can do here."

"We could send a medic to examine him."

"For what purpose? He'll be dead before too long anyway. Perhaps, he's caught a blight of some sort with all the undead they battled?" Boldair replied. "Or perhaps his madness stems from losing the rich ore veins along the mountain ridges?"

Forboud frowned. "Shouldn't his trial take place before the Dwarven Council and *not* before a half-elf queen? Her throne does not supersede ours."

Two Hoffnung guards turned and faced Forboud and Boldair with their hands placed on the hilt of their sheathed blades.

"Careful, brother," Boldair said with a firm gaze. "Speaking ill of Queen Taube will have you in the dungeon with father. Even though the war against the Vykings has ended, the Hoffnung Guard remain on high alert. Probably will be for quite some time to come."

Forboud glanced at the guards, shook his head, and lowered his voice. "Having father's trial in Hoffnung won't settle well for Nagdor, and you know it."

Boldair sighed. "Bah! It'll have to suffice."

"Why?"

"Because I'm not about to attempt transporting father across Aetheaon for another trial. Staggnuns and Thorgum agree dat father's execution takes place *here*. He betrayed Hoffnung. Therefore, it's their right to punish him."

"I suppose you cast the third vote?" Forboud asked.

Boldair frowned. "I do not oppose their judgment, which by every means is sound through and through."

Forboud shook his head. Tears burned his eyes.

"I know this is difficult, Forboud," Boldair said. "I wish there be a better way, but there's none."

"Your heart isn't as heavy as mine."

"Your assumption's correct," Boldair replied. "I've no doubt in the future dat today will turn to one of regret. A time will come when I'll wish to consult his advice, and I won't be able. When a father dies, his children become adults. We must make our own decisions and hope they're correct."

"Boldair, you don't know Nagdor's council like I. Should word get to them of your quickness to allow father's execution without an outright protest and petition before the Dwarven Council, you'll lose favor with them. Father never spoke highly of you to them."

"Ah, dat's no secret."

"They'll view you with utter hostility, brother. Mark me words," Forboud said.

"I've the feeling you do already," Boldair said.

"Not true."

"Isn't it? You're 'aving difficulty hiding your loyalty to father."

Forboud formed fists and hammered the top of the wall. He grunted and struck a fist to his chest. "Aye! I'm torn in me feelings. I don't want to believe our father's a traitor. I can't fully accept it but know I must. Dat part saddens me most. I spent more time with him than you. He trained me. We talked daily, except when I traveled with you. And somehow, at some unknown time, his mind altered. You'd think I'd have seen it long ago. Blasted! I can't even see it now!"

Boldair placed a hand on Forboud's shoulder. "Aye, he's not the same. Though you may not believe me, I ache inside. Nowhere as deeply as you. Regardless of he and I's differences, he's still me father."

"Then 'ave compassion enough to remain for his execution," Forboud said. "He's betrayed Hoffnung's crown, but if we're not there during his last moments, we've betrayed him as well."

Boldair let his hand slide from Forboud's shoulder. He shook his head. "Brother, it's not the same thing. I cannot wait behind to see his final moments. It's not something I wish to see, and not a memory I wish to keep, either."

Tears brimmed in Forboud's eyes until they spilled, trickled down his cheeks, and soaked into his thick beard. "Brother, me heart's heavy at your decision."

"I'm sorry, Forboud. Truly, I am."

"As am I. But I'll honor your wishes and return home with you. No animosity, I swear. But my grief will burden me for some time to come."

"Understandable," Boldair said.

"If it seems I hold anger and hatred, dat be toward me-self. Not you."

"Good to know. Perhaps in time, we'll understand the truth behind our father's actions and what distorted his mind beyond return."

"Aye." Forboud gave a firm nod.

Six

"Let's gather our belongings and travel to Meadwyrm Pass. Drinks are on me," Boldair said.

Forboud stared at the bay from the lift's ledge. His blue eyes shimmered, greatly resembling the water, but without the enlightened radiance. His eyes toiled darker, like a storm brewed overhead and a destructive whirlpool was forming beneath his feet. Despair consumed him.

Boldair frowned. "Did ya hear me?"

"Aye," Forboud whispered. "Drinks plummet the sorrow of a heart far deeper than it should suffer. Leave me to me pain."

Boldair left Forboud to stare at the bay. Dwiskter and Drucis talked to an old peddler, so Boldair joined them. The old man wore a tattered robe with the hood pulled over his head. His wiry white beard twirled down his soiled, frayed tunic. He patted the side of his packhorse's head. The horse was weighted down with heavy wares, and its knees almost buckled.

As Drucis spoke, he raised his hands in the air. "Aye, dat be when the Horned Beastlord hefted his axe and came at me full speed. His giant hooves beat the ground with such vibrating force, I almost lost me footing. His eyes blazed like hot coals and smoke streamed from his nose. In seconds, he was on me."

The peddler puffed his pipe with a half grin. "What happened then, dwarf?"

Drucis' eyes widened, his cheeks flushed, and spittle flew from his mouth. "Ah, I sidestepped him. He brought down his axe and sliced through his right knee. He bleated and toppled face first. His anger boiled so much dat flames flickered from his nostrils. Before he could hop on one leg, I lopped off his horned head, which is now mounted in the Gorefest Tavern."

"That's all?"

"What do ya mean, is dat all? You think you'd do better?" Drucis asked. "A crazed Beastlord? Nah, there's no way—"

"No, I meant, was his head the only trophy you took?"

"*O-o-oh*? Oh, no." Drucis shook his head. He turned the hilt of his battle axe to show two large polished topaz stones and a blood ruby. "These were in his coin pouch."

The peddler cast a greedy gaze at the gleaming gems. His shadowed eyes flashed a brief glimmer of red.

"Ah, now, don't be coveting these."

The old man held his pipe and shook his head. "Those stones don't draw my interest."

"Rare gems draw *anyone's* interest," Dwiskter said, stepping closer to Drucis.

"No?" Drucis asked.

"No," the man replied. "I'm more curious where you encountered a Beastlord. They're quite rare."

"Depends on where you're at. Beastlords are most common near active volcanoes," Boldair said.

The peddler regarded Boldair with sudden interest. He pointed an aged, crooked finger. "You ... you look familiar. Perhaps I've seen you during my travels. A tavern, maybe?"

Boldair offered a bold grin and chuckled. "Aye, I've visit a vast number of taverns. Some are like second homes."

"Before he became king," Drucis said.

"King?"

The man bowed slightly. "Your Highness. I'm honored."

Boldair regarded the man suspiciously. "Forget the formalities. We're not in Nagdor."

"Nagdor?"

"Aye."

The peddler stood in silence for several seconds. His hood prevented them from seeing his face or eyes. "But you're still king, regardless of what kingdom or hamlet you visit?"

"Aye." Boldair's face reddened. "Not quite used to the title. Dat's all."

"I see," the man said. "So you've recently been crowned king?"

Dwiskter frowned and stepped between Boldair and the peddler. "What business be it of yours?"

"Pardon?" The peddler stepped back and grabbed the packhorse's halter.

"Dwiskter," Boldair said firmly but softy. "It's all right."

"No, Sire, he asks too many questions," Dwiskter said. He frowned fiercely at the old man and gripped the heel of his axe. "You've another game at play, don't you?"

The peddler studied Dwiskter for a few moments before shaking his head. "No, I don't. Sorry to have troubled you. I'll be on my way. Lots of wares to sell and no need to waste *my* time or yours by being held suspect by dwarves outside their own kingdom."

"Hey!" Dwiskter pulled his axe slightly out of the sheath.

Boldair placed his hand on Dwiskter's shoulder and squeezed. "Let 'em go."

Boldair pulled Dwiskter to the side of the cobblestone path. The peddler led his packhorse past. Boldair waited until the old man was out of hearing range. "What be the meaning of dat?"

"Not sure." Dwiskter sheathed his axe. "I've an uneasy feeling 'bout him."

"He didn't pose any threat," Boldair said. "Not in any regard."

"Perhaps not," Dwiskter replied. "But mustn't take chances this far from Nagdor."

Boldair nodded. "Let's not be so ready to alienate passersby. After all, a king must show diplomacy. No need to create unnecessary enemies."

"Aye," Dwiskter said. His shoulders drooped. "I want ya to know dat I've got your back."

"No need to tell me," Boldair said with a broad grin. He patted Dwiskter's shoulder. "I know ya do, and I greatly appreciate it."

The peddler led his packhorse through the morning vendor tables and never offered a glance over his shoulder. The citizens approaching the lifts were dressed finer than the vendors in the market square. They were merchants who came to the port, perhaps to trade or wait for goods unloaded from the ships. Some were more arrogant than any aristocrat.

"Dat sight should fill anyone with delight." Boldair looked down at the harbor.

"What?" Drucis asked with a curious smile.

"Every kingdom knows the devastation the Vykings caused, but merchant ships haven't abandoned Hoffnung. The charred Vyking ship hulls stand a reminder to the victory Taniesse and her sisters won in this harbor."

Dwiskter grinned. "Aye, I was down there when the filthy Vykings rush from their ships the night they invaded. I must admit, the fleets of vessels stopping at the docks almost paralyzed me with fear. *Almost.*" He cackled. "But me fury quashed my fear. I killed several Vykings before reaching the lifts. I wish I could've seen the dragons setting the ships and their sails aflame."

Boldair laughed heartily and nodded. "Aye. But we see the aftermath."

"Yes. It's doubtful the Vykings will recover from their losses," Dwiskter said. "But on dat night. One thing still haunts me."

"What's dat?"

"How close I was to the Plague-bringer but I couldn't get to him before he vanished."

"We'll cross his path again," Boldair said.

"Dat I've no doubt," Dwiskter replied. "But had I reached him, I could've killed him dat night."

"Possibly." Boldair nodded. "Or worse, he'd 'ave inflicted you with the plague, and you'd be one of his."

Dwiskter thought about Boldair's statement for several seconds.

"Mors' power has weakened, thanks to Zauber. Hopefully, we can destroy him before he regains his strength."

"I wish we could've gone with Riese and Prince Manfrid to attack King Obed," Dwiskter said. His eyes gleamed with the thought of returning to battle. "Obed's tied to Mors."

"I know. I greatly considered joining Riese's battle, too," Boldair said. "If not for other commitments."

"Taking the throne?" Drucis asked.

"Aye," Boldair replied. "'Tis time I took my role more seriously. Less drinking and tavern tales, though I'll sorely miss *those* occasions. It's time I settle down and seek less adventures."

"Wait now," Drucis said. "We're not skipping the Meadwyrm Pass drink dat sets your bowel on fire, are we?"

"Goodness sake's, no!" Boldair grinned broadly. "A king mustn't go back on his word, now should he?"

Drucis released a heavy sigh. "Good. You had me worried for a moment."

"Sorry," Boldair said. "No, I'd not make a dwarf suffer such worry, especially over the promise of drinks. I'd wager you only manage half a shot of the molten drink."

"Bah! If it's a wager ya want—"

"Boldair!" a female said.

Boldair turned to see a tall, muscular woman dressed in armor with her midriff exposed. The golden dragon belt studded with various gems encircled her waist and hugged her right side. Her black sword hung on her belt.

"Taniesse?"

"I'm surprised you've tarried in Hoffnung. I expected you'd left for Nagdor days ago," she said.

Boldair nodded. "Aye, we planned to be gone before sunrise this morning, but I needed to visit father one last time before his execution."

At the mention of his father, Forboud turned his brooding attention away from the bay and joined them.

Drucis and Dwiskter stood to each side of Boldair and studied Taniesse's face.

"Far be it for me to offer bad news concerning Ulthor's execution," Taniesse said, "but the four of you need to accompany me."

"To where?" Boldair cocked a brow.

"We need to discuss your father's destiny," she replied.

"Why?" Forboud asked, stepping behind Boldair.

"All will be explained, but not here. Not in public."

"Then where?" Boldair.

"Come," she said.

The dwarves followed Taniesse from the lifts and through a narrow alleyway. She stood a good three feet taller than they, so she lessened her strides as she walked.

"So tell me, treasure-hunter, how do you feel as king?" she asked.

Boldair stared at his feet while walking. "Ah, it be no different."

"None?"

"No. Not yet, anyway."

"I suppose it's too early for the realization to strike you, but a king's weighted burden will become apparent soon enough," Taniesse said.

"What do ya mean?"

She laughed but never slowed her pace. "You'll see. You've yet to sit on the throne, give commands, or enact judgment. You're far from your kingdom, but I assure you, once you've ascended the throne, your life changes forever."

"*Now*, ya 'ave me worried."

"Worried? Actually, worry's the best frame of mind for a new king to possess."

"How so?"

She grinned, looked down at him, and stared into his bright, curious eyes. "You're less likely to make hasty decisions and learn what true wisdom is. You've matured since our first meeting. I'm impressed."

"Bah! I don't know about dat." Boldair shook his head. For her every step, he hurried two to keep her pace. The other dwarves worked hard to match his pace.

"Every decision you make as king has consequences. Weigh each mandate for its advantages and disadvantages before finalizing any resolution."

"Tis true," Boldair said.

Forboud rolled his eyes. "Phht!"

Boldair's jaw tightened and his eyes narrowed. But trying to match Taniesse's pace, he didn't scowl at his brother. "Where are we going?"

Taniesse turned right on Market Street. "Queen Taube requested your presence."

"Me?"

Taniesse nodded. "All of you, actually."

"Why?" Forboud asked.

"To further discuss your father's fate," she replied.

"What?" Boldair's brow furrowed. "I thought the decision had already been decided."

"In ways, it has," Taniesse said, "but an execution's never rushed."

"Why not? Even if the crime has been proven?"

"Even if the guilt has been proven," she replied.

"Father confessed before Staggnuns and Thorgum," Boldair said in a gruff voice.

"Yes, we know."

Boldair huffed his disdain but offered no words.

"You're not wishing to rush his death, are you?" Taniesse asked with a side-glance.

"He is," Forboud said.

"Is that true, Boldair?" she asked without a tinge of judgment.

"No," he replied. He turned and pointed a sharp finger at his brother. "If I need your input, Forboud, I'll ask ya. Now, pipe down!"

Taniesse glanced at Boldair without slowing her steps. "I sense great hostility between you two. Is this because the Northern Dwarven Alliance named you king instead of he?"

"Partly," Boldair grumbled.

"Aye, it is!" Forboud said. "Nothing *partly* about it."

Taniesse shook her head. "I never expected such."

"What?" Boldair asked.

"That the two of you would come to odds over the throne."

"I'm not at odds. *He* is. I never asked for the throne," Boldair said.

"Forboud believes he deserves it because father trained him as a warrior and a potential diplomat."

"I see the logic in his ambition," Taniesse replied.

"But tis not true, O' Great One," Forboud said. "I don't covet the crown. I don't feel entitled to replace father. The roots of this go much deeper."

Taniesse nodded slightly. "I see."

"Oh, *much* deeper!" Boldair said.

"In what way?" She stared at Boldair.

"Forboud's against father's execution, even though father's undeniably guilty. He wishes to turn a blind eye to father's crimes."

"Dat's *not* true!"

"Forboud," Taniesse said softly. "You had a more intimate relationship with Ulthor than Boldair?"

"I wouldn't call it *intimate*." Forboud snarled the word with bitterness. "But he and I spent a lot of time hunting, training, and discussing Nagdor's defense. I know the mining maps like the back of me hand. Father even discussed the plans for digging deeper mines to find better ore veins."

"So his execution proves more costly to you than Boldair," she said.

"Aye."

"Boldair," she said. "I recall how your father belittled you before we went into battle. But, before that, were you and your father ever close?"

"Never," he replied in a low voice.

"So the division between the two of you is jealousy over his affections?"

"Affections! Bah!" Boldair balled a tight fist. "Father has *no* affections. None except for himself. The way dat I see it, he should pay the price for his crimes and betrayal. So I don't see what this meeting has to do with dat. He's admitted his guilt. Death's the price."

"No one's questioning his guilt or his sentence," Taniesse replied.

"It seems dat way," Boldair whispered.

Drucis gave a side-glance stare at Taniesse. "Didn't Staggnuns and Thorgum already place the sentence?"

"They did," Taniesse said.

"So is dat going to change?" Dwiskter asked.

"Probably not," she replied.

"Then what's to discuss?" Boldair asked.

"That will be acknowledged once we sit with Queen Taube," Taniesse replied.

"Is there any chance he'll escape his fate?" Forboud asked. "Or dat his sentence could be lessened?"

"Doubtful," Taniesse said. "Let's discuss this no further. Not until we've met with Taube."

SEVEN

B oldair and Taniesse stood at the railing of the high balcony overlooking Queen Taube's Royal Garden.

"The city's destruction is barely noticeable," Boldair said, studying the gardens and streets below. "Hard to believe a war took place."

Taniesse smiled. "The peasants and citizens worked hard to erase the damage."

"Aye," Boldair said.

"Elven artisans from Woodnog offered their services to replace the statues and the decor the Vykings destroyed."

"Icevale and Nagdor 'ave metalworkers to reinforce the archways and gates," Boldair said. "The scorched ramparts are almost repaired."

Dwiskter and Drucis sat on a stone bench with various Elven rune symbols carved in the artwork. Forboud stood near a fountain with his hands clasped behind his back. His sad eyes warned of the unsettled turmoil churning in the depths of his mind and soul.

Queen Taube entered the upper patio, adorned in a sparkling gold gown. A deep sapphire stone set in gold hung on a thread of silver around her neck. She wore a glimmering ruby ring on her right hand,

and an onyx ring on the left. Almost hidden by the long sleeves of her gown were several turquoise tattoos of protective runes.

Dwiskter and Drucis stood. They offered slight bows of reverence and respect for the half-elf Queen. From the corner of his eye, Forboud noticed their homage, turned, and did the same.

Boldair and Taniesse smiled in response to Taube's radiant smile. The Queen's eyes matched the sparkling gems she wore. A web of magic enveloped her. Tendrils of her magic swept outward, reached and searched—it seemed—to detect the slightest trace of unseen malice or inner hostility any of her guests might harbor.

Although Boldair was unable to cast magic, he recognized and sensed its touch. When he stepped within several feet of Taube's proximity, the magical gems set in his weapons glowed in response to Taube's magical aura.

Taube's face didn't express any uneasiness or fear, but her detecting magic indicated she was on high alert, even though she reigned on Hoffnung's throne.

"Please, be seated," Queen Taube said.

Boldair and Taniesse left the balcony and approached the table. Taube motioned two servants with a graceful wave of her hand. The servants carried heavy wine pitchers, and promptly filled the prearranged flasks on the circular oak table.

"I extend my thanks to you, Taniesse," Taube said, "for finding King Boldair before he and his party left Hoffnung."

Taniesse acquiesced a nod.

Boldair lifted his flask and sniffed its contents. Despite his want to snarl his nose in protest to the drink offered, out of respect for Taube, he sipped the wine. He greatly wished it contained Dwarven Stout or something stronger. To his surprise the wine was pleasantly sweet, but not enough to mask the bitter taste of hops, causing his sip to progress into a larger gulp. He set the tankard down on the table, and out of habit, wiped his mouth with the back of his hand.

Amusement danced in Taniesse's eyes. She bit her lower lip, obviously holding back her laughter for the new king's crude mannerism. Boldair met her gaze and blushed.

Under his breath, Boldair muttered, "Sorry."

Taube smiled. "No apologies necessary. I wish to thank you, King Boldair, for your aid in retaking Hoffnung's throne. Taniesse and Lady Dawn informed me of you and your comrades' bravery. Dawn's truly impressed by your valor."

"Aye," Boldair said with a sheepish grin. "Happy to help. How's Lady Dawn?"

Taube's eyes met his for a moment. She smiled before laughing softly. "Proud to *not* be Queen, I suppose. The last raven message stated she and Caen are exploring every crag and forest in Aetheaon. A little taste of the outer world spurred her curiosity. Her spirit's too wild to accept the obligations of the throne. For now, at least, and of course, I cannot blame her. Her wanderlust is far greater than mine ever was."

"She's a valiant fighter through and through." Boldair raised his empty flask in a toast.

"Aye!" Dwiskter and Drucis said in unison.

Forboud observed in silence, not offering any comment or physical response.

"Her need to avenge your betrayal by Lord Waxxon was ruthless and boosted our morale," Boldair said. "I fought proudly beside her."

"As did I!" Dwiskter said.

Taube's face beamed with pride. "A princess gown ... she's outgrown. She never seemed to fit the role of a princess. She's more like her father than I. Rambunctious and free-spirited." She laughed. "I cannot count the number of times she snuck to hunt rats with the sewer rat-killers. Wearing one of her best dresses, too. She once brought back a string of dead rats and showed them to me with great pride."

Boldair, Dwiskter, and Drucis roared with laughter.

Taube shook her head. Her eyes were lost in memories. "No matter how much I tried to explain what it meant to be a princess, she paid me no mind. Nessa had a difficult time keeping track of her. Dawn was like the son Erik never had. Perhaps with her, he got the best of both, a daughter who served as both. He took her stag hunting in the forests many times when she was little, thinking I didn't know where they'd gone." She sighed. "I cannot rightly call her a princess now. Perhaps I never could with complete honesty. I find it difficult calling her a warrioress, though that's what she is in heart and spirit."

"Indeed." Boldair stared into Taube's eyes. A slight grin parted his thick beard.

"Dawn insisted you be knighted into the Dragon Skull Order, and rightly so." The radiant smile on her face faded. Sadness filled her eyes. "In spite of your father's betrayal to my husband, my heart holds no animosity to you. You're not responsible for Ulthor's actions."

"Aye, milady," Boldair said. "I knew nothing of my father's state of affairs. To put it bluntly, I still don't. Rest assured dat once I return to Nagdor, I'll overturn any of his affairs dat are damaging to Hoffnung or the other peaceful kingdoms. And, because of his greed and the ... his contribution to King Erik's ... death, I expect you'll carry out his execution promptly."

Various emotions struggled on Taube's face. "In time, he'll be executed, but I'm afraid not in the *immediate* future."

"How's dat?" Boldair straightened in his seat. His eyes narrowed. "Why not? He confessed and admitted his guilt in King Erik's demise."

Taube and Taniesse both nodded.

"He did," Taube said.

"Then why delay his execution?" Boldair asked.

"While it's true he confessed," Taube said, "I need *more* than his confession."

Dwiskter downed wine, set the flask on the table, and winked at the female servant. The servant blushed, filled his flask, and offered a slight curtsy.

"What more do you need?" Boldair asked.

"A trial," she replied.

His eyebrows rose. "A trial? Why?"

Taube folded her hands and rested them in her lap. "Regardless of his admission of guilt, a trial's necessary."

"What do you expect to discover from a trial dat you don't already know?" Boldair asked.

"That's what I hope to find. Discovery."

Boldair frowned.

"Ulthor didn't act alone," Taube said softly. "He couldn't have."

Boldair thought for several moments. His brow tightened. His eyes brightened and he looked into hers. "You think others in Nagdor aided him?"

"It's possible," Taube replied.

Boldair gave Forboud a shrewd, momentary stare. Then, he placed his fists on the table and leaned forward. "I shall find them."

Taniesse shook her head. "Undisclosed enemies are not readily found, especially when they don't wish to be discovered."

"Father knows more of what happened," Boldair said, "but he'd never confess it to me."

Forboud adjusted in his seat and cleared his throat. "He might to me."

Boldair glared at his brother and pointed a stern finger. "Oh, you'd like dat, wouldn't you? Father's scheming to put you on the throne. Perhaps you've conspired with him and *dat's* why you're so insistent to talk to him?"

Forboud shook his head.

"No, brother, I forbid it," Boldair said. "I cannot risk letting you speak in private to him."

Taniesse raised one brow. "I understand why you don't trust your brother but you need to set your differences aside, at least for now."

"I wish I could." Boldair fumed. "Father told me dat he'd rather have Forboud on the throne. Ever since I went to the prison and spoke to father this morning, Forboud won't stop his insistence to visit him. Like me brother said earlier, there's something *deeper* at hand."

"You think they're in cahoots?" Queen Taube asked.

"I won't put that past them."

"You don't think Forboud can get the answers you need?" Taniesse asked.

Boldair spread his stubby fingers wide and his hands to the sides of his head, adding his dramatic expression like he did when telling his tavern tales. "Father's mind's scattered. Forboud knows it, and apparently Thorgum and Staggnuns do, too. Otherwise, I don't think they'd have declared me king."

Taube frowned. She looked from Taniesse to Boldair. "Do they have such a right?"

"Aye, they do," Boldair said with a firm nod. "The Northern

Dwarven Alliance oversees all three of our kingdoms. But to answer your question, Forboud would be no more successful in getting honest answers from Ulthor than myself."

"There are ways to get answers from him without a trial," Dwiskter said. His hand rested on the hilt of his axe. "Give me a half hour with Ulthor. I'll make him talk. I swear it."

"You're speaking of the *former* king," Forboud said. His eyes narrowed, his face flushed red, and he placed tight fists on the table, slightly rising from his seat.

"Yes, *your* former king," Dwiskter said. "Now, he's nothing more than a dwarf without a crown and without a throne. He's no longer king. He tarnished the crown, and now, the punishment—"

"No!" Taube rose to her feet. "I won't allow Ulthor to suffer such treatment while inside *my* prison. That's *never* been tolerated in the past, and it most certainly won't come into play *now*."

"You've my permission." Boldair gazed at Dwiskter.

"It's not permission I seek," Queen Taube said. Her eyes narrowed with anger and wrath.

Boldair flicked his angered gaze to Taniesse. "You're okay with this?"

"Why shouldn't I be?" Taniesse shrugged.

"My father tried to kill you in order to keep his ties with the Dredgemen a secret."

"Believe me, Boldair, no one seated here would like to see your father executed for his actions more than Queen Taube and I. We've every right to seek his death. If I relied on revenge, I'd side with you, Boldair. But as you already know, had I wanted your father dead, his charred remains would be buried under feet of snow by now. Perhaps sparing him wasn't the best decision, but killing him wouldn't have gained me any better advantage. Had I done so, we'd have lost the truth. Forever. We'd have never known about his secret alliance."

"Then let me propose an alternate solution," Boldair said. He relaxed his fists and placed his palms on the table.

Taniesse sat in silence for several long moments. "What?"

"*You* visit him in his cell. Reveal to him who you are and what you will do should he not give you the answers you seek."

Taniesse entertained a smile for several seconds. Her eyes indicated her mind was tracing possible outcomes of visiting Ulthor in private. But then the coldness of a serpent darkened her eyes. She shook her head. "I'm sorry, but I must decline such an opportunity."

"You'd kill him, wouldn't you?" Boldair asked with a shrewd grin.

Taniesse looked away. She folded her hands on her lap. "That would not be my first solution."

"Then what?" Drucis asked. "You thought of something."

Taniesse nodded slightly. "My meeting him would never come to the proper fruition."

"Why not?" Boldair asked.

"Because Ulthor would say practically anything to *make* me kill him. He'd arouse my anger beyond the point of no return, and sadly, he'd suffer less by my fire than he does by staying alive and being confined in a prison cell."

"Meaning?" Queen Taube asked.

"His death would be instant," Taniesse replied coldly.

"It'd save us the agony of a trial," Boldair said.

Taniesse shook her head. "Never act in haste, Boldair. Your father's more stubborn than you and less likely to offer any information, no matter how severely Dwiskter or I tortured him. He'd probably die before he'd divulge further confessions."

"Trust me," Boldair said. "A trial won't get you the desired answers, either."

"Perhaps not," Taube said, "but my conscience will be clear."

Boldair placed his elbows on the table and leaned forward. "So dat's what this is all about, eh? *Your* conscience?"

Taube's jaw tightened. Fury darkened her eyes.

Taniesse shook her head. "Careful, Boldair. You're both rulers. Don't breach your relationship with the queen this early in your rulership. Your kingdom needs her as well as she needs yours."

"Aye," Boldair said with an abrupt sigh. "My apologies, milady. I've let me emotions get the better of me."

Taube took a deep breath, held it, and slowly released it. Her anger subsided and tears crested in her eyes. "As have I."

Taniesse offered an aristocratic smile. "I think it's fair to say, with everything that's occurred recently, our emotions are running high."

Taube straightened her gown with her hands, nodded, and seated herself. "You're right, Taniesse. Some of my wounds are still tender."

"Aye," Boldair said.

"Is it necessary dat I be present for his trial?" Boldair asked.

Taube shook her head. "No. Not at all."

"Good." Boldair stood. He eyed Dwiskter and then Drucis. "Let's go."

"Boldair," Taube said. "By no means am I attempting to put you at odds with me. I must attempt to get necessary answers, if possible. Should he refuse to comply, judgment falls in the courtyard. I promise no further delay."

"Aye, no bitterness or anger from me, Your Highness," Boldair said.

"One thing you should understand." Taniesse stood and placed her hand on her sword's hilt.

"Yes, Ol' Great One?"

"Whatever secret alliances your father holds are not only Queen Taube's enemies, they're also yours. Which means, most likely, these enemies reside nearer to Nagdor than to Hoffnung. They might not take too kindly in your assuming the throne. In fact, they might want you dead."

Boldair frowned and chewed his lower lip. "Aye. If father doesn't give the information you seek, I highly suggest you take Dwiskter's suggestion to find the answers we all seek."

"Whatever becomes necessary will be decided in court," Queen Taube said.

Boldair's eyes narrowed. He nodded his disgruntled agreement. "As you wish."

"Boldair," Taniesse said. "Where shall I find you, should I need to speak with you?"

"We be headed to Nagdor, although not immediately. I've a few side places I wish to visit first."

"Then you need to understand my warning."

"What warning? Dat there could be enemies within Nagdor?"

"Yes," Taniesse said.

"Aye! I've taken dat to heart."

"No," she said. "Until we find who's aligned themselves with your renegade father, you cannot return to Nagdor. Until they're removed, there'll be no coronation for you to assume the throne."

Boldair cocked a brow. "What?"

Taniesse nodded slowly. "Don't return to Nagdor until I deem it's safe. No sense having a king murdered before he's properly placed on the throne."

"If I don't return to Nagdor, I'll be viewed as a coward," Boldair said. "I'll have no one think such of me."

"How will your death prove otherwise?" Taniesse asked. "Nothing's foolhardy by avoiding unknown enemies."

"Then I should reside as king in secret?"

Taniesse shrugged. "For now."

Boldair shook his head and grumbled under his breath as he left the table and headed for the stairs. Dwiskter, Drucis, and Forboud followed.

EIGHT

"Dat went well," Boldair grumbled and marched through the palace gate.

Dwiskter eyed Drucis with a confused expression. "Ya think?"

"Bloody Hell! Of course not!" Boldair clenched his fists and growled.

"So what now?" Drucis asked. "Are we leaving Hoffnung?"

Boldair waved his finger in the air. "You bet your arse we are. I'd rather shave me beard than listen to more of dat—"

"Just go on an' say it, brother," Forboud said. "You want father dead. Admit it outright already!"

Boldair spun in an instant with his double-edge battle-axe drawn and the razor-edged blade inches from Forboud's face. Boldair's cheeks flushed red and fury narrowed his eyes. "I've had enough of your meddling."

Forboud's eyes widened. His hands rose to his sides in surrender. "Have I offended ya with me words, brother? Is dat it? Or does the truth make you despise me even more?"

"Ya know not what ya talk about." Boldair stepped closer. "There's no truth in your words, so stop your prickling and prattling. Else, you're going find out what my anger and wrath are truly like."

Dwiskter placed his hand against Forboud's chest and eased him back. Dwiskter stepped between Boldair and Forboud and shook his head furiously while staring at the axe. "Boldair, this isn't like you. Sheath your axe. King or not, I'll not allow you to slay your brother."

"Then bloody keep him the Hell away from me. If he presents further lies, neither you nor Drucis or the both of you combined shall stop me."

"What lies have I told?" Forboud asked. "Explain, brother."

"Aye," Dwiskter said. "I agree with Forboud."

"As do I," Drucis said. "Explain or I refuse to accompany you any farther."

Boldair glared harshly at Drucis. "Is dat so?"

"Aye," Drucis said with a firm jaw and an unflinching gaze.

Boldair huffed, and he ground his teeth. He turned his attention to Forboud. "Explain what exactly?"

"You said dat I have presented mistruths." Anger tightened Forboud's gaze. "I've done no such thing. And if ya think dat I 'ave, tell me *what* I've lied about!"

Boldair took a deep breath, held it, and slowly exhaled. His jaw tightened. "Father told me dat he wanted you on the throne, dat he'd prepared you to take his place, and yet, you keep denying dat. I've no choice but to believe *dat's* why you want so badly to visit him in private. You deny it?"

Forboud gave a firm single nod. "I do. I doubt you believe me, but I've no reason to lie. But since your appointment set by King Staggnuns and King Thorgum to replace father, you've viewed me as your enemy. For the life in me, I don't understand your sudden hostility or why—" Forboud shook his head and looked down.

Boldair's shoulders slumped. He kept his eyes fastened on his brother for a few seconds more before glancing away. "Go on. What else?"

Forboud lowered his hands. "Explain *why* you want father dead so badly. I understand his betrayal and his lies being a reason for his imprisonment, but why do ya push so hard for his *immediate* execution?"

Boldair lowered the axe and sighed. He placed the head of the axe on the path and propped his hands atop the heel. He shook his head. "It's not so much you, Forboud, dat bears me anger at father or dat he'd rather you rule over Nagdor than I."

"Then what?"

Boldair stood in silence for several minutes. His eyes grew distant, deep in memory, until finally he snapped to attention and cleared his throat. "Unprovoked, father tried to kill Taniesse. There's the possibility dat he might've been successful, which angers me greatly."

"Why does dat anger you?" Forboud asked. "He didn't succeed. Why does dat remain an issue?"

"*Why*? Had he killed her, I'd 'ave never known her. She wouldn't 'ave become my friend." Boldair's eyes saddened. "I'd 'ave never led a battalion into battle for Lady Dawn. I'd be tavern-hopping and telling tales to entertain drunken peasants. I'd not be king. Taniesse is the major reason I became king. Father tried to kill her. His failure changed my destiny. For his misdeeds, he should never be pardoned."

Dwiskter's eyebrows rose. "Pardoned? I understand your feelings. Dat's never going to happen. Ulthor won't receive *any* pardon. You heard dat, from both the Queen and Taniesse."

"Aye. Dat's what they *say*." Boldair's brow furrowed with concern. "But the more Forboud presses the Queen and Taniesse—"

Drucis shook his head. "No. No amount of persuasion could alter Ulthor's sentence. Taube would never allow it. Such a thing would spike a titanium wedge between the Dwarven Kingdoms and Hoffnung forever. Dat won't be happening."

"Aye," Boldair said. "Maybe not a pardon as we know them to be. But there's the chance he might somehow escape."

"From Hoffnung's prison? Are ya serious?" Dwiskter asked. "No. Dat's not possible. Dat prison's the most secure in all the kingdoms."

"From physical attacks, perhaps," Boldair said. "But ... magic ... magic could penetrate the walls, unlock locks, mesmerize guards—"

Drucis gave Boldair a shrewd stare.

Forboud placed his hands on Boldair's shoulders. "Brother, I swear to you I've no interest in the throne. Never have I known you to worry such, nor have you ever threatened my life. You've faced numerous dangers exploring dark dragon caves while searching for treasure, without ever a fear or worry. Father placed himself into condemnation. And yes, I ache with grief at losing him, but I've accepted what his fate has become. My last words dat I would've spoken to him, had you allowed it, would 'ave been to express my sorrow for the reprehensible damage and divisions he's caused. Nothing more did I wish to disclose to him. I swear it. So, you 'ave no need to worry o'er what you thought I *might've* said. Let's go. Wherever you lead, I follow, and ya 'ave me axes at your disposal."

"What has you so uneasy, Boldair?" Dwiskter asked.

Boldair shook his head and stared at his thick hands folded atop the heel of his axe. "Maybe father was right about me not being worthy to be king. I fear I'll disappoint Taniesse, King Staggnuns, and King Thorgum. They might discover dat I be a better treasure-hunter than a ruler."

Forboud slammed his hands firmly on Boldair's steel pauldrons. Boldair met his brother's eyes. "You'll do fine, Boldair. And ya got me at your side for guidance should you need it."

"Us, too," Drucis said. He winked. "Now 'bout dat drink you promised us."

"Aye!" Dwiskter said with a broad grin. "Don't think we've forgotten 'bout dat."

Drucis howled with laughter. "Aye, we best be heading on, eh?"

Boldair straightened, sheathed his axe, and nodded. "I could use a strong drink. I'll hold to me promise of buying the rounds, and let no dwarf say otherwise."

NINE

At the royal stables, the four dwarves went inside to retrieve their mounts.

Boldair approached the giant dire wolf, Ember. Ulthor had raised Ember from a cub until he was mature enough to become the king's mount. The wolf's outer, thick fur was black with an orange-red undercoat. When brushed back, the fur's blended colors resembled glowing, windblown embers of smoldering coal. The brilliant, contrasting colors were the reason for the wolf's name.

Boldair reached for Ember's bridle. The wolf's eyes narrowed and focused on Boldair. Ember's huge muzzled snout snarled, and he exposed its huge teeth. A low growl rumbled deep inside its throat.

"He's taken a fondness to you." Drucis grinned and winked.

Dwiskter laughed.

"He has." Boldair huffed without the slightest hint of a smile. "At least he's stopped trying to rip my arm or leg off with his massive jaws."

"I think the muzzle prevents dat," Drucis said with a howling laugh.

Boldair laughed. *"Dat's* why he's muzzled. The first time I attempted to mount him, he bit and dented my steel bracer. He damn near dragged me to the lifts. It took six Hoffnung guards to pry his mouth open so I could get free. Bloody Hell, I won't go into detail about what happened to one of the guards. His sacrifice to free me won't be soon forgotten."

Dwiskter shook his head. "So dat explains the nasty bruises on ya forearm, eh?"

"Aye, it took two smiths to pry and cut the bracer off me forearm. Almost lost me hand."

Drucis reared his head and howled with laughter. "Did ya not inform Ember dat you're king?"

"Dat doesn't matter to Ember," Dwiskter said.

Boldair shook his head. "Probably not. I doubt any amount of persuasion will ever change his feelings toward me."

Dwiskter winked at the other dwarves. "Dat wolf's contempt for Boldair is the same as Ulthor's."

Boldair chuckled and pointed a stern finger. "Now *dat* be true."

"I don't know, brother," Forboud said. "The wolf holds *more* affection for you than ya think."

Boldair turned to his brother. Forboud offered a slight, kind smile. "Maybe in time Ember will soften his outlook for me. Doesn't look too promising at the moment."

Drucis and Dwiskter chuckled.

Boldair took the reins, grabbed the steel handle welded to his saddle, and pulled himself up. Ember snarled and shook his head. "Settle down, you big heap of fur and teeth!"

"Are ya capable of getting him to obey?" Drucis asked while leading his giant, gray ram from its stall. The ram was equal size to a full-grown horse. Its curled black horns were the size of a vendor pushcart's wheels. The ram's goatee was braided neatly and looked freshly groomed. Drucis looked the ram in the eyes. "Someone's gone to a lot of effort to fancy ya up, Tusk."

Angrily, the ram blew air through its flared nostrils. Drucis laughed. "Aye, don't be getting mad at *me*, Tusk. Trust me, I never paid anyone to sissify ya."

"Nor I." Dwiskter frowned, shook his head, and held his ram's reins. His ram's horns were flat and were shaped like large pinchers with the sharp tips pointing forward. The beard of his ram was also separated into different braids. "Though it'd 'ave been a great joke, except ... Will ya have a look at this?"

Boldair looked at the pair of ram mounts and bellowed a hearty laugh. Forboud joined his laughter until he noticed his ram wore similar braids.

"What in blazes!" Forboud's face flushed hot red. "What dainty, elf-kissing prancer's been messing around with our rams?"

Despite Ember's low rumbling growl, Boldair scratched the fur behind the wolf's ears. "Think I'm beginning to like having a wolf now. Ember'd 'ave taken a couple of arms if anyone tried dat to him."

Forboud turned and pointed a finger. "You? Did ya have someone do this?"

"Me?" Boldair shook his head. "I had *nothing* to do with this. Nor, 'ave I 'ad the time. I've been with you the entire time."

"Doesn't mean ya didn't pay some peasant to do this though," Forboud said.

"With everything occupying my mind ... such a prank never occurred to me. But, tis a good one, if ya ask me," Boldair said.

Ember growled and fought his muzzle.

"What's eating him?" Drucis asked.

"Bah! I never know," Boldair said.

"Something's angering him a heap," Dwiskter said.

"Easy, Ember." Boldair scratched behind the wolf's ears even harder.

"Just get him out of here," a high-pitched voice said from behind a stall door.

"Who's there?" Boldair asked. "Show yourself!"

Drucis and Dwiskter readied their hands on their weapons.

"Come out, whoever you be!" Drucis pulled his axe from over his shoulder.

"I can't unless you take the wolf outside."

"It's me you should worry about, more than the wolf," Drucis said. "Unless I remove his muzzle, dat is. At dat point, we're probably *all* in trouble."

Ember growled fiercely. A small shadow moved behind the stall door and the furry face became more visible.

"Viorka?" Boldair asked. "What're you doing 'ere?"

"Trying not to get eaten by your wolf," she replied.

Boldair pulled back the reins. "I'm holding him back. Come on out."

Dwiskter cocked a brow. "You sure you 'ave him under control? I tend to believe he's much stronger than you."

"Oh, I hold no doubts 'bout dat," Boldair said. "Come out of the stall, Viorka, but keep your distance from Ember."

Viorka, a magical catlike fynx who could turn invisible, stood a bit taller with a tad more bravery. She stepped from the door of the stall and walked a wide sweep away from the growling wolf.

"Why are ya 'ere?" Boldair asked.

"Looking for Taniesse," she replied.

"Here? She doesn't have a mount. She doesn't need one."

Viorka offered an embarrassed smile and shrugged her narrow shoulders. "Have you seen her?"

Boldair nodded. "She's in the palace."

Her furry brows rose and her nose scrunched. "She is?"

"With Queen Taube," Drucis said.

"Oh."

Boldair stared at her with curiosity. "What'cha need her for?"

"Adventure, if she plans on traveling soon and doesn't mind a tagalong."

"Ahh, little cat," Dwiskter said, "if it's adventure you seek, you should travel with us."

Viorka stared at Ember with wide eyes. "I've a feeling I'd be safer *not*."

Boldair grinned and tugged back on the reins. Although Ember made no attempt to lunge at Viorka, his resistance to Boldair's hold indicated he'd not given up on the idea. "I think you'd be right 'bout dat."

"The wolf likes him about as much as you." Drucis winked at Viorka.

She offered a sheepish grin.

"Were you the one who tied all the fancy knots in my ram's beard?" Dwiskter's eyes narrowed beneath his furrowed brow.

She nodded. "Yes."

Dwiskter frowned. "I oughta smack ya with the flat side of me axe."

"It was *you*?" Forboud asked. "What prompted you to do such a thing? Are you trying to soil our reputations? Or do you wish to shame our rams into thinking they be unattractive sheep?"

Viorka shook her head. "Sorry, I got bored."

"Bored? Ya couldn't find anything *else* to do?" Forboud said.

"Ah, let her be," Dwiskter said. "No harm done."

"Not until we meet other dwarves," Forboud said. "We'll be mocked beyond scorn, especially if they've been drinking."

"By then, the knots will have unravelled."

"Doubtful." Forboud rubbed the bridge of his black ram's nose. He took the side of its bridle and led the ram to the wide stable door.

Boldair looked at Viorka. "Ol' Ember would've wolfed ya down if ya tried dat on him. How'd you get past him, anyway?"

"I came inside invisible."

"Invisible?" Dwiskter asked curiously.

She nodded. "Yes."

Dwiskter smiled. "Dat's interesting."

"Then how'd Ember find you?" Boldair asked.

"He smelled my scent. I was invisible the entire time I braided the rams' beards."

Drucis shook his head. "Do you habitually braid others' mounts without permission?"

"I can unbraid them if I've caused you trouble," Viorka said.

Drucis ignore her offer and looked at Boldair. "What route are we taking?"

Boldair pulled the reins and turned Ember around. Even though the wolf obeyed Boldair's direction, it never took its hungry stare off Viorka. "North, toward Icevale."

"Icevale?" Drucis frowned. "Meadwyrm Pass is close to Damdur on the other side of Glacier Ridge. The quicker route would be to travel south, then head west to Bridgebarrow. We can drink our fill and stay the night at the inn."

"Dat's true," Boldair said, "*if* we travel on the surface. But I know some underground tunnels—"

"Icevale has tunnels, but none burrow dat direction."

Boldair laughed. "We're not going to Icevale."

"Then where?" Drucis asked.

"It's a secret tunnel I found during one of my treasure hunts."

Dwiskter's eyes widened. "You must tell us!"

"I'll do better than dat. We'll travel through an abandoned goblin cavern dat leads to Frosthammer."

"Frosthammer?" Drucis said. "Dat city actually exists?"

"You've never been?" Boldair asked perplexed.

Drucis scratched his beard. "No. I've always believed the place to be legend."

"As have I," Dwiskter said. "So it does exist?"

"Aye," Boldair replied. "Getting to Frosthammer is difficult. It requires more dedication and determination than what most surface-dwellers are willing to sacrifice. Ya got to cut through the heart of the frozen mountains. Dat's why most believe Frosthammer's nothing more than a bard's tale. But I've been there."

Dwiskter and Drucis looked at him in awe as did Viorka.

"Is it true dat Frosthammer's the city o'er the edge of the Lava Pits?" Drucis asked.

Boldair rode a disgruntled Ember to the open stable doors. "I must confess dat I didn't venture to the deepest floors in Frosthammer. Too many to count. I saw a gated titanium wall riveted and chained. Off limits, I suppose. Either they don't want anyone passing through dat gate, or they don't want *whatever's* on the other side to *escape*. But a river of molten steel divides the great city in half."

"Ya 'ave me curiosity," Drucis said.

"Mine, too," Dwiskter said.

Viorka shivered.

Boldair chuckled. "We'll only pass through the city. No extended stay. They don't welcome outsiders too often. When I was there, they requested my extended stay so they could hear my treasure hunting tales."

"Since your king, they'll more than welcome you, eh?" Drucis asked with a grin.

"Ahh, don't be mentioning dat," Boldair said, scratching his chin.

"Why not?"

"Let's just say dat my departure wasn't on the best of terms and leave it at dat."

"Wait," Dwiskter said. "You expect us to pass through the city dat holds hostility toward you? Do you want us on the other side of metal bars like your father?"

Boldair waved his hand. "It's nothing like dat. No hostility. Frosthammer's king holds no grievance with me."

"Then what's the problem?" Drucis asked.

Boldair looked away and cleared his throat. "Perhaps it be nothing, but I'd rather not speak of it, for now. We best not waste any more time."

TEN

B oldair rode Ember ahead of his Dwarven companions on the narrow forest trail, but the wolf's temperament was no less forgiving. Boldair half expected the wolf to charge through low branched trees to dislodge him from his saddle, so he kept a tight hold on the reins, as a precaution. Boldair glanced over his shoulder. "I thought you wished to speak to Taniesse, little cat."

Viorka followed the forest trail behind the dwarves, out of Ember's sight, and remained partially invisible at times. "I said I want adventure. What could be greater than seeing a city I've never heard of?"

"What happens if you become Ember's supper?" Drucis winked at her with a sly grin.

"He'd have to catch me first." Viorka laughed nervously. Her fearful eyes met Ember's hungry gaze. "I plan to stay outside his reach at all times."

"I hate to tell ya," Boldair said, "but the goblin cave's first series of pathways before we reach Frosthammer is tight and narrow. We'll be packed together and it'll be nearly impossible to turn around once we enter."

Viorka nodded. "Then I'll stay at the rear. If it's that compacted, Ember cannot possibly turn on me."

"This wolf's full of surprises," Boldair said.

Viorka's voice saddened. "Do you not want me to travel with you? I'll behave. I promise."

"Dat's *not* what I'm implying," Boldair said.

"Ya aren't bothering me," Dwiskter said.

"Viorka," Boldair said, "You were a great asset when you traveled with me and Taniesse. Honored to 'ave you with us. Besides, you're the perfect scout. I doubt a forest elf could hide any better."

"Thanks," she said with a confident grin.

Forboud faced her. "You must promise not to tie fancy knots in me ram's fur."

"I agree with dat myself," Drucis said.

"Deal!" Viorka said. "If I'd known it'd offend you, I'd have not tied them. Sorry."

Dwiskter smiled at Viorka. "It might be handy to 'ave a fynx dat turns invisible. Ya never know what type of creatures we might encounter."

"I'll help any way I can," she said.

Boldair tugged the reins, and Ember stopped. His companions followed suit.

"What's the problem?" Dwiskter asked.

"We leave this path and head through the trees." Boldair untied his helm from the saddle pack and placed it on his head. "I advise wearing your helm."

"Why?" Viorka asked. "I don't have one."

"You 'ave no worries," Boldair said. "Us, on the other hand, have to worry about bashing our heads on branches."

"Which wouldn't happen if you walked on foot like me," she said.

"Hey!" Drucis pointed a stern finger. "Dat might be true. Just because you're shorter, doesn't mean you can poke fun at our *height*."

"I'm not poking fun," she said. "Sometimes, being shorter has its advantages."

"Don't I know it!" Dwiskter said. "Our height gave us the upper hand against those blasted, oversized Vykings."

"Don't forget about the orcs we fought long ago," Drucis said.

"Aye," Dwiskter said. "Still trying to get dat stench out of my nostrils from battles long ago."

"Is it necessary for us to leave the forest trail so soon?" Forboud asked.

"Aye," Boldair replied. "The forest floor's rocky and unpredictable the farther south it goes. With nightfall approaching, we can't take unnecessary chances."

"Viorka," Boldair said. "Do you mind traveling ahead through the treetops. Alert us should you find any bandit camps?"

"How great's that possibility?" she asked.

"Bandits and thieves don't like to be seen. The dark cover of the trees conceals them. You know dat," Boldair said. "Once we enter the wilderness, we might encounter bandits or wolf packs. Receiving a forewarning could prove quite helpful."

"What about ... goblins?" she asked. "You mentioned the goblin cavern. Are any still there?"

Boldair, Drucis, and Dwiskter laughed. Forboud observed their response, grinned, and then reared his head and joined in.

"We've ne'er seen a goblin in any of our underground cities in more than a century," Boldair said.

She shrugged and her eyes narrowed. "Doesn't mean they *don't* exist. How can you be so certain they're all dead? Look at me. If you asked anyone in Aetheaon about whether they'd ever seen a fynx, only a minor few could say they have. Most have never heard of my kind. I've never encountered another of my kind, but I'm not so foolish to think I'm the only one. Whenever I've worried I might be the only fynx, I'm overshadowed by gloom."

Boldair said, "You've never seen another fynx?"

She grimaced. "No. We're good at concealing ourselves within our environment, which prevents hunters from killing us for trophies. It wouldn't do a hunter good anyway. When we die, we turn invisible, which is why no one's ever found a fynx corpse. Since I'm often on edge and stay hidden, others like me have done the same. I might never see another fynx. If I don't, I'll offer no offspring to continue my species."

"Goblins were obliterated during the Battle of Final Rest dat's known as the Vale of Frozen Tears," Forboud said. "Dat's when the three major Dwarven cities—Damdur, Nagdor, and Icevale—formed the Dwarven Alliance. All three cities sent massive battalions into the valley. They trapped the goblins at the mountain base, where they were all slaughtered. So you needn't worry about goblins."

"Dat good enough for ya?" Boldair asked Viorka. "Me brother's a great historian."

She nodded.

Forboud blushed at Boldair's unexpected compliment.

Boldair pointed at the nearest tree. "On with ya, then. Into the trees. We need to reach Whirled Forest before sunset."

"Whirled Forest? Why?" Drucis asked.

"We can take shelter and camp for the night at the bluff."

"No tavern before we camp? Now, you're getting on me bad side," Drucis said.

"What's eating you?" Boldair asked.

"Need you ask? No tavern means no drinks."

Boldair smiled. "Don't get testy. I always pack a tankard or two. Don't you?"

"Of course!" Drucis said. "But I don't aim to *use* 'em unless we're in dire circumstances, which we're not."

"We're headed to the Whirled Forest," Forboud said. "If dat's not dire—"

Dwiskter nodded. "From what I hear, the climate's almost as bad as Glacier Ridge, except Glacier Ridge *has* a tavern, an inn, and residents. It has shelter against the blasted, icy winds."

"Not anymore," Boldair said.

"You're right," Drucis said with a glum expression. "Not after the Plague-bringer. No places to buy a drink is quite dire, if ya ask me."

"Not to worry. You shall all drink from my skins," Boldair said. "Now, get off the road before highwaymen see us. We don't want any bandits trying to rob us after dark."

"Ahh, let 'em try," Dwiskter said. "They'll breathe their last."

Viorka altered her appearance into a large cat and scampered through the underbrush that carpeted the trees. She scaled the wide oak trunk and disappeared into the foliage.

Boldair turned Ember with a gentle tug of the reins. To his surprise, the wolf didn't resist, left the worn forest path, and stepped into the forest underbrush. "Ah, there we go. Thanks for listening, Ember."

Ember growled deep inside his throat. The wolf's back muscles tightened beneath Boldair. He expected the wolf to bolt and attempt to dislodge him from the saddle. Boldair scratched the nape of the wolf's neck to soothe the giant beast, but the wolf stopped in his tracks. Ember arched his head partway around and bore teeth.

Boldair pulled back his hand. "Easy, I know ya don't like me. Perhaps you don't trust me. But for now, for *this* journey, we're sorta stuck together. I hope ya can see past your repulsion for me to get to our destination. We can reevaluate our relationship later, if dat be all right with you."

"All well up there?" Dwiskter asked.

"Aye," Boldair replied.

"You're moving painfully slow," Dwiskter said. "Is dat your doing or the wolf beneath ya?"

"A bit of both, to be honest. You could say we're working through our differences," Boldair said.

Drucis laughed. "Have you reached a mutual understanding?"

"What do you think?" Boldair huffed.

"Your courtship's a bit too slow. Maybe a serenade's in order?" Dwiskter said.

Boldair glared at Dwiskter but said nothing. Drucis laughed.

"What do you expect, brother?" Forboud asked. "Ember has been father's mount for ten years. He won't forget father and possibly senses your resentment for father."

Boldair chuckled. "Ember and I must come to terms somehow. I don't expect he'll forget father. Their bond's still strong. I only hope his resentment is short lived."

"Give the furry bag of bones a chance to adjust to your ... scent," Dwiskter said.

"You've poked your fun at my expense," Boldair said. "But now, it's time we listen more than we speak, just in case we're not alone."

ELEVEN

Whirled Forest set atop a narrow ridge overlooking the steep, descending mouth of the valley. The ridge divided the Frosted Peaks and separated Glacier Ridge to the southwest. Woodcrest lie directly east.

The harsh, cold winds cut through the valley, blew fiercely upward, which, over time, had forced the massive pine branches to whirl in unnatural directions. Because of the never-ending winds, the trees grew in irregular whirled patterns with twisted trunks and branches.

Massive gnarled, icy roots clung to the cliff's jagged edge. Climbing the roots was impossible. The severe, cold winds were deafening for anyone to withstand for an extended period of time. Traveling parties that hoped to shorten their journey to Glacier Ridge by attempting to climb the ridge fell swiftly to their deaths. Their frozen corpses were a warning to travelers that climbing the ridge was suicide. Those who witnessed the falling deaths of their comrades retreated farther south to the warmth of a tavern. After rounds of strong drinks, they spun their sorrowful tales of the treacherous Whirled Forest to anyone willing to listen.

Boldair remembered a young drunken lad—Mosser—tell his tales in

Bridgebarrow Tavern. Mosser's slurred words could've easily been a tale spoken to draw sympathy from the patrons in order to receive gratuity to buy more drinks. Boldair almost discarded the story, except for the haunted fear Mosser's eyes possessed. His face withered as he talked. One couldn't fake such terror easily. With pity, Boldair offered the young bard a gold coin for sharing his loss.

Mosser sat at a tavern table with Boldair for a short spell. He explained the greatest danger was the harsh, howling winds. The wind whistled through the jagged rocks and through the whirled tree branches. Sometimes the winds luringly whispered, too, and had encouraged his comrades to blindly disregard the dangers. The winds spoke and hinted of great treasures for whomever reached the whirled pine plateau. But the whispering voice frightened Mosser, so he chose *not* to risk his life.

The coarse, wailing winds made it impossible to hear anything other than its banshee howls. Mosser named the rough mountainside Banshee's Bluff. Unlike his friends, he resisted the baleful summons. When the last of his dangling friends dropped and vanished into the valley below, Mosser ran through the forest and headed to the safety of Woodcrest.

Days later, Mosser's story plagued Boldair's mind. Boldair's curiosity gnawed at him. He decided to view the gruesome nature of the Whirled Forest for himself. Looking back, it'd been a foolish endeavor, especially *alone*.

The hint of possible treasure didn't lure Boldair to the rough mountain's edge. He needed to know the tale was true. When Boldair found himself overlooking the mouth of the valley, he realized Mosser's fears were genuine. Although Boldair held no fear of the crude cliffside, he greatly respected its dangers. No amount of treasure was worth gaining if he were dead.

He imagined the bottom edge of the jagged bluff was littered with broken, frozen bodies of those blinded by their obsessions and unable to ascertain their doomed fate until after it was too late.

These were victims of their own demise, partly due to the arrogance of overcoming any obstacle no one before them had ever achieved. This type of haughty, stubborn nature was common with most dwarves, elves, and humans. The less intelligent races, like goblins and orcs, held more common sense whenever they approached such terrain. At least, Boldair would wager a large portion of gold that his assumption was true. But, he'd never risk his life to see if he could scale the wicked mountainside.

TWELVE

The last fragments of the sunset smoldered over the mountain. Boldair dismounted. He led Ember by the reins while keeping a fierce side-glance on the wolf. Even though the wolf hadn't challenged Boldair after leaving the forest path, Boldair didn't fully trust the giant. Not this soon. Possibly never. But he hoped the wolf's distrust and resentment would eventually fade.

"Now what?" Drucis grumbled and climbed off his ram. "You led us out 'ere for our deaths?"

Boldair ignored him and led Ember to the side of a large boulder that blocked the swirling winds.

Drucis shook his head and followed. "I'm beginning to dislike the prospects of this powerful drink you've tempted us with. The price of *getting* to it is far too steep, and for a dwarf, *steep* isn't something we like. Ya should've warned us we might die *before* we ever wet our throats with this lava-like concoction."

Boldair glanced at him and leveled a stern frown. "Are you done with your elfish-whining?"

"Hey!" Drucis pointed a stern finger. He released the reins of his ram and took several quick steps toward Boldair. His face reddened. "What's the point of leading us out to one of the most dangerous terrains in the Frosted Peaks? Blasted, we passed dozens of nicer places in the forest where we could've set up a cozy camp. Instead, you 'ave us facing winds cold enough to freeze the heart of an Ice Ogre."

"You can turn back, if you like," Boldair said angrily. "The whole lot of ya, if dat's the way you see it. But if ya remember, Taniesse warned I should keep a low profile until we discover who's aligned with father dat might want me dead. If you choose to leave, go back the way we came. I'm done with ya."

Dwiskter placed a hand on Drucis' shoulder. "Careful how you speak to our king, Drucis. It's easy to forget he's no longer a treasure-hunter, but a ruler."

Drucis lowered his hand. He sighed and nodded. "Aye, forgive me, Your Highness."

"We're all beat. The path to the Whirled Forest is filled with pitfalls and low branches. But ya shall be rewarded for your efforts," Boldair said with a broad smile.

"How's dat?" Forboud led his ram to where they stood. "I agree with them. I can't see camping on this windy cliffside without freezing our arses off. Our mounts can withstand this weather better than we."

Viorka scampered from the trees to the boulder where they stood. The wind flung her into the trees. With her second effort to reach Boldair, she clung to protruding roots until she reached the boulder blocking the wind. She pressed her back against the cold rock and rubbed her arms.

"Ya can't possibly make a roaring fire," Forboud said. "Even with the boulder's protection, the whipping wind prevents it."

Boldair chuckled. "Aye, we're *not* camping here."

"Then where?" Drucis said. "Don't tell me we've got to ride along the ridge in the dark."

"No-o-o," Boldair shook his head and sighed. "I've learned a few things over the years as a treasure-hunter."

"Well, if it be magic," Drucis said, "how 'bout whipping us to Meadwyrm Pass and save us further torture?"

"Everyone stand back." Boldair knelt behind the rock.

"Why?" Forboud asked.

"I've got to release the traps," he replied.

"I can't move away from the rock," Viorka said. "If I do, the wind's going to carry me away."

"Okay, Viorka," Boldair said. "Climb on my back and firmly hold my armor. You'll be safe there. The rest of ya, give me some room."

The dwarves backed away. Boldair ran his stubby fingers along a large, flat rock next to the boulder.

"Ah," he said. "There we go."

A distinctive click sounded and he stood. He stepped back a few steps. The flat rock sunk. In the fleeting daylight, a set of stairs became visible.

"Go down before we lose what daylight we've left. Otherwise, I won't be able to find a torch to light."

"What about our mounts?" Forboud asked.

"There's room for them, too," Boldair said. "Viorka, you go first."

"Why?" she asked.

"Ember's probably gotten fairly hungry carrying me all this way. To him, you're a tasty morsel. Put some distance between ya. Besides, you can see in the dark. I need ya to find my torch."

"What's down there?" she asked nervously.

"Since I've disarmed the traps, nothing dat can hurt you," Boldair replied. "I promise."

Viorka climbed off his back, dropped into the hole, and landed promptly on her feet. A second later, she disappeared down the steps and returned with an old pitch-covered torch.

"Thanks, lil' cat."

She beamed a smile.

Boldair glanced at the dwarves. "Forboud, if you'd be so kind as to lead Ember down the steps, I'll follow ya and light the torch. Viorka follows me."

Forboud nodded solemnly.

"Thanks."

Boldair and Viorka disappeared down the rock steps.

Thirteen

The flickering torchlight brought strange contours to Boldair's face. After Forboud brought Ember down the steps, Boldair waited for the rest of them to descend. Then he walked to the side of the steps and pushed an iron lever up. The large stone that had lowered into the ground slowly rose until it was flush with the ceiling.

Forboud watched the heavy stone move into place. "Since when 'ave you learned engineering skills?"

Boldair chuckled. "With all the traps and snares I've encountered throughout the years, ya get a knack for how they work."

Viorka stood outside Ember's reach and rubbed her arms to warm them.

Boldair took the torch and touched it to a pile of dried firewood in the center of the room. "Ah, is this better?"

She nodded.

The fire rose in a matter of minutes. The smoke masked the dusty smell the room contained. A small hole in the ceiling near the outcrop of the bluff acted like a flue and sucked the smoke from the room. Boldair grabbed a thick, dry log and placed it on the rising flames.

The room was quite large. Several flat stones were covered with hay for beds. Near the room's center was a table with benches made from stacked stones. Several unlit torches were inserted in crude rock sconces on the walls. Boldair made his way around the room and lit each one.

"If you will," Boldair said to Forboud, "tie Ember near the far wall. The rest of ya can tie your rams along beside him. There's hay in the corner for them to eat, and Ember's saddlebag has some dried meat you can feed him."

Drucis offered a shrewd stare. "How'd you find this place?"

Boldair paused from lighting a torch and smiled. "I built it."

Forboud studied the room. "*You* impress me, brother. How'd ya do all this?"

Boldair laughed heartily. "You and father might think I never listened to the things I was taught, but dat's not true."

"The stonework's quite good, considering." Drucis looked around the room.

"Thanks," Boldair said. "In a few minutes, the fire will take the chill out of the air."

"*Why'd* ya build it?" Dwiskter asked.

"Ah, 'ave a seat, and I'll tell ya."

The dwarves seated themselves at the table. Boldair rested his torch in a small hole at the center of the table. He walked to Ember and took two wineskins from the large saddlebag. He set those on the table, along with several strands of elk jerky, and a quarter wheel of hard cheese.

Boldair said, "Help yourselves."

As the dwarves drank, Boldair shared Mosser's story about how the seductive, siren winds disguised their true banshee screams and led the misfortunate to their deaths.

Dwiskter took a long drink, wiped his mouth with the back of his hand, and handed the wineskin to Drucis. "Knowing what happened to all the people who died on this cliffside, why'd you travel to check it out?"

"Curiosity."

Viorka's eyes widened. "Didn't you fear these winds might lure you to your death, too?"

Boldair shrugged. "Treasure hunting always has risks. Certainly no greater than awakening a dragon inside its lair though."

"You've done that?" Viorka asked.

He shook his head. "No. But I've always *feared* the possibility. Now dat Taniesse and her two sisters have shown their might in battle, I suppose the possibility of encountering a dragon has become far greater. Dat is, if they've disguised themselves as human. But the danger existed despite my ignorance."

Drucis passed the skin to Forboud. "So what happened when you arrived at the Whirled Forest?"

"While the wind speaks harshly to the humans and elves who've ventured here, the mountain spoke *louder* to me than the wind possibly could. Cause we're dwarves, rock and stone are where our hearts belong, right?"

Forboud, Dwiskter, and Drucis nodded.

Boldair pointed a finger at the ground. "Under the mountains are our homes. It's where we abide and where our strength's its greatest. We're part of the mountains. But, something odd happened when I came to this point facing the mouth of the valley."

"What?" Viorka asked.

"I wasn't dressed for the journey. The cold wind bit me arms and face. I'd been on foot dat day, too. The large boulder we stood behind to shelter us from the wind lie on its side then. With all my might, I pushed until it stood upright. I used it as a shield to block the wind. After moving it, I noticed a small crevice, so I took a blunt rock and dug. A bit of warmth touched me hands, so I dug faster. The next thing I knew, I fell inside this pit."

"Nothing was set in 'ere like now, was it?" Dwiskter asked.

Boldair shook his head. "Before the large boulder had fallen flat, it's possible some type of creatures used this pit for shelter or to hibernate, but I found no trace of 'em. Luckily, I keep flint in me pockets. I broke off some dead tree roots to start a fire. I used loose stones to build those steps. I had fallen ten feet or more from the opening. It took me more than a day to stack enough rocks to reach the top. I traveled to Woodcrest and traded for masonry tools to chip and fashion the stones into smoother steps. Then I made the table and benches."

"But why? Why'd you want to make this place more hospitable?" Forboud asked. "Certainly, you didn't plan to meet your death by trying to climb the bluff. You've often taken great risks to find treasures, but nothing as foolhardy as dat."

"You're right, brother. I've no intention to ever make such an attempt up dat ridge, or *down* it for dat matter, but having a hidden place to stay overnight on long journeys is always a plus. After all, who'd look for this room?"

Forboud frowned. "There's nothing out *here*."

Boldair smiled. "I built this *after* I discovered Frosthammer. It's a midway point. Within a few hours tomorrow we'll come to the old goblin cavern, and a few hours after dat, we'll be in Frosthammer."

"I see," Drucis said. "I'm surprised you never hid any of your treasure here."

"I thought about it, but carrying the masonry tools on foot was difficult enough. Gold and silver are *much* heavier, but this would be the perfect spot to hide treasure though. Of course, hefting loads of gold would prevent the wind from blowing ya away." Boldair gave an odd grin and chuckle.

"You built the crank that lowers and rises the stone platform?" Dwiskter asked.

Boldair nodded. "Aye. The iron lever I found discarded at an old cemetery sepulcher, but it proved useful. The gears and chains I found in the narrow creek we crossed. No telling why they'd been left there, but no one was coming back for 'em. The rest of assembly was simple mechanics. I've used enough gadgets in old dungeons and cemeteries to know how they work. That's also how I learned to set me traps. After disarming dozens of them, one learns how triggering mechanisms work. It doesn't take much more to build ya own afterwards. I reset some traps in the hopes of spearing a few nasty Ratkins."

Dwiskter and Drucis laughed.

"I've never heard your tales in the taverns," Dwiskter said. "But before we met, I'd heard plenty *about* you."

Boldair chuckled. "Word of me adventures travels faster than I. Peasants and townsfolk enjoy my stories."

"Some say your a blowhard," Forboud said with a shrewd grin before sipping from the skin.

"Oh, do they now?" Boldair asked.

"Actually, brother, they do." Forboud nodded.

"He's right," Drucis said. "I've heard some whisper such names when they see you. Ha! They're probably jealous of your treasures."

"Bah, let 'em talk," Boldair said with a dismissive hand. "I pay 'em no mind. Besides, why should I worry about 'em anyways? I'm a king now."

Dwiskter pulled out his pipe, tapped dried herbs into it, and lit it. A sweet scent lofted above the table. After a few puffs, he looked at Boldair. "Tell me how you hunt for your treasures? Do you have a process, or a secret for discovering large gold and gem deposits? Most dwarf miners have a keen sense for which rocks contain rich ore deposits. Is it similar for you?"

"Thinking of becoming a prospector?" Drucis asked.

Dwiskter chuckled and shook his head. "No, just curious."

"I've never mined, so I can't compare the two. However, whenever I'm near a large amount of gold, a strange feeling arises in the pit of me stomach," Boldair replied. "It's best described as a tinge of excitement. My heart hammers in me chest. I know treasures are nearby. This probably sounds strange, but precious metals and gems cry out a strange melody, like a song."

"Been hitting the hard stuff already?" Drucis rose from his seat, pressed his hands atop the rock table, and looked for a bottle. "Where'd you hide dat?"

Boldair shook his head. "No, I'm serious. Gold and all these other treasures came from the earth. I believe they wish to return."

Viorka cocked her head. "In a way, that makes perfect sense."

"It does," Boldair said.

Dwiskter cocked a brow and looked at Viorka. "Careful not to inhale the smoke off me pipe. The herbs can disorient the minds of smaller creatures."

"Let her alone," Boldair said.

"You're agreeing with a cat," Forboud said.

"A *fynx*." She huffed and glared.

"Ah, no matter," he replied. "You look like a cat to me."

"Seems your brother, Boldair, has inhaled too much from me pipe.

Viorka's isn't shaped like a feline. She looks mostly human," Dwiskter said.

"Boldair was the one who said gems and gold sing!" Forboud said. "Maybe's *he's* too close to your pipe, too."

Drucis laughed. "Bah! I wasn't going to say anything since he's the new king."

Boldair frowned. "Dwiskter asked. Dat's the best I can describe it. How else do you think I found Taniesse and her sisters' dragon lairs? Treasure hunters searched unsuccessfully for years to find them. Their lairs held so much gold and gems dat I was overwhelmed by the cacophonous volume. The excitement was so overbearing I almost collapsed."

"You returned all of dat to them, didn't you?" Dwiskter asked.

"Aye." Boldair nodded. His eyes went distant, as he recalled the stacks of gold he'd stood atop. Gems of every color. Silver. Tears formed at the sides of his eyes. He flicked his gaze to Dwiskter. Sadness of loss coated his voice. "But, returning it was the right thing. The treasure is theirs, not mine."

Forboud straightened on the crude rock bench and lit his pipe. "Not one gold coin ya kept for yourself?"

"No." Boldair shook his head. "None except the reward Taniesse gave me after we destroyed the Vykings."

"No possible way you hauled all her treasure to Legelarid and Oculoth by wagon when you hired those armies," Forboud said. A tinge of angered jealousy flowed with the words.

"Of course not!" Boldair said. "I drew maps for her to follow to find the rest of their accumulated treasures. You think I'd be alive if I'd tucked away any portion of their treasure for myself? A dragon knows to the last shilling how much treasure it owns. They'll abandon their lair to scorch any thief dat steals from them. The *only* reason I ventured inside any dragon's lair was because dragons were believed to be dead."

Drucis and Dwiskter looked at Forboud with narrowed gazes.

"Are you making accusations against Boldair?" Drucis asked.

"No, of course not!" Forboud shook his head.

"Because your line of questions seem headed to presume Boldair's guilty of something," Drucis said.

Forboud cleared his throat and set his pipe on the table. "Dat's not my intention at all."

"Then what's your intention?" Boldair rose from his seat.

"None, brother. I swear it! I didn't accompany you on dat trip after we got separated near Bridgebarrow Tavern."

"Doesn't seem you spent too much time looking for me," Boldair said. He studied Forboud shrewdly.

"The lot of us ran for our lives when Taniesse threw fireballs at us. I returned to find you."

"When?" Boldair asked.

"The following morning."

"Dat soon?" Boldair shook his head. "How *long* did ya search for me?"

Drucis cocked a brow and took a puff from his pipe.

"A few hours. After not finding you, I assumed you headed north to Damdur or perhaps decided to hunt more treasure without me."

Boldair's brow tightened. "Where'd you go?"

"I joined our comrades and headed to Nagdor."

Boldair chewed the tip of his pipe. "Seems I worried much longer about ya than ya did me."

"Surely, you jest," Forboud said.

"No. I thought you were the charred dead prisoner in the cell next to mine when I awakened. Taniesse insinuated it were you," Boldair said. "I pleaded with her. Do ya think I'd be so foolish to horde any piece of her treasure when she lopped fireballs at all of us?"

Forboud shook his head. "No, I suppose not."

"Ya *suppose*? While the rest of you ran from Bridgebarrow, she knocked me unconscious and took me prisoner. She locked me in a tiny prison cell at the top of a high cliff and waited for me to awaken. When I awoke, she told me the dead body in the neighboring cell was you, and I'd suffer the same fate if I didn't agree to give back her treasure. For the period of time I thought the charred body was yours, I grieved deeply. I wept. You only searched for me a few hours? Did you ever consider dat I might've been killed or taken prisoner?"

Forboud shook his head. "The thought never crossed my mind."

"Oh? Why not?"

"To my knowledge you've never had an enemy. Father's the only one who views you negatively. Well, he was nowhere around."

"And yet, you ask accusing questions about whether I withheld any of Taniesse's treasure for myself."

Forboud opened his mouth to speak, but Boldair raised a stern finger and shook his head.

Boldair leaned forward and rested his elbows on the stone table. "No doubt her intentions were to frighten all of you away with those fireballs. She came for me, to find where I'd hidden her treasure. She hurled more fireballs at me in dat prison cell. After I told her where the treasure was, I figured I'd become a burnt corpse anyways. But she spared me. For her mercy, I'm forever grateful. And because of her mercy, I'd never in the remainder of my life ever give her any reason to doubt my loyalty to her."

Forboud lowered his gaze and shook his head. "I'm sorry, Boldair. I never saw her take you. To be blunt, I ran to save me own hide. I cannot apologize enough."

Boldair grinned. "Brother, I cannot blame ya for dat. I don't blame ya at all! She took us all by surprise. Not one of us had any idea what her itinerary was." He laughed heartily. "Anyone would've fled. My point isn't to make you feel guilty. My aim's to ask if ya noticed any hostility from Taniesse toward me when we sat with Queen Taube?"

Forboud lifted his head and looked at Boldair. "No. None at all."

"Dat's my point. I was fully honest with her before I was released and am so, even now. If she harbored any grudge at me, or if she believed me a thief, she'd 'ave never warned me not to return to Nagdor, nor would she've allowed me to leave Hoffnung. Dragons aren't creatures you betray and not expect repercussions. I'm surprised she set aside father's attempt to kill her."

Forboud nodded. "Dat surprises me, too."

Boldair stood and grabbed another log to place on the roaring fire. "We'd best sleep. Tomorrow's trip has its share of hardships."

"Unlike today?" Forboud asked.

"A bit worse in places, I'm afraid."

FOURTEEN

The following morning Boldair stood at the bottom of the stairs. Dwiskter, Forboud, and Drucis brought fallen deadwood they found on the forest floor and handed them downward. Boldair took them and set them at the side of the stairs.

"And your purpose for this?" Forboud asked.

"So we've dry firewood ready for whenever we return. No sense tripping around hunting for firewood should it be dark if we return," Boldair asked.

"We won't be heading this direction after we reach Meadwyrm Pass, will we?" Forboud asked.

"No."

Forboud shook his head. "Good, 'cause I've no intention of ever seeing this fierce mountainside again. I'm surprised we're not up to our necks in snow with how cold it is."

"The winds prevent snow from sticking," Drucis said, "but the ground's frozen solid. Beyond this peak are the snow hills of the Frosted Peaks."

Boldair set down a log and dusted his hands. "All right. Dat be plenty."

"So much for staying warm throughout the night," Forboud said. "Gathering all this wood has gotten me cold again."

"Ahh, come back inside," Boldair said. "The ashes are giving off heat."

"I'd just as soon be headed on our way," Forboud replied.

"If you weren't my brother, I'd swear you were an elf the way you constantly whine," Boldair said.

"I'm *not* whining. I see no reason for taking the path we're currently on. All for a drink?"

"It's not just *any* drink." Boldair hurried up the steps. "And what would you propose we do?"

"Since you're the new king, you should meet with the Northern Dwarven Alliance's council," he replied.

"You heard Taniesse. She advises against it."

"Yes, against us returning to Nagdor. She said nothing of visiting King Thorgum and King Staggnuns. Seeking an out of the way path for a rare drink is pure foolishness, if ya ask me."

"I didn't ask, did I?" Boldair said with a fierce glare.

Drucis laughed. "You fail to see the point, Forboud. The drink's a powerful one dat tests whether you're worthy of claiming dwarf heritage or if ya 'ave traces of gnome in your blood."

Forboud frowned. "I wouldn't go dat far."

"Then let's see if *you* pass the test, eh?" Drucis' eyebrows rose, and he beamed a daring smile.

"Boldair," Forboud said. "Please reconsider this bizarre quest."

Dwiskter laughed and shook his head. "Quest? A quest would be us undertaking a series of Tavern-hopping to see which dwarf's the most resilient afterwards."

Boldair turned a metal handle, which activated the gears to bring the heavy stone flush with the ground. After the stone set in place, he placed several smaller stones atop it to better conceal the opening. He rose and placed a hand on Forboud's shoulder. "My days of these *quests* as ya call them are limited. Once I'm seated on the throne, my duties change forever. These next few days are the last of my freedom."

"Freedom?" Forboud asked. "Are you suggesting being king is like a prison term?"

"Isn't it?" Boldair said. "A king's bound to his kingdom, or 'ave you never considered dat before?"

Forboud rubbed his chin. "No, I haven't. But, yes, I understand what you mean."

"Good, then let's not continue shivering our arses off and be on our way."

Dwiskter nodded. "I agree. But, might I ask a question?"

Boldair glanced at him. "Sure."

"Do you perceive any treasure dat lies in the valley's edge below or upward beyond the gnarled roots of those whirled pines?"

Boldair stood and faced the valley. The harsh breeze made his long hair flow like ribbons. The braids in his long beard struggled not to become untied. He stared to the foggy bottom of the valley. After a few moments, he shook his head. "If any treasure awaits, it's small. The sound of the winds silences it. To risk death for whatever small amount of coins the dead carried ... isn't worth it."

Dwiskter stared at the trees and nodded. "I agree. Such a shame those never heeded the risks."

"Mount up," Boldair said. "The temperatures might not improve, but at least we won't 'ave to contend with this fierce wind much longer."

FIFTEEN

The dwarves rode an hour before the wailing winds diminished enough to speak without shouting to be heard. Boldair untied and unrolled a mottled bear hide from his saddlebag and wrapped it tightly around his shoulders.

His blood-red cheeks were numb. "All well behind me?"

"Aye!" Drucis and Dwiskter shouted in unison.

Seated behind Dwiskter, Viorka peered around the dwarf. "Where are we?"

"We're riding along the Lost Pass," Boldair said, straightening on Ember. The wolf's heavy paws kicked up snow with each step he took.

"Lost Pass?" Forboud shouted. "Determined to lead us to our deaths, are ye?"

Boldair let the question linger in the frozen air. Suddenly, his growing anger at Forboud's constant, challenging remarks warmed him more than the thick bear hide draped around him. Boldair lit his pipe, puffed it, and then combed bits of ice and snow from his beard. Lost Pass narrowed ahead. Biting his tongue and not lashing out at Forboud was painful.

The path scaled between two steep mountainsides. Hanging from the rugged cliffs were long, bluish-white icicles that whistled when the higher, gusty breezes flowed between the cliffs. Several brown eagles glided overhead, possibly looking for concealed snow hares. Their shrieks echoed between the ridges.

Although not a treacherous road, few ventured this narrow pathway. The Lost Pass led into the heart of the Frosted Peaks, which was frozen, uncharted wilderness. The few prospecting dwarves that had ventured deeper into this mountainous terrain, on their quest to map out the ore veins, were never seen again. Such bizarre disappearances inspired bards to spin tales about flesh-eating Frost Giants and ogres or something far worse. Tales included mysterious creatures none had ever encountered before.

The unknown mysteries didn't concern Boldair. The darkening skies above the higher peaks indicated heavy snow would soon fall. His party didn't need to be trapped between these two towering mountains and they were in desperate need to replenish their rations.

Boldair estimated another half hour of riding lie ahead before they cut northeast onto a smaller path. The intersecting side path was the farthest he'd traveled into the Frosted Peaks. Such bold expeditions were never wisely done alone, especially when previous explorers never returned.

"Shield your eyes!" Boldair shouted.

A harsh wind gust whipped downward and swept a blanket of loose snow and ice crystals from the pass and through the air. It approached at full force.

Pellets of snow and splinters of ice bounced off the bear hide Boldair had wrapped around his face.

Ember growled slightly and bowed his massive head. He braced himself and refused to take another step forward.

As quickly as the gust passed, it faded, and continued in the direction they'd traveled. These harsh gusts were probably why the Lost Pass pathway remained visible and never accumulated impassable walls of snow.

Boldair lowered the bear hide. Ember was covered in a thick layer of white ice crystals. The wolf shook his head and body before groaning a long yawn.

"Not much farther," Boldair whispered to Ember. The wolf replied with an agitated growl. Boldair shook his head, chuckled, and looked over his shoulder. "How are ya faring?"

The rest of his party dusted and shook away the snow from their hair and beards. For a moment his companions resembled the elder dwarves who'd advised Ulthor decades ago.

"Looking forward to a warm place to camp, or a small tavern where we can drink and perhaps eat warm stew," Dwiskter said.

"Ah, sounds great!" Boldair agreed. "We've not much farther before we cut off this pass."

"And then we have the warmth of a *cozy* goblin cave, right brother?" Forboud said.

Angry, Boldair turned in his saddle and stared at Forboud. "Nah, we've at least another three hours before we *reach* the cave!"

His voice boomed between the mountains. Several hanging icicles crackled. Small pieces of ice trickled downward and clinked like broken glass at the base of the mountain ridges. Some icicles were larger than spears and capable of splitting an armored dwarf in half. These swayed slightly at the echo of Boldair's voice.

"Careful," Drucis said. "The mountains are sensitive. Let's not make our presence any more *unwelcome*. Might prove costly."

Boldair kept his fierce gaze fastened on Forboud until his brother looked away. Boldair shook his head and turned around. *Must you increase this contention between us, Forboud?*

They rode in silence for the next quarter hour, listening only to the crunching steps of their mounts walking on the thin layer of snow and ice.

Boldair hummed a tune he'd once heard in Bridgebarrow Tavern. He didn't know the words, as the song was in an Elven tongue, but the sweet melody endeared his heart and brought him peace whenever strife sought to torment him, like now. The song had been sung by a pixie, and she lured the peasants and tavern patrons seductively with her physical beauty and soothing voice. Humming the tune led his mind to a place sorrow never knew. He smiled.

"What's dat song?" Drucis asked, riding alongside Boldair.

Boldair shook his head. "I'm sorry. What'd you say?"

"Dat noise. Did you hear it?"

"Oh, I—I was humming."

Drucis shook his head. "No, not dat. I heard your melody, but no, the sound echoing along the ridge."

Boldair pulled back the reins. A soft thudding riveted in the distance, almost like a woodpecker tapping a rotten tree. He shrugged. "I've no idea."

The sporadic sound held no constant rhythm.

"What's the problem?" Forboud stopped beside them.

"Dat sound," Drucis said.

Forboud cocked his head to the side and listened. "I hear nothing."

"Wait," Drucis said. Again, the thudding echoed. "Dat."

Forboud frowned and shook his head. Dwiskter reacted in the same way.

"It's got me curiosity up," Boldair said. "Let's go see."

Forboud sighed. "Brother, it's best we be on our way to *wherever* you wish to take us. Side journeys not only place *your* life in danger, but *ours* as well."

"We've yet to reach the road dat leads away from the Lost Pass," Boldair said. "Unless, of course, you wish we return to Banshee Bluff and then south? Or perhaps, maybe we should trek our way to one of these high peaks and cross over and down the other side?" Boldair frowned. "Or is *dat* too much for your sense of adventure?"

Drucis and Dwiskter stared at Forboud with mild agitation.

Forboud looked at the steep mountainside and shook his head. "Head on, brother."

Boldair's eyes narrowed. "By what authority are *you* commanding *me*?"

Forboud stiffened in his saddle and lowered his gaze. "Apologies, brother."

"Still playing prince?" Boldair asked. "Perhaps exile from Nagdor is your best option since you seem unable to accept me as the new king."

Forboud bowed forward on his saddle while gazing in Boldair's eyes. "Again, apologies. I'm tired, cold, hungry—"

Boldair waved his hand and shook his head. "As are we all. No one else is complaining. Only *you*."

Forboud closed his eyes and sighed.

Boldair clicked his tongue twice, but Ember ignored the command. Boldair nudged the heel of his boot against the wolf's thigh. Ember released a low guttural growl of stubborn protest but stepped forward and walked. "Seems too many resist my requests as king."

Drucis frowned at Forboud, tapped his ram's side, and moved in behind Boldair. Dwiskter followed. Viorka sat on the high saddlebag behind Dwiskter with her back pressed to his where she kept sight of Forboud.

Another half mile and the terrain on both sides of Lost Pass drastically changed. Large stumps remained where trees once stood. Deep trenches cut away the side edges of the pass where the massive trees had been dragged away.

"Odd," Drucis said.

"Very," Boldair said, nodding.

"I smell smoke." Viorka scrunched her nose.

"As do I," Dwiskter said.

"A stew of some kind," she added. "An odd aroma that I don't recognize."

The thudding sound grew louder and more consistent around the bend.

"Bloody Hells!" Drucis said.

Boldair tugged the reins. "So, you see it too?"

"Aye, and I swear I've not drank a drop this morning."

SIXTEEN

Snow-dusted logs were piled against the mountain base beside a large sawmill. Stacks of freshly cut planks were on other side of the mill. An iron kettle bubbled over a roaring fire, and black smoke curled upward.

Atop two large balance beams rested an almost completed hull of a large wooden ship. Inside a small section of the frame, a dwarf hammered rivets into the planks.

"Greetings!" Boldair said.

Startled, the dwarf paused. With wild eyes, he frowned at Boldair sternly. Then he studied the party of dwarves. His skin was dark with a slight, icy-blue tint. His beard and long hair were whiter than snow. He stood and huffed. "Be on ya way!"

"Is dat any way to speak to Nagdor's king?" Dwiskter said.

"King? Ha! Now, if ya said dat he were da *queen*, dat'd impress me far more. Be gone!"

Dwiskter, Boldair, and Drucis exchanged confused glances.

"You've no respect for our king?" Dwiskter placed his hand on the hilt of his axe.

Boldair placed his hand atop Dwiskter's and shook his head.

The dwarf frowned and scanned the Lost Pass. "I see no throne. He wears no crown. As far as *I'm* concerned, he's not a king here! Be gone now, the lot of ya. I've work to do. No time to prattle!"

Boldair chuckled. "Why are you building a ship at the side of the mountain? You're nowhere near a body of water."

The dwarf flung his hammer against the side of the hull, cursed under his breath, and stormed to the edge of the platform. He looked down at them. "What concern is it of yours, Ol' King?"

"No concern," Boldair said with a frown. "Just a bit ...peculiar."

"No more peculiar than a *king* traveling unprotected with a party through the Frosted Peaks."

"Fair enough. What's your name?" Boldair asked.

"Dat concerns you, *how*?"

"I only ask out of curiosity."

Dwiskter leaned close and whispered to Boldair. "He's a bit unhinged."

"I agree," Forboud said. "We should keep going, brother."

Boldair grinned.

The dwarf retrieved his hammer from the floor of the hull and sighed. "My name's Ice'ik. What else do ya need?"

"What kingdom are ya from, Ice'ik?" Boldair asked.

Ice'ik tilted back his head, stared at the sky, and shook his fists. "I don't see how dat matters, but if you absolutely *must* know, Frosthammer *was* my home. But no more! Those dwarves are daft!"

"As though *he* has room to talk," Drucis whispered with a smirk.

Boldair and Dwiskter laughed.

"Is dat funny?" Ice'ik asked. "You wouldn't think so, after you've tarried there long. Dat's why I'm building this ship, so I can get as far away from them as possible."

"Good luck with dat," Drucis said.

"I've no need of luck," Ice'ik said. "I'm a master carpenter."

Boldair stared at the ship hull with feigned admiration and scratched his chin. "I won't argue with dat. Quite good. Tell me, are you building this ship by yourself?"

"What do you think?" Ice'ik crossed his arms.

"To be truthful, I'm not certain *what* to think of a dwarf building a ship on the side of a mountain," Boldair replied.

"We have company." Forboud nodded at a small party approaching on the path ahead.

Four dwarves balanced and carried a midsize log on their shoulders. When they noticed Boldair and his party, they dropped the log. Their complexions were dark and tinted icy blue like Ice'ik's. Their hair and beards flowed to their waists and were the color of snow.

"Is all well, Ice'ik?" one dwarf asked.

"Aye!" Ice'ik said rather frustrated. "Just some *king* wandering around the Frosted Peaks. They should be on their ways now. Or does *Your Highness* 'ave more questions to delay our work?"

Drucis put his hand on the heel of his axe, tapped his ram's side, and rode a few steps closer toward the ship. "I've had it with his disrespectful—"

"Ah, let 'em be, Drucis," Boldair said. "As Forboud suggested, we should head on."

"Perhaps, you'd sell us some of your stew?" Viorka asked.

"Viorka," Boldair whispered in a scolding manner.

"What?" she asked. "It smells good."

Ice'ik's eyes widened when he noticed the fynx. He looked to his carpenter companions. "Fill 'em some bowls. No one will e'er say dat Ice'ik refused passing travelers food in such freezing conditions. Of course, I'm sure Halmick would like to know if his stew's fit for a king."

Halmick laughed.

Dwiskter and Drucis roared with laughter.

Halmick handed a tin bowl of bubbling soup to Boldair.

Boldair nodded his appreciation. "I suppose you'll have your answer in a few minutes."

Dwiskter took the bowl from Boldair.

"Hey!" Boldair said.

Dwiskter raised a finger in protest. "Allow me, just in case."

Halmick looked hurt.

Boldair frowned and harshly whispered, "You actually think they'd poison me? *Us?* You think they keep a large cauldron of bubbling, poisonous stew out in subzero temperatures, just waiting for the first unsuspecting party to arrive? I doubt they've seen any travelers for weeks."

"We cannot take such chances," Dwiskter said.

Boldair yanked the bowl from Dwiskter. "My apologies, Halmick. Dwiskter has my best interests at heart, though his manners in the situation could be more proper."

"Boldair," Forboud said. "You really should heed what Dwiskter said."

Boldair blew the steam from the bubbling stew. He carefully placed his lips to the side of the bowl and took a sip. He chuckled. "Hot! But tasty. Is this rabbit?"

Halmick shook his head. A sly grin parted his beard. "Kobold with yams, ice-root, and secret spices."

Boldair gave an old side-glance at Dwiskter. "Never eaten Kobold before; not dat I ever plan to again."

"How is it?" Halmick asked with eager eyes.

"Different. A bit ... gamey."

Halmick nodded. "Aye, yeah. They're a bit stringy, too. Not a lot of critters around. Sometimes, we're lucky enough to trap an occasional snow hare. But the kobold wandered into our camp and tried to kill and rob us. A mistake he won't e'er make again."

"Yes." Boldair swallowed hard and tried not to spew the tough meat from his mouth. "I imagine he won't."

Viorka held out her catlike hands for a bowl. "You have to make due with what you have sometimes."

"Aye." Halmick handed her a bowl. He looked at Drucis. "Come on. The rest of ya gather round. Eat before heading on your way. After all, you're hours away from any villa or city."

With a look of bewilderment, the rest of Boldair's party approached cautiously.

"It's really not bad at all." Boldair pulled a long strand of curled white hair from his mouth, winced, and let it fall on the frozen ground.

The rest of his party took bowls and leaned against the stack of logs. Each watched the other to see who was brave enough to take the first bite. Drucis sniffed the stew and then he jammed a large spoonful into his mouth. He chewed for several seconds, paused, and his eyebrows rose. He shrugged, swallowed, and took a second bite.

Ice'ik set his hammer on the hull floor, made his way down the ladder, and joined his group at the boiling pot. "What's your verdict, king?"

"I'll never tell anyone outside our circle dat we ate kobold. Considering how nasty and foul-smelling those creatures are, Halmick has done a remarkable job to make a delicious stew. No offense, but ... a kobold isn't something I'd ever consider eating again," Boldair replied.

Ice'ik laughed. "Nor would we. Dat's chunks of snow hare in the stew, not kobold. We set traps each day and get lucky e'er so often. You caught us on a good day. Kobold's stink worse than a skunk. Ain't ne'er a way we'd become *dat* desperate for food. Tree bark and sap is far tastier. Besides, kobold hide is quite tough. I imagine their meat's the same. They're filthy beasts ridden with disease."

After hearing the meat was hare, Drucis and Dwiskter ate the contents in their bowls with vigor, complementing Halmick for his incredible culinary abilities. Even Boldair ate a bit more at ease, but couldn't shake the thought of the long white hair, which must've been Halmick's.

Boldair set his empty bowl on a small table beside the cauldron. "Why'd you leave Frosthammer? Were you exiled?"

Ice'ik studied Boldair's concerned face for several moments. "The particulars aren't important. Do you plan to travel to the city?"

Boldair nodded. "It's where we're destined now, but only to pass through."

"No diplomatic appointments?"

"No," Boldair said. "We need a quick pass under the mountains."

"I see. So you've been to Frosthammer before?" Ice'ik asked.

"Aye, but a long time ago."

Ice'ik's icy blue eyes shimmered like sapphires struck by a bright ray of sunlight. "I wish you well on your visit, but things have changed in the underground city. If all you desire is to get to the other side of the mountain, be quick. Tis a shame my ship isn't yet completed. I'd be honored to take your party to wherever your journey ends on our first voyage."

Boldair glanced at the ship hull. The bow and stern were virtually complete. Two large masts were set in place with unfurled sails. To Boldair, the ship looked near completion but the Lost Pass was far too narrow. After a few moments, he expected Ice'ik to burst into laughter, but he didn't. His blue eyes and facial expressions remained serious.

"How long 'ave you worked on this ship of yours? It looks almost finished," Boldair said.

Ice'ik sighed. "Aye. A ship takes a lot of time to build, especially when only eight carpenters left Frosthammer with me. We've been working day and night for the better part of a year. If you tarried with us a few more days, you'd witness our maiden voyage, perhaps even sail with us."

Boldair exchanged side-glances with Drucis and Dwiskter. They strained not to burst into laughter.

"Indeed, dat would be a fantastic ... event to ... witness." Boldair bit the tip of his tongue until it hurt. He hoped the pain thwarted the rumbling laughs wishing to escape his mouth. After tasting blood, he attempted to redirect the conversation. "I doubt we could survive the cold nights."

"The ship's quite insulated," Ice'ik said. "Ya get used to the cold after awhile."

"You mentioned Frosthammer had changed. What made you *flee*?" Boldair asked.

"Lots of things, actually, the least of which would be political."

"Like what?"

"I'm afraid if I told ya, you wouldn't believe. Nor would I, had I not witnessed firsthand such abnormalities. It's why I spoke warnings to all who are dear to me. They chose not to listen and remained behind. I pleaded with my broken heart for them to come with me. Dat ache hasn't lessened, but I'm compelled to build this ship, so we can get farther away. I hope they'll come to their senses before the ship's finished."

"What'd you see?"

Ice'ik's lips twitched. His brilliance of his haunted eyes dimmed, as though sunken beneath murky water. "King, I must bid you and yours safe travels. Don't tarry in Frosthammer. Be quick about your business. Stay on the higher levels and you'll be safe. Rumor is Frosthammer's gates will soon close under King Rigrim's orders. Those caught inside won't be allowed to leave."

"Why?"

"Some of the dead are alive once more," Ice'ik said. "But they're not the same. Some believe a plague. Others like me, a curse. A few suggest the magic of a dark wizard has created these undead. There be worse things, too, but until you see them for yourself, words can't explain them. So heed my warning and journey to the other side quickly."

"You left Frosthammer a year ago?"

Ice'ik glanced over his shoulder at the ship. "Aye, about dat long."

Boldair marveled. "You've done dat much construction?"

"Aye."

"With only nine of you, dat's incredibly fast."

"When time's limited, and the cold keeps getting colder, you work faster and harder and through many nights. Unlike now, with you delaying us."

"My apologies," Boldair said.

"All's fine, dear king," Ice'ik said. "Of course, if you and your companions cared to use a hammer or two, we'd be done even faster."

"I'd love to offer my help," Boldair said. "But none of us are carpenters. Our *help* would only slow ya down."

Ice'ik chuckled. "I appreciate the candor. Your brief company has been pleasant, but we must return to our labor. Again, I wish this was completed, so we could aid you in your journey."

Boldair appreciated the sincerity in Ice'ik's voice and in his mannerisms. His attitude was completely different than a half hour earlier. He wondered if some sort of plague had occurred deep in Frosthammer. Was disease responsible for Ice'ik's delusions and his urgency to build a ship so far from the sea?

Boldair smiled and extended his hand. "You've done more than enough with your hospitality. I wish we could return the favor. Perhaps, whenever you complete this, you could visit me in Nagdor."

"I appreciate your offer. But I'm afraid once my ship's completed, I travel east to the Hoffnung Sea."

"Might I ask another question?" Boldair asked.

"If it won't take too long."

"Did a man driving a black carriage ever visit in Frosthammer?"

Ice'ik shook his head. "Frosthammer's a huge city with many levels, so it's possible but not someone I recall. Why?"

"His name is Mors. He's known as the Plague-bringer and might've cause the dead to rise from their graves. He's a necromancer."

"Sounds like you've dealt with him," Ice'ik said.

"Recently. He brought an army of undead to the surface and even an undead dragon. The Dwarven Alliance defeated him in battle, but he isn't dead. He escaped."

"I see." Ice'ik shook Boldair's hand firmly. "Safe travels. Perhaps one day we'll meet again."

SEVENTEEN

Once Boldair and his party traveled a half mile farther, the hammering on the ship returned to a hollow echo, but with a chorus of nine hammers instead of one.

"So Boldair," Drucis said, "what did *you* think of Ice'ik?"

Dwiskter laughed. "Yeah, he called everyone else daft?"

Boldair kept his gaze focused on the path ahead. Other than the darkening clouds and different numbers of soaring eagles and swooping hawks, the Lost Pass hadn't changed. If anything, the path seemed endless.

His mind couldn't shake the fear he'd seen in Ice'ik's eyes, especially after Ice'ik's dismissive, hardened attitude when they addressed one another. He'd pressed rather rudely for Boldair and his company to keep moving and not to stop and visit. Perhaps, Ice'ik's urgency to construct a ship was his hope to rescue his friends and family in Frosthammer. But why and *how*? The ship was on the side of a mountain far from any body of water.

The idea was ludicrous, and nothing more than the dream of a maddened dwarf. Yet, Ice'ik's sincerity and devotion held more stubbornness than the silence of a monk. But Ice'ik's intentions never hinted a religious tone.

"He's seems a bit deranged, don't you agree?" Drucis asked.

Boldair shrugged. "His actions are a bit ... *unbalanced* ... if you judge from what you see, I suppose."

"Or perhaps he drank one barrel too many." Drucis grinned.

"I never saw any barrels," Dwiskter said.

"Ah, my point exactly. Nor did he offer us a drink, which for a dwarf lacks hospitality."

"Maybe rations are low?" Viorka rubbed her full stomach and licked her lips.

Drucis chewed his lower lip, thought for a few seconds, and then nodded. "Dat's probably true. Still, I'd wager he's stashed several barrels behind the hull of the ship and out of sight. Who could blame him? I must admit, though, if what he said's true, they've accomplished quite a bit in a short amount of time."

"But building a ship on the side of a mountain? I suppose if ya pushed hard enough, it might slide down the ice-covered Lost Pass," Dwiskter said with a chuckle. "But once it broke free, how could ya slow or stop it?"

Drucis howled with a fit of laughter until a tear edged down his cheek. He grabbed a handful of his ram's hair to keep from falling off his mount. "My, what a sight dat would be! Can you imagine them tugging back on the ropes while the heavy ship dragged them down the slope! Of course, it'd crash into the mountainside or plow a road through the trees. Should it reached thawed earth beyond the forests, it'd mire down. And *he* thinks the dwarves in Frosthammer are daft!"

"Oh, my! Yup. I can picture the ship dragging 'em!" Dwiskter wiped tears from his eyes. "Enough! I need to see where we're going." He tried to regain his composure but shook his head and wailed heartedly.

"He's sincere in his beliefs, Drucis," Boldair said, in a quiet, serious tone.

"Oh, is he now?" Drucis' grin remained wide. Tears flowed.

"Aye, he is," Boldair said. "You remember the Plague-bringer?"

Drucis and Dwiskter nodded. Their laughter ceased.

"It's possible Mors has been to Frosthammer. Ice'ik mentioned dat the undead are roaming the lower levels of the city," Boldair said. "Dat's the biggest reason for why he left."

"Perhaps dat's what's driven Ice'ik to madness?" Drucis said.

"Perhaps. I can't think of anything more batty than building a ship in the mountains," Boldair said.

"And for what purpose?" Dwiskter asked.

"He wishes to flee quickly."

Drucis cackled. "Walking on foot for the past year would've been much faster, don't ya think?"

Boldair nodded. "Of course."

"Or crawling," Dwiskter said. The two returned to their laughing fits.

Boldair sighed but didn't join their laughter. "His family's in Frosthammer. The deranged notion of building a vast ship might be his way of prolonging his stay and hoping dat his family will leave Frosthammer to join him. At least it's shelter from the cold."

"It'd take a lot of dwarves to hoist dat ship," Drucis said.

"You're missing the point," Boldair said.

"Dat being?" Drucis asked.

"Leaving family behind," Forboud said sourly. "Even when they don't see things the same way. Or if their minds have altered slightly. Family's the strength of all dwarves. It always has been and will always be."

"Aye," Boldair said. "But not all transgressions can be forgiven or forgotten."

"They should be, if one has the heart to forgive," Forboud replied.

"Forgiveness has little to do with it, brother. Trust lost can seldom be earned back," Boldair said. "Such a division can't ever be bridged together in the same manner it was, either."

Forboud straightened in his saddle and puffed his pipe. "One needs to allow those wounds to heal."

"Wounds heal," Boldair said. "The scar, however, is a constant reminder of the injury and pain."

Drucis gave Dwiskter an odd side-glance. "I don't think we're talking about Ice'ik's dilemma anymore."

"You be right about dat," Dwiskter replied. "How 'bout sharing one of your treasure hunting tales, Boldair?"

Forboud groaned slightly.

"It'll help pass the time." Drucis eyed Forboud. "And let us forget *your* current tensions for a while."

Viorka perked up. Her eyes widened with excitement. "Have him tell you how we destroyed the Orb of Misfortune!"

"Is dat a good one?" Dwiskter asked.

"Not about treasure," she replied.

"And not the way *she* tells it!" Boldair said fiercely, before turning and giving her a broad smile. "But I 'ave you know, had it not been for her bravery, I might not've survived. She looks tiny at times, but her heart's dat of a warrior. The worst part, though, is dat I nearly killed her."

Viorka smiled and blushed. "The orb held you under its spell. You weren't at fault."

"You tell them what happened," Boldair said.

"You sure? I wouldn't want to tell it incorrectly."

Boldair smiled. "You'll do fine. Besides, after I took the orb, I don't remember a lot of what happened."

Viorka turned on the saddlebag to tell the story, which turned out to be a more optimistic tale than Boldair would've told.

EIGHTEEN

After several hours riding along the bottom edge of the Frosted Peaks, Boldair pulled the reins. Ember stopped. When Boldair slid off the saddle, the snow went above his knees. A chill shot through Boldair. Without thinking, he exposed his back to Ember. The dire wolf growled and lunged at him.

Boldair turned, tried to move out of Ember's reach, but the deep snow prevented him from moving. He raised his steel-gloved fist. "Wait until I turned my back, eh? Back up, you mangy mutt! You want to wear dat muzzle forever? 'Ave some respect or find yourself missing teeth."

Boldair's heart hammered in his chest, but he stared fiercely into Ember's eyes without showing fear. The wolf's eyes glowed like red coals. Neither broke their gaze with the other. Boldair pointed his finger. "I'm a warning ya! Get back!"

"Ember!" Forboud shouted and slid off the saddle. Fury reddened his face. "Yield!"

Ember's ears backed. Ember looked at Forboud and stepped back. The wolf lowered his head in submission and licked his chops.

"Dat's better!" Boldair glared at the wolf. He nodded at Forboud. "Thanks, brother."

Forboud shrugged and loosened the wolf's muzzle.

Boldair turned his attention from Forboud and took a difficult step forward in the snow. Two fir trees stood at the base of the snowy mountainside. Snow weighted and made the tree branches sag almost to their snapping point.

"We're here." Boldair grabbed a lower tree branch and shook it. Snow plummeted around the base of the tree in thick clumps. With several feet of snow covering the area, they didn't need to contend with the harsh winds like they'd endured at Banshee Bluff.

Viorka sat on Dwiskter's saddle and her cat eyes widened. She expressed her hatred for the snow. Since she was too short to walk through it, she didn't reject Dwiskter's offer to remain on his saddlebags while they traveled.

"This is it?" Drucis asked. "I don't see any cavern."

"Aye," Boldair replied. "The snow's hidden the opening. These two firs are the landmark I was looking for."

Forboud frowned. "They look like all the others."

Boldair nodded. "Except, for my carving on this one's trunk." He slapped his hand against the smooth bark. Above his hand was a dark colored groove cut deeply with the hammer symbol Boldair used in his signature.

"Ahh." Dwiskter dismounted. "I'd have never seen dat, had you not pointed it out."

Boldair walked to the snow-covered entrance, pounded his fist against it, and stepped back. More snow fell and formed another small pile on the ground. "Step back. I gotta release the trap."

"Do you set traps on everything?" Forboud asked.

"On the things I value the most."

"You *value* an old goblin cave?" his brother asked.

Boldair laughed. "I value what's inside."

"O-oh," Dwiskter said. A smile spread across his face. "You've hidden treasures inside."

Boldair looked over his shoulder and grinned. "Not much, but some. The good news is dat no one's triggered the trap. At least no one on the outside."

Boldair fumbled with a small device, removed it, and slid his hand into a small hole. He squinted. A gear clicked. He exhaled a sigh of relief. "All's safe now."

"I suppose dat's *until* we step *inside*?" Forboud asked. "Careful, all, it'd be a shame if the trap misfired. Nothing's worse than being killed by a king when no crime's been committed, don'cha think?"

Boldair's brow narrowed and his jaw tightened. "Dat's not going to 'appen."

Forboud grinned. "How can ye be so certain?"

"I didn't find the switch for the second trap."

"What does *dat* mean?" Forboud asked.

"Perhaps I didn't set it properly and it's already fired. Or, a rat triggered it from the other side. Bah, who knows? The trigger's been tripped. Dat good 'nuff for you?" Boldair frowned.

"Didn't mean to rile ya up, brother, but it seems you're losing your knack for setting these traps. Perhaps it's time you retired from treasure-hunting to become king."

Boldair sighed.

Forboud's tone defined the resentment in his voice. Regardless of how much Forboud insisted he wasn't jealous or he didn't want to be crowned king, Forboud continued spewing his disdain whenever he spoke. He couldn't seem to help himself. Boldair wondered if Forboud even realized it. Drucis' and Dwiskter's facial expressions revealed they detected Forboud's bitter undertone.

Boldair was saddened he might have to part ways with his brother. Until their father's imprisonment, the two always seemed to get along, though their interests were never exactly the same. Boldair was more inclined to hunt for lost treasures than to partake in military exercises. Despite their differences, they were still close.

Forboud often traveled with Boldair on the shorter journeys, but now, after discovering Ulthor's plan to place Forboud on the throne, Boldair wondered if Forboud was a spy for their father.

Protest all ya like, Boldair thought. *But, the truth's in your tone, Forboud. Can't you see the disgrace father has placed on our name and our lineage by his betrayal to one of our dearest allies? Will ya ever realize how he's tarnished the crown?*

Boldair hated not trusting his brother, but until he was certain he could fully trust Forboud, Boldair needed to keep a watchful eye and be on guard.

Boldair gave a side-glance to Ember. The giant wolf wagged its tail as Forboud scratched behind its ears. Forboud smiled and held the muzzle in one hand. He fed the wolf a strand of jerky. Ember gulped down the dried meat and nuzzled Forboud's hand. Boldair's brow furrowed. A new worry came to mind.

The wolf hated Boldair, but held affection for and obeyed Forboud. What prevented Forboud from commanding the wolf to attack, maim, or kill Boldair whenever Dwiskter and Drucis were away? They knew the wolf's underlying resentment and distaste for Boldair. Should the wolf kill Boldair, no one could argue the wolf had not purposefully done so on its own. The blame would never fall on Forboud because of the wolf's hatred for Boldair.

Boldair pulled a lever. A set of gears squeaked and turned. The faux rock door pulled slightly inward.

Viorka leapt from the saddlebag and landed facedown in the snow. The deep snow swallowed her. Only the outline of her body was visible. Dwiskter waded through the snow to where she landed, reached in, and pulled her out.

Her lips shivered and she shook snow off her face. "Uh, thanks."

Dwiskter laughed and shook his head. "Any deeper and I don't think my arm could've reached ya."

Boldair stepped beside the door. "Viorka, you go first."

She peered at the narrow opening with nervousness. "I—I don't know."

"Oh, come now," Drucis said, "Boldair's inside trap has been released. Nothing's gonna hurt you."

"I'd rather not," she said.

"And after I boasted so greatly of your bravery earlier," Boldair said, "you're going to prove me wrong?"

"Can you prove the goblins aren't inside the cavern?" she asked.

Boldair shook his head. "Ya don't believe Dwiskter and Drucis, either, then?"

"Or *me*," Forboud said with a firm brow. He tapped his pipe against the wall to dislodge the burnt herbs.

Boldair pushed the door farther inward, turned sideways, and walked through. He returned a moment later with an unlit torch. After several scrapes of his flint against the side of the rock doorway, the pitch on the torch flared. A ribbon of smoke curled upward.

"There!" Boldair grinned. "Satisfied?"

Viorka nodded. "Mostly, yes, but that doesn't prove there aren't goblins inside."

"I'm afraid I misspoke your bravery, lil' cat," Boldair said.

"I see no reason to risk *my* life in a situation where bravery isn't called for. I choose not to die for *your* curiosity," she replied.

"You're not the least bit curious?"

"Not when I might get eaten by goblins. Besides, you don't know why the other trap was released."

Boldair grumbled under his breath and entered the narrow doorway with Drucis and Forboud following behind. Dwiskter carried Viorka inside and set her on the dirt cavern floor.

"Boldair?" Viorka said softly.

"Yes?" he replied.

"I know how your second trap was disarmed," she said.

"How?"

"You might rethink your thoughts about the goblins being dead."

Boldair turned. "Why?"

Her eyes widened and she pointed.

NINETEEN

Boldair swung the torch in the direction Viorka pointed. Speared into the rock wall was a scrawny goblin. The spear wasn't what had killed it. Its shriveled skin stretched over its bones indicated the mottled, green-skinned creature had starved to death.

Dwiskter and Drucis drew their double-edged axes.

"It triggered the other trap," Boldair said with a slight grin.

"I see nothing amusing," Viorka said with a frown.

"So ya know what dat means," Dwiskter said.

"What's dat?" Boldair asked.

"More goblins are probably in the cavern," Dwiskter replied.

"Could be a straggler trying to find its way outside," Boldair said.

Drucis shook his head. "Doubtful."

Dwiskter glanced at Boldair. "Is what you hid still here?"

Boldair used the torch to scan the dirt floor. Old crates had been strewn and some had been smashed against the wall. Splintered fragments of planks littered the dirt. Boldair grumbled. "Thieving varmints!"

"What'd you have?" Dwiskter asked.

"A few small bags of gold coins and some gems. Not a great loss, really," Boldair said. "But too much to tote without a mount."

"Where'd you find them?" Viorka asked.

"An abandoned goblin alcove deeper in the caverns," Boldair said.

"You stole the loot from them?" Drucis asked.

Boldair shook his head. "No. No goblins were there."

"Apparently, they were, brother. They stole whatever you took from them."

Dwiskter frowned and shook his head. "Dat's not good. They must've been hidden in other dens dat you didn't see. If they followed you to the surface, they'll be more violent if we use this cavern for a shortcut."

"Perhaps we should find a new route to Meadwyrm Pass?" Forboud asked.

Viorka nodded and pleaded. "Yes, let's."

Boldair shook his head. "No. We continue our route to Frostham-mer. There's no turning back."

"Why?" Forboud asked in a challenging tone. "Can't you see the odds be far greater against us entering a cavern where these goblins live?"

Boldair crossed his arms. "No. If you wish to go back, then go. There's the door. I'll lock it once you're out. But understand, as king, I need to know dat Frosthammer's not suffered their demise from these fiendish imps. We also need to know how badly the undead infestation has become. *We* need to know. If somehow the goblins 'ave returned in greater numbers, we need to warn the other kingdoms. The Dwarven Alliance needs to know."

Forboud pointed at the goblin speared to the wall. "You 'ave more than enough proof with dat corpse."

"One dead goblin isn't sufficient evidence to have our allies send troops to investigate," Boldair replied. "We're already here, so we can explore the cavern and its alcoves."

Frustrated, Forboud headed to the door. "I doubt the Alliance will be pleased with your decision to risk your life."

"I've been through this cavern twice and never saw a goblin," Boldair said. "I saw no recent evidence of their camps. Besides, their horrendous stink gives them away."

"It doesn't mean they didn't see you." Forboud walked to the crude entrance.

"Are ya leaving us?" Boldair asked.

"No," Forboud said. "If you're so foolish to continue down into a maze of goblins, I cannot allow you to go without me. You're still king. I pledged my life to save yours, even if you ignore our sound advice. Should we both die, though, who'll rule our grand city?"

Boldair ignored the snide comment. "Then why are you going outside?"

Forboud sighed. "To fetch my mount and Ember. So, Viorka, you might want Boldair and the others to stand between you and Ember. Even though Ember's muzzled again, he can still hurt you." He studied the narrow corridor that led deeper into the cavern. "Judging by the low ceiling, we'll have to lead our mounts."

"The ceilings are higher once we get past the corridor," Boldair said.

"Until then," Forboud said, "we must lead them."

Boldair looked at Viorka and grinned. "Looks like you go first after all."

Her eyes narrowed. "I'm not certain *which* danger I prefer less. Ember or the possibility of goblins gnawing on me."

Drucis chuckled. "For now, we know Ember's real. Not sure about the goblins, but you alert us when they appear."

"I won't be *that* far ahead of Boldair," she replied.

"You'll smell them long before you see them," Drucis said.

"What do they smell like?"

"Acrid sweat and musty ol' rat-eaten rags with a hint of burnt oil and kobold feces. If their jagged blades don't kill ya, the smell most certainly will sicken ya."

She scrunched her nose and looked at the dark passageway. Frigid air flowed through the corridor and engulfed them.

Viorka rubbed her arms vigorously. "It feels as cold in here as outside."

"Aye," Boldair replied.

"Most caves are warmer than this," Drucis said.

Boldair nodded. "Usually. Even though we're going deep underground, the temperatures stay like the dead of winter. How do you think Frosthammer and the Frosted Peaks got their names?"

Dwiskter brought his ram and Drucis'. Forboud entered the cavern with Ember and his ram. After the wolf and ram were clear of the door, Forboud twisted the device at the side of the door. The narrow doorway sealed. Darkness consumed them. Boldair's flickering torch was their only light.

Ember's eyes glowed red in the swaying light.

"Viorka, head on." Boldair motioned to the path ahead.

"No turning back now, huh?" she replied.

"Not unless you wish to be a tiny morsel for a hungry wolf," Forboud said in an ominous tone.

Viorka gasped.

"Pay 'em no mind," Dwiskter said. "Ember's muzzled. As little as the wolf likes Boldair, it's more likely to attack him first."

Boldair shook his head and chuckled.

Dwiskter smiled. "We won't let dat 'appen either."

Viorka took a few hesitant steps. Boldair held the torch overhead so the light was cast around them. The flickering flame licked the frozen rock and melted ancient spider webs.

"Ya know," Drucis said, "there be times when I wish I could cast light spells."

"How long will we remain squeezed tightly together like this?" Dwiskter asked.

Boldair said, "Not too much longer. Twenty yards or so."

"I can't hold me breath dat long," he replied.

"Why would you need to?" Boldair asked.

"These rams' are quite gamey."

"I thought dat was you!" Drucis said, before howling with laughter.

Inside the narrow passageway, their voices and laughter echoed.

"Tease all ya like, Drucis," Dwiskter said. "But for a moment, I thought maybe dat stew had made its way through ya already."

"Ha! I'd never confess if dat's true."

"Shh-hh!" Forboud said. "The point of heading deeper into the cavern is to *not* be noticed."

"Ah, now—" Drucis said.

"You realize." Forboud interrupted Drucis. "Any forces dat choose to rush us headlong while we're confined in this tight huddle can destroy us quite readily."

"Let 'em try," Dwiskter said, holding his axe over his shoulder.

"He's right," Boldair said sternly. "The least sound is greatly magnified inside this narrow passage, possibly booming outward into the cavern. If goblins live here, they know we're 'ere. They'll be waiting for us."

The group walked in silence until they reached the end of the narrow corridor. Viorka stepped into a vast open room. The path ahead was a narrow stone bridge with no walls at either side.

"Wait," Boldair said to Viorka. He reached to the side of the corridor passage and grabbed an old torch stuck in a hole. He placed it against the lit one until the second torch flamed. He handed it to Drucis. "Dat should help some."

"Aye, much better."

"Watch the path carefully. One misstep and you won't escape death. I've no idea how far down the bottom is. I don't think any of us want to know."

"Shouldn't we mount up?" Dwiskter asked. "The rams are more surefooted than we are."

"If you trust dat better, so be it." Boldair thought for a moment. "As for me, I continue on foot. Forboud, if you wish to mount up, tether Ember behind you. Should I attempt to ride him across this bridge, he'll find a way to send me to the depths below."

Forboud laughed softly. "You're starting to understand him better than I thought you might."

Boldair took a deep breath and held it. *I'm afraid I understand more about you and the wolf than you realize.*

Drucis climbed on his ram and held the torch. "You mind me asking you a question, Boldair?"

"What's on your mind?"

Drucis cleared his throat. "What e'er possessed you to journey beyond this point? With either side of this bridge dropping into oblivion, I'd have turned back."

"Why would you even enter such a place alone?" Forboud asked.

Boldair sighed. "My goal during those days was to find Frosthammer."

"What led you to believe it'd be through these caverns?"

"On occasion I've found old, crude maps in the treasures I've discovered."

"Treasure maps?" Dwiskter asked.

"Sometimes," Boldair replied. "I found one particular map dat revealed a passageway to Frosthammer. I wanted to know if Frosthammer actually existed or if it was only a myth. Dat's why I chose to pass through here."

"Do you ever weight the dangers of your travels?" Forboud asked.

"Aye, I 'ave every time."

"I've difficulty believing dat," Forboud said.

Boldair held his torch high, which allowed more light to spill on the path ahead of Viorka and himself. "Believe as you wish. It's obvious you do anyway. But entertain me with why you think I'm not weighing the dangers now."

"Blasted! Isn't it obvious? You're leading us on a folly-fallen, fool-hardy trek across Aetheaon for a bloody drink," Forboud said.

"Dat be *half* true," Boldair replied.

"Then, brother, do tell. What be the other half?"

Boldair's voice deepened with anger. "Unfinished business I should've tended to in Frosthammer years ago, if dat's *any* of your concern."

"But you weren't king then."

"Right you be!" Boldair shrugged and nudged Viorka to keep walking across the bridge. "King or not, it's something I should've already take care of. It's none of your concern."

Forboud sighed. "Fair enough. But at least answer this, since I am part of your council. Did the map indicate this cavern was once occupied by goblins?"

"No."

"So other than the dead goblin at the entrance, what caused you to believe goblins inhabited it?" Forboud asked.

"Brother, the treasure I found in the alcove and hid near the entrance had several silver daggers with various rare gems in the handles." Boldair sighed. "Goblin daggers. I wish I had taken them with me. The jewels were worth more than all the gold coins combined. But the daggers ... there's no mistaking their origin. No other race crafts them in dat manner."

"What if these goblins had swarmed and killed you?"

"You'd be king," Boldair said with a short laugh. "Erm, wait. I'm wrong 'bout dat assessment."

"Why?"

"Because, most likely, father would still be king."

"Why do you say that?" Forboud asked.

"Everyone believed father when he boasted about killing Taniesse. It wasn't until after she revealed who she was dat I let others know father had *not* killed her. King Staggnuns and King Thorgum pressed father about his lies and his purpose for lying about his *great dragon slaying*. Dat's when his lies about King Erik surfaced and *why* he was stripped of his reign. Are ya done with your questions? After all, you were the one who insisted we remained quiet, so the goblins can't hear us."

"You're right," Forboud said. "I said dat. But your actions for exploring these caverns seem careless, even now. Regardless of my warnings, you insist we—"

"Enough, Forboud!" Boldair drew his axe from its sheath. "I gave you the choice of following or leaving. You chose to follow, yet you yammer on and on. Why question *my* reasons for seeing if the map led to Frosthammer years ago?"

"I think any one of us would've had held major qualms of further exploration without seeking aid from others."

"I imagine *you* do," Boldair replied. "But you're *not* me. You don't have the fortitude necessary to search through the dark crevices deep inside the hearts of mountains. Dat's the huge difference between the two of us. It's also why *I* have the crown. If you wish to take this battle beyond words, me axe is ready. What say ye?"

"I don't wish to lift any weapon against you," Forboud replied. "Regardless of whether you're king or not, you're my brother. I couldn't ever attack you with a weapon."

"No weapon other than the sourness of your words," Boldair said. "The bitterness of your heart spills through your lips and your actions."

"Aye," Dwiskter said. "I attest to dat! Forboud, I've bitten my tongue for some time during this journey about your questioning our king and his decisions. It's one thing to advise, but you're close to treason with your words. Whether you've noticed or not, my axe is drawn at the ready to remove your tongue if you speak further ill words to King Boldair. You know me reputation well enough. Dat's not an idle threat but an action I *won't* hesitate to carry out. Do we 'ave an understanding?"

"Aye, duly noted," Forboud said.

"Boldair," Drucis said. "Could I ask you a question?"

"Go on," Boldair said.

"Why would Frosthammer allow goblins to live in such close proximity to them? Is there a treaty between the two?"

"None I know of."

"It seems odd though," Dwiskter said.

"Aye," Boldair agreed. "It's a question worth asking. If nothing else, the goblins are a strong deterrent to prevent outsiders from finding Frosthammer."

"There's no way Frosthammer's dwarves don't know this goblin cavern neighbors their city," Drucis said.

Viorka dove forward on the narrow bridge. "What was that?"

"What?"

A small creature fluttered in the darkness outside the torch's radius, swooped past Viorka, and then darted into the darkness once more.

"A bat," Boldair said.

She peered over her shoulder. "You're sure?"

"Yes. Quite harmless."

"How much farther do we worry about where we step?"

Boldair extended his hand to Viorka and helped her stand. "We've almost reached a giant column dat descends from the cavern ceiling into the dark abyss below. A spiral path encircles the column. It's not much wider than the natural bridge ahead, but we can brace ourselves against the solid column while we get our bearings."

"What about our mounts?" Drucis asked. "Is it wide enough for them?"

"Aye," Boldair replied.

"Once we're on those spiral stairs, where do we go from there?" Dwiskter asked.

"We descend into the darkness below," Boldair replied. "We continue downward until we reach a level rock ledge. Dat's where another tunnel leads to Frosthammer."

"The map gave you detailed instructions for how far down we are to go?"

"Yes."

Viorka increased her pace. "Dat smell you warned about earlier?"

"Goblins?"

"Yes."

"I don't smell anything," Boldair said.

"Nor I," said Drucis.

"Trust me," she said. "My sense of smell is greater than all of yours combined. Goblins are nearby, unless something else reeks that badly."

"Not my doing." Dwiskter grinned.

Bursts of fires appeared at different levels of the cavern at the outer perimeters. Dozens of them. Mad squeals and angered growls echoed. Metal bolts fired and struck the rock bridge at their feet.

"They see us," Boldair said. "Move to the column quickly. Once we head down those stairs, we should be out of their view."

TWENTY

Boldair tried to match Viorka's swift pace but couldn't. Metal bolts struck the rock bridge in rapid succession. Her keen night vision aided her nimble steps. She seemed to guess where the bolts were going to hit, and her feet moved a second ahead of their strikes. The bolts chipped bits of rock off the bridge.

In seconds, she stood with her back against the center column. A large, circular stone platform encompassed the stairs. Should they get down the stairs unharmed, the platform could block the goblins' view from overhead.

Boldair moved his stubby, muscular legs swiftly. Metal bolts struck his steel plate-legs and ricocheted off. He released a burst of crazed laughter, spun his two axes in windmill fashion, and thwarted several bolts destined to strike him above the belt.

Behind him, the ram mounts bleated in pain. Ember yelped and snarled. The hides of the rams and the giant wolf were thick, but their skin wasn't impenetrable.

Drucis, Dwiskter, and Forboud dismounted, grabbed the halter of their mounts, and hurried along the narrow bridge. Metal bolts continued to strike the mounts.

Boldair joined Viorka at the circular platform where two more stone bridges intersected into the platform encircling the spiral stairwell. A line of torches approached from each of these roads. At least two dozen crazed goblins growled and snarled with weapons drawn. Their eyes glowed crimson, but a few had snotty green eyes.

"So you *didn't* 'ave this problem the last time you were here, eh?" Drucis pulled his ram on the circular platform.

"No!" Boldair readied his broad axes.

"Well, they're giving ya a hearty welcome today!"

"Let 'em come!" Boldair shouted. "I'll sharpen me axes with their bones."

"I'm with you!" Drucis slid his shield off his back and hefted his massive axe in his right hand.

Viorka screeched like a mountain lion and growled.

Drucis glanced her direction. "What the—?"

She was no longer the smaller version of herself. She stood taller and more slender, nearly five feet in height. Her claws extended into long, needle-pointed nails, and her face altered. Her teeth became sharpened fangs. A madness swirled in her emerald eyes.

"You've not seen dat side of her before?" Boldair asked.

Drucis' brow furrowed. "Uh, no. Dat's new. I'd remember *dat*."

Dwiskter and Forboud reached the circular platform.

"They'll be on us in the span of a few breaths," Boldair said. "Keep your backs against the stairwell! We've no time to descend. We can't retreat, so don't get backed to the outer edge. We're outnumbered. They can overpower us and knock us into the abyss. Goblins don't care to sacrifice themselves to kill their enemies."

Dwiskter led his mount to the center near the stairs. He hooked the reins around a metal bolt embedded in the rock column. Drucis did the same. Forboud held Ember's reins and his ram's and positioned himself near the mounts to hide.

The stench of the vile goblins was on them before the scuttling creatures even reached the platform.

"Steady yourselves!" Boldair shouted.

Dwiskter laughed. "Seems this trip has a few highlights before we get to Meadwyrm Pass."

"Keep telling yourself dat," Forboud said in an angered whisper.

"Tryin' to work up our thirsts *before* we get there?" Drucis said.

Dwiskter took his shield and positioned it to one side of Boldair to lessen the chance a metal bolt striking their king.

The goblins' eyes glowed in the light of their torches. Their narrowed slits displayed their fury and demonic hatred. Their rapid footsteps thudded without any apprehension in their approach. Perhaps they viewed the odds in their favor?

Drucis and Dwiskter lowered their shields and prepared for the onslaught. As the goblins neared, they leapt, snarled, and swung their daggers madly as they descended.

Before the first goblin touched the platform, Viorka sprang upward, spun, and sliced her long, sharp claws through a goblin's throat. Its squeal of pain ended in less than a second. Its head left its body and bounced across the platform.

While still in the air, she spun again, dropped, and kicked her feet off Drucis' shield. She propelled herself at the next two goblins. Their angered expressions widened into brief fear. Viorka plunged her claws deeply into their chests. She landed atop them, yanked her claws free, and readied herself for the next goblins.

"Hey!" Dwiskter shouted. "Leave some for me!"

Viorka grinned. "From what I see, there's no shortage."

"From the rear!" Forboud shouted.

Boldair faced the adjoining rock bridge. A dozen small torches danced and lit the crazed goblins' eyes. "Ye 'ave an axe, brother. How 'bout using it!"

Forboud released the reins of Ember and his ram and fumbled to pull his axe from its sheath.

Boldair growled and rushed to the rock bridge. He hoped to cut off the goblins' advance before they reached the platform. By the time he got past the ram and Ember, two goblins lunged from the bridge at Forboud.

Boldair growled in fury. He spun with both axes outstretched and jumped forward. When he landed, a goblin's arm dropped to the platform still holding its torch. The goblin squealed. Black blood spurted from it shoulder. Boldair kicked its chest and sent it toppling off the ledge into the darkness below. The second goblin clutched its throat and gurgled. Blood leaked profusely between its fingers. Even near death, it gnashed its teeth. With the flat-side of his axe, he smacked it. It staggered, slipped on its blood, and dropped off the platform.

Viorka was midway down the other bridge. She slashed and dismembered several goblins. Frustrated, Drucis hurried on the bridge to help. Boldair chuckled. *Not dat she needs any help.*

Dwiskter left the two of them on the bridge. He didn't have enough room to join them without accidentally knocking one another off the bridge. He hurried past Forboud who struggled to unsheathe his axe. Dwiskter shook his head in disgust, flung his shield in front of Boldair, and blocked several metal bolts before they struck Boldair's chest.

Boldair and Dwiskter took turns swinging their massive axes. They struck and toppled the approaching stream of goblins. As more and more goblins fell into the chasm, the goblins farther up the bridge slowed their pace, possibly realizing they held no advantage in their swarm tactic.

"Hold your positions!" Boldair shouted. He glanced at Dwiskter. "They're having second thoughts now."

"Seems so," Dwiskter replied.

Fireballs glowed from a higher ledge. Seconds later, the fireballs glided at them.

"Bloody Hell!" Boldair shouted. "Sorcerer!"

Dwiskter lifted his shield and blocked two fireballs. Several metal bolts flicked off the shield immediately after.

"We've no way to stop their firing from this distance," Boldair said.

Forboud whispered, "Behind you."

Boldair turned and looked. On the ground was a goblin crossbow. He glanced at Forboud. "You know how to use it?"

Forboud nodded.

"Then do so. It's apparent you can't use an axe!"

Forboud frowned at the comment. He grabbed the crossbow and several bolts off the platform.

"Aim for the sorcerer," Boldair said.

"I can't see him," Forboud replied.

"Whenever he creates a fireball, dat's where you aim!" Dwiskter frowned. "Ya sure your father trained you for battle?"

"Quite," Forboud said.

"Then bloody Hell prove it!" Dwiskter said.

Six goblins charged in pairs at Boldair. They struck Dwiskter's shield, and knocked him and Boldair backwards on the platform. Another half dozen goblins scrambled down the bridge and sought to encircle them.

The crossbow twanged.

Boldair blocked the downward dagger attack from a goblin and caught its wrist with the handle of his axe. He shoved and sent the goblin into its companions behind it.

Fireballs lofted on the higher ledge. Forboud fired again. The sorcerer shrieked in sudden pain, and the fireball engulfed the sorcerer.

Boldair and Dwiskter fought to hold back the goblins. But before he realized it, the goblins took advantage of the dwarves' brief distractions and moved to overpower them.

Boldair swung his axe and ripped a goblin in half. He glanced at the other bridge. Viorka and Drucis backed to the platform as a huge wave of goblins pressed across the bridge. Viorka slashed but these goblins carried tiny iron shields, which prevented her claws from reaching them.

Ember howled fiercely and ripped the muzzle off his snout. The sound echoed greater than thunder and struck fear into the goblin mob. The wolf growled and lunged at the goblins surrounding Boldair. Its massive jaws clamped on a goblin. The goblin squealed. Ember held it tightly and shook the goblin until its bones cracked.

Ember flung the lifeless goblin on the bridge. The line of approaching goblins paused to inspect their dead comrade. Two goblins nudged the body with the tips of their daggers. With widened eyes, they peered at Ember and the Dwarven warriors fighting on the platform.

Ember snapped the next goblin and repeated the process. Then in a frenzy, Ember mauled and bit his way through the remaining goblins standing on the platform. Several goblins jumped off the platform, preferring to fall to their deaths rather than being ripped apart. Ember stepped partway on the bridge with a fearsome growl rumbling in his throat. He faced the line of goblins that stood frozen. They contemplated whether to continue their attack or turn and flee.

Boldair decapitated a goblin with a swift swing of his axe and pushed his way to the next one. Goblin corpses piled around his feet. Slick pools of black blood spread and dripped off the edge of the platform. With Ember blocking the approach of the frightened goblins, Boldair hurried to the other side of the platform to aid Viorka and Drucis.

"Some help, please!" Viorka panted. She pressed her back against the column. Blood dripped from her long, sharp claws.

Dwiskter turned, stepped beside her, and eyed the blood dripping to the rock platform at her feet. "You okay?"

She nodded. "The blood's not mine, but ... I'm winded. I've killed sixteen."

"Ah, now, I counted fifteen!" Drucis teased. "The one *jumped* to his death."

Viorka grinned. "It still counts. He jumped because I stepped toward him."

While Ember faced the perplexed goblins on the opposite bridge, Drucis, Dwiskter, and Viorka faced a determined line of partially armored goblins with daggers and shields. Although their armor was flimsy at best, it didn't allow for swift kills.

"How many have you killed?" Dwiskter asked.

"Erm, ten, I think, but *she*'s blocked my path pretty much the entire time."

She grinned and shook her head. "Excuses!"

"Move aside and let me show you how it's done," Dwiskter said. He glanced at Viorka. "Catch your breath and rejoin us."

"Ah, find your own!" Drucis placed his right foot forward and readied his axe.

The band of armored goblins advanced in odd, jumpy steps. They sprang upward from one foot to the other and bounded toward the column platform. They seemed to defy gravity, or they somehow landed on floating, unseen steps in the air.

Drucis and Dwiskter stood side by side and battered their axes through the goblins' helmets. The crushing impact bent the helmets into their skulls and the goblins collapsed where they stood.

These goblins, like those on the opposite bridge, realized that while they held a far greater number, they weren't capable of making a wide lunging attacks due to the narrow bridge. After the two dwarves killed another half dozen goblins, the goblins stopped advancing. They grumbled and shouted obscenities at the dwarves and one another. Their heated bickering escalated and some fought each other.

Viorka screeched with a high-pitched growl of pain. A moment later, Ember yelped and whimpered in a horrible series of cries.

"Viorka!" Boldair yelled.

She lie on the platform, clutched her side, and curled into the fetal position. Ember staggered away and wiped its bleeding left eye with its paw. His whining yelps frightened the remaining goblins, and they scurried deeper into the darkness.

Ember shook his head and sprayed warm pellets of blood across the platform. The pain angered the dire wolf. He growled and snapped savagely at the air. His nostrils flared and he panted. The wolf sniffed across the platform until he found Viorka.

Already in pain, she pushed herself upright and scooted her back against the column. Ember lunged at her. His massive jaws barely missed. In response, Viorka slid to her side, flailed her long claws into Ember's left shoulder, and sank her nails deeply.

Ember yelped. He yanked back and dragged Viorka's limp body with him. She pressed her free hand against the rock platform for leverage and yanked her claws free.

"You shall die for this!" Forboud shouted with his axe held overhead with both hands.

Boldair leapt and caught the axe handle right beneath the sharp blade and yanked downward. Forboud spun and landed on his back. "*Now* you choose to use your axe?"

"Look what she did to Ember!"

"To Ember? It attacked her! The wolf's lucky *I* don't kill it," Boldair said.

"The wolf attacked me!" She winced with each breath. Blood leaked through her fingers.

Spittle flew from Forboud's lips. "A shame it didn't!"

Boldair placed his boot atop Forboud's chest and pressed the sharp edge of his axe to his brother's throat. "I've a good mind to slit your throat in front of our enemy. Viorka's my friend, and a friend of the king outweighs your loyalty to me; which, as it appears, has been next to nothing."

"How can you say dat?" Forboud asked.

"How?" Boldair cocked his head. Fury reddened his cheeks. "You never lifted your axe to kill one goblin. You don't think I could tell dat you left us to our demise? You hid like a coward amongst our mounts."

"I couldn't free my axe."

"You think me a fool, brother?" Boldair pressed the blade harder and cut Forboud's skin. Boldair looked into his brother's frightened eyes. "I thought father taught you how to fight, but you're a coward to the core. You did nothing against the Vykings. Cowards on the battle-field must be punished for such weakness."

"Please, brother, don't."

"Other than striking the sorcerer with a metal bolt, you lingered from the battle while the rest of us fought for our lives. Rest assured, Forboud, we *weren't* fighting to protect *you*. Are you wishing my death so you can claim the crown? Is dat why you refused to draw your weapon?"

Forboud opened his mouth to speak, but Boldair shook his head and pushed the blade harder. Tears formed in Forboud's eyes and spilled. The tears meandered down his face into his ears.

"Now, you listen. Your words mean nothing to me. Your actions reveal everything about you, do they not?" Boldair asked. "Tell me something, brother. When Drucis, Dwiskter, and I fought for Lady Dawn, *where* were you? I didn't see you on the front lines, nor did I see you with father dat night. In fact, I'll wager dat if I ask King Staggnuns and King Thorgum about your whereabouts during the battle, they'll be clueless as well."

"I—I was—"

"Save your breath, brother," Boldair said. He knelt atop Forboud and peered into his eyes. "Your lies cannot save you. Drucis, Dwiskter, did either of you ever see Forboud during the Battle of Hoffnung?"

They shook their heads and glared at Forboud with disdain. Both said, "No."

Boldair shook his head and ground his teeth. His breathing grew heavier with each deep breath he took. "See? None of us saw you in battle. You kept father fooled, didn't you? All those years of training, you made him believe and boast about ya. Yet, none of dat ever gave you the bravery to face an enemy on the battlefield. You can't even kill a stinking lil' goblin, but you can try to kill my friend after dat bloody wolf almost killed her. You're a disgrace to Nagdor. And as such, you'll pay the appropriate price."

Fear widened Forboud's eyes even more. Tears leaked rapidly. His breathing shuddered.

"Only if father could see ya now," Boldair set his axe aside and it clanged on the rock. He drew a sharp dagger from the sheath on his belt.

"Brother, please," Forboud said with a shaking voice. "Please reconsider."

Boldair shook his head. "Reconsider what? Don't struggle. Just close your eyes, take a deep breath, and be quiet. It'll end in seconds."

Boldair pressed one hand around Forboud's throat and placed the dagger to his brother's neck.

"Boldair," Forboud sobbed. "Please."

"Sh-hh-hh," Boldair said. "Close your eyes."

Forboud obeyed and offered a slight nod.

With one swift stroke, Boldair sliced with the dagger. Confused, Forboud opened his tear-filled eyes. Boldair lifted his left hand. Clutched in Boldair's fist was Forboud's long braided beard.

A hurt sigh expelled from Forboud's mouth. He closed his eyes. His body fell limp. Tears flowed.

"Boldair," Drucis said. "Viorka isn't moving."

Boldair pushed himself to his feet, grabbed his axe, and clung to Forboud's beard with his other hand. "Dwiskter, take Forboud's weapons. Make certain he doesn't even possess a lock pick. Then bind his hands behind his back. If the goblins return, leave him to their mercy."

Dwiskter nodded, eyed Forboud's beard in Boldair's fist, and stared at Forboud.

No greater shame was known to the dwarves within the Dwarven Alliance than for one to have his beard removed. It showed everyone, regardless of rank or race, the dwarf's great dishonor.

Boldair knelt beside Viorka and placed the back of his hand against her furry cheek. Blood leaked from her nostrils and at the edges of her mouth. Her breathing was shallow. If she didn't get to a medic or a healer soon, she'd die.

Gently, Boldair scooped her in his arms and stood. "Have the goblins fled, or do we still need to defend our position?"

Drucis had been gathering coin pouches off the goblin corpses. He looked and took a few moments to study the bridges. "They're retreating, for now. We probably killed a hundred of them by my estimate. They'll reconsider a second attack for a while."

"Good," Boldair said. "I must get Viorka to Frosthammer before she dies."

Dwiskter shoved Forboud toward the stairs. Forboud's hands were tied behind his back. "And what of him?"

"Tether Ember to walk behind him. Should either jump or fall, they both suffer the same fate." Boldair eyed Forboud fiercely. "Not much of a loss either way."

"You could execute him here, if you so wish," Dwiskter said. "Toss his body in the ravine. You 'ave dat right. No one but us would know."

Forboud's eyes hollowed. He peered at Dwiskter and then flicked his gaze to Boldair.

Boldair nodded and pondered the thought. "Aye, I do. But living in shame's a greater punishment than immediate death."

"I agree." Dwiskter placed his hand atop Forboud's shoulder. "Come on."

Boldair looked at Drucis. "I must go first. If you could, please lead our mounts down the stairs. You'll come to another platform like this except there aren't any bridges connected to it. Only a large double-door dat leads into Frosthammer. I'll wait for you there. Please hurry."

TWENTY-ONE

At each side of the locked, double-doors were two glowing Elven stones. These offered enough ambient lighting to see from the entrance to the stairwell column. Boldair held Viorka and paced in front of the steel doors. He mumbled incoherently. Anger and rage shortened his patience.

Ember's harsh attack had left no bleeding wounds. The caked blood around her mouth and nose indicated she'd suffered serious internal injuries. Depending on the severity of the injuries, death could be quicker than he expected.

No guards stood outside the doors. On Boldair's last visit, the guards were inside. He needed to rap the proper knock sequences at the exact pace for them to open the doors. Since no one else in his party knew the code, he needed to wait until the dwarfs arrived.

"You're going to be okay, lil' cat," Boldair said. "I promise. I'll get you help."

He shook his head and exhaled. Puffs of white flowed from his mouth. The frosty air bit his nose. Frozen tears filled the wrinkles around his eyes.

"Boldair!" Drucis shouted. "Are we near?"

"Aye!"

Their steel boots scuffed harshly against the steps as they came around the last spiral.

Drucis led his ram and Forboud's off the steps and onto the platform. He stared at the double-doors with uncertainty. "Don't tell me we're locked out?"

"Aye," Boldair said, "but they'll let us in."

"How can you be certain?"

Boldair shrugged while holding Viorka in his arms. "They opened the doors for me the last time I was here."

"Will she survive?" Drucis asked.

"Don't know yet. I pray so."

Drucis sighed. "She's not dead. You'll know when she is."

Boldair frowned. "How?"

"She'll turn invisible. Remember?"

"Right," Boldair said.

"Is this her true form?" Drucis studied her face and gently touched the fur on her forearm. Raising her limp hand, he inspected her long needle-like claws. He shook his head, possibly thinking about how painful having those claws thrust into one's flesh might feel.

Boldair said, "I'm not sure which form's dominant. She alters, based on the circumstances. She's a dangerous fighter when in this form."

"But she's not changed back. Is dat normal?"

"Perhaps it's because we're *not* out of danger. Her life's in the balance, so it's safe to say dat she's still in danger."

Dwiskter stepped on the platform, reached behind and grabbed Forboud's mail tunic, and tugged him to follow. Forboud offered no resistance or words. His eyes expressed his shattered spirit and loss of hope. Since Ember was tethered to Forboud, the dire wolf stood closely behind. Blood dripped from the three deep grooves Viorka slashed through its left eye and into its skull during the few moments she had to defend herself.

Ember must've rushed her from behind and wrapped his powerful jaws around her waist. He possibly shook her like he had the goblins he'd killed. She'd done nothing to provoke the wolf. Raking her razor claws was her natural instinct to defend herself. It was possible her aim was off the first time she struck. But slashing through the wolf's eye was a tender vulnerable spot, enough to distort and disorient her attacker. Ember probably dropped her due to the pain.

During Ember's second attempted attack, Boldair figured Viorka's aim was for the wolf's heart. Apparently, she was too weak to accurately strike the proper spot or plunge her claws deep enough.

Boldair cradled Viorka in his left arm and did the series of knocks with his right from memory.

"You learned dat code from the map?" Dwiskter asked.

Boldair nodded. "Aye."

The double-doors rattled slightly and pulled inward. Two dwarf guards stood dressed in armor fashioned from Ice Dragon scales. These dragons were rumored to have lived in the highest elevations of the Frosted Peaks. From Boldair's previous visit, he learned this insulated armor was light weight and almost impenetrable to most weapons, other than those enchanted with fire spells.

The Frosthammer guards looked at Viorka with grave concern before they noticed who held her.

"Boldair!" One guard exclaimed. "I never expected you to return after such a long absence!"

Yotram! Brandrum!" Boldair said with a forced, hearty laugh.

"With your treasure hunts, I figured a dragon might've eaten you," Yotram said.

"Almost, my friends! Almost!"

"Good dat you've returned."

Boldair forced a quick smile. "I planned to pass through the city, but my friend suffered a vicious attack. Her life's fleeting."

"This fynx is your friend?" Yotram marveled and peered closer. His icy blue beard was neatly tied into long braids. His hair was sheered short on the sides but a long ponytail tied into knots hung down the center of his back. "I've only seen paintings of these unique creatures. Never thought they really existed."

"It's obvious they do," Boldair replied.

Yotram shrugged. "No denials now, I must say."

"I don't suppose dat you're aware," Boldair said, "but ya 'ave an army of goblins outside these doors. You might consider placing more guards to stand watch at the gate."

Brandrum was bald with a dark bluish-black beard. He reared back his head and roared with laughter. His voice thundered deeply. "Oh, Boldair, it's much too early and too little stout for ya to begin telling tales this soon!"

"No, not a tale. Tis the truth. The goblins 'ave returned." Boldair's voice was grim and his gaze, stern. "In far greater number, it seems."

"You're not hoodwinking us? No lie?" Brandrum cocked a brow.

"I never lie," Boldair said with a slight frown. "I might exaggerate from time to time, *after* a few tankards, but my friend, this isn't one of those times. I speak truthfully and without exaggeration. The goblins have returned."

Dwiskter nodded. "Boldair speaks the truth. We killed at least a hundred of 'em before they retreated to the higher ledges of the cavern. In the pitch darkness, we've no way to properly estimate how many there are."

Concern overtook Brandrum's and Yotram's facial expressions.

Drucis held up several coin pouches and shook them. "This be some of the loot I retrieved off their stinking corpses."

Brandrum and Yotram cautiously watched the outside stairwell column while they hurried to shut the heavy doors. After sealing it shut, they latched several heavy steel planks into position and locked them. It was doubtful the best Dwarven cannon could destroy the gate.

"Goblins? Did they do this to the fynx?" Brandrum asked.

"No," Boldair replied. "The wolf mount tried to kill her."

"She's not faring well at all," Brandrum said.

"Aye," Boldair replied. "She needs a medic or a healer quick, please."

"Yotram," Brandrum said. "Could you escort him to Telsia?"

"Of course," Yotram said.

Two patrol guards approached the locked gate, studied Boldair for a few minutes, and broad smiles broke their stern faces. "Boldair! Come for more of our frostbitten stout?"

"At the moment, no," Boldair replied.

"I'm escorting him to the medic," Yotram said.

"Drinks at the Ice-Slurry Tavern later?" A guard asked. He carried a heavy hammer in his hand and an octagon bronze shield was slung over his back. He wore a patch over his left eye. A long scar began above his left eye and ended at his lower jaw, which cut a bare path through his bluish-gray beard. "Or perhaps, you'd prefer Hogshead Splatter Grog?"

"Perhaps later, Kairun. Let's see how things go with the medic first," Boldair replied.

The two guards nodded.

"Can I or Bathil aid you in any way?" Kairun asked.

Bathil crossed his thick muscular arms. Sheathed on his belt were two short swords. His braided beard and hair were dark blue, which appeared almost black in color. Several tattoos marked his face and massive forearms. He studied the fynx with great curiosity.

"Actually," Boldair said. "Place Forboud in a cell until we're ready to depart."

"Your brother?" Bathil glanced at Forboud and grimaced.

"Aye," Boldair said.

Forboud looked at Bathil. "How do you know my name?"

Bathil ignored him. "What's he done to bring himself such shame?"

"Partly, what happened to my little friend here," Boldair said. "If you can place him in a cell until Viorka's healed, I'd be grateful."

"Aye." Bathil frowned at Forboud with disgust. "We'll make certain he's well taken care of."

"Good. Trust me. You can't believe a word dat falls from his deceitful tongue. He's as bad as father in *not* telling the truth and almost cost us our lives." Boldair showed the horrible bruising around his wrist where Ember had attacked him. "And it might yet cause her death. He'd best hope she survives."

"May I ask what he did?"

"He betrayed the king of Nagdor," Boldair replied. "And cowered when we fought the goblins earlier."

"Your father? I thought the two of them were close?"

Drucis shook his head. "Boldair's king now."

"Boldair?" Yotram said in disbelief. "You've taken the throne?"

Boldair held a grim gaze and nodded solemnly. "We've much catching up to do. Now's not the time. I'll share with all of you my endeavors since we last spoke. Drinks are on me."

Bathil nodded and laughed. "I hope you've deep pockets, if you're buying the stout."

Viorka's body shook. Boldair couldn't tell if it were due to the frosty temperature or if she were near death.

"Follow me, Boldair," Yotram said.

TWENTY-TWO

Boldair followed Yotram. Drucis and Dwiskter walked alongside Boldair. He cradled Viorka in his arms. Other than occasional tremors, she hadn't moved since they entered the gate. Her breathing was shallow and she sweated profusely.

Their steel boots thudded on the metal roadway while they marched at a rapid pace. Thick steel panels with treaded grooves for traction were riveted to the roads throughout the upper levels of the city. They walked along the Pinnacle Path at the edge of a deep chasm, which divided the great city into nearly equal halves. The pungent scent of brimstone lofted in the air. Every eighth of a mile, a bridge crossed the deep divide. At the bottom of the ravine, the fiery river's radiant glow cast an orange light.

The river's appearance was deceptive. Contrary to the heat the river should've provided Frosthammer, the city remained frigid, though warmer than the constant winter outside the mountain. Braziers burned outside each shop, tavern, and inn. Even these offered little heat, unless one stood close to the flames. Lanterns hung from polished metal posts along the edge of the roadway, the awnings of buildings, and along the bridges.

The Frosthammer dwarves were hearty. The cold didn't affect them.

The only ones standing at separate braziers were a few visiting forest elves and some gnomes. The elves regarded the passing dwarves with slight suspicion, but when they noticed Viorka in Boldair's arms, they turned with keen interest.

Drucis peered over the edge at the river below. "Ah, the legend be true?"

"What legend?" Boldair asked.

"Dat Frosthammer's built above the lava flows?"

Yotram glanced over his shoulder. A slight grin broke through his thick beard. "Dat, my friend, is the River of Steel. It's a river of molten steel. It runs from our smelters. The river flows and separates into different channels farther down into the lowest levels of the city. There, it's poured into various molds, depending on what we need."

"For dat much molten steel to be flowing through a vast channel, you must 'ave a mighty furnace for heat," Drucis said. "Either dat, or your using the heat from Hell's belly."

Yotram laughed softly. He came to an intersection. The left path led to a bridge that crossed the River of Steel. He walked to the right, which led them to an open lift. The rising platform elevated and stopped before them. "Come. We're almost at Telsia's shop."

Boldair and his party followed Yotram onto the lift. After several seconds, the lift lowered and descended at a moderate pace with clicking gears and chains. The lift stopped at two different floors, and when it stopped at a third floor, Yotram stepped off and onto the street.

The glowing river beamed brighter. Several dwarves pushed carts of goods. Some led burros packed with large sacks of grain and other odds and ends wares. A couple of wagons passed with freshly sawn logs.

Dwiskter studied the passersby. "What cities do you trade with?"

Yotram turned right at the next street. "Frosthammer's essentially self-sufficient."

"How?" Drucis asked. "We're far deeper under a mountain than any Dwarven city I've ever visited. How do you maintain food and where'd those logs come from?"

"We have farmers. A large pool of water has a variety of fish. Over time, we've adapted, learned how to obtain our own resources without the aid of outsiders, but we still trade some goods. There's not sufficient time to explain it all," Yotram said. "But if you're with Boldair in a tavern later, I'll try to answer your questions as best I can."

"Aye, thanks," Drucis replied. "Sounds like something worth listening to while downing a few tankards."

Yotram pushed the door of a small building inward. "This is Telsia's shop."

"Thanks," Boldair said, walking past Yotram.

Boldair stood before a polished wooden countertop similar to a tavern's bar and unlike what he imagined in a medic's or healer's bazaar. The only exception was the carved runes in the counter's surface. He studied them. *Elven?*

"Where is she?" Boldair paced and scanned the room.

A chandelier made from four medium-size dragon tusks hung above the counter. Large candles burned at each of the four flattened ends. Boldair cringed. Between the guards who wore Frost Dragon armor—from dragons long believed extinct—and dragon tusks used for ornamental purposes, he wondered where they'd obtained these materials. Had they discovered the burial grounds where these dragons once prospered? Or were they the ones who drove the Frost Dragons to extinction?

He averted his attention from the tusks to prevent his curiosity and anger from increasing. Since his friendship with Taniesse, his view of dragons was far different than most of Aetheaon's population. He wondered what Taniesse would do if ever she entered Frosthammer. Would she torch the city in an unyielding rage?

Boldair turned from the counter and gazed around the room. Bottles of powdered herbs, dried leaves, and ground roots lined the shelves from the ceiling to the floor on two walls. Each bottle was labeled with penmanship unlearned by the hand of most dwarves. The writing resembled that of the dedicated monks in the Ruins of Sturn, which had been destroyed centuries earlier by the dark elves. However, some of their scrolls were antiquities kept in different libraries and temples throughout Aetheaon.

A double-sided bookcase acted as a partial wall to divide the main entrance and formed a tiny room in the corner. The decorative book spines were written in various languages of Fae, elves, dwarves, humans, and gnomes.

Almost hidden in the nook was a small round table that set in the corner where the two shelves filled with the bottled ingredients met. A black cloth weaved from pure spider-silk draped the table. At the table's center were Fae crystals, used to divine one's future or more commonly, to find a lost loved one. Sweet incense billowed in tiny streams from a silver burner shaped like a dragon's head. The eyes were deep red rubies that glinted ever so slightly whenever one gazed at them.

A silver birdcage hung from a golden hook on the ceiling. Several odd looking sprites hovered inside the cage. Their eyes shifted with mischievous curiosity while they studied the three dwarves. Their hideous, bitter faces prevented anyone from staring at them for more than a few seconds.

Telsia pushed a hanging purple drape across a silver curtain rod, stepped through a narrow doorway, and offered an endearing smile. The brightness of her amber eyes was mesmerizing. "Sorry to have kept you waiting."

Her long flowing, black robe shimmered when she walked. Like the delicate tablecloth, her robe was made from exquisite spider-silk. Her brown hair was tied in a series of knots down her back. With her given name and the decor of the room, Boldair had expected the medic or in this case, the *healer*, to be an elf, *not* a dwarf.

"Welcome." Her eyes darted at Viorka and her brow rose. She gasped. "A fynx? She's injured?"

"Aye," Boldair said with a firm nod. "Can ya help us? Quick?"

"My goodness!" Telsia placed a hand over her mouth. "Bring her to the back."

She turned and hurried through the curtained door. Boldair followed without hesitation.

Telsia waved her hand toward a small cot. "Place her there."

Boldair gently placed Viorka on the bed and stepped back. A gentle fire burned in a fireplace. More bookshelves with magical tomes lined the walls.

"What happened?" Telsia asked.

"A dire wolf attacked her," he replied.

Telsia placed her hand to Viorka's forehead. She shook her head. Tears moistened her eyes. "Fynxes are the rarest of creatures. She has a fever. Where'd you find her? Did you plan to sell her?"

Boldair shook his head and glared. "Sell her? Hell no! She's my friend."

"Your friend?"

"Aye, she's traveled with me on a couple of journeys now, but nothing as tragic as this."

Telsia searched his eyes and was possibly attempting to discern whether he was telling the truth or not. "I see. When did she last speak?"

Boldair shrugged and looked at Drucis and Dwiskter who stood right outside the door.

"More than a half hour ago," Dwiskter said. "Perhaps a bit longer."

"Hopefully, you've brought her in time," Telsia said. "Leave her with me and I'll tend to her."

"If it's all the same," Boldair said, "can we wait with her for a bit?"

Telsia smiled and offered a slight nod. "You may, but she'll be here for a day or more at best. I'm sure you're weary from your travels. Across the bridge is an inn with a steam room and other amenities. Take a hot bath to soothe your aching muscles. Of course, dozens of taverns and pubs are on each side of the steel river. As for your friend, she needs immediate attention and lots of rest. She probably won't awaken for some time. May I have her name?"

"Viorka," Boldair said.

She looked in Boldair's eyes. Her amber eyes soothed him, as did the gentle tones of her voice. "Rest assured. She's in good hands. You may visit her at any time, day or night. My door's always open."

Telsia placed her warm hand on his elbow, and then looped her arm in with his. She walked him to the door where Dwiskter and Drucis stood.

"Ya know," Boldair said. "When first told your name and then seeing all the various books ya 'ave in other languages, I never figured you to be a dwarf. I thought maybe an elf."

She laughed in a near seductive tone and squeezed his biceps. "While elves occasionally visit our grand city, we never expect any to set up shop in Frosthammer. We're tolerant of their kind, but not *dat* tolerant."

"Many believe Frosthammer to be a mythical city," Boldair said.

"I did," Dwiskter said.

Telsia nodded and beamed a smile. "We're not offended by dat error. In fact, it's something we're rather proud of."

"Why's dat?" Boldair asked.

"Because we don't deal with the skirmishes of the clashing kingdoms on the surface." She caressed the inside of his arm. "Of which, I'm certain you've witnessed. I'm certain the three of you fought in a recent war?"

"Aye," Boldair said.

Telsia walked through the doorway with Boldair. "I detect great valor in you, Boldair. Your boldness has made you a leader, has it not?"

Boldair frowned. "H-how'd ya know dat? How'd you know my name? No introductions 'ave been given."

Telsia smiled softly. Her eyes held his in a warm gaze. "I see a lot of things, and I'm far more than a healer."

Boldair cocked a brow. "I-interesting."

Drucis stood near the exit and counted coins from a goblin pouch. He slid the coins inside the pouch and tightened the drawstring. He tucked the pouch behind his belt and pulled out another one. Frowning, he shook it. "What the—?"

He opened the pouch and looked inside. Carefully, with his forefinger and thumb, he pulled out a stack of dried leaves and held them up.

"What have you there?" Telsia asked. If she'd wanted to mask her interest, she failed miserably.

"Leaves of some sort," Drucis replied.

"May I see?"

"Of course." He shrugged and handed them to her.

She carried the leaves to the counter and set them down. Her eyes widened. "How'd you find these?"

"From a goblin's purse," he replied.

"Goblins?" Her brow furrowed with concern and she turned her attention from the herbs to Drucis.

"Aye," Boldair said. "We battled our way through the filthy beasts in the cavern to reach the gates."

"No goblins have been seen in ... ages." She spread the leaves on the countertop. "May I see the pouch?"

Drucis slid the pouch across the counter to her.

She looked inside the bag. "The goblins had these leaves in their possession?"

Drucis nodded. "Most of their pouches held coins, but dat one had leaves. I probably should've 'ave tossed them rather than keep them."

"To the contrary," she said, "these are quite rare. In fact, if I used a sliver of one in my healing salve for Viorka, her healing might occur quicker. What's your price for these?"

Drucis shrugged. "You can 'ave them. They're useless to me. If they aid Viorka, all the better. Her healing's worth more than gold."

"While I greatly appreciate your generous offer, I can't accept them for free. I'd become indebted to you. But, I'd gladly pay whatever your tab is during your stay in Frosthammer for all of you—dat's the cost of the inn, your food, and all your drinks at any or all taverns."

Drucis' brow rose, and he exchanged glances with Dwiskter. They laughed heartily until tears formed in their eyes.

Partially offended, Telsia said, "I wasn't joking. I'm serious."

Drucis wiped a tear. "Ah, now, ya be puttin' us on. The tab we'd build on drinks alone would cost a fortune."

Boldair nodded. "He's not exaggerating."

"But, I'm willing to pay the price." She crouched behind the counter and clicked a few devices. She rose and tossed a heavy bag on the countertop. Gold coins rattled and spilled from the top of the bag.

"What are the leaves?" Boldair asked.

"Frostroot."

"They're dat hard to come by?" Drucis asked.

"Yes, especially if the goblins have returned to reside in the cavern. These herbs grow in crevices along steep inclines, which are most difficult for a dwarf to scale. An elf or human could do so much easier, due to their thin statures. I've offered a high reward for dwarves to collect them, but some of the younger dwarves have fallen to their deaths. I quit sending dwarves to find them after we learned how to cultivate them.

"But a blight wiped out our supply. The reason I'm willing to pay such a high price is because the pouch also contains seeds. With the proper care, I might be able to sprout seedlings in my shop to transplant in the darker recesses of Frosthammer. Should I succeed, I can harvest more seeds and replenish our cultivation." She placed her hand on the bag of gold coins. "However, I refuse to take these for free, so do we have an agreement?"

Drucis nodded. He scooped the loose coins and put them inside the bag. "If ya insist."

"I do," she said before turning her attention to Boldair. "I need you to do something for me."

"What?" Boldair asked.

"Stick your index finger in the pixie cage," she replied.

Boldair responded with a curious frown. "Why?"

"Trust me." Telsia smiled.

"No offense, but I find it difficult to yield my trust to anyone since my father and my brother have betrayed me."

"I understand betrayals within families more than you might think," she said. "Often one learns to rely more on strangers than those bound to us by blood. All the same, it's only a simple task. It's necessary in case I need to find you quickly. Frosthammer's a huge city. To find someone based on chance, you might wander for weeks before crossing paths."

Boldair removed his glove and placed his finger through a small hole near the top of the cage. A pixie lighted on the edge of his finger and jabbed his finger with a short quill. He yanked his finger from the cage. Blood pooled where he'd been pricked. He frowned at Telsia. "What's the meaning of dat?"

The pixie placed the hollow end of the quill to its lips, tilted it back, and drank Boldair's blood.

"Now, if need be, should Viorka's health worsen, and we pray it doesn't, Frizt can locate you for me. Preferably, all shall go well for Viorka's recovery. But if not, I'll send Frizt to fetch you."

Boldair rubbed his finger and nodded. He looked at Drucis and Dwiskter. "Let's go."

TWENTY-THREE

Boldair left Telsia's shop and stepped on the bridge that crossed to the other half of the city. Drucis and Dwiskter walked behind him.

"You trust her?" Dwiskter asked.

Boldair stopped mid-stride and glanced at Dwiskter. Frustration creased his brow. He shrugged. "What choice do I 'ave? I'm not a medic, nor a healer, and to be honest, I don't know who else to leave Viorka with. You 'ave any suggestions?"

Dwiskter shook his head. "No. I know no one here."

Boldair forced a tired smile. "Then the rest is fate."

"Know dat I'm 'ere for you, regardless of the outcome. My axe and shield are to protect you for as long as I breathe."

Boldair nodded. "I appreciate your devotion, but while we're in Frosthammer, let's not mention me being king. Safety reasons and all."

"Aye, as you wish," Dwiskter said.

Boldair turned and walked halfway across the bridge.

"You've only been to Frosthammer once before?" Drucis asked.

Boldair stopped and stepped to the side of the bridge so the city's inhabitants could continue to their destinations without stepping around him. He nodded. "Aye."

"The guards know you quite well," Dwiskter said. "How long did you stay?"

"A couple of weeks."

"Why'd ya stay for so long?" Drucis asked.

"To be truthful, I was tired of searching for treasure after the map led me here. Getting to the goblin cave through the mountains exhausted me. After two weeks of *recovery* ended, I was almost out of gold. Drinks are expensive at most of the Frosthammer taverns, especially when you're *not* a citizen. With my funds depleting, I left to get more gold from my troves, so I could stay longer."

Dwiskter leaned against the bridge's steel rail and looked down. Icicles snapped off the rail, tumbled downward, and melted before they were even close to the molten steel. "But you never returned until today?"

"No, I didn't."

"How many levels does Frosthammer have?" Drucis asked. "This is a massive city."

Boldair grinned. "Aye, it is. When I visited before, I counted eight levels on each side of the river." He laughed. "Of course, dat might not be accurate with all the tavern-hopping I'd done. Occasional blurred vision and all. If your goal's to drink at each tavern before we leave, we'd be here longer than an average elf's life."

Drucis laughed. "In the heart of the mountains lives the hearts of the dwarves, and in the hearts of the dwarves live our love for hard stout. I could die a happy dwarf in Frosthammer."

Dwiskter pounded his fist on Drucis' shoulder. "I'll drink to dat!"

From the rail of the bridge, Boldair counted the closest sets of bridges downward. Four levels of the city were below their position, as best he could tell. Three levels were above them. Following the River of Steel into the heart of the mountain, he counted the number of bridges outward, but his limited vision prevented him from seeing how wide the city expanded. Frosthammer seemed unending.

Of course, the colossal statue of King Rigrim Dragonbane stood with one foot planted on each side of the molten river and blocked the view of what else was downriver. Balanced in both hands was King Dragonbane's massive warhammer with simulated icicles hanging from the hammer's head. Atop his helmet were wings like a majestic eagle. His eyes were insets of enormous amber stones set in the sockets. Burning braziers behind these huge stones made the eyes glow ominously. For any visitor, the statue was menacing. Its feet were on the ground floor and the winged helm rose above the rooftops of the highest level.

Most kings possessed egos, but none, it seemed to Boldair, was greater than Dragonbane's.

During Boldair's previous visit, he never met or saw Rigrim, but the Dragonbane's massive warhammer was the reason for the city's name. From stories belted by the bards in taverns, Dragonbane's hammer could not only crush his enemies, it froze their bodies beforehand and their flesh shattered and exploded like crushed ice after the heavy hammer struck them.

Nothing caused loyalty better than fear. Perhaps this was why the residents seldom left Frosthammer, and why the few visitors never left. Somehow over the centuries, other kingdoms dismissed Frosthammer. The less the city was mentioned, the quicker it faded from memory and became whispered legend. Because few dwarves ever moved outside the mountains that housed Frosthammer, the city's population steadily multiplied.

From Boldair's estimation, Frosthammer easily outnumbered the combined populations of the three cities in the Dwarven Alliance: Nagdor, Damdur, and Icevale. Why'd this magnificent kingdom isolate itself from the other Dwarven cities? Had the three kings shunned and forbade Frosthammer from joining the Alliance? Or had King Dragonbane refused to join the Northern Dwarven Alliance? If the latter were the case, evidence of such a withdrawal was stricken from the history ledgers and tomes.

Had Boldair not succeeded his father on the throne, he could've moved to Frosthammer without a single regret. But such a decision would have had to occur *after* he was too decrepit to explore Aetheaon in his treasure hunts or when the mountains were ready to reclaim him.

He was still young for a dwarf. Too young to become king, he reasoned. Oddly, his heart was torn three different directions: king, treasure hunter, and settling in Frosthammer. Being king negated his other two desires. He couldn't shirk his responsibility overseeing Nagdor. His father's execution was near and Forboud had proven he was no more fit to rule than their father.

"Boldair!" Dwiskter said.

Boldair jerked and flicked his gaze at Dwiskter. Drucis opened another goblin purse and examined its contents with eager eyes.

"Your mind's taken you elsewhere," Dwiskter said with a short laugh.

"Apologies. A lot weighs heavily on my heart and my mind."

"Indeed. I understand. With all the places to explore in Frosthammer—the beautiful monuments and fountains, the various merchants and shops—I could get lost in Frosthammer. In a good way! I don't see why you never came back," Dwiskter said. "Why've you never told us about this city?"

"I've wanted to return." Boldair sighed and lowered his gaze. Again, his mind drifted. "I truly have. My heart and mind 'ave battled fiercely over the decision. I didn't wish to forfeit my adventurous life." He chuckled. "It's true dat one can get lost in this city's beauty. One can also get lost in—" He cleared his throat and changed the subject. "If one's not careful, one might never leave. I grieved a long time after my departure. Dat's mostly why I never returned. Frosthammer continually tugged at me heart to return. Dat dull nagging desire never faded completely. My mind lost its strength to resist any longer. Perhaps dat's why I took the opportunity to cross through the city on our way to Meadwyrm Pass. I might regret returning though."

Dwiskter gave Boldair a curious smile. "Why's dat?"

"I 'ave me reasons," Boldair said.

"He's avoided his return to Frosthammer because of *me*," a voice said from behind them.

The three dwarves turned to see a female dwarf. She stood near the center of the bridge with her muscled arms crossed. Like the guards at the gate, she wore icy-blue armor made from frost dragon scales. Her dark, bluish-black hair was tied with fancy knots down her back. She peered at Boldair for several long moments with anger flaring in her amber eyes. Then, without warning, her anger subsided and her gaze softened. Her eyes moistened.

"Wynneffin?" Boldair said.

"Did you think you could visit Frosthammer and I *wouldn't* find you? Dat I wouldn't sense your presence?" she asked.

Boldair smiled. The wrinkles at the sides of his eyes creased deeper. "I'm glad you found me, actually. I had no idea where to start looking for you."

"Is dat the truth?" she asked.

"Aye, it is." His sad tone matched the regret in his eyes.

Wynneffin sighed and shook her head. "I doubt I've crossed your mind over the years. I don't think you'd have searched for me, either."

"Wynnie, dat's not true."

Her attention moved to Dwiskter and Drucis. "Tell me, gents, has Boldair *ever* mentioned anything about me to either of you? One word even?"

Taken back by the question, Dwiskter pushed back from the rail, glanced at Drucis, and said, "It's time you and I explore the city. We don't want to tread into this ... *long* avoided conversation dat doesn't concern us at all."

"Aye!" Drucis chuckled. "The goblins we fought were mild to the battle Boldair's about to face."

"Hey—" Boldair pointed a stern finger at them.

Dwiskter laughed under his breath and winked. "This battle's yours and why I've never pursued a wife."

Drucis winked and whispered, "Seems *she's* pursuing him."

Dwiskter nodded. "Ya might be right."

Drucis offered a slight bow to Wynneffin. "Best tavern nearest us?"

"The Cunning Midget." She pointed. "After you pass the third bridge on the other side, take the alleyway about three blocks back. You'll see it."

Drucis nodded. "We wait for you there, Boldair. Whenever you're done ... *reminiscing*."

Boldair offered a sheepish smile. His face flushed red and his throat tightened. Breathing became difficult. "Aye, meet up with cha later."

After Drucis and Dwiskter walked away, Wynneffin placed her hand atop Boldair's muscled forearm. Her strong grip tugged him to her. He didn't resist. She slid her hand into his and squeezed.

"I oft wondered what became of ya." She stared into his eyes. "And why you forgot me so easily."

"Aww, Wynnie, I've never forgotten you," Boldair said. The truth of the words hurt. Looking in her eyes, he realized how much pain he'd buried by avoiding her.

"So you've returned for me?" Wynneffin said with an optimistic gaze. "I hoped ya'd come back, but your visit's not for me. It doesn't concern me at all, does it? The fact you never mentioned me to your companions tells me all I need to know. It explains plenty."

She took his hands in hers.

"I didn't know how to explain—"

"Explain what exactly?"

Boldair sighed. "With the huge gap of time dat's passed, Wynnie, I —I figured you hated me too much for me to even hint dat you're the greatest treasure I've ever found. My extended absence got longer and longer because I didn't know how to face you. I'm ashamed I've waited this long."

"Have you returned to stay then? With me?"

Boldair sighed and shook his head sadly. "I'm only passing through. I wish I could stay. I do. But things for me have changed—"

"Passing through?" Wynneffin said. "To where exactly? Our city's far out of the way for any dwarf or race to consider 'passing through.'"

"We're headed to Meadwyrm Pass."

"Why?"

"Ya see, a vendor sells a drink made from a poisonous vine and well—"

"A drink!" She frowned and shook her head, appalled. The amber in her eyes flashed like flickering lightning. He tried to step back, but she squeezed his hands painfully tighter. "A drink? You've come all this way as a shortcut to get a drink? This stout, mead, grog, or whiskey means more to you than I?"

"Of course not!" Boldair's brow tightened.

"So it appears, you had *no* intentions of finding me at all."

"Dat's not true," Boldair said. "If it were, this conversation would be over and I'd join my comrades at the tavern."

"Then tell me. What do you see dat's wrong with me?"

"What do ya mean? The situations dat changed in my life aren't about you or us, but," Boldair took a deep breath and sighed. "But these are things dat affect my future and my friends' future for the rest of our lives."

"Do I not figure into your future? We shared our hearts the last time you visited, Boldair. Within your words and mine, we shared our dreams of a future together. You expressed how you felt about me. Have your feelings for me changed?"

Vendors with drawn carts and other passersby pressed around them and ignored them and their conversation.

"Could we *possibly* discuss this in a more private setting?" Boldair asked. "Perhaps over a tankard or two of stout?"

"Numbing the pain already?" Her voice deepened and the rage in her eyes blazed. "We've not even *scratched* the surface."

"No, it's not dat. My friends and I 'ave traveled a long ways to get here. We even fought and killed several dozen goblins in the cavern."

Wynneffin pressed her index finger against his lips. Her eyes widened. She looked around to see if anyone heard his statement before returning her attention to him. "Shh! Don't announce such news in public. Are ya trying to cause a panic?"

"Ya know 'bout them?"

She nodded. "I've heard the rumors, but what you've spoken lets me know dat it's true."

"Where can we talk?"

"The Dragon Pit is a tavern one level down. Or, the Dungeon of Dragons Pub is across this bridge and in the opposite direction of where I sent your friends. Your friends will be okay for a bit without you?"

"Of course."

Twenty-Four

A llowed the choice for which tavern they should sit, drink, and catch up on the events in their lives, Boldair decided to visit the Dungeon of Dragons because he liked its name, and because he found himself missing Taniesse. She wasn't only his friend, but she was a great advisor. However, he doubted she'd have the proper advice to alleviate his current inner turmoil.

He understood why he'd avoided his return to Frosthammer the moment Wynneffin's voice caressed his ears and he looked in her eyes. Excitement shot through him, as did the pain and ache of missing her that he'd kept more secretly buried than his most prized gems. His mixed emotions were nothing compared to the sudden fear overshadowing him. He wasn't certain what her feelings for him were after all this time.

It was odd to feel less fear of a dragon's fire than the fear of contemplating his future life with someone he truly loved. His sole reason for avoiding Frosthammer sat directly across from him.

He could deny his feelings all he wanted, but Boldair knew without any doubt she was the strongest pull on his heart. A dwarf's life changed drastically when he finally settled with a spouse.

Short of funds, Boldair had left to get gold from one of his coffers and intended to return to her immediately. And he would've, had he not *overthought* the stirring feelings of love inside his heart and mind. These foreign emotions weren't something he understood. He didn't know how to work through them. Rather than confront them, he pursued other goals instead.

His decision to take a spouse was as daunting as assuming the throne of Nagdor. Settling with Wynneffin meant he must abandon his hunts for treasure. At the time he left her, he was younger, mentally immature, and couldn't acknowledge which he loved more—her or his freedom to scout for gold. Looking at her from across the table, he realized he'd made a foolish mistake. He had chosen wrongly. Her eyes and her voice showed bitter affection for him. She seemed willing to look past his childish, hasty decision and perhaps, she'd forgiven him.

Boldair glanced around the quaint tavern. Sconces made from hollowed dragons' teeth were fastened to the walls with candles burning softly inside. The chandelier balanced similar sconces atop long, sharp dragon claws.

Where had they gotten these teeth and claws?

Dragons shed their teeth yearly, but their claws never regenerated. Taniesse was proof of this. The black sword she carried was the claw she'd lost fighting Boldair's father, King Ulthor. In her human form, she was missing her finger where the claw had been.

With so many dragon claws and teeth being used for ornamental purposes in Frosthammer, Boldair worried. Had dragon hunters in the past sold these teeth after successfully killing a dragon in its lair? But those hunts could've been ages ago. However, with dragons masked in human form, they might've been recent kills. These relics were seldom seen in other kingdoms. Boldair had never seen so much dragon-scale armor than in Frosthammer, and *that* disturbed him.

He understood why Taniesse and her sisters had chosen to disguise themselves as humans. Such usages for a dragon's body parts was savage, but until Taniesse befriended him, he'd never actually given it much thought.

A mural of raiding dwarves rushing into an ice dragon's lair with their shields and axes covered the wall across from their table. The horrific scene most likely was recorded as a time in Frosthammer's history. The dwarves in the picture wore mithril and steel armor, and *not* dragon-scale.

Fires softly roared in the corner fireplaces. Behind the large U-shaped bar stood the barkeep. His bluish-white hair flowed across his shoulders. He wore an onyx ring on his right hand and a ruby one on his left. A black headband kept his hair from falling over his face.

A female dwarf bard stood near the hearth and sang tales of woe. Her delicate voice spun subliminal sorrow along with the magical sound of her lyre. The tone and pitch added more sadness to her story. Several elder dwarves seated at the tables wept and wiped tears from their eyes. Their bodies shook. She sang better than any bard he'd ever listened to and she captivated her small audience.

Though he couldn't sing, nor entertain the notion, Boldair hated tales that offered no hope or lacked triumph. His stories were always about his travels and finding treasures. Such stories were hailed in the poorest taverns where only peasants gathered. For those without gold or adequate necessities, hearing the possibility of *finding* wealth beyond means often stirred the embers of hope enough to get them through another day.

His most popular tales were retold by other bards, and his reputation in Aetheaon often preceded him. He was quite popular at the taverns he frequented the most. The recognition was flattering in some ways, but he also hated the notoriety. Often, those who sought to gain quick wealth followed him after he departed, not to befriend him, but they hoped to discover his secrets. Thieves had been known to shadow him, and he almost lost his life to an overly greedy thief who demanded a coffer of treasure to spare his life.

The glint in the thief's eyes revealed he'd kill Boldair no matter what amount of gold and gems Boldair gave him. Boldair took the thief to his largest coffer in a cemetery where he'd set numerous deadly traps. A skilled thief should know how to disarm any trap. This thief was more violent than skilled, apparently, and when he didn't recognize the most obvious trap, the bullying rustler died instantly.

Boldair shook his head and dismissed those thoughts.

With few patrons in the tavern, the barkeep took a broom and swept the floor behind the bar. He paid little attention to others in the tavern.

His eyes were distant and deep in thought. By speculation, this dwarf had never labored in the mines, nor had he ever partaken in a bloody battle, which was a stark contrast to dwarves in any Dwarven city.

Frosthammer lacked diversity. All the patrons were resident dwarves. Unlike Hoffnung, Nagdor, and Legelarid, where it was common to see almost every race except Vykings, goblins, Orcs, and the disease-ridden Ratkin, Boldair noticed few outsiders visiting Frosthammer. Of course, the vast city might have more attractive areas for elves, gnomes, and humans to frequent and gather. But Telsia had been rather blatant with her comment of how elves were *tolerated* in Frosthammer.

The Frosthammer dwarves held common traits in their appearance, which were unlike any dwarves in the three kingdoms of the Northern Dwarven Alliance. Regardless of their dominant hair color, their hair gleamed a bluish tint. Their eyes were various shades of amber. Their statures and physical characteristics made them unmistakably dwarves, but their skin tone, eyes, and hair meant they were a separate race of dwarves altogether.

Two female dwarves carried trays with tankards of dark stout, bread loaves, and brie to various tables. Another server stood behind the bar and filled a tankard from a large balanced barrel of stout set on its side. A line of unopened barrels set near the storeroom door. A grayish-white mouse poked its head cautiously between the barrels.

With all the amenities this tavern offered, Boldair expected a larger number of patrons. Perhaps the tavern bustled later in the evening? Of course, the singing bard's sorrow-filled songs might have caused some to retreat. No being could withstand constant inner turmoil for extended periods of time.

Boldair lowered his gaze and stared at the tankards on the table. He grabbed the loaf of bread and ripped a corner off. He took the dull knife and sliced a hunk of brie. He smiled at Wynneffin. She patiently waited for him to break the silence. He wasn't certain how to even begin the conversation.

"Wynneffin, the last we spoke, I explained dat I'm—I *was* a treasure-hunter. Marriage wasn't right for me. I wasn't ready to settle down. My heart and devotion for hunting treasures prevented me from being a proper husband. You deserved far better than I could offer."

"Shouldn't you have had enough courage to at least tell—" she said. She cocked a brow and studied him for several moments. "Wait. You said, '*was* a treasure-hunter'. What's changed, Boldair? Are you ill?"

"Nothing like dat. More things than I've time to explain." He chewed the bread and brie and swallowed. "When I said we're passing through, dat's true. Believe me, it's not to avoid this conversation we partake in now."

"There's always time. Nothing rushes you except yourself. You're more carefree than any dwarf I know."

Boldair forced a smile. "At one time, aye, dat was true. *Not anymore.*"

"What changed?" she asked.

He sighed and held up his palms, which indicated for her to stop pressing the issue. "Please. If you'd give me a few moments to finish me thoughts—"

"Apologies."

Boldair tilted back his tankard and emptied its remaining contents. He held the tankard up for the server and nodded his head.

Boldair sighed. "I've been tasked with other major obligations dat prevent me from hunting treasures any longer."

"How so? What are these obligations?"

"I'm Nagdor's new king."

Her eyebrows rose and her mouth hung open. She took in his words and sat in silence, while studying his face.

"It's not a farfetched tale, if dat be the reason for your surprised lack of words," he said with a wide grin. "It's the truth."

"No, your words ring true. Your honesty showed in your eyes when you spoke. I've always detected whenever your boasts were exaggerations. Your eyes have always revealed the truth to me."

The server set a tankard of stout in front of Boldair. "Thanks."

Boldair stared at Wynneffin. "You think my tales are filled with lies?"

She shook her head. "No, not lies, but ya *inflate* the stories for—how shall I politely put this? To add *gumption* to the story!" She pushed back in her chair, crossed her arms, and laughed heartily.

Boldair laughed for several moments and his face reddened. The beauty of her laughter was contagious. He roared from his gut in a fit of laughter and slapped the table with palm of his hand before pointing his index finger at her. "*Gumption*! Yes, dat be the word! Ah, Wynnie, for what little time we've known one another, ya know me too well."

Her laughter ceased, and she wiped a tear from her cheek. Seriousness overtook her expressions. "Wait, your father was king. What happened? Did he die?"

"No." Boldair shook his head. "Not yet."

Wynneffin sighed. "Dat's good."

"Actually, his death might've been far better for all of us."

"Why?"

He explained how his father had betrayed Hoffnung and was locked in Hoffnung's prison awaiting trial before his inevitable execution.

"Dat's horrible."

"Aye, and then me brother—" Boldair shook his head. "I'll leave dat story for another time."

She watched him with saddened eyes. "I've missed you so, Boldair. I realize dat we only spent two weeks together, but not a day has passed when I've not thought of ya. But I suppose those feelings were, one-sided?"

"Not entirely," he replied.

"Not entirely?" She stared at her tankard for a moment. Her eyes darted back and forth with mixed emotions, and then she huffed. "Your flattery overwhelms me, Boldair."

Boldair reached across the table and placed a hand on hers and gently squeezed. "Apologies, Wynnie. I didn't mean dat like it sounded. I've thought of you often."

"But not daily?"

"Wynnie," Boldair said. "Recently, I've had some rough days and weeks at times. I was nearly roasted by a dragon."

She gave him a shrewd, almost questionable, stare.

He grinned. "It's not a lie."

"I see dat to be true. You sure you weren't drunk at the time?"

Boldair frowned. "Of course not! Well, I was *when* she abducted me, but not after I awakened and she hurled fireballs at me."

Wynneffin laughed softly. Her eyes sparkled brighter than any gem he'd ever unearthed. "I can still vex ya, after all this time."

"Aye, you do. I suppose it's because you read me so well."

"I do, Boldair, and dat's why I should be your queen." Her face showed no hint of a smile, nor did her voice. He was stunned by her immediate proposal.

Boldair leaned back from the table and swallowed hard. His mouth felt dry.

She said, "Do you deny those feelings we shared when you last visited? It wasn't the effects of the stout dat caused you to say dat you love me. We hardly drank anything."

Boldair nodded slightly. Fear rose in the pit of his stomach. "I know, Wynnie. I know."

"Has dat changed?"

"Circumstances have changed," Boldair said.

"But your feelings haven't?"

"Look—"

She shook her head, never taking her eyes from his. "No, Boldair, you're not changing the subject, no matter how hard ya try. I gave my heart to ya dat night for many reasons. I'll never share what I have with you with another dwarf. Either you've returned to propose or I *insist* you *leave* Frosthammer *never* to come back."

Even though her words were icy, her eyes remained warm and caring. Nervously, he tore a hunk of bread from the loaf and stuffed it in his dry mouth. As he chewed, she folded her hands on the table and met his eyes.

Boldair couldn't remember a time when he felt more pressure, or when his stomach twisted from intense nervousness like it did now. He swallowed but the dryness of his mouth and throat caused the bread to lodge halfway down. He grabbed the tankard and gulped a huge swallow. The bread washed down with the stout. He sputtered and coughed.

He stared at her for several more seconds. "Wait a minute. Shouldn't *I* be the one proposing instead of you ordering it?"

"The decision's all yours, Boldair, but the last time you fled rather than propose. Remember? At least you hinted dat your interests in marriage were to be discussed when ya returned. Did I misread dat? If I did and ya can't ask me today, there's no tomorrows for asking in the future. Do you think I won't be a good queen?"

"I don't know dat I'll be a good king," he replied.

Wynneffin smiled. "The greatest kings have always had strong queens to council them."

Boldair cupped his tankard between his two hands and stared at the frothy head stuck to the top. "I don't recall my mother."

"Not at all?"

He shook his head. "No. Father seldom spoke of her after her death. I was told dat she was a great person. I wish I knew based on my memories. But those don't exist."

"Sorry."

Boldair shrugged. He gazed in her eyes and found himself lost in them. He smiled. His courage prompted him to finally tell her what he wished he'd said so many years before. But before he could let the words flow, they were interrupted.

"Boldair!"

He turned in surprise. Telsia's sprite, Frizt, fluttered near his ear. The sprite's voice was much deeper than he'd ever expected such a tiny creature to emit.

Boldair's heart pounded. "What is it? Is Viorka okay?"

"Come quickly," Frizt said. "She's been taken."

TWENTY-FIVE

"Taken?" Boldair rose to his feet. He pulled gold coins from his belt pouch and set them on the table.

In confusion, Wynneffin stood. "Who's Viorka?"

Boldair faced the sprite. Anger and fear stirred in his troubled eyes. "What do you mean she's been taken?"

"Exactly what I said," Frizt said.

"By whom?" Boldair asked, walking swiftly to the door. His steel boots thudded hard.

"Who's Viorka?" Wynneffin asked, following behind.

"Best I could tell," Frizt said. "Viorka was taken by two forest elves."

Boldair frowned with fury. He remembered passing the elves when he first entered Frosthammer. They'd seen Viorka in his arms, and their facial expressions revealed their keen interest in the fynx. They were the only elves he'd seen thus far.

"Boldair!" Wynneffin said. "Who's Viorka?"

"She's my friend!" Boldair replied with frustration. He glanced at Frizt. "Go tell Dwiskter and Drucis at The Cunning Midget."

Frizt cocked a brow. "Being a dwarf, even you should know not to jest over height."

Boldair frowned and gritted his teeth. "It's a tavern."

Frizt laughed in a high-pitched squeal. "I know!"

Boldair's face reddened and darkened to near purple. Now wasn't the time for humor. If he didn't need the pixie's help to retrieve Drucis and Dwiskter, he'd have smacked the pixie across the room with the back of his hand and regretted it later.

The pixie noticed Boldair's dark mood and zipped out the door and disappeared into the alleyway. Boldair hurried as fast as his thick stubby legs could move. Wynneffin kept pace with him.

"Where are you headed?" she asked.

"Telsia's shop, if I can still find it."

"I know where it is," she said. "Come on."

She led him to the bridge and they headed across. "So who is Viorka exactly?"

"Are ya jealous?"

"Should I be?"

"No. She's a traveling companion who set out with us for adventure. But she nearly died in the goblin caverns. I feel horrible because I 'ave only myself to blame."

"The goblins attacked her?"

"No, my wolf mount, Ember, did," he replied.

"Odd your mount attacked her."

"The damn wolf has tried to kill *me* twice," he said.

Wynneffin gave him a perplexed side-glance. "Really? Didn't you have a better trainer?"

A soured expression claimed Boldair's face. "The wolf was my father's, and he's more resentful dat I'm king than my father is. The wolf's loyalty to me is equal to dat of me brother. Neither, it seems, support my reign."

"Get a new mount. If Ember's determined to kill you and your female companion, the wolf's not safe and reliable enough to keep. I can't believe it attacked a female dwarf."

"Viorka's a *fynx*," Boldair said. "I'm supposing dat since she often resembles a cat dat Ember didn't like her and dat's why he tried to kill her. Of course, she didn't go down easily."

"A fynx? Dat'd make more sense for why someone would steal her. Few have ever seen them."

"I know." Boldair formed fists and growled. "I knew not to leave her unguarded with Telsia. *Trust me,* she said. I trust few individuals. Foolishly, I lowered me guard and ignored me gut."

"Boldair." Wynneffin placed her hand on his arm as they walked. "Telsia's trustworthy. She wouldn't betray your trust. I'm certain she didn't 'ave anything to do with Viorka being taken."

"Maybe not. I'm not necessarily implying dat, but had we remained in the shop, we could've stopped these forest elves from ever taking Viorka."

"They couldn't have gotten far," Wynneffin said. "And most likely, they've not left the city."

"In this city? They don't *need* to get far," Boldair replied. "There's so many places where they could hide. They don't need to leave, either."

Wynneffin hurried through Telsia's shop door. Boldair followed and drew his axe. She looked at Boldair and shook her head. "Dat's not necessary. The elves aren't here."

"I refuse not to take precautions."

"Telsia?" Wynneffin cried out.

A muffled groan came from the small room behind the counter where Boldair had left Viorka. Wynneffin entered the room.

"Boldair, come quickly," she said.

With a bit of caution, Boldair stepped to the door and peered through with his hands tightened on his axe. Books, scrolls, and other objects were strewn across the floor. The blankets on the cot were tossed aside. Telsia sat in a corner with her wrists tied together and a cloth stuffed in her mouth. Her face was battered.

Wynneffin stooped and pulled the cloth from Telsia's mouth. "What—?"

Boldair stepped closer. "What happened?"

Telsia took several deep breaths. "Two female forest elves rushed me while I was tending Viorka. I fought them, but one struck me in the face. I—I lost consciousness. When I awakened, they had taken Viorka."

Wynneffin offered her hand and pulled Telsia to her feet.

"Thanks, Wynneffin."

"So you hadn't treated her?" Boldair asked.

Telsia nodded. "I was spooning her medicine."

"Where could they have taken her?" Boldair asked.

Telsia rubbed the bruise above her right eye and winced. Slowly, she shook her head. "Lower levels of the city, I suppose."

"I'll put on some tea," Wynneffin said.

"Thanks, Wynnie." Telsia placed one hand to the wall for support. "Make twindle-root. It's in the—"

"I know where it is," she replied, walking past Boldair.

"Wait," Boldair said to Wynneffin. He gently took her hand.

Wynneffin turned and her brow furrowed with curiosity. "What?"

He eyed them suspiciously. "How do the two of you know one another?"

Surprised, Wynneffin said, "I've lived 'ere all my life, Boldair. I know hundreds of dwarves."

"Well enough dat you'd know *exactly* where a particular type of tea was notched away in a cupboard? I know lots of folks in a lot of hamlets and cities, but I've never snooped their cupboards or closets to know where they store things."

Miffed, Wynneffin turned and walked out the door. Boldair followed with Telsia slowly making her way behind them.

"Oh, no!" Telsia leaned against the counter while Wynneffin placed a kettle over the small fireplace. "They took my Fae stones."

Wynneffin looked at the table in horror where the crystals had set when Boldair first entered the shop. "Those will be impossible to replace."

Boldair frowned. "Worry less about your crystals and more about where Viorka might've been taken. I placed her in your trust. Whatever happens to her, you'll pay the price."

"Apologies." Telsia rubbed her temples. "Yes, she's top priority."

Boldair sheathed his axe and crossed his arms. He stared intently at Wynneffin. "Now, tell me what I need to know. The two of you ... how long 'ave you known one another?"

"What's dat matter?" Wynneffin asked.

"I find it a bit odd dat only a few minutes after I left this shop, you *found* me, and during dat short amount of time, two forest elves attacked Telsia and took Viorka."

Wynneffin's brow furrowed with confusion. "Are you implying dat this wasn't done by elves and dat I had something to do with it?"

"No," he replied. "I'm certain forest elves took her because I saw them when I entered Frosthammer. They couldn't hide their interest in Viorka. Dat much I believe. But as for the two of you knowing one another and Wynnie finding me so quickly in a population so vast? You cannot convince me *dat's* a coincidence. Like I told you, Telsia, I trust few individuals."

Wynneffin sighed, drooped her shoulders, and stared at the floor. "I met Telsia a few weeks after ya left Frosthammer and didn't return. She used the Fae stones to look for you because I feared you'd died."

Boldair met Telsia's eyes. Telsia nodded.

"She found ya," Wynneffin said. "You were okay, but had moved on to another city. My heart broke. So I paid her to check your where-abouts once a week. Telsia and I soon became friends. Once I realized ya weren't returning, I stopped having her locate you. Why further torture myself? She taught me mystical ideology, but neither of us has the ability to cast magic."

"Then how'd you know I returned?" Boldair asked. "Were you hiding here when I brought Viorka?"

Wynneffin shook her head. "No, Boldair. But, like Telsia did for you, she linked me to a pixie. When you arrived, she recognized you from the Fae stone visions and summoned my pixie to inform me. Since I was already on my way to the shop, I wasn't far from where you and your friends were on the bridge. *Dat's* how I found you. I hadn't visited Telsia yet."

Drucis and Dwiskter stepped inside the shop door with their hands on the heels of their axes.

Boldair stared at the caged pixies. "Could a pixie find where Viorka was taken?"

Telsia shook her head. "They'd have to drink her blood to become bound to her."

Boldair's shoulders slumped. "Then it's hopeless."

"What happened?" Dwiskter asked.

Boldair told them.

Telsia straightened and walked to the room with the cot. She returned several seconds later with a wet cloth. She held it up. "I washed blood from the fynx's nose and mouth with this. I cannot promise, but I might squeeze out enough blood for a pixie to drink."

She took a small steel bowl from a cabinet, wrung the cloth over the bowl, and pink liquid formed a small pool. Boldair could only hope it worked.

Telsia set the bowl inside a cage with a greenish-blue winged pixie. "Hexis? Drink this and tell me if you can find Viorka."

Hexis lighted beside the bowl. She cupped and drank a handful of the liquid. She made an odd face and shook her head. "No, nothing."

"It's mixed with water, so you might need to drink more," Telsia said.

Hexis cupped more and drank, shook her head, and drank a bit more. Her eyes widened and she smiled with a nod.

Telsia opened the cage door and allowed Hexis to fly out. "Don't let Boldair lose sight of you, okay? He's the one who needs to find Viorka."

Hexis smiled at Boldair. "Better be moving those stumpy legs if you wish to keep up."

"Hexis," Telsia said in a scolding tone.

Hovering in place, Hexis held her hands outward and shrugged with a grin.

"Thanks," Boldair said to Telsia.

Telsia forced a smile and massaged her temples. "A word of caution, Boldair. Even if you find the forest elves, don't kill them in Frosthammer. Although their kind's moderately tolerated in our city, you mustn't kill them. If you do, you'll stand trial regardless of what crimes they've committed."

Boldair nodded. He turned to Drucis and Dwiskter.

"Here." Telsia handed him a small vial. "This is the medicine I was trying to give Viorka when I was attacked. If you find her in time, try to get her to swallow it. It won't completely heal her, but it should aid her recovery."

"Thanks," Boldair said.

"Boldair," Wynneffin said. "I'd like to accompany and help you."

"It's a shame those elves stole Telsia's Fae crystals. You could've viewed the happenings without setting foot outside the shop."

"Boldair—"

"Wynnie," he said, "I don't like dat you spied on my whereabouts while I was gone."

"I wasn't *spying*," she said, angrily. "I was concerned and needed to know you were alive."

"Once a week?"

"I stopped after I realized you weren't coming back," she said. "I didn't want to torture myself over you and your broken promises."

"Come on," Boldair said to Drucis and Dwiskter. "Let's find Viorka so we can leave Frosthammer."

"Do you want me to come or not?" Wynneffin asked.

Without glancing back, Boldair said, "Do whatever suits ya."

TWENTY-SIX

B oldair stood in the center of the lift with Hexis seated on his shoulder. Drucis stood to his left and Dwiskter was on his right. Wynneffin insisted on coming, even though Boldair hadn't given his opinion either way. Before the lift rose, she spoke to a pair of patrolling guards and informed them of the situation. While she talked softly, the guards peered over her at Boldair with a slight look of confusion. One guard stayed with Telsia and the other hurried to find a medic to tend Telsia's injuries.

Wynneffin rode the lift near the front but didn't look at Boldair. He couldn't tell if she was angry or worried about how he'd reacted to the news of her using Fae stones to watch his activities. The tension between them stood like a towering steel wall.

Boldair sighed, while watching her from the corner of his eye. If she happened to face him, he could stare ahead and pretend his mind was elsewhere. His heart, though, was torn. He still loved her, but he wasn't certain either of them could ever gain an equal level of trust.

He admired the beauty of her bluish-black hair and the time she'd taken to fashion the knots. He found it odd she was dressed in armor. They'd never gotten the chance to discuss her duties in Frosthammer during their brief romance. Was she a warrioress or one in training? She wore the armor but didn't carry a great axe or sword. Tucked into sheathes on her belt, she carried long, curled daggers.

When he last saw her, she favored libraries, and wore thick leather robes and a skirt. Her rough demeanor was the same. Her stubbornness reminded him of his father, which led him to remain cautious because the last thing he wanted in a relationship was someone to constantly butt heads with.

He half grinned.

Boldair liked that she was spirited. But he'd learned never to trust what was on the surface. The true person was hidden inside. Often the worst monsters were the most beautiful in appearance. They lured unsuspecting prey to its doom. Those with a pure heart were quite the opposite sometimes.

Boldair placed his thumbs behind his belt and watched each floor slowly pass. He wasn't certain why Wynneffin's spying made him uneasy after he'd departed. He could understand her worry. If the situation were reversed, he's have wondered about her welfare. He doubted he'd have gone to the trouble of spying on her.

He wondered what else the two might've conspired. Even though Wynneffin claimed she and the healer weren't capable of using magic, he wasn't quite convinced.

The pixies drank blood to link with someone and then had the ability to track the person. If that wasn't dark magic, he didn't know what was. What more was at Telsia's hand?

Boldair understood he'd wronged Wynneffin by promising to return and not doing so. He'd broken his promise and lied. He hadn't deliberately lied. After some thought, he changed his mind due to fear and uncertainty. His actions were wrong, and he'd hurt her. He acknowledged that. She shouldn't have been left wondering and worrying. But she should've respected his privacy.

What had she witnessed through the stones' usage? Did she suspect he was seeing someone else? He hadn't because he wasn't looking for a companion. He'd never expected to find and fall in love with her. His obsession with hunting treasure ruled his life. Well, until Taniesse tapped him to lead a battalion into battle.

He didn't understand why, but her secretly watching his activities without his permission was spying and infringed on their trust. While she didn't view her actions as spying, he couldn't see it as anything less.

"Seems to be getting colder, the farther down we go," Drucis said. "Aren't we getting closer to the River of Steel?"

Hexis nodded. "We are."

"So why doesn't the temperature increase?" Little white clouds puffed from his mouth with each word.

"Some believe it's the mountain's curse," Wynneffin said, without looking in their direction.

"You believe dat?" Dwiskter asked.

"Seems possible," she replied.

Drucis said, "Icevale's inside a different set of frozen mountains, but it's nice and balmy near the forges. Dat heat warms the fortress. But not here. I find *dat* particularly odd."

"Where do you see Viorka?" Boldair asked the pixie, choosing not to join their conversation.

"She's on the eighth level," Hexis said. "The area we call the Ruthless Pits."

"A bad place?" Drucis asked.

"Ruthless," Hexis said with a sly grin.

Wynneffin looked over her shoulder at him, and deliberately cast her gaze to *ignore* Boldair. "Not so much bad, but the entire level is under construction."

"How do ya mean?" Dwiskter asked.

"Each level of Frosthammer started as a mining quarry. As the ore was removed, steel beams and shaft walls were placed to support the city levels above. Once all the ore and excess rock has been removed, architects start constructing buildings," she replied.

"Odd. I never noticed any beams or supports," Drucis said.

Wynneffin smiled. "They're good at concealing those in the city's construction."

"Why would they take Viorka to the Ruthless Pits?" Boldair asked. "If there are no buildings?"

Wynneffin sighed and a worried expression came to her face. "Thieves often make shady traces in the building hulls at night. It's a place where thieves and murderers gather. Darkness is the best shield for such activities."

"You think they're trying to trade her?"

"No. They're probably trying to find a way to sneak her out," Wynneffin said.

"How? The main exits are on the top floor where we entered," Boldair said.

"The old mining tracks haven't been removed. They lead out through various tunnels to ventilation traps. They'd have to figure a way to climb them, but dat wouldn't be easy for most. Thieves, though, are crafty and use ropes quite effectively."

"For what purpose? She's almost dead. If she dies, what good would she be to them?" Boldair asked.

"I hate to say it, but it's possible they could sell her body as a trophy for a hunter's collection," Wynneffin said. "Let's hope dat's not the case."

"Aye," Boldair said sternly. "Dat won't 'appen."

"Oh? We'll do everything to find her before they escape," she said.

"If she dies, they won't 'ave a trophy. Fynxes turn invisible when they die."

"Really?"

Drucis nodded. "Dat's what she told us."

Boldair's jaw tightened, and he formed fists. He wanted to find whomever had taken Viorka and cause them immense suffering and pain. He hated to feel helpless, and not knowing where Viorka was, frustrated him to the core.

The elevator slowed and stopped. Wynneffin stepped off the platform.

Boldair said, "This is it?"

"Yes."

A few sconces flickered along the massive steel beams that supported the city level above, but didn't offer enough light to see any clear paths. Instead, the wash of lighting created more shadows for those with unruly intentions to hide and carry out their illegal endeavors.

Every major city housed places where thieves and murderers gathered. Usually, they met in the darkest places. Only those interested in seeking to hire underhanded scallions dared to abandon the safety of the light to enter uncertainty. Most first time visitors became victims robbed of their gold and often lost their lives.

With his anger building inside, Boldair came to find Viorka. When the fynx traveled with him and Taniesse, Viorka was irritating, but after proving her worth and loyalty, she was someone he'd sacrifice his life to protect.

"Should we follow the sconces and see where dat leads?" Boldair pointed.

"It's probably wiser, Boldair, for you to follow us," Dwiskter said.

"No," Boldair said firmly. "She's my responsibility."

"She's all *our* responsibility. If you're killed," Drucis said, "Forboud assumes the throne. Imagine the disservice to Nagdor you'd impose then."

"So be it," Boldair said.

"Boldair—" Wynneffin said.

His harsh gaze was a combination of anger and determination. He took a step toward the first massive steel pillar. What eventually would become alleyways and streets were crude walkways with jagged, protruding rocks. Stacks of large granite blocks, carved into cubes, were set on flat railcars. Possibly to build walls. Since the builders didn't have the greater luxury to access trees for large amounts of lumber, the buildings were constructed with steel and granite, which reinforced the levels above better than wood. In regard to building materials readily attained, lumber was rare and more expensive than using steel.

The rough ground shook beneath them.

Boldair looked at Wynneffin. "Blasting sticks?"

She nodded.

"Ya think dat's safe?" he asked.

She shrugged. "The city's fortified with massive columns of steel."

Drucis chuckled. "Doesn't mean those blasts aren't weakening it."

Gears and chains creaked. The lift rose behind them. Boldair turned. A massive titanium wall rose about forty feet in height. "Is dat the outer dam of the molten river?"

"Yes," Wynneffin replied.

"Whoa!" Drucis looked up. "Best hope those walls never give way while we're down here."

Dwiskter laughed. "Ah, now, you won't remember, should dat happen."

"Hexis, can you locate Viorka?" Boldair asked.

"Yes," she whispered.

"She's near?"

"Not near, but in the general direction you pointed earlier," she replied.

"Don't fly ahead," Boldair said. "I'll lose sight of you. Stay on my shoulder and tell me which direction to go."

"Straight ahead," Hexis said. "Follow the lit sconces."

"Wait." Dwiskter grabbed something off one of the flat carts and caught up to Boldair.

"What did ya find?" Boldair asked.

Dwiskter said, "An extinguished torch a builder must've left behind."

Dwiskter walked to the nearest sconce and touched the torch to it. He turned with the flaming torch in his left hand, which allowed enough light to see the crude floor. "The only problem with this, Boldair, is dat a moving torch gives our position away."

Boldair nodded. "Under the circumstances, though, we've no other alternative."

"I suppose you're right," Dwiskter said.

Boldair pulled his axe. "Be on guard."

Drucis pulled both axes and readied them. Wynneffin slid one dagger from its sheath.

"Allow me to the front," Boldair said.

"Aye," Dwiskter said, stepping aside. "You should allow me to lead."

"Those behind me need the light, too. With you behind me, enough light spills so I can see."

"As you wish," Dwiskter said.

Hexis slid closer to Boldair's ear. "Follow the lit torches."

"Aye," Boldair said. "Let's find Viorka and bring her back safely."

TWENTY-SEVEN

The jagged rocks made Boldair glad his boots were steel-plated. Even with the boots, walking was cumbersome. Soon, they stood on the excavators' metal tracks where they pushed carts filled with ore and rock chunks out of the mining tunnels.

"Ah, dat's a bit better," Boldair said.

"Much smoother," Drucis agreed.

"These tracks seem endless," Boldair said.

"At least our path's marked by the line of sconces," Dwiskter said.

"Dat means someone has been here recently," Wynneffin said. "Or we're being intentionally led into a trap."

Dwiskter said, "I agree. To give us a marked path is suspicious."

"Aye," Boldair slid his shield from his back and held it in his left hand. "Quite odd. Ready yourselves. It's a trap."

Wynneffin said, "Then we should get guards to aid us."

Boldair shook his head. "Nah. Dat'd be a waste of time. Viorka could die by the time additional help came. I can't allow it."

"Keep going," Hexis said.

"How far?" Boldair asked. The line of lit torches stretched endlessly ahead. Dozens of them, with each fire progressively appearing smaller until the last one in view was nothing more than a speck of light.

A wind encircled them. Boldair paused mid stride. The sconces behind them extinguished in the blink of an eye. The one immediately ahead was snuffed and then the next.

"Run!" Hexis said in Boldair's ear.

"Which direction?" he asked.

"Follow the lights before they're gone, or you'll lose Viorka forever," she replied.

Boldair leaned forward and rushed into a sprint. As he neared each torch, the fire vanished. He hurried to the next and the next, but before he entered the slightest edge of a torch's arc, the fire was snuffed. An obvious trap, but he refused to stop his pursuit.

Their need to stay with the lit sconces bordered on sheer desperation. With nothing but darkness behind them, turning back was foolish. Perhaps not as foolish as chasing the series of extinguished torches. Those who'd taken Viorka might not even be responsible for the inevitable trap, but Boldair needed to discover and confront whomever lured them.

The rest of his party followed with equal speed. Their boots and mail rattled.

"Be careful, Boldair!" Drucis yelled. "No doubt this is a trap, but where we spring the trigger could be anywhere."

"I know." Boldair panted. "Keep alert. We'll find out one way or another."

The swirling harsh wind was tainted with magic. The priest-blessed gems on his axe and shield glowed, detecting the essence of a sorcerer's touch. The engraved runes on his armor and axe gleamed.

All the torches suddenly extinguished. Other than Drucis' torch, a blanket of darkness surrounded them.

"Halt!" Boldair skidded to a stop. He leaned to catch his breath. Drucis' torch burned. The wind teased and flickered the flame. "Now what?"

Drucis stood beside him and swept his torch across the floor where they stood. "We stand at a crossroads where two rail paths cross."

"So pixie," Boldair said. "Are we any closer?"

"Yes," she whispered.

"Directions, please," he said.

Before the pixie replied, a light brightened down the right pathway of the crossroads. The size of the light was too large to be a torch.

"Dat way?" Boldair asked.

"Yes," Hexis replied. "You've been given an invitation."

"Boldair," Wynneffin said. "You don't have to go."

"You're right, Wynnie. I don't *have* to. I *must*."

"Boldair—"

He turned to Drucis. "Put out your torch."

Drucis' brow rose. "You're not serious?"

"I am. Now, put it out. We approach in darkness. The torch only lets them know where we are."

"And if their light goes out, too?" Wynneffin asked.

"We're on equal footing," Boldair replied.

"No," she said. "You're not. This is their territory, currently. Slowly they'll be squeezed out once the new shops, taverns, and homes are built. Dat could take years. Until then, this is *their* terrain."

Boldair grinned. "Time to evict 'em, then."

Dwiskter chuckled.

Drucis placed the torch on the ground and gently turned it beneath his boot to quash the flame.

"Let's go," Boldair said.

Boldair stepped ahead of the others. Dwiskter walked to the left of Boldair and Drucis protected his right. Wynneffin stealthily crept along behind them.

The light ahead dimmed.

"Is Viorka there, Hexis?" Boldair asked.

"Yes. We're getting closer."

"What's happening to the light?" Drucis asked.

"Not sure," Boldair said in a near whisper. "Walk quietly."

"In steel boots?" Dwiskter said.

"I know. It's not easy. But try. Hopefully, we'll get closer without them noticing," Boldair said.

The light dimmed even more, but illuminated enough they could slowly advance. Had they not been able to walk on the steel tracks, they could never hope to approach without tripping or stumbling.

Boldair gripped his axe tighter. He eased closer to the light. Its brightness hadn't actually dimmed but was in a deep, unleveled round pit. The excavators must've found a deep ore deposit or gems embedded in hard stone and decided to pick the deposit until they removed all the valuable ore and gems.

Voices whispered in the deep pit. Boldair looked over the edge but couldn't see anything, except where the light shone from a small adjoining room.

"Viorka's down there?" Boldair whispered to Hexis.

She nodded.

"You mind getting a closer look?" he asked. "So we know what we're dealing with?"

"That wasn't my duty," she replied. "You only requested I lead you to where she is. That I've done. I won't risk my life for her or you."

And with those words, she whisked off into the darkness.

Boldair grumbled. He couldn't rightly blame the pixie. Without her help, though, they were blind to the number they'd confront when they went into the pit. He could only trust Hexis had been truthful in saying Viorka was there.

"Look there," Drucis whispered and pointed.

"What is it?" Boldair asked.

"A crude set of stairs."

Boldair eased around the edge of the pit to where Drucis stood. "They've already dug out another room."

"It happens in large caves," Wynneffin said. "Sometimes areas are hollowed out due to underground water erosion. I'm sure it's the same in Nagdor."

"Aye, it is," Boldair said.

"Usually the houses or shops built over these pits have the luxury of a naturally formed cellar."

Drucis placed his index finger to his lips. Below, the whispering increased. Two or more individuals argued. Drucis was the first to start down the steps. Boldair offered no protest. Reconsidering their advice, Boldair was foolish to place himself directly in the line of attack. Even though he'd led a battalion into battle, his experience as a warrior wasn't any comparison to Drucis and Dwiskter. They'd been trained for battle.

Both wore battle scars with pride and honor. He was thankful they were willing to fight and protect him.

After Drucis reached the third step, Boldair stepped down, careful not to scrape the bottom of his steel boots against the stone.

Wynneffin stepped behind him.

"We seem to 'ave a problem, Boldair," Dwiskter said from the rear.

Boldair looked over his shoulder. "What's dat?"

Dwiskter stepped on a step with his axes held out and above his head. Behind him yellow eyes glowed. Sharp teeth gleamed in the faint glow of the light in the pit. The creature snarled, squealed, and pressed a long spear to Dwiskter's back.

"Goblins?" Boldair whispered.

TWENTY-EIGHT

Boldair heated with intense anger. He wanted to charge past Wynneffin and decapitate the goblin. He was almost certain its blunt-tipped spear couldn't penetrate Dwiskter's armor, but it wasn't something he'd risk. And besides, more goblins might be waiting in the darkness above and possibly below.

The goblin's high shrilling voice sounded like an alarmed cat, but Boldair wasn't able to interpret what it said. The crazed goblin poked Dwiskter's back twice and then pointed for Drucis to go farther down the stairs. Drucis looked at Boldair with uncertainty. Boldair nodded.

Drucis continued down the steps. Boldair followed. He descended sideways to keep an eye on the goblin.

The goblin chattered with a small fit of laughter and waved his spear in the air triumphantly, but the creature lacked the intelligence to disarm Dwiskter.

"The goblins 'ave found a way into your quarry," Boldair whispered to Wynneffin.

"So it seems." She slid her hands over the hilts of two daggers.

"I hear rumor dat the undead roam these lower levels of Frosthammer," he said softly.

She frowned. "Really? By whom? I've heard nothing of the sort."

Boldair offered a firm grin. "You didn't expect goblins, either?"

"No, but who told you this?"

Boldair took another step and pressed his back to the wall. "A dwarf we met on our way through the Lost Pass. Ice'ik is his name."

Wynneffin laughed and shook her head. "He's a bit touched about a *lot* of things."

"So it seems," Boldair said. "He's building a ship on the side of the mountain."

Her mouth gaped.

"It's true." Drucis grinned.

"Hold up, Drucis," Boldair said.

Drucis stopped. Boldair stood beside Wynneffin at the wide corner where the crude stairs turned and continued downward.

"Nah! Nuh!" the goblin shouted. It poked the blunt tipped spear against Dwiskter's back.

Dwiskter rolled his eyes and stared upward. He looked at Boldair, indicating he could kill the goblin, if Boldair okayed it.

Wynneffin slid a dagger from her belt and Boldair nodded.

She turned and flung the dagger before the goblin or Dwiskter noticed it leave her fingers. The blade sunk to the hilt in the goblin's left eye. Its body stiffened and fell limp. It tumbled and almost dropped off the side of the stairs. Dwiskter grabbed and pulled its arm to prevent the goblin from splattering at the threshold below. He placed its dead body on the stairs but the spear fell from its loose fingers and struck the rock below with a dull thwack.

No other goblins rushed down the stairs, but the voices below silenced.

Drucis readied his axes.

Boldair eased down the steps behind Drucis. Dwiskter stopped at the wide corner step.

"Get ready to charge," Boldair said.

"I wouldn't advise it," a voice said from above.

A figure dressed in black robes held a short staff in his left hand. The gnarled finger-like roots of his staff curled around an onyx orb. The forest elf slid back his hood. By his complexion, he looked more like a dark elf. Rune tattoos marked his face, which meant he was a sorcerer. But something more darkened him.

Dwiskter turned with his axe.

The elf shook his head. "Again, I wouldn't advise it."

"Well," Boldair said. "We're not going to drop our weapons."

The elf laughed and shrugged. "Your weapons don't concern me. I can shrivel your insides and kill you before you get near me." He glanced at the dead goblin. "Nicely done."

"He's one of yours?" Boldair asked.

"A goblin?" The elf grinned and shook his head. "They stink to us no less than to you. We've no treaty nor do we bargain with their filth. Its inconvenient death came only because it entered the wrong place."

Wynneffin slid another dagger from its sheath.

The elf pointed a stern finger. "You pull the dagger, and I inflict a slow agonizing death on all of you. Understood?"

She shoved the dagger in its sheath with her thumb and frowned. Her jaw tightened.

"Now, move forward. We have something you want. Otherwise, you'd not have entered *our* chambers."

"Ya 'ave a name, elf?" Boldair asked.

"Rhuse," he replied.

"Fitting, no doubt," Drucis said.

"Go!" Rhuse pointed to the doorway below. His eyes were black. The glow spilling from the room below revealed the deep festered pocks on his face.

"I suppose you're responsible for extinguishing the torches on our way along the rails?" Boldair asked.

"It got you here, didn't it?"

"So you wanted this meeting?"

"We have mutual needs we can help one another with," Rhuse replied.

"Doubtful," Boldair replied.

"Listen to our terms before hastily disregarding the offer."

Drucis stood at the doorway and waited for the others to step behind him before crossing the threshold. The room was much larger than Boldair anticipated. Small fires burned at each corner of the room.

At the room's center was a large, rock altar like those Boldair had seen in temples. Viorka lie on the altar. The two female forest elves he'd seen near the underground entrance stood at the head of the altar.

Boldair pushed past Drucis and walked in the room. The female elves fastened their attention on him. One raised her hand and a glowing, blue fire danced on her palm.

"That's close enough," she spat. Her eyes were solid black like Rhuse's.

"Release her to me," Boldair said, "and ya shall live to see tomorrow."

Rhuse appeared on the other side of the stone slab beside the two females. He laughed softly. "You're far bolder than you need be. Your threats are idle. You're not native to Frosthammer and hold no power."

"Neither are you," Boldair replied. "You a thief. The fynx is my friend. She's not an object for negotiation. She's injured, and I was given something to heal her."

The one female elf flicked her gaze to Wynneffin. A sly smile spread across her face. "You? I guess you found what you wanted, Wynnie." She glanced at Boldair and then at Wynneffin.

Stunned, Wynneffin jerked a dagger free of its sheath. In a low, gruff tone, she said, "Myriel."

"You know one another?" Boldair asked in surprise.

"Not in the manner you assume," Wynneffin replied.

Myriel laughed. "Yes. You stole his heart like you stole so many things in the past."

Wynneffin drew back the dagger to fling it, but Boldair grabbed her wrist.

Rhuse and the other dark elf shot waves of bluish flame at Wynneffin. Boldair brought his shield around and blocked both paths of flame. His shield glowed and absorbed the magical fire.

Drucis readied both axes, and Dwiskter gripped his axe with both hands.

Behind the protection of his shield, Boldair stared in Wynneffin's eyes for several seconds. He tried to read her thoughts by her reactions, but he wasn't able. She looked away. Boldair lowered his shield.

"One more misstep," Rhuse said, "and you all perish."

"Not before I cut at least one of you down," Dwiskter said with a harsh glare.

Rhuse ignored Dwiskter and his eyes fastened on Boldair. "You're the one in charge of this party. What do you say?"

"Tell me what you want," Boldair said. "All I want is Viorka. No blood needs to be shed. You let me take her, and we forget this entire ordeal."

"You really think your weapons can harm us?" Rhuse asked.

Boldair shrugged. "Your magic has little effect on us."

"So we're at a standstill?"

"Doesn't 'ave to be. Why'd you take her? Is it because of whatever sickness dat's eating you up from the inside?" Boldair asked.

Wynneffin gave him a puzzled expression and then set her gaze on Rhuse's face.

"How did you know that?" Rhuse asked. His facial expressions softened with surprise.

"The infection's coming out your pores. Death's claiming you, but it won't be successful."

Rhuse lowered his staff and cocked a brow with the briefest glimmer of hope in his eyes. "What do you mean?"

"You won't die. Not a normal death, at least. You've been cursed. The whole lot of you."

Rhuse rolled up his robe sleeve and revealed the black sores. Some festering scabs leaked pus. "You've seen this before?"

Boldair nodded. "It's as I feared. Mors has been here."

"Who?" Rhuse asked.

"Mors is the Plague-bringer."

"I've never heard of him." Rhuse's eyes darted as his mind thought.

"He's related to Tyrann," Drucis said.

The three elves gasped.

Drucis nodded. "Mors released his plague in Glacier Ridge. Nearly all of them perished. A few of us, myself being one of them, were fortunate enough to escape with our lives."

"We have this plague?" Myriel asked.

"Aye," Boldair said. "Do you have any memory of how you might 'ave contracted this disease?"

Rhuse stared straight ahead, in deep thought.

"Not to throw accusations your direction," Boldair said. His attention was on Mariel. "But I gather dat you're thieves. Not particularly stealing fynxes, but perhaps pickpocketing those who are misfortunate enough to pass close enough to ya? Like when you're warming yourselves by one of the fire pits?"

Embarrassed, Myriel swallowed hard and nodded.

"Did you happen to rob someone and find something unusual in the bag's contents?" Boldair asked.

Rhuse cringed. "Yes, but not from any of the city floors above. I found a bag on a corpse near our thieving guild hideout. When I opened it, a swarm of strange beetles scurried out. They bit all three of us."

Boldair stared at Dwiskter. "The Plague-bringer."

"Is there a cure?" Rhuse asked.

"If I may ask, have you seen wandering dead bodies down here?"

"No," Myriel said. Her eyes widened with fear and uncertainty. "None."

"Only the dead body I took the bag from," Rhuse said. His eyes widened. "But it was gone last I looked. You think it's wandering around?"

Boldair shrugged. "Quite possibly. But if you've not seen a large number of them, dat means the infected ones are most likely on the other side of the River of Steel. Why'd you take the fynx?"

Myriel reached over to the other female elf and gently placed her hand on the elf's shoulder. "Syvil?"

Syvil cupped her hands together at her waist. She took a raspy breath and exhaled. Blood trickled from her nose.

With concern, Myriel stared at Syvil. "We hoped her blood might heal us."

Angry, Boldair took a step forward. "What exactly did you plan to do to Viorka?"

"We weren't going to kill her. We only needed a small amount of her blood to add to a concoction I hope can cure us," Myriel replied. "Then we were going to return her to the mystic shop."

"The fact ya took her before she was healed has nearly killed her."

Wynneffin said, "You almost killed Telsia in the process, too."

"Is that what you think?" Myriel asked. "*She* helped stage the attack."

Boldair gave Wynneffin a sharp glance. Wynneffin shook her head.

"Dat can't be true," Wynneffin said.

"Boldair, you might concern yourself with Wynnie's friendship," Syvil said. "Circumstances often aren't what they seem."

"You had a part in this, Wynnie?" Boldair asked.

She shook her head adamantly. "No, not in *this*. I swear it! Telsia didn't, either! They're lying."

Syvil laughed.

"Is there a cure you know of?" Rhuse asked Boldair.

Boldair nodded. "One dat never fails."

Rhuse looked hopeful for a moment. "And that is?"

"Your body must be burned."

Rhuse snarled. He held his staff tightly. Bluish fire glowed around the onyx orb.

Boldair shrugged and raised his shield. "You asked. There's no other way. None dat I know. Not with how far it's progressed for the three of you."

"You don't think Syvil's potion will work?" Myriel asked.

"Honestly, I've no knowledge if any potion might work. I'm not a herbalist," Boldair replied.

"Can we at least try?" Rhuse asked.

Boldair sheathed his axe and reached inside a pouch on the side of his belt. He took out the vial Telsia had given him. "Allow me to administer this to Viorka first."

"What's that?" Myriel asked.

"The potion Telsia gave me dat should at least stabilize and help her heal faster," Boldair replied.

Dwiskter frowned. "You trust dat it's safe, after all they've revealed about Telsia's hand in abducting Viorka?"

Boldair held up the vial and studied it. "Good point."

Wynneffin placed her hand on his elbow. "No, Boldair, Telsia wouldn't have given you something dat would kill Viorka."

"How can ye be sure?" Boldair asked.

"Because I know her. She's my friend," Wynneffin said. "And the accusations they hurled against her, saying dat she helped them take Viorka, are all lies. You must believe me. You know I tell you the truth."

"I used to think so, Wynnie. But sometimes, folks get lost in their emotions."

The sting and hurt of his words brought tears to her eyes. "Boldair, think about it."

"I've been thinking about a lot of things since I arrived in Frosthammer. I find my disappointment is in distorted memories. Perhaps my gut warned me long ago and *dat* was why I chose *not* to return."

"Look," Wynneffin said. "Telsia has no reason to stage the attack for them to steal Viorka. Think about it. If she conspired with them, they didn't need to take Viorka outside the shop and place Viorka's fragile life in danger. Did she? If all Syvil needed is blood, they could've easily gotten dat in the shop."

"Dat's true," Drucis said.

Dwiskter nodded. "Besides, Boldair, when 'ave ya ever known a thief to tell the truth?"

Boldair's mind raced. He tried to discern between possible truths and lies. One could never trust a thief, but no one could ever have faith in someone who lied and betrayed, either.

However, Wynneffin was correct in her evaluation. If Telsia was involved with this trio, she had no reason to suffer a battering, be tied to a chair, and allow her precious shop to be torn asunder. Such a plot needed more time to stage.

From the moment Boldair noticed the lustful greed in Syvil's and Myriel's gaze, he recognized their desire to take Viorka. The lustful stares were similar to what he'd seen in treasure-hunters. Short of death, little could be done to persuade them not to take her. These two must've followed him in the shadows without any foresight of where Boldair was taking Viorka. It could've been any medic or healer's shop. So it wasn't coincidence. These thieves were lying. With the disease consuming them, they were desperate to do almost anything to find a cure.

Boldair wondered if they only needed a little blood, as they insisted. Perhaps that much of their story was true. But what if a little amount didn't work? Would they've taken more? Maybe they'd have drained Viorka when the potion didn't work? They were forest elves, vile and underhanded, to say the least. The sacrifice of a fynx was nothing to them. And if the blood benefited them, and Viorka survived, they could've filled their pockets with gold by selling her.

Boldair walked to the edge of the stone slab. Viorka looked peacefully asleep. Her long tail curled around her left leg. He placed his hand to her stomach. Her chest rose and fell slightly. Her breathing was shallow.

Drucis and Dwiskter stood close behind Boldair with their weapons drawn. Boldair wasn't worried the dark elves would attack. Their interest was on the vial he held in his hand.

Carefully, he tilted Viorka's head and cradled it in his hand. With his teeth, he yanked the cork from the small vial. Her mouth was slightly open, so he tipped the vial and allowed the liquid to trickle into her mouth. The small bottle emptied quickly. After he was certain she'd ingested the contents, he lowered her head carefully. Her whiskers twitched.

"Now what?" Syvil asked.

"We wait," Boldair replied.

"We don't have much time." Syvil wiped blood from beneath her nose.

"If you need her blood, it's *her* permission you need. Not mine."

Rhuse frowned. "You want us to wait until she's awake? We'll die!"

"How else will you get her permission?" Boldair asked.

"What if we take what we need now?" Rhuse asked.

"Dat would not be in your best interest," a voice said from overhead.

Rhuse turned and looked upward.

Boldair and everyone else did the same. Several armored dwarves stood on a narrow balcony. They must've found another way into the room.

"Is all well, Boldair?" he asked.

"Yotram?"

"Aye."

"How'd you know we were here?"

Yotram said, "Frosthammer's a massive city. However, not much occurs dat we're not aware of, especially in these unfinished sections."

"Could it be dat Wynnie sent message to ya?" Boldair asked.

Yotram laughed. "Dat would be a better analysis. But we 'ave enchanted bats dat send out shrill alarms to inform guards when shady activities are taking place down here. Some things don't concern us, but abduction and sacrifices do."

Bluish flames engulfed the orb of Rhuse's staff. His eyes darkened. "Enough! Syvil, take her blood!" He turned to Yotram and the guards atop the narrow balcony. "I'll turn you all to ash if anyone interferes."

"Rhuse," Yotram said. "I strongly insist you abstain from what you're doing."

"By the time any of you reach me, the task will be done. Besides, your axes and swords cause me no fear," he replied. "Syvil, you've delayed long enough."

TWENTY-NINE

Boldair shook his head. "Rhuse, we freely offered our aid to help you find a cure, but not like this."

Rhuse studied Boldair's eyes and offered a gracious nod. He rolled up his sleeve. "While I believe your words ring truth, time isn't something we have. You see the pustules on my face and arms. This plague's crippling my insides. We have no other hope."

Syvil stepped to Viorka and slipped a dagger from the inside of her robe. Blood trickled from Syvil's nose and down the sides of her mouth. She coughed and paused in step. She slapped her hand on the stone slab to steady herself. Her head wobbled. She peered at Boldair, disoriented.

Boldair guessed the undead plague was in its latter stages with her. She was more *undead* than alive.

"Syvil?" Myriel said, placing a hand on Syvil's shoulder. "You okay?"

Syvil staggered, gasped, and fell in Myriel's arms. Myriel hugged her and held her limp body. A black arrow shaft protruded from Syvil's back.

"Perhaps, Rhuse," Yotram said, "you'll fear arrows?"

Rhuse scanned the balcony, confused.

Confusion creased Boldair's brow. He'd never known a dwarf to use a bow. Dwarves took pride in close combat because they could watch the fleeting life escape an enemy's eyes.

Myriel eased Syvil to the floor. Tears of blood leaked from Myriel's eyes.

"I warned you!" Rhuse summoned bluish flames from the staff.

Boldair leapt on the stone slab and dove at Rhuse.

"Boldair!" Wynneffin said.

Boldair struck Rhuse with the side of his axe. The blow interrupted Rhuse's spell and his concentration. The staff fell and spun across the rock floor.

Drucis and Dwiskter rushed them.

Boldair reared back his fist.

"No!" Myriel said. "Don't strike him. Syvil's still alive."

Rhuse looked at Boldair's steel-gloved fist and his eyes widened. He must have read the rage in Boldair's eyes and realized the strike was a destined deathblow. Rhuse relaxed and allowed his arms to fall at his sides.

"Myriel," Wynneffin said in horror. "Syvil's *not* alive. Get away from her. She's undead."

Myriel scooted across the floor and shrieked. She pushed to get away from Syvil. Syvil awkwardly stood. Strange, gurgling sounds came from her mouth. She fastened her attention on Myriel.

Three arrows pierced Syvil's back, jolting her, but ineffectively stopped her advance.

"Myriel!" Rhuse said. "Move away! Hurry!"

Myriel rolled to her side and tried to stand. Before she could, Syvil clasped a tight hand around Myriel's ankle. Myriel screamed.

"Do something," Rhuse said. He fought unsuccessfully to get free of Boldair. "Please."

Several arrows struck Syvil. One went through the center of her head, but none affected Syvil.

"I told you," Boldair said, "only *fire* destroys the undead."

"Then allow me my staff," Rhuse said with tears in his eyes. "Please."

"I don't know dat I can trust you."

"Please," Rhuse pleaded. "It's the only way I can save Myriel and myself."

"Very well." Boldair pushed himself to his feet. "But know, if you do anything other than burn Syvil, I'm close enough to remove your head."

"You've my word." Rhuse scrambled across the floor to get his staff.

"For what dat's worth," Drucis said.

Rhuse grabbed the staff. "Everyone stand back."

"I cannot do dat," Boldair said.

Rhuse faced Boldair with fury in his eyes. Blue sparks glowed on his fingertips. Sincerity coated his words. "You must. If they think I'm casting to hurt others, they'll send an arrow through my heart. You're standing too close. The hazard's too great with this spell. You'll be engulfed, too."

Drucis grabbed Boldair's forearm and nodded. "Come on."

Boldair walked to the stone slab beside Viorka. He gripped his axe and stood ready to hurl the blade at Rhuse should it become necessary. The throw might not decapitate the sorcerer, but he figured the blow was enough to kill Rhuse.

Viorka stirred slightly. The medicine seemed to be working. Boldair watched her from the corner of his eye, but kept his focus on Rhuse.

Rhuse placed both hands around the staff and thrust it against the rock floor. Blue flames rose around the onyx orb. Small strands of lightning and tendrils of fire spiraled and grew and spread outward.

Myriel kicked at Syvil and tried to break free of her grip.

Rhuse spoke deeply. The words were foreign but held a poetic, pleasant melody. The blue flames flickered, hissed, and rose higher from the floor. The flames slowly built a wall around the sorcerer. The fire was cold like the purest blue ice found in the coldest regions of Glacier Ridge. The fire swept in a cylindrical wave and resembled a cyclone. Rhuse cried out in pain. His body convulsed. He leaned forward and pressed his body against the staff, which was now frozen to the floor.

Drucis looked at Boldair questionably. Boldair shrugged. He'd never witnessed such a spell being unleashed and wasn't certain what might happen. He readied his shield between him and the dark sorcerer. He hoped the hidden archers in the shadows held their aim on Rhuse.

The spiraling flames rose higher and higher. The circling wind rushed with a wailful whistle.

Rhuse's mouth moved, but his voice was absent. His brow narrowed. Frost thickened on his forehead. His skin turned dark blue, almost black. His jaws tightened. He continued leaning forward, but the pressure inside that wind column sapped him. His shoulders slumped and his knees bent. Boldair wasn't certain exactly what the sorcerer was doing.

Rhuse reared back his head. His intense facial expressions indicated he was shouting but no sound emitted. The blue wall of fire blazed forward across the rock floor and settled over Myriel and Syvil. The frigid air was consumed by intense heat. Boldair stood closer to Viorka and shielded her helpless body.

Myriel screamed. Her eyes widened with confused fear. "Why, Rhuse?"

Her body dropped lifelessly. The flames engulfed Syvil. Her flesh and robes smoldered before fire burst out of her body. The intense magical fire dissolved her into a pile of ash and then crawled along Myriel's leg and consumed her. She didn't struggle. Moments later, her body was ash.

Rhuse dropped to his knees. Black tears streaked his cheeks. The consuming wave of fire rushed to him. He turned long enough to make eye contact with Boldair. The sorcerer's eyes were void of hope. He smiled slightly with a nod of appreciation before falling victim to the magical fire.

Yotram and the dwarves on the balcony descended the stairs to Boldair. "Why'd he kill them and himself?"

"They were infected with the undead plague," Boldair replied. "He killed them out of mercy."

"At least he saved us from disposing of their bodies," Yotram said.

Boldair retrieved Rhuse's charred staff, which still glowed in places. He stared at the onyx orb for several moments and grinned. Once he found a smith, he'd have the new stone fitted into his shield.

"Rhuse understood they were altering into the undead," Boldair said. "Syvil had turned, which was why ya arrows didn't affect her."

Brandrum stared shrewdly. "Is this one of your concocted stories? It's hard to tell with you sometimes."

"It's every bit the truth," Boldair said. "Ask Drucis and Dwiskter. We've seen it before."

Yotram and Brandrum looked at them. Drucis and Dwiskter nodded.

"Who's your archer?" Boldair asked. "Never known a dwarf to use a bow."

Brandrum laughed. "Keerla is a forest elf in our army. Several hundred forest elves 'ave joined us."

Boldair searched the balcony and found her standing in the shadow of the doorway above. She nodded and held her bow to her side.

"Are you preparing for war?" Boldair asked.

Yotram smiled. "One must always be prepared. Dat's why our alliance with these Elven archers is most beneficial. No enemy can reach Frosthammer without first going through the forests. These thieves didn't expect range weapons, did they?"

Boldair shook his head while studying the three piles of ash. "Have you found undead roaming these unfinished sections of the city?"

"From time to time, the miners have reported small groups of them," Yotram said.

"Undead dwarves?" Drucis asked.

Yotram nodded.

"And dat doesn't concern you?" Boldair asked.

"Of course it does," he replied. "We're not certain how it happens since we don't bury our dead in stone like the other Dwarven kingdoms. We conclude burial ceremonies by placing the bodies in the River of Steel. The molten steel consumes them."

Dwiskter and Drucis gave Boldair a stunned look.

Boldair frowned. "You're fine with dat?"

Yotram shrugged. "Why shouldn't we be? The majority of our steel is used for our city's construction. So our dead are part of the city forever. No necromancer can resurrect our ancestors to attack us. Dat's why encountering undead dwarves is troubling. We've no dead buried here."

"What do the miners do when they find the undead?" Boldair asked.

"They immobilize them with their pickaxes and toss the wriggling bodies into the River of Steel. Why?" Yotram asked.

"Good. Fire's the only way to completely destroy them," Boldair said. "I suppose what Ice'ik told me is true."

Brandrum chuckled. "Don't tell me you spoke with the mad dwarf? Bah! Half of what he speaks ya gotta ignore. He's never been the same since he struck his head on a steel beam in a mining tunnel. The only reason the blow didn't kill him is because of his enchanted helm."

Boldair crossed his arms. "Dat's what happened to him?"

They nodded.

"All I can say is dat he's right about the undead." Boldair sighed. He glanced at Myriel's ashes smoldering on the stone floor. He wished he could've spoken to her before Rhuse incinerated her. He wanted to know what she knew about Wynneffin. She knew vital information, and specific details Wynneffin didn't want him to discover. Wynneffin became uneasy when Myriel mentioned that Wynneffin had gotten her wish. Wynneffin's reaction was to silence Myriel with death, if necessary. Why else was Wynneffin so eager to pull her dagger? What did Wynneffin *not* want him to know?

Had Wynneffin used a love spell to inspire Boldair's return to Frosthammer? With Myriel dead, he'd never know what information died with her.

Other than aiding Rhuse in taking Viorka, Myriel had posed no immediate threat at the moment Wynnie was ready to kill her.

Boldair sighed. What information had Myriel taken to the afterlife?

Yotram stood over Rhuse's ashes, sheathed his weapon, and clasped his hand on Boldair's shoulder. "Our business is finished 'ere. How 'bout those drinks you promised us?"

Boldair nodded and a smile parted his beard. "I'm a bit parched myself, old friend. I could down a tankard or two."

"A tankard?" Drucis said with a hearty laugh. "After *this*, I won't settle for less than a barrel!"

"My pockets aren't dat deep." Boldair laughed.

Yotram frowned. "No? I've never known a poor king."

Boldair looked uneasy.

"Why didn't you share your good fortune with us on your arrival?" Yotram asked.

"There's no need for a fuss, as the coronation ceremony has yet to occur," Boldair replied. "I'm not convinced dat it's good fortune to chain oneself to a throne."

"Never known a *modest* king, either," Yotram said. "Come, drinks be on me this night."

Boldair laughed. "Nah! They be on me. Can't welch on me promise. Besides, who knows when I'll have the luxury to revisit me ol' friends?"

THIRTY

While they waited for the lift, Boldair studied the architecture of a large titanium gate beside the River of Steel's levee. The massive gate blended with the surrounding fortified wall in such a way he hadn't noticed it when they'd stepped off the lift earlier. His focus and worry to find Viorka had probably prevented him from seeing the obvious.

Despite his intense worry, he didn't understand how he'd failed to notice such a huge object. Each rivet holding the massive gate together was larger than a dwarf. The gate's handle was too high from the ground for the tallest elf, human, or land giant to reach. A huge chain hung from the handle. Even if the handle was within grasp, Boldair guessed a small army of dwarves was required to open or close the gate. The weight for this barrier was immense.

No guards were posted along the gate perimeter, which increased Boldair's curiosity.

"Is dat a huge gate?" Boldair adjusted Viorka in his arms. Her breathing was nearly normal, but she'd yet opened her eyes.

"Aye, it is," Yotram replied.

"Where does it lead?"

"I doubt dat's used anymore," Yotram said.

"What's its purpose then?" Boldair asked.

Yotram shrugged. "Beyond dat wall, The River of Steel separates into various channels. Each leads to various types of molds for support blocks, weapons, gears, and so forth. From my guess, the gate was fashioned after all the necessary equipment for the forges were installed. Since our city sets so deeply, it acts as a reinforcement barrier to support the mountain wall. More than a hundred years 'ave passed since it was last opened. It seals off the city from the forging processes."

Boldair studied the giant gate a bit longer. Between the gate and the river's levee was a small door. Several floors up from the door, a balcony crossed the River of Steel. "So ya access your forges through the smaller door?"

"Yes," Yotram replied.

"Perhaps you could escort me through those channels, so I can see how your process works?"

"Ah," Yotram hesitated. "I would, but I don't have access to enter."

"Why not?"

Yotram smiled. "I'm not an engineer or a miner. I'm a guard. Only a few guards 'ave ever gone inside."

"Just out of curiosity," Dwiskter said. "How does one even open a gate dat size?"

Brandrum laughed. "We've never seen dat occur. Like Yotram said, 'more than a hundred years 'ave passed since it was last opened.'"

Boldair frowned while he studied the detail of the titanium gate's construction.

Yotram laughed. "Your curiosity eats at ya, eh?"

"All the time," Boldair said in a harsh whisper.

"I 'ave a pressing question at the back of me mind," Dwiskter said.

Yotram cocked a brow. "What's dat?"

"We're so close to the river, which is molten steel and yet, it's damn cold in Frosthammer?"

"Mysteries abound everywhere, don't they?" Yotram grinned.

"I suppose," Dwiskter said. "I'll wager dat you don't know why?"

"The cold's something everyone in Frosthammer has acclimated to.

Even before my birth, da climate's been frigid. Since we know no difference, why should we let it bother us?"

"Fair enough. Though my curiosity remains, I 'ave no more questions."

Boldair also wondered about the odd, cold temperature. Yotram avoided answering the direct question, which made Boldair more suspicious. Being this far under the mountains, the temperature should increase more than the arctic surface. Dwarves favored underground cities because the mountains buffered the cold, but oddly, not in Frosthammer.

Yotram clasped Boldair's shoulder. "Dat gate's still troubling you? You could stare at it for a year and never gain the proper understanding to satisfy your curiosity. Better things to do than worry about mysteries dat've never been solved."

"Let's take some worries off ya, now dat you 'ave your fynx back," Brandrum said.

Boldair nodded. Arguing for more clarity was a waste of time, since Yotram and Brandrum obviously didn't plan to disclose any additional information.

"Then lead the way to the best tavern," Drucis said.

The lift's gears squeaked slightly and the platform thudded against the ground floor of the city.

"Drucis has the right idea," Yotram said. "We should relax and forget our troubles for a bit, eh?"

Boldair half smiled, but he didn't take his eyes off the gate. He stepped on the lift platform. "Aye. I'm for dat!"

The lift chains rattled and the gears ground. Slowly they rose. Once they were above the River of Steel's fiery orange flow, Boldair said, "While we hunted for Viorka, we came to a crossroads in the rails. So the ore's taken to the other end of the river?"

Yotram nodded. "Yes."

Boldair smiled and chuckled. "It's quite obvious dat I don't know a lot about the smelting processes. Not dat it bothers me because I'd rather explore Aetheaon and hunt for treasure and ores. I can hire a smithy whenever needed."

Brandrum laughed. "Wouldn't we all? You probably won't believe this, but I've never been outside Frosthammer."

"Never?" Dwiskter asked.

Brandrum shook his head.

"Nor have I," Yotram said.

"I've often dreamed of what it's like outside our mountains," Wynneffin said.

Boldair stared at her from the corner of his eye, but he didn't address her comment, nor did he look directly at her. Her blatant hint lingered in the air, but for the moment, he was unable to get past her use of magic to spy on him during his absence. Or, what she and Telsia conspired.

"Why would you stay in this city forever?" Drucis asked Yotram. "Ya missing out on so much in the forests and other cities."

"We're self-sufficient," he replied. "We've no need to venture. Since we keep to ourselves, and few visitors ever pass through our gates, we don't have problems with the politics of war disrupting our lives. We 'ave chosen to be a peaceful city. But, should Frosthammer ever suffer attack, we've a massive army dat prevents us from ever being defeated. An enemy's entrance is too narrow. No way to send massive forces all at once. No offense, Boldair, but dat's why King Rigrim forbade Frosthammer from joining the Dwarven Alliance."

"No offense taken," Boldair said. "However, Yotram, since undead are turning up, Frosthammer's already been attacked, albeit discreetly."

Yotram acquiesced a slight shrug. "If anything, it's a minor threat."

"No, it isn't," Boldair said. "You saw the three forest elves. Syvil had *already* changed. She was undead. Had Rhuse not consumed himself and his female companions with magical fire, they'd have infected others. It's a plague. Not one dat kills the entire body. Rather, it kills the mind and overtakes the body. They spread the plague to others. It's not a situation to take lightly."

Yotram's jaw tightened. "Duly noted. I'll report this to King Rigrim. It's more his concern than yours."

"Yotram." Boldair shook his head and raised a hand. "In no way was I admonishing you or trying to dictate what actions should be taken.

Viorka and I encountered an entire hamlet where the plague had turned them undead. Drucis, Dwiskter, and I witnessed Mors, the Plague-bringer, raise an undead army and an undead dragon from the ground. Should the undead multiple in Frosthammer, the devastation will be unlike anything you've ever seen. You won't stop it."

Yotram turned and stared in Boldair's eyes. "I'll make a report, King Boldair. My report will have a greater bearing if you accompany me to see King Rigrim.

After the lift stopped, Wynneffin stepped off and walked away.

Boldair watched her leave without offering any words. Although he truly wanted to speak with her in private, he didn't know how to start the conversation. He wasn't certain he could place his trust in her again, and perhaps parting ways now eliminated the possibility of bitter words later.

"Everything okay?" Drucis asked her.

"I need to check on Telsia," she replied without looking back.

Drucis glanced at Boldair and whispered, "Perhaps you should go talk to her?"

Boldair cradled Viorka in his arms and shook his head.

"Ya sure?"

"At the moment? Yes," Boldair replied.

No anger echoed in Wynneffin's tone, nor did she sound saddened. She refused to make eye contact or to tell him goodbye. For him, it indicated she either understood his lack of trust in her or she was too embarrassed for spying. She might not have known what actions she should take. Either way, he needed to sort through his problems without adding more.

"Boldair?" a dwarf said in his approach.

Boldair turned. "Yes?"

"I'm Burr, the stable-master. I came to inform you about your wolf." Burr was a husky dwarf with a wild unkempt beard and frazzled hair. He wore a coat made from striped bear pelts and a cape fashioned from bat leather, possibly from the giant bat swarms near the Woodnog swamp.

"Oh?" Boldair studied Burr. With so few visitors to Frosthammer and few residents ever leaving the city, how had Burr obtained such furs?

"Yes. He's strong and healing, but he's lost his left eye. The deep gashes caused too much damage. An Elven healer could remedy the eye much better than us, but by the time you journeyed to such a place, there'd be nothing an elf could do, either. The wolf's shoulder where he was pierced should heal readily, provided he has no infection."

Boldair nodded. "Thanks for informing me. Ember, I'm afraid, has served his purpose for me. Do you think he'd be much use for you 'ere?"

The stable-master cocked a brow. "What do ya mean? You don't want him?"

Boldair nodded at Viorka in his arms. "Dat wolf almost killed her. I can't turn my back to him. He's attacked me several times and nearly took my hand. It's best I part with him."

"Odd," Burr said. "He's well-behaved, considering the amount of pain he endured with his injuries. Quite gentle."

Boldair chuckled. "Aye, he's favorable to *anyone* other than myself. You see, he was my father's mount. After my father's imprisonment, I took the wolf for my own. But Ember despises me."

"If you're in need of a new mount," Yotram said, "I'm certain we'll 'ave no problem finding you a new one. We 'ave dire mount breeders and excellent trainers. Of course, we 'ave rams as well."

"I definitely need to trade Ember for a new mount, but with only one good eye, I doubt anyone would take interest," Boldair said.

Burr said, "I've a young dire wolf mount I'd trade for Ember. He's trained well, obedient, and more loyal than any other wolf pup I've ever reared."

Boldair frowned and thought about the offer. "Why would ya want a wolf with only one eye?"

"Breeding purposes, Boldair," Burr replied. "Ember's coat is remarkable. I'd love to get pups with the same coloring. If so, they'd be easily traded or sold."

"I see," Boldair said. "I've some important ... uh, pressing issues with Yotram and Brandrum first, but if it pleases you, I could view your wolf tomorrow and possibly work a trade?"

"Of course," Burr said with a slight grin. "There's no hurry. But if you decide to keep Ember, I truly understand. He's recovered enough dat he could leave tomorrow."

Boldair smiled. "Oh, don't worry. We'll work a trade somehow. I've no intention to keep Ember since he's so unpredictable."

Burr grinned eagerly. "Good. I'll leave ya to your affairs."

With that, Burr turned and hurried to the lift.

THIRTY-ONE

B oldair sat at a corner table in Hogshead Splatter Grog and roared with laughter. The entire tavern was rowdy and filled with raucous chatter, so his hearty laughs weren't noticed by the dwarves seated at neighboring tables.

Some dwarves challenged and dared patrons to compete in various displays of strength. While Boldair enjoyed listening to new tales and watching their feats of strength, he was happiest being in their midst without them knowing he was Nagdor's new king.

He held up his tankard and clicked it against Drucis'. On the table was a firm, loaf of bread and a fresh peeled wheel of hard cheese. A young boar on a spit roasted over a roaring fire. A barmaid cut through its golden skin and sliced away big hunks of meat.

Across the room, grimy dwarf miners downed tankards and conversed with one another but with less energy than the guards who were off duty.

Viorka lie curled on the bench beside Boldair. Despite their loud laughter, she remained asleep. Occasionally, she turned and readjusted her position. Her breathing was stronger and her ears twitched at their overzealous laughter.

"You told the stable-master we had *pressing* issues?" Drucis howled and grinned at Boldair. "Ya don't even drink wine!"

Yotram choked and turned to spit his stout on the floor. "Wine presses? We don't serve Elven drinks 'ere!"

Boldair wiped a tear from his eye. His laughter subsided. "What else should I 'ave said? The whole reason we came this direction was to get to Meadwyrm Pass for drinks, but then no need to *press* on until we've had our fill 'ere first."

"Meadwyrm Pass?" Yotram set down his tankard. "What's dat place?"

Boldair shrugged. "Nothing but a narrow trail through the forest, but vendors sell a rare drink dat'll nearly burn your insides out. But the drink's not important. The journey was simply something to pass the time until I'm able to return to Nagdor for my coronation."

Brandrum frowned. "What prevents you from doing so now?"

Boldair sighed. "Word has reached me dat my life might be at risk when I return."

"Why?" Yotram asked.

"Loyalty to my father," Boldair replied. "There are some, my brother included, who don't view me worthy of the throne."

"Your brother—" Brandrum shook his head and took a deep gulp of his stout. After wiping the foam with the back of his hand, he looked at Boldair. "None of us could ignore dat his beard was cut off. Did you cut it?"

Boldair nodded. "Aye."

"Was it because he doesn't favor you as King?"

"No. Well, partly. He tried to kill Viorka for slashing Ember's eye. She merely defended herself, but Forboud has undermined me ever since father was imprisoned."

Yotram rubbed his bearded chin. "You think he vies for the throne?"

Boldair cleared his throat and motioned for a barmaid to bring him a fresh tankard. "Father told me dat he wanted Forboud on the throne, which is all the more reason why me brother should never become king. Father betrayed Nagdor and Hoffnung. If Forboud became king, Nagdor would still lack a worthy king."

"What are your plans for him?" Brandrum asked. "Why not try him for treason and execute him."

"Dat's harsh, don't you think?" Yotram glared at Brandrum. "You're speaking of his brother."

"Aye, tis sad. But I've thought about doing dat," Boldair said. "However, being alive is a greater punishment."

"If he lives, he's always a threat to your rule. He'll plot on how to overthrow ya," Brandrum said. "When it comes to ruling a country, your chiefest enemies can be family and those you once trusted the most."

"Where do you come up with this?" Yotram asked. "We've known only one king our entire lives."

"Aye." Brandrum nodded. "But King Rigrim's *lost* three sons in weapons training, too, hasn't he?"

"They died in training?" Dwiskter asked.

Brandrum nodded.

Yotram shook his head and set his tankard down. He lowered his voice. "You honestly think King Rigrim had something to do with the deaths of his own sons?"

Brandrum shrugged. "If you think it's mere coincidence—"

"Silence your tongue," Yotram said. "Or you give me no choice but to drag you away in shackles for treasonous accusations."

Brandrum glared at Yotram but bit his lip and cradled his tankard between his thick hands.

Boldair frowned and studied the growing tension between the two guards. Brandrum's jaw tightened. He tore a piece of loaf bread and dipped it in broth. Boldair always thought they were best friends, but they seemed to tolerate one another. Quite similar to how the dwarves *tolerated* outsiders visiting Frosthammer. They'd not drunk enough to go to fists over minor arguments. If they were already at odds with one another, more stout was the last thing they needed.

"Ah, there ya be!" Kairun walked to their table. "Ya got room for two more?"

"Of course." Boldair gently eased Viorka into a seated position in the corner and allowed her head to rest against his shoulder.

Kairun adjusted his ponytail and squeezed into the corner seat opposite Boldair, so he could view anyone's approach to the table with his right eye.

Bathil sat between Kairun and Brandrum.

Boldair said, "Have any of you ever ventured outside of Frosthammer?"

Yotram, obviously still perturbed by his brief argument with Brandrum, flicked his gaze to Boldair. His glare softened and he shook his head. "I've not, as I've mentioned before."

Brandrum chewed his bread. "No."

Bathil shook his head and motioned for a bar maiden.

Kairun studied Boldair for several moments. "Nah, not interested in what lies outside Frosthammer. This is my home. I was born 'ere, and I'll die 'ere, never once to gaze upon the sun. Why do you ask?"

"Is such forbidden?" Boldair asked. "Are you bound to remain in Frosthammer because you're guards? What permissions must you secure to venture to another city?"

"To request a leave isn't forbidden," Kairun said. "But actually taking a leave ... *dat* would draw scrutiny from higher level guards and of course, King Rigrim."

"Scrutiny, eh?" Boldair asked. "Is dat why Ice'ik's viewed as a mad dwarf?"

Drucis reared back his head and laughed.

Bathil, Kairun, Yotram, and Brandrum stared at him, perplexed.

"Ice'ik made himself look mad," Drucis said. "Building a ship on the side of a mountain is insanity at its worst."

Boldair laughed. "Okay, so he's not the best example."

The bar maiden set several tankards of stout on the table, grabbed the emptied ones, and hurried away.

Kairun sipped his stout and set down the tankard. "Ice'ik's an odd one. Some say he was touched *before* his head injury. Always talking about Deities and what 'appens after the mountain claims our bodies. He had a good following and could've easily built a temple to cause an uprising, if he'd chosen to do so."

"What happened?" Dwiskter asked.

"He warned of doom dat would befall Frosthammer," Kairun said.

"Doom?" Boldair asked. "Like what exactly?"

"The River of Steel would swell and rise above its barriers to consume us all. He caused terror for a while, but then he was exiled. I was one of the guards who escorted him through the goblin cavern, along with six of his loyal followers."

"Only six?" Drucis asked.

"Aye," Kairun said, nodding. "He was heartbroken 'cause he thought *dozens* would follow him based on his prophecies. They were more afraid of the unknown outside our mountains. They remain inside the city. Ice'ik's message though, continues to be told in small circles. However, they're not as convincing with the message as Ice'ik. But if he's building a ship on the side of the mountain, like you say, he's even madder than they've stated. Frosthammer's better off without him."

"His prophecy doesn't alarm you?" Boldair asked.

"No," Yotram said. "Not one bit."

"You don't think such could 'appen?"

Kairun shook his head. "No. The river's channels 'ave plenty of safeguards. Besides, we're the ones feeding the ore into the smelters. *We* control the river's levels to ensure the molten steel never overflows."

Yotram set his tankard down and peered around for several moments. "Boldair, where's Wynneffin?"

"She went to tend to Telsia," he replied.

"Ah, I figured she'd be here by your side. You seem to have captured her attention."

"A bit *too* much, I'm afraid," Boldair replied.

Yotram raised an eyebrow. "What ya mean?"

Boldair explained what had happened after he left Frosthammer and Telsia using the Fae Stones to spy on him. "How would you fellows feel 'bout someone doing dat to you?"

Kairun rubbed his bearded chin. "Dat be a bit much. You hardly knew her at the time, correct?"

Boldair sighed. "Time-wise, aye. Only the couple of weeks. But, we'd grown rather close in dat short amount of time. Too close, perhaps."

"Ah, she be scorned," Brandrum said. "You riled up her interest in ya, and then wandered away. But this might be more 'bout her than ya."

Boldair met Brandrum's gaze. "What'cha mean?"

Brandrum offered an uneasy smile. "The way you left without returning or sending an explanation made her believe she wasn't good enough or dat you didn't find her attractive. You left her with a lot of unanswered questions. So perhaps dat's her true reason for consulting Telsia? You could've made her self-doubt her own qualities." Brandrum shrugged slightly and reached for his tankard. "Dat's how I see it."

Boldair chewed his lower lip and nodded. "I never thought 'bout it like dat, but ya might be right. What I did and how I did it is unforgivable. Signs of a coward, now dat I look at it."

Yotram smiled. "I wouldn't go *dat* far. But, you should definitely discuss your true feelings about everything to resolve whatever problems you two 'ave. At least, if you don't feel the same way about one another, you won't leave Frosthammer with unsettled business this time."

Thirty-Two

Boldair sliced a narrow piece of the wheel cheese and placed it on a torn piece of bread with a chunk of boar meat. Before shoving it into his mouth, he said, "So, this isn't what we'll be talking 'bout tonight, right?"

Yotram chewed bread.

Brandrum said, "Ya don't think the advice is sound?"

"I'm not implying dat," Boldair said, "but what do the lot of ya actually know 'bout love?"

"I know we don't 'ave it!" Kairun grinned shrewdly.

"And ya think I do?" Boldair scoffed.

"Better than the rest of us," Drucis said. "Not dat I'm looking."

"We're always *looking*," Yotram said.

Dwiskter shrugged. "Maybe. Maybe not. But what I've noticed is dat when you *stop* looking, dat's when it finds you."

Boldair chewed the bread and cheese before washing it down with stout. He set his empty tankard on the table. "Let's bring the subject to something else."

"Like what?" Kairun asked.

"I thought your interests were in my telling of the treasures I've found since we last met." Boldair's eyes gleaned and he hoped to change the subject.

"How 'bout the treasure you'll let slip away, if ya don't act on it," Yotram said with a smirk.

Boldair frowned. "Like I said, let's bring the subject to something *else* for the time being."

"No greater treasure than love," Brandrum said.

Boldair formed fists and set them atop the table. He glared at them. "Okay, I can take a good jesting from time to time, but enough for the evening, if it suits you. Cause even if it doesn't, it suits me perfectly. So, no more."

Yotram glanced at Kairun and shook his head. "His defensiveness proves his heart aches for her."

"Aye," Kairun replied. "No denying dat."

Boldair leaned partway across the table with fury in his narrowed eyes. "Enough, while we're still able to call one another friends."

"Sorry, Your Highness." Yotram offered a slight bow.

Boldair pointed a stern finger at him and shook his head. "Dat's to remain a secret for now."

Kairun sat back against his chair and frowned. "Did I miss something?"

Brandrum whispered to Kairun, "Boldair is Nagdor's new king."

"Ah, ya see, I didn't know dat," Kairun said. "Then your situation's entirely different."

Boldair turned his attention to him. "What'cha mean?"

"I mean, Wynneffin could become your queen if ya don't mess this up."

Frustrated, Boldair lowered himself into his seat and sighed. "Ya not going to let this go, eh?"

Kairun chuckled. "We've not held a better conversation since your departure."

Boldair rolled his eyes and huffed.

Kairun adjusted the patch over his eye. "Look, I'm being serious, friend. The most valuable treasure you 'ave is the one your heart yearns for. Right? You want to tell us a story about finding your *greatest* treasure, but Boldair, your story's not yet complete. You must secure the treasure or ya 'ave no tale to tell."

"You're probably right," Boldair said softly.

"No, he *is* right." Viorka opened one eye to stare at him.

"Viorka." Boldair turned to her with a broad smile. "You're finally awake."

She opened both eyes and slowly sat up. "Who can sleep with all this noise?"

Boldair cupped her furry face in his hands and stared at her emerald eyes. "You had me worried, lil' cat. I thought Ember had killed ya."

"He didn't hold back in his attempt." Viorka pulled her head from his grip and held her side. "I'll be bruised for some time. I only hope I returned some pain to him. I don't recall what happened after his jaws wrapped around me."

"He lost an eye to your claws but ya missed his heart," Boldair said.

She shrugged. "Pity. Under better circumstances, I wouldn't have missed."

"Ember won't be traveling with us from this point forward," Boldair said.

"Won't see me weeping tears." Viorka sniffed the air and looked at the boar meat on the table. "Could I have some meat?"

Drucis set a juicy hunk of boar on the table before her. She retracted her long slender claws and took the meat in both hands. She sat back and gnawed it.

"So, Boldair," Yotram said, "when will you finish your quest."

"What quest?"

Viorka paused in eating and glanced at Boldair with a look of disbelief. "Overcoming your fears to tell Wynneffin dat you love her. Sheesh. I've been asleep for hours and yet I even know what you need to do."

The dwarves at the table laughed.

"It's not dat easy," Boldair said.

"Not if you continue to postpone the inevitable," she said.

"It's not supposed to be easy," Drucis said. "Probably be one of the hardest decisions you 'ave to make as king."

Kairun shook his head and laughed. "No, telling her is far easier than asking Wynneffin's father for her hand."

Boldair's eyes widened with fear. "What?"

"Aye," Kairun said. "I'd love to witness King Rigrim's face when you ask for his daughter's hand."

"No? You jest!" Boldair said.

"No joke. Her father's the king," Yotram said. "Don't tell us ya didn't know dat?"

Boldair paled. His mouth dropped open.

Kairun's brow furrowed. "She never told ya?"

"No-o-o." Boldair shook his head. "Ya putting me on. Dat can't be true."

"Oh, but it is," Yotram said.

Brandrum nodded.

"She never told me," Boldair said.

"Perhaps she thought telling you would scare you off," Kairun said.

"And then he fled," Yotram said with a wide grin, followed by a bellowing laugh.

Brandrum nodded. "Now, it's making more sense."

"What?" Boldair asked.

"She might think you left her because you found out dat her father *is* king."

"Dat's something she should've told me, don'cha think?" Boldair asked.

Kairun laughed. "She never makes a big issue out of her royalty, much like yourself."

"Hey!" Boldair said. "I've not even had a coronation ceremony yet, so it's rather foolhardy to announce it to anyone I come in contact with."

"Then ya need to talk to Wynneffin 'bout everything dat's happened," Kairun said. "If she decides to become your wife, you can join the two kingdoms."

"O-oh." Yotram shook his head.

"What?" Boldair asked.

"As much as King Rigrim hates immigrants, I wonder how he'll view such a marriage proposal?"

Kairun glared at Yotram. The patch over his missing eye made the stare even more intimidating. "Don't scare Boldair off a second time."

"You think *dat's* why she didn't tell me earlier today?" Boldair asked.

"Possibly," Yotram said with a shrug. "Rigrim can be quite ... overbearing and frightening, even to her, I imagine."

"Did you tell her dat you were Nagdor's king?" Brandrum asked.

"Aye." Boldair nodded. "And she practically *asked* to be my ... Queen."

"Ahh," Kairun said. "She's not lost interest in you or the fact she's a princess. I can tell by your reactions dat you're not over her, either. What's holding ya back?"

"I—I don't like dat she spied on me," Boldair said.

"Do you not think it's because she might have been worried dat something happened to ya?" Brandrum asked. "Or, like I said before, she might've thought you found fault with her?"

Kairun shook his head. "I think it might be dat she feared Boldair had learned she was a princess more than dat. And at the time, he wasn't a king."

Brandrum said, "Since you're king, at least you'll be on equal levels with her father when you ask for her hand in marriage."

Drucis roared with laughter. Everyone stared at him in question. He quieted himself. "Apologies, but no one, king or otherwise, is ever on equal ground when asking for a daughter's hand in marriage. Suitors are *always* met with the utmost scrutiny. Few ever meet a father's expectations on the first meeting."

Boldair swallowed hard. His eyes revealed his nervousness.

Viorka swallowed the boar meat and licked her paw-like hand. "Ya know, Boldair's never going to find out why she chose to spy on him unless he gets brave enough to *go talk to her*! Stop speculating and go find her, Boldair. Have the courage to ask her. Clear the air. Worry about speaking to her father *afterwards. Not* before."

Kairun laughed. "Couldn't 'ave said it better myself. Boldair, go find her. We'll still be here if she rejects and runs you off. I'm betting she won't. But if she does, we'll buy a barrel of stout to drown your sorrows."

Boldair took a deep breath and his eyes met each dwarf's individually as he scanned the table. Each dwarf displayed the same eager hope that he'd act on his heart and feelings and express those to Wynneffin. He stood and nodded. "Wish me luck."

THIRTY-THREE

Boldair entered Telsia's shop. At first, he thought no one was inside. Glass shards rustled and clinked on the other side of the bookcase. He walked around the bookcase to find Wynneffin sweeping up broken glass vials and dried herbs.

Boldair cleared his throat. "Here you are. How—how's Telsia?"

Wynneffin set the broom against the bookcase. She shrugged. "I don't know. She's with another healer."

"Look," Boldair said softly. "I think it'd be good for us to talk."

"I agree." She nodded.

"When can we?"

"Now's as good a time as any."

"Here?" he asked. "The place's a mess."

"I'll tend to cleaning while we talk."

"Dat's no job for a princess."

She frowned and released a small gasp, which could've been from shock or relief. "Who told you?"

"Is it such a grand secret? All the guards at the tavern who sat with me knew. Did you think they'd not tell me?"

Wynneffin shrugged. "It no longer matters."

"And why not?"

"I've thought a lot about you since you arrived. But I view our situation in a different light now."

"How so?"

"For one." She walked to the front counter. "You didn't return to Frosthammer for me. You made it clear dat you were only passing through the city as a shortcut to get a drink." She shook her head and looked away. Tears formed in her eyes, but she took a deep breath, and with determination, she prevented them from maturing. "A *drink*! In importance to you, I fall behind a measly drink. You 'ave any idea how *dat* makes me feel? Dat you'd venture to our grand city, not to *find* and visit *me*, but to pass through to get a rare drink?"

Boldair lowered his gaze to the floor and nodded. "Aye, I understand how dat makes you feel. Again, when I had spoken those words, they didn't come out like I intended."

She glared at him. "You never intended to find me when you arrived, did you? Don't lic. I'll know. I'd rather be hurt over the truth than angered over a lie. The hurt I'll survive and can forgive. A lie? Never."

"From the moment I told my companions dat we were going through Frosthammer, I thought about you." Boldair looked in her eyes. "But understand, as vast as the city is, I never thought I'd find you, even if I scoured each level of the city looking for you. Truthfully, I didn't 'ave the time for such an endeavor. I was surprised when you approached me on the bridge."

"I could tell," she said.

"But it was a *good* surprise, Wynnie," Boldair said. "It stirred my heart and all the feelings I've held for you awakened."

She closed her eyes. "It's good dat you can tuck them into slumber whenever I'm not around."

"Wynnie—"

She shook her head. "No! I've *ached* for you, Boldair. I've stayed up nights wondering about ya and why ya chose not to return. Treasure hunting outweighed your feelings for me. A drink does, too? How many nights 'ave you stayed awake thinking and wondering about me?"

Boldair frowned while his mind raced.

"Dat's what I thought." Wynneffin brushed past him and headed for the door.

He gently placed his hand on hers and turned her. "Look, Wynnie, I don't profess to be an honorable dwarf in how to court a lady, *especially* a princess. But I think I've matured a bit since I returned."

"No, Boldair, you haven't. The distance between us is too great to bridge the gap."

"I'm sorry my shallow stupidity hurt you. Dat was never my intentions. Honest," Boldair said.

"While dat may be true," she said, "my heart no longer yearns for you."

The coldness in her voice cause his skin to pimple from the chill.

"Fine," Boldair said softly, nodding in surrender. He sighed. "Perhaps it's best this—whatever it is between us—ends this evening, then. Might I ask you something before I leave?"

Wynneffin nodded.

"How long 'ave you been practicing magic?"

She was taken back by the question. "I've not."

"Wynnie, you 'ave. The fact dat you had Telsia use the Fae Stones to spy on me is enough proof."

Her face tightened with anger.

"Wait, I'm not trying to offend you," Boldair said. "But the use of such stones *is* channeling magic. Using those sprites to keep tabs on one's whereabouts by having them drink the blood of the person they're required to watch is dark sorcery. You realize dat, don't ya?"

She sighed. "The sprites ... I could see dat as dark sorcery, but dat's something *she* did. I've no part of it. But it really bothers ya dat I chose to have Telsia use the Fae Stones to see if you were okay?"

He nodded. "Yes, it did and still does a little now."

"Why?"

"Because ya invaded my privacy."

"You 'ave something to hide?"

Boldair shook his head. "No, but it still makes me uncomfortable, like you were *hoping* to discover me doing something unruly. And—" His eyes widened.

She stared at him curiously. "And what?"

He turned away and ran his hand along his beard. "How often did you spy on me?"

"I told you."

"No, how often? How many times? What was I doing when you viewed my activities?" He turned to her with angry eyes.

His sudden anger startled her. "I don't recall."

"Give an estimate then," he said.

Wynneffin crossed her arms. "A few dozen times, I suppose."

"Are you able to use these stones by yourself or did Telsia summon their power for you?"

"She did. I told you dat I know no magic."

"Dammit!" Boldair shook his head.

"What?"

"Dat means *she* could've been watching me on a daily basis without you being present."

Wynneffin frowned. "Why would she want to do dat?"

"Tell me what I was doing when she viewed me," he said.

"Different things, why?"

"It might well be dat she knows where I've stashed some of me treasures."

"So?"

"Wynnie," Boldair said with a firm stare. "*Where* is she?"

"Why?"

"I don't think the forest elf was lying when she said dat Telsia had a hand in Viorka's disappearance."

Wynneffin frowned. "Why must you assume the worst about her? You don't know her."

"You don't know her as well as you think."

"Ya barely know anything about me," Wynneffin said.

"Aye, you 'ave secrets of your own, too, dat we've *not* discussed."

"You believe she'd actually allow them to pummel, gag, and leave her behind like they did?"

Boldair nodded. "I'd wager my entire cache of treasures on it."

"You realize the degree of your paranoia?" she asked.

"It's a gut feeling dat she's taken advantage of the information she's gathered 'bout me in her supposed *offer* to help you."

"Preposterous."

"Where is she?"

"I'll not tell you," Wynneffin replied.

"Then you're in on it, too."

"Boldair!" Fury blazed in her amber eyes. "How dare you—"

"Either you take me to where she is, or I'll have no choice but to believe you and she are in cahoots to rob me. Dat's an offense I won't take lightly." His eyes narrowed, and he awaited her answer.

"Fine," she said coldly. "I'll take you to the healer where she is. You'll see dat I've been honest. When you see dat, I want you to leave Frosthammer and never come back. Is dat understood?"

"Either way, Wynnie, I've no intention of ever setting foot inside Frosthammer again." He motioned to the door. "Lead the way."

THIRTY-FOUR

If Boldair had thought he'd seen Wynneffin at her angriest, he quickly learned he hadn't. She fumed and marched across the bridge. They descended three floors on the lift. Her knuckles on her tightened fists had whitened. The entire way, she refused to glance his direction, and worse, she was so silent he could almost hear the brassiness of her thoughts.

Anger radiated energy and the harsh vibes undulating from her let him know to remain silent. If he were wrong about Telsia, he'd readily accept a verbal thrashing afterwards. No need to sample her desired unrelenting tirade beforehand.

But now, Boldair was certain the forest elf had not lied. Elves and dwarves were never the closest allies, but in the search to better one's knowledge in the realms of magic, barters and schemes were common to advance to a higher plateau, regardless of race. With thieves, this was also true. Stealing a magic scroll from a sorcerer without being detected and killed was richly rewarded by other wizards and sorcerers. This was the situation he assumed Telsia had involved herself in. These forest elves had been supplying her with scrolls, potions, and rare herbs to advance Telsia's knowledge and power in a tradition better known by elves than dwarves. With the possibility of gaining greater riches, Telsia must've offered a substantial amount of gold and gems to increase her abilities, only *she* didn't possess such wealth.

Although Boldair wasn't absolutely certain this was Telsia's arrangement with the forest elves, his strong premonition linked their mutual benefits of their working together. The elves needed Viorka, or at least her blood, to concoct the perfect potion to rid themselves of the plague. But the disease had already gone past the point of healing and slowly consumed their minds.

It seemed by chance Boldair entered Frosthammer at the exact time with Viorka to allow the forest elves to abduct her. But if Telsia was an oracle or had direct access to one, she could've told the forest elves about the injured fynx. That explained how the forest elves were lying in wait when he and his party entered the gates. Viorka suffering great injury and her need of a medic didn't matter. What mattered was Telsia knew he was coming with Viorka. The elves would've still found a way or attempted to take Viorka even if she'd been healthy.

Because Wynneffin completely trusted Telsia, Telsia needed to make herself appear innocent when the elves came for the fynx. A feat she pulled off with success.

After the lift stopped, Wynneffin brushed past Boldair and shoved him with her shoulder to push him aside. Her lips curled in a snarl. All the loveliness he'd once seen in her was gone. Seeing this side of her was hurtful, but had it not been for his gut accusation toward Telsia, Wynneffin would not openly display such countenance.

Even if his instinct about Telsia was correct, Boldair was finished with Frosthammer for good. Too much contention divided Wynneffin and he. Nothing could mend their severed friendship.

Wynneffin's anger caused dwarves along the street to step aside and allow her to pass. Who she was, a daughter of King Rigrim, was not a mystery to the citizens like it'd been for him. They knew who she was, and if the king's daughter held intense anger, none were safe should anyone unintentionally cross her path or inconvenience her.

Boldair realized asking her father for her hand in marriage might be a lot easier than surviving a lifetime of walking on brittle eggshells and hoping never to provoke her darker side. In her defense, Boldair could not picture a more perfect queen whenever the situation with a neighboring city became hostile. Any foreign ruler would think twice and perhaps a third or fourth time before acting undiplomatic.

They walked past a vendor shop that reeked of strong cheese. The aroma caused Boldair to hold his breath until they were several shops away. The sulfur in the deepest pits near a smoldering volcano was far more pleasant. It didn't surprise him the shops on either side were empty. How anyone went inside the shop to purchase a wheel of cheese was beyond him.

A carved picture of a vial and herbs was posted above a door a couple of blocks from the cheese shop. Wynneffin stormed to the door and flung it open. Several birds in a steel cage chirped their alarmed cries and thrashed against the bars, trying to escape.

An old dwarf with silvery blue hair adjusted his brass-rimmed goggles and frowned at her intrusion. She crossed her arms and glared at the birds and then at the old dwarf. When he recognized her, nervousness widened his eyes. "Yes? How might I help you, Wynneffin?"

"Xyle, I need to speak with Telsia," she replied firmly. She walked to the polished countertop and set her tightened fists atop it.

"Telsia?" He lifted his goggles and rubbed his tired eyes. He adjusted his goggles again. "She was only here for a short time."

"She was injured and said you'd attend her injuries."

Xyle shrugged. "A guard escorted her here, but soon after he was gone, she told me she was okay and left."

The anger vanished from Wynneffin's face. She was instantly pale. "You didn't give her any remedies? Salve?"

"No, nothing. She didn't act injured in any respect."

"When I last saw her, her face was battered. She could barely walk."

"Well, she sorta *limped* inside the store with the guard but afterwards, she didn't."

"So she faked her injuries?"

"Dat would be my assumption, Wynneffin," Xyle said.

Shocked, she turned to Boldair.

"I told you," Boldair said. He turned on his heels and exited.

"Wait!" Wynneffin rushed out the door and followed him.

Boldair marched with abrupt steps. "I'm gathering my party together. We're leaving Frosthammer. I'm good for my word this time, Wynnie. I won't return. Not for *you* or anything else. I hope ya understand dat."

"Look, Boldair, I honestly never thought Telsia would do something like this."

"None of dat matters now," Boldair replied. "I've me safeguards in place to protect my treasure. After my coronation, I'll send troops to gather all my treasures and have them stored in Nagdor's vaults where no one can possibly steal them."

"Boldair," Wynneffin said in a softer tone. "We shouldn't part ways like this."

He turned with fierceness in his eyes. "You were fine with it a few minutes ago, weren't you? When *you* were right and I was wrong! Now, dat it's the other way around. We should never 'ave crossed paths again. And in the future, I hope we never do."

She grabbed his forearm.

He yanked it free. "I'm warning ya. I'm in no mood to discuss this further. You couldn't even consider my advisement concerning the underhandedness of Telsia until *after* you discovered the truth. If ya think so little of my observations, why should I ever consider any future with you? There's no trust between us, nor will there ever be. Dat's *not* what I need in a queen."

"I was hasty in my actions, Boldair."

"In every single way, Wynnie. First by spying on me, which probably gave Telsia enough information to attempt to steal my treasures. And then, regardless of what I said, you deny her of any possible wrongdoing."

"I thought she was my friend, Boldair. I trusted her, and she was always loyal to me."

"Is dat right?"

"Aye, it is!"

Boldair kept his gaze straight ahead as he walked. The strength of his anger was enough, he didn't even notice the stench of the cheese shop. "Tell me something."

"Anything, Boldair." She hurried along beside him.

"Did you know her before you tried to find my whereabouts? Now, I mean *know* who she was and not in name or reputation only. Did you?"

"No. But we became quick friends."

Boldair nodded. "I imagine so, once she learned about my passion for hunting gold and treasures."

"She never mentioned anything about your treasures or where you kept them hidden," Wynneffin said.

Boldair paused to glance angrily at her and then continued walking. "Do ya really think dat she would? If her goal was to get wealthy by somehow robbing my caches, she's not going to clue ya in 'bout it. Just like she let you believe she needed to see another medic when she didn't."

"You need to remember dat you told me you were going to return," she said. "Dat's why I consulted her in the first place."

"I would've returned eventually. Dat was never a lie. Not returning quickly was wrong. I've admitted dat. But I would've returned like I promised. Now, though, I regret ever having come to this city in the first place."

"You really mean dat?"

"You bet'cha I do."

She halfway growled in frustration. "Turn around and talk to me."

"I'm done talking," he replied. "And to think I'd returned to Telsia's shop to discuss our future together."

"You really came to talk about dat?"

"Aye, but then you showed me how little you believed my observations. I can't have a queen who doesn't believe in me."

She huffed. "Gut feelings are not absolute."

"Mine are. They've always been. They're the reason I'm still alive. I've survived against some insurmountable odds, and it was due to what I felt in me gut."

"What's your gut telling you now?"

"To get as far from this frozen hellhole as possible," Boldair replied.

"Without me?"

"Without you."

"Why?"

Before Boldair stepped on the lift platform, he turned and faced her. "I promised ya when we left Telsia's shop, I was leaving Frosthammer either way. Whether Telsia was where she told you or not, I was leaving. And I am. A promise is a promise."

"Sorry dat I caused you to possibly lose your treasures."

"The issue isn't about the treasures, but more about your lack of trust and whether I could ever trust you after you spied on me."

"You can't talk through our differences?" Wynneffin crossed her arms.

"After your display of anger earlier when I expressed my concerns about Telsia, there's no logical benefit in trying to discuss anything further with you. You're not rational."

She shook her head in exasperation. "And *you are*? Boldair, I'm sorry. I felt you were challenging me and I reacted in kind. It was as if you didn't believe I was capable of discerning the true motives of ... my friend."

He shrugged. "Friend? How do ya feel now dat you know the truth?"

"Humiliated," she replied. "As well I should be, since I was wrong. Not only did I misjudge her, I misjudged you. And for dat, I'm truly sorry."

"I'm sorry, too, Wynnie, but to be honest, it's dat kind of misjudgment dat lets me know you could never be my queen. A queen must have the ability to read others effectively in order to council me about decisions. You've failed miserably." He stepped on the lift and turned to face her. "This is goodbye ... forever."

Fury heated her gaze. Her amber eyes brightened from her rage. "You'll regret walking away from me. You'll return to Frosthammer to face your doom."

Before the lift rose, he was certain her fingertips glowed like he'd seen wizards right before they summoned a spell into action. Did she know how to cast magic? Had she lied about that? Were her capabilities something she and Telsia had learned to accomplish together? Few dwarves held the ability and knowledge to become sorcerers or wizards.

And if she were lying, she was holding back far more information than he ever had.

Regardless of her potential powers, he realized by her quick temper that she and he would never remain compatible enough to marry. One of them would surely die, and he was certain it wouldn't be her.

THIRTY-FIVE

Boldair returned to the Hogshead Splatter Grog and was hailed by Dwiskter, Drucis, and the Frosthammer guards. Still seated at the table where he'd left them, they raised their tankards in his honor before downing the contents.

Their broad grins shrank when he came to the table. His anger and disappointment weighed his facial expressions. The heaviness of his footsteps hammered his frustration.

"Things didn't go like you hoped?" Kairun asked.

"It went as badly as I expected *before* the lot of ya convinced me to talk to her. I'd 'ave been better off never seeking her out," Boldair replied. He glanced at Dwiskter and then at Drucis. "It's time to gather our belongings and travel on."

Yotram frowned. "So soon? Boldair, at least sit and drink. Stay the night and be fresh for your travels on the morrow."

"No. I appreciate the offer and invitation, but we really must be heading onward."

Yotram stood and placed his hand on Boldair's shoulder. "The nights are far colder than the days in the Frosted Peaks. Even a hardy dwarf can freeze to death beside a bonfire. Besides, predatory animals roam in the darkness, so even if you set a sheltered campfire, these beasts would rip you apart in the dead of night."

"What sort of beasts?" Drucis' thick eyebrows rose. "I like a good challenge. Besides, it might be nice to have some new trophies on Nagdor's dining room walls. Eh, Boldair?"

Boldair grinned and nodded, but his eyes never met theirs. Inside, a harsh whirlpool of emotions tugged his thoughts downward into his aching memories. Had he done the right thing in how he left Wynneffin? Were his sharp words from his heart or due to the anger he held for his father and brother and their betrayal? Add Telsia's deceit to the mix, and perhaps his anger was misplaced. Wynneffin had been betrayed by Telsia, too. Boldair had lashed out at Wynnie without fully letting her explain her side.

Boldair stood and was about to leave when Kairun gripped his shoulder and pulled him to sit. He placed a tankard on the table before Boldair. "Here, don't go yet. Drink up!"

Yotram looked at Drucis. "What sort of beasts, ya ask? Some say dat they're part human and part bear. Others have spoken of strange Owl-beasts dat roam during the night. Both of these creatures are blood-thirsty terrors. Along the cliffside are ice spiders dat blend in with the snow and icicles. The extreme cold doesn't bother them, but the heat of the living attracts 'em. They slowly spindle down their silken strands to drain travelers of their blood while they sleep."

"Bah! You've never even left Frosthammer. Ya said so yourself," Boldair said. "How do ya know such is true?"

Yotram laughed. "Expeditions are sent out for the logs dat we saw into lumber. We can't make *everything* out of steel. We trade with peddling caravans from time to time, and these are the kind folks who offer their tales of terror. Some have survived the attacks and have the scars to prove it."

Boldair sighed. "I'd rather face those odds than—"

"Look, rejection's difficult for the best of us."

"No. She didn't reject *me*. *I* rejected her and left. And dat's what I want to do now. I want to leave Frosthammer."

Viorka slid from behind the table and came closer. "*Why'd* you reject her?"

"It'd take too long to explain," Boldair replied. "Besides, I'd rather not get into the particulars. But, let's just say dat Telsia did more than help Wynneffin spy on me."

Drucis frowned. "What do ya mean?"

"Telsia used the Fae Stones to view where I stashed some of my treasures."

Kairun took a sharp breath. "You're sure?"

"Aye. I'm positive."

Dwiskter said, "Did she tell you dat? I thought she'd been injured by the forest elves."

"Dat's what she wanted us to believe. Wynnie and I went to see the medic Telsia was to get treatment from. He said dat Telsia had already left and had never been injured at all. My guess is she'll leave Frosthammer to seek my closest hidden treasures."

"Not if we can help it," Yotram said. "We only have three gates dat lead out of the city. I'll inform the guards to not allow her to pass and to retain her. Dat way, your treasures remain safely hidden."

Boldair grinned. "I appreciate dat. But if she finds my stashed treasures, she can't release the traps without dying. If she's escapes Frosthammer, her life will be short."

"Boldair," Yotram said, "no residing dwarf in our city would dare attempt to leave during the coldest hours of night. I assure you. We know the fate of doing so. Please, 'ave a seat and your tab's on me."

Yotram waved at two guards from the bar and met them halfway between their table and the bar. He spoke to them briefly before returning. The two guards left their tankards and exited the Grog.

Boldair sighed and reluctantly took his seat with his back to the wall. Yotram motioned a bar maiden. She brought him a tankard. Boldair wiped the excess froth from the top and pressed the tankard to his lips. He tipped it and downed half the contents.

Dwiskter sat beside Boldair. "I'm sorry things didn't work out."

"Ah, don't worry over it," he replied. "I tell ya dat I've a better understanding of her than what I've pictured in my mind all these years. I like a strong female dat's spirited. I do. She's one dat can stand her ground against the worst ruffian, but she can't control her temper. Much like myself. Imagine the two of us with volatile tempers. Bah.

Worse is dat she didn't believe me when I told her the truth about Telsia. Instead, she hurled her anger and mistrust at me until *after* she realized Telsia wasn't the friend she believed her to be. Then her demeanor softened as though I'd forget the fiery anger she'd displayed minutes earlier. Suddenly, she wanted to side with me because she was a victim, too."

"But wouldn't anyone think that way?" Viorka asked. "Wouldn't you place stronger trust in someone you've known for a long time over someone you didn't? In some ways, Telsia's betrayal cut Wynneffin worse than your suffering, because you saw what she could not about Telsia."

Boldair shrugged. "Perhaps. And it depends on the circumstances. Wynnie's always butting heads with me. Her stubbornness doesn't allow her to trust me and my instincts. She'd rather oppose me until she's proven wrong. As king, I can't 'ave dat in a queen. Our kingdom would be quickly divided."

"Dat's true," Drucis said.

Boldair sighed. "Ya know, I truly hoped for a better outcome with Wynnie. I did. Like a fool I believed what all of you had convinced me."

Viorka's eyes narrowed. "Boldair, things between you and her might yet change. I don't think she's ever deliberately set out to hurt you. Give it time. You might see the circumstances differently tomorrow."

Boldair turned up his tankard and emptied its contents. "The damage between us might be too great to repair. I'll bear the sorrow for a time."

Dwiskter held his tankard up firmly, nodded, and finished off its contents. "Not everything goes as planned."

"Aye," Boldair said softly. "But it's good having friends who 'ave ya back regardless of the disappointments. And those of you gathered 'round this table with me, I count you as the closest of them all."

Kairun, Brandrum, and Yotram grinned.

Boldair looked at Yotram. "If ever the three of you venture outside Frosthammer, I invite you to visit me in Nagdor. Dat's a king's invitation. We can hunt or you can enjoy the finest ales and stouts our city makes."

Kairun nodded. "Dat's an invite worthy of examining, friend."

"Agreed," Yotram said.

Brandrum looked at the door with an uneasy expression. "I must say dat we have some unexpected company."

Kairun said, "Royal guards? Never seen 'em enter here."

Two dwarf guards were dressed in heavier, ice dragon armor. The sharp tusks on their pauldrons were gold-plated and more distinctive in appearance than regular guards or soldiers.

They approached the table where Boldair sat.

"King Boldair," the one guard said.

"Aye?" Boldair said.

"King Rigrim requests your immediate presence."

Boldair glanced at Yotram. Yotram shrugged.

"If you would accompany us—"

Boldair rose slowly. He wanted to decline the invitation, but since the request was from King Rigrim, he couldn't. Refusing a king's invitation was a direct insult. As a new king, Boldair couldn't afford making enemies, especially not with a king he needed for an ally.

Yotram exchanged nervous glances with Brandrum and Kairun.

Boldair offered a quick wink to those at his table. "Save some stout for me for when I return."

THIRTY-SIX

King Boldair entered King Rigrim's private library behind the two royal guards. King Rigrim sat in a fine cushioned, high-back chair with his frost warhammer propped against the chair's right arm. He wore a nightshirt and bearskin leggings. The king seemed ready to retire for the night.

Rigrim's thick hands gripped his chair's armrests. Swollen veins on his muscled forearms resembled small ropes. His frost-blue, long beard curled on his lap. For an elder dwarf, he lacked any signs of age or weakness. His amber eyes reflected his vigor and his intense stare chilled Boldair. Wisdom bore in his eyes, and for the better part of a minute, Rigrim seemed to be trying to invade Boldair's mind and read his thoughts.

Bluish-white waves of frost filtered into the air from the magic of his weapon. A thin layer of frost formed around the warhammer's head where it touched the floor.

Boldair had seen magically enhanced weapons before, but none more intimidating. Such a weapon combined with King Rigrim's brutal strength would make an Orc army momentarily freeze in their advance. From the tales he'd been told about the power of the warhammer, it'd freeze the Orcs into large cubes of ice as well.

"Have a seat." Rigrim pointed at the chair opposite his. His cold tone indicated it wasn't a request.

Boldair nodded. The cushion sank beneath his weight, but then its buoyancy suspended him slightly as though he hovered on air. Boldair adjusted on the cushion until he found the perfect balance. Before daring to met Rigrim's harsh gaze, Boldair observed the bookends on the bookshelves.

Above the books were mounted heads of strange beasts, which adorned the top shelves where no books collected dust. Some of these heads resembled the creatures Yotram had mentioned minutes earlier in the tavern. They were intriguing beasts but their fangs, beaks, and claws could easily inflict more damage than Yotram described. Yotram hadn't exaggerate the accounts. If anything, he gave a modest description of the beasts.

After Boldair finished admiring the different mounted heads, his gaze froze on Rigrim's piercing eyes. Rigrim didn't blink, nor did he seem to breathe. He appeared a predator surveying its prey.

Rigrim studied Boldair in uneasy silence. He offered neither a smile nor a frown. His peering eyes, though, spoke volumes. The quietness made Boldair even more uncomfortable, despite the lofty chair cushion. The room grew icy cold even with the small fire in the hearth. Rigrim looked at the two escort guards and motioned them away.

"Leave us," Rigrim said.

The guards bowed and backed through the door, promptly closing it behind them.

"King Boldair," Rigrim said in a thunderous voice. The high ceiling allowed the deep resonance of his words to echo. Boldair wondered if the room's architecture was deliberate for such intimidating purposes. "I find it odd for a king to enter Frosthammer without first announcing his arrival. Is dat the proper way for a king to behave?"

"My apologies. No. You're right. But my reign as king is not yet official, King Rigrim."

Rigrim frowned and peered at him. His amber eyes glowed. "What do you mean, *not* official?"

"My coronation has yet to occur."

Rigrim tilted his head back without breaking their gaze. "I see. What brings you to my kingdom?"

Boldair explained how he and his party simply wanted to pass through Frosthammer to reach the other side of the mountains more quickly.

"How'd you learn about Frosthammer?" Rigrim asked. "Most believe the city's a myth."

"From a map I found in a vault. Directions to the underground gates and the proper pattern of knocks to get inside were written on it. Due to my overpowering curiosity, I came to investigate and stayed a couple of weeks."

Rigrim nodded slightly. "Is this when you met my daughter, Wynneffin?"

"Aye," Boldair said, nodding slightly.

Rigrim frowned. "What are your intentions with my daughter?"

"None."

"I was told you had come to ask her hand in marriage. Is dat true?"

"Not officially, no."

"Is anything ever *official* for you?" Rigrim's brow tightened and his eyes gleamed. "Was your intention to join our kingdoms through marriage?"

"No," Boldair replied.

"No?" Rigrim's brow narrowed.

Boldair shook his head. "Until a few hours ago, I never knew Wynnie was your daughter."

"She never told you?" Rigrim looked surprised.

"No."

"What are your intentions now?"

"To continue on my journey with my party," Boldair said. "We set out in the morning."

"Without her?"

Boldair nodded. "Aye."

"If I may ask," Rigrim said, "had ya ever considered marriage to my daughter?"

"Yes." Boldair sighed. "For a long time after I left Frosthammer, I considered the possibility. When we first met, we had an immediate attraction for one another. A strong one, but I was too immature to settle then. I sought adventure, not commitment. And with all your mounted trophies, you 'ave fond adventures as well. Me? I'm not much for hunting, other than what I need to eat. I've always sought treasure to pass me time."

Rigrim formed a bridge with his fingers and rested his chin atop them. He leaned forward. A slight smile spread on his lips. "You and I should hunt sometime."

"Like I said, I've not done much hunting, but the opportunity to hunt with you would be quite enjoyable," Boldair replied.

The library door opened. Boldair glanced at it. A servant brought in two tankards. She handed one to Rigrim and offered the other to Boldair. He took it and nodded his appreciation. The servant smiled before turning to leave.

Rigrim waved his hand at several of the beasts' heads on the wall. "Hunting creatures, such as these, proves one's courage. The next worst creature to hunt is a dragon. Not many dragons nowadays, are there?"

Boldair met Rigrim's eyes with slight anger and didn't flinch. With Taniesse as his friend and ally, he'd never hunt a dragon and instead, he'd butt heads with anyone who suggested doing so. "I've seen a few."

"Lately?"

"Aye."

Keen interest claimed Rigrim's facial expressions. "Might I ask another question regarding my daughter?"

"Depends on the question," Boldair said, smiling slightly.

"Aye, I suppose so." Rigrim chuckled and eased back in his chair. "What changed your opinion about marrying her?"

Boldair explained how Wynneffin had Telsia use the Fae Stones to spy on him, how Telsia had taken the opportunity to learn where Boldair stored his treasures, and he believed Telsia had fled to find and steal them.

"So you've lost your trust in my daughter?"

Boldair nodded. "Because of dat, yes. Likewise, she apparently holds little trust in me and my assessments anyway. A king's wife must 'ave me back instead of haggling over every decision and evaluation. Besides, *any* relationship without trust is doomed for failure."

"Yes, quite true. I understand your reasoning. Marriage consists of equal footing, even for a king. Too many struggles exist outside the throne room for a king to have to deal with strife within his marriage."

"Aye," Boldair said.

"Wynneffin!" Rigrim looked at the dark corner of the room. "Present yourself."

Wynneffin stepped from the shadows of the corner bookcases. Embarrassed, she stared at her feet while she walked to stand between Rigrim's chair and Boldair's.

Boldair felt the blood drain from his face. He swallowed hard. First spying, and now, eavesdropping. He wanted to show anger, but held back. He couldn't believe she'd somehow gotten her father to probe him for information. Was no one worthy of trust anymore?

His heart dropped. The entire time he'd spoken with her father, she'd been hidden in the shadows. His mind raced. Had he implied any insult to Wynnie? No, he hadn't. But still he worried. He felt hollow inside. Rigrim had betrayed his confidence. He was fearful of what Rigrim might do or say. But Wynnie's eyes indicated she was more fearful than Boldair.

"Is it true, Wynneffin? You sought a known sorceress to spy on your potential suitor?" Rigrim asked.

Known?

"Yes, father," she replied.

"For how long?"

"Months."

Anger rose inside Boldair but he reined it in.

"Then Telsia betrayed you?" Rigrim asked.

She nodded.

"What magic do you know?" Rigrim asked.

Wynneffin dared to look into her father's amber eyes, but she didn't answer.

"Are you capable of using magic?" he asked.

"No less than you are." With agitation, she crossed her arms.

Boldair gave an incredulous stare at Rigrim but Rigrim offered a dismissive frown and shrugged. For the moment, he kept his attention on Wynneffin.

"Telsia taught you?"

"Aye, father," she replied.

"Why abuse such power to watch someone's activities without their knowledge? What had you hoped to gain?" Rigrim asked.

"At the time, I never considered it as abusing my magical abilities. I was genuinely concerned about Boldair's welfare in the beginning because I thought he planned to return immediately. He promised he would."

"So you know how to use the Fae Stones to view others' activities?" King Rigrim asked.

"Yes, father."

"Return to Telsia's shop and use those stones to find *where* she's hiding. Have two of my guards escort you. When you locate her, send them to apprehend her."

"I cannot," she replied.

Fury tightened Rigrim's brow. "Why not?"

"The Fae stones were taken. Telsia probably packed them away."

"Then report this to each guard at our entrances," Rigrim said. "Give them orders dat Telsia's forbidden to leave Frosthammer."

"Yes, father." Wynneffin offered an embarrassed smile to Boldair in passing. Her smile spread into a sly grin once she turned from her father's view. Her eyes darkened with threatening mischief.

What's she up to?

Boldair watched her leave. He offered no words and wondered how he'd failed to see her true nature from the beginning. Perhaps subconsciously he'd detected it and that was why he'd chosen his treasures over her. And *she* faulted him for lying when she'd denied having the ability to use magic when he asked?

After she left the library, Rigrim shook his head. "King Boldair, I offer my apologies. Should Telsia somehow escape Frosthammer before we arrest her and she steals any of your wealth, I will recompense your losses."

Boldair waved a dismissive hand and shook his head. "Dat won't be necessary. Most likely, the first trap she encounters in my troves will kill her."

"Nonetheless, my offer stands."

"Appreciated," Boldair said. "Might I ask you something?"

"Sure."

"In the Dwarven kingdoms I've journeyed to, I've seen only two other dwarves capable of wielding magic. Yet, you, Telsia, *and* your daughter have this ability?"

Rigrim smiled, but not pleasantly. "I'm convinced dat most races possess the ability, if the individuals seek to tap into the well. For dwarves, since we're capable of using runes to nullify magic's effects, dwarves are conflicted to channel magic as a weapon." He placed his hand on the handle of the warhammer. "As you see, magic has great benefits for me."

"You enchanted the weapon?"

Rigrim nodded. "Yes. The magic dat flows into this weapon comes from the core of our city. The city's named after my weapon, Frosthammer. The warhammer is connected to me. No one else can wield it. Doing so is instant death. Anyone else who touches it turns to a block of ice. Dat's why I always keep the weapon close at hand. Curious folks often don't think before acting. An eager hand is death awaiting."

Boldair smiled. "Good to know."

"Another thing I need to ask about my daughter, Wynneffin."

"What's dat?"

"She's my only daughter dat's never married. In beauty, none are fairer, but in temperament ... I wish my living sons held half the stubborn zeal she displays in weapons training. She's defeated all my sons in practice duels. Believe me, they never held back. Their frustration in trying to defeat her was too great. None ever bested her. Because of her dominant display to outdo those around her, she repulses male dwarves who wished to court her in the past. Has she done such with you?"

"Her zeal and spirit were what attracted me actually. But I've never seen anyone who could go from gentle to burning hatred within the blink of an eye."

Rigrim's brow rose. "She did dat?"

"Aye. She spoke—practically insisted—of becoming my queen. But when I discovered Telsia's underhanded plot to steal my treasure, Wynnie turned utter disdain toward me. Volcanoes burn with less intensity. The moment after she learned the truth about Telsia, her hate-filled attitude vanished as though she'd never gotten mad. She made no excuses for her behavior."

"Dat explains a lot."

King Rigrim stood and Boldair followed suit. They firmly clasped hands. "King Boldair, I've kept you long enough from your affairs with your friends, but you're always welcome in Frosthammer."

"Aye," Boldair grinned and nodded. "Once I reach Nagdor, I shall send word by raven. If you'd accept the invitation, I'd be honored for you to attend my coronation ceremony."

"I appreciate the invitation and shall consider it. I've not made any journeys outside the Frosted Peaks for half a century or more." He released Boldair's hand and waved toward the door. "Please enjoy the remainder of your stay."

THIRTY-SEVEN

Boldair awakened the following morning. His vision was blurred and his thoughts, murky. He blinked several times and tried to clear the fuzziness, but everything around him remained unclear.

He rubbed his eyes. Viscous tears etched from the corners, meandered down his cheeks, and soaked into his beard. The hazy, flickering torch at the edge of the wall caught his attention.

"Bloody hell!" He swung his feet over the side of his bed. "How'd I get 'ere? More importantly, where am I?"

Boldair massaged his temples. The last thing he recalled after leaving King Rigrim's library was returning to join his party, Yotram, and the other guards in the tavern. They had drunk, sang, and he told some of his more popular treasure tales while standing atop the table. The other patrons gathered around, listened, and cheered to his triumph during his ordeals, but then ... He didn't remember anything further.

He hadn't drunk enough to lose consciousness. The strongest drink he consumed was the frosty dark stout Yotram insisted to be the best brew under the mountains. How could he refuse such a boast? It was good, Boldair recalled, but cold like swallowing huge chunks of ice. The drink gave him a tremendous headache. Stabbing his brain with the icy tips of hard icicles was how he'd explain the pain. But after those harsh effects waned, he drank different stouts with better taste and less unpleasant effects.

"Behold, the King! Morning, brother."

Boldair turned in the direction of the familiar voice and opened his eyes. His vision was a bit clearer. Boldair rose to his feet, stunned. Bars separated him from his brother, Forboud.

"What the—?" Boldair staggered to the cell bars. He was in the prison cell beside Forboud. "How'd I get in 'ere?"

Forboud grinned, clearly amused, and chuckled. "Doesn't set too well, does it, oh kingly brother of mine?"

Boldair frowned. "What happened? Why am I in 'ere?"

Forboud shrugged. "No entirely certain, but those guard friends of yours dragged you in during the night, despite your adamant protests."

Confused, Boldair gripped the cell bars and fought to remember. "What'd I do?"

Forboud laughed and shrugged slightly. "You were a raving lunatic, madly shouting, kicking, and fighting to break free. Dat soon passed after they tossed you in the cell and locked the door. I don't recall ever seeing you quite so hostile. It took three guards to haul you inside dat cell."

Boldair released the bars, turned, and placed his hands over his face. It hurt to think. "Where are Dwiskter and Drucis? Were they arrested, too?"

"No," Forboud said. "Not dat I know about, at least. They weren't here when you were arrested."

"Did Yotram say anything to you or me when they locked the door?"

"No, but *you* said plenty. I've never seen you so angry."

Boldair shook his head. "This makes no sense."

"You were a bit tipsy."

Boldair shrugged and waved Forboud off. "I've been dat way plenty. I've been arrested before, too, but I usually recall the reasons why. But not ... this time."

"I've no clue, but your friends weren't pleased with you, either."

Boldair sighed, returned to the cot, and plopped down. He grumbled and kicked straw on the floor. The last time he found himself in such a predicament was when Taniesse had taken him prisoner. Only then, he'd been shackled to the prison wall while she threw fireballs at him until he promised to return her treasure.

"Brother," Forboud said, softly. Boldair glanced at him. "How'd we get to this place?"

"What do ya mean?"

"At such odds against one another."

"Bah!" Boldair shook his head and waved him off. "Brother, my head hurts too badly to discuss this now."

"Boldair, we've shared many adventures together. I've always admired your free spirit and how you hunted for treasure. I don't possess those skills. I was honored whenever you asked me to join you. I truly would never cause you harm. I'd give my life to save yours. What are your plans now? Will you have me face death like our father does?"

"Father's situation is far more different than yours. I didn't place father into custody. The Dwarven Alliance Kings did."

"I realize dat."

"Father dealt himself his fate. You've dealt yourself your own as well."

"Death?" Forboud asked quietly.

Boldair frowned and looked at Forboud's beardless face. Boldair's stomach tensed. He fought looking away, because it'd appear Boldair's actions had been rash. Perhaps cutting Forboud's beard was irrational, but Boldair needed something drastic to catch Forboud's attention. His constant undermining infuriated Boldair, and when Forboud tried to kill Viorka, he'd gone too far. Forboud knew Viorka was Boldair's friend. Friends came before an out of control beast. Boldair refused to ignore or forgive Forboud's actions.

Boldair sighed. "Brother, I don't know. Death comes for all eventually."

Forboud maintained a meek appearance, similar to an animal being beaten down by a stronger pack member. It didn't mean his brother had lost his bite or his teeth had lost their edge. Serpents, when cold, accepted the warm coddling of a compassionate human, only to turn and bite their savior when their strength returned.

"Boldair, I must confess it bothers me dat the Alliance chose ya to replace our father when my qualifications—"

Boldair raised his palm at Forboud and shook his head. "Not *now*."

"Please, when will we ever get a better time to talk heart to heart in privacy."

Boldair sighed, rubbed his temples, and nodded. "Carry on, then."

"Thanks. Even though my qualifications are greater because father taught me diplomacy—"

"To the point, brother. My head aches."

"Yes. Sorry. I accept my place beneath you and serve you as my king." Forboud knelt on his cell floor.

"Come off it," Boldair said. "Dat's not necessary. Rise."

"Is there any way I can prove my submission to you?"

"Look, our journey after we leave Frosthammer is long yet. Prove yourself during our trip to Nagdor, so I see your change of heart. Your actions dictate the trueness of your heart and mind. But, after you attempted to kill Viorka, it'd take a mountain's worth of proof to ever bend my mind in your favor."

Forboud stood and held the bars. He nodded. "Quite right, brother. I should've never gone after her, but unlike you, I helped father rear Ember from a pup. He's like my own, too."

"You understand dat Viorka was only defending herself?"

"Aye, I've thought about dat since they locked me up. I wasn't thinking about my actions though. She, or no one else, had any reason to let Ember kill her. I'm truly sorry. How is she?" Sadness dampened his eyes. "She survived?"

Boldair nodded. "Aye, but barely. A lot transpired after we got her to the healer. We got medicine in her though. She awoke before they put me 'ere."

Forboud looked relieved. "Dat's good news. Again, I'm sorry."

"Something you should express to her," Boldair replied.

"Yes. If we ever get out of these cells."

Boldair stood and walked to his cell door. Outside their cells was a large circular room. In the room's center several crow's cages hung. Two cages held dwarf prisoners. More prison cells encircled these cages. From the two prisoners' tattered clothing and their thin, emaciated faces, they'd been caged for quite some time. "We shouldn't be 'ere too long."

"Why do you say dat?"

"We have better boarding than others."

"Ah, ya mean the cages outside?"

"Aye."

"I suppose," Forboud said. "They've said nothing and haven't the strength to rattle their cages. Can ya ever forgive my transgressions?"

"In time, I hope I'm able."

"I hope to prove myself to you."

Boldair wanted to believe his brother enough to forgive him, but it was too premature a decision this soon. Before their father lost the throne, Boldair had never viewed Forboud negatively. They were, at least to his knowledge, close. But now? The divide was vast without any chance to connect them. The fondest memories between them were tarnished. The luster of those times might never gleam again. To Boldair, the loss was worse than Telsia finding and stealing his treasure. One could always find new treasure, but one could never replace the loss of a sibling. And worse, it seemed, was an estranged sibling.

Footsteps echoed from the stairwell beyond the cages. The determined thudding steadily descended. He hoped it was Drucis or Dwiskter and they could somehow aid his release. He still couldn't remember what actions led to his arrest. The footsteps stopped outside his cell door.

"Morning," Yotram said from the other side of the barred, cell door. He yawned and pulled a ring of keys from his belt. "Have you calmed down enough for us to release you?"

Boldair stood. "Calmed down? I've no idea what I've done to be locked up."

Yotram smiled curiously. "Not at all?"

Boldair shook his head. "No. My memories of what transpired escape me. *Why* was I arrested?"

"This wasn't an arrest. You've no charges against you."

"Then why?"

Yotram unlocked the door and swung it outward. He motioned Boldair to step out. "More for your safety than anything else."

"My safety? From whom?"

"Aye, dat last story ya told angered quite a few of the tavern patrons. Several guards wanted your head for your insulting comments."

Boldair frowned with confusion. "For which story? What'd I say dat was so offensive?"

"You belched a long tirade over Frosthammer's dragon ornaments and our armor," Brandrum said from the outer prison hall. He laughed. "You went on about being friends with a trio of female dragons and how they'd set Frosthammer ablaze for our atrocities."

"Good job, brother." Forboud shook his head.

Boldair ignored Forboud and frowned. "I said all dat? Out loud?"

Yotram and Brandrum nodded. Their bluish complexions seemed darker, and their amber eyes were brighter in the dim lighting.

Yotram shut the prison door and smiled at Boldair. "I 'ave to say dat was quite a story you told. We tried to convince the other guards dat you had drunk too much strong stout. I bought them several rounds to calm them down. We wanted to ensure your safety, so we put ya 'ere. Since you and your party are leaving today, we'll escort you through the gates before those guards 'ave slept it off."

Boldair leaned against the wall and shook his head. "I never meant to offend anyone. You know me. I'd never do something like dat."

"We know," Brandrum said.

"Ya also know dat I don't lie," Boldair said. "I might embellish—"

"But dragons?" Brandrum said.

"Aye," Boldair said with a nod. "They exist."

Yotram frowned with uncertainty. "Again, you drank a *lot* last night."

In thought, Boldair frowned with confusion. "I did, but no more than normal. What'd I drink dat'd make me totally forget what happened after my telling stories? The tavern crowd getting offended escapes me. My being dragged to the prison cell ... I've no recollection of dat, either. So which drink caused me to lose consciousness or spout off offensive words to those not interested in my stories?"

Yotram thought for several seconds before he shook his head. "You didn't drink anything stronger than the rest of us. What do you think, Brandrum?"

Brandrum shrugged. "Nothing comes to mind for me, either."

Boldair rubbed his eyes. "The last story I remember telling was the one of the kobold trying to kill me in a mine. You say the guards became offended about my statements over their armor?"

"Aye," Yotram said.

"Hmm. I don't recall mentioning dat. Ya know, when I first arrived yesterday and while I sat in the Dungeon of Dragons tavern, I noticed a lot of dragon parts were used for the sconces and the chandeliers. And all the guards' armor, of course. I never spoke a word about it though. Might I ask where ya acquired so much dragon scales and claws?"

"Dat, my friend," Yotram said softly, "is something we've been sworn to secrecy by Royal Order of King Rigrim."

"I see. But the scales for your armor are from Frost Dragons, are they not?" Boldair asked.

"Aye," Yotram said with a nod. "More than dat, we cannot say."

"My apologies for my behavior last night," Boldair said, still baffled by his lack of memory. "I don't recall those outbursts."

"We've all had too much to drink at times," Yotram said.

"While I'd agree with your assessment, I assure you dat I've drunk far more without forgetting my actions."

Yotram nodded. "Perhaps, in time, all will become clearer."

"I hope so. I hate to feel like I've lost time."

Yotram turned toward Brandrum. "Shackle Boldair's brother securely and meet us at the stables."

Brandrum nodded.

"Boldair needs a new mount," Yotram said. He turned to walk across the room with Boldair to get to the stairs. "Indeed, quite a story ya shared last night. I wish those guards hadn't so easily taken offense by it."

Boldair forced a smile. Inside, he knew what he supposedly had said —though he didn't remember saying it—were words he would've freely spoken *without* drinks. He took offense to any race using dragon claws and scales as ornaments.

Before meeting Taniesse, he'd have never given it a second thought. He wondered why the guards were sworn to secrecy over how they obtained such large quantities of dragon anatomy. He couldn't risk saying more without angering King Rigrim or turning these guards he regarded as friends against him. Boldair wanted to be as far from Frosthammer as possible, and the sooner, the better. He certainly didn't want any animosity between himself and Rigrim. Nagdor had always sought peace, especially with other dwarves. The longer he stayed in Frosthammer, the more likely he would do or say something to worsen the damage than what happened the night before.

Thirty-Eight

B oldair met Burr, the stable-master, at the stables. Unlike most dwarves who took pride in their appearance with the proper grooming of their beards and long hair, Burr spent no time primping his. In many ways, his wildly frayed beard and hair reminded Boldair more of a beast than a dwarf.

Burr ran a hand through his beard. His dark eyes were unlike the majority of Frosthammer dwarves. Only a pinpointed speck of amber glowed, encircled by inky black, in his eyes. He studied Boldair with eagerness. "Welcome. 'ave you come to consider my offer?"

Boldair nodded. "Yes. Might I see Ember beforehand though?"

"Sure," Burr said. "This way."

The stables were housed inside a long, bored tunnel that went deeper into the mountain wall. Overhead lanterns glowed brightly. At the corner of every stall were smaller lanterns.

The harsh smell was as unpleasant as any other stable he'd ever entered. Nothing dispelled the thick, soured aroma of urine and fecal matter. Often the acrid stench hit one like a sledgehammer well before reaching the stalls and pens.

Not even magic could put a dent in dat. Boldair's nose snarled in protest.

Several young dwarves with short beards used rakes and shovels to clean the stalls. The smell didn't affect them, but Boldair guessed they'd worked in the stables long enough to ignore it.

Boldair passed several individual stalls where large mountain ram mounts chewed straw over their troughs. The rams gnawed with bothersome expressions when the visitors entered the stable hall.

"Your wolf mount's in the next stall." Burr pointed.

Before Boldair came into view, Ember caught Boldair's scent. The dire wolf snarled, curled its upper lip, and faced Boldair with an indignant growl. A patch covered Ember's left eye.

Burr shook his head. "He's *not* fond of you, is he?"

"The feeling's mutual," Boldair replied. He leveled a shrewd glare at Ember.

"You cannot place your trust in such a beast. A good mount's one dat protects its rider. It *never* turns on him." Burr climbed over the gate. For a moment, Boldair almost yanked Burr back, fearful Ember would rip the stable-master apart. Instead, the massive dire wolf wagged its tail and licked Burr's face and hand.

"Traitor," Boldair whispered.

Ember turned and growled fiercely at Boldair. The wolf stood between him and Burr, acting protective of the stable-master he'd only met the night before. Boldair shook his head.

Burr rubbed between the wolf's ears and calmed him. "I've never seen a mount act this way toward its rider."

"It's evident he doesn't view me as *his* rider," Boldair said, softly. "I doubt he ever will since my father and brother reared him."

"Aye," Burr nodded. He scratched the sides of Ember's head. The motion of his fingers brushing through the wolf's unique fur looked like a gentle breeze arousing the red fire in dying coals. "Those early years of rearing a mount are crucial, but even so, a mount should adapt quickly to accepting a new rider. Wolves are sociable, so if you treat them right, you'll gain their loyalty."

"No one's told 'em." Boldair pointed at Ember with his thumb. "I've never given him a reason to be hostile to me."

Burr climbed over the stable gate. Ember chuffed and wagged its tail. "Come, I'll show you other wolf mounts. They're young, but they're trained. Each wolf has multiple riding trainers so the wolves don't imprint to one rider. They're less temperamental, too."

Boldair laughed. "An immediate plus!"

Burr joined in with an odd cackle. "Yes. I'm surprised Ember's allowed you around him for as long as he has."

"I agree."

Burr walked away and Boldair stepped closer to the stall. Ember bared his teeth.

In spite of Ember's attempt on Boldair's life, Boldair still viewed the great wolf with admiration. He hated exchanging the wolf because of its brilliant fur and magnificent stature. Ember was an incredible beast, but Boldair couldn't picture a mutual understanding ever developing between he and the wolf, regardless of Boldair's coaxing. The wolf's hostility would always challenge Boldair's authority. Ember would never allow Boldair to be his rider or master. The wolf was a true alpha with a mule's stubbornness.

With a regretful gaze, Boldair whispered, "I truly wish you had a change of heart, Ember. I hate leaving you 'ere."

The wolf's growl ceased. It panted. Sadness overwhelmed its facial features, as though it understood Boldair's words. It whined a long, sorrowful cry.

"Look, Ember," Boldair said, "sorry 'bout your eye. Viorka was only defending herself. You should've never attacked her. You could sense dat she was a part of our group."

Ember chuffed softly and licked his chops.

"When I return to Frosthammer, perhaps you'll hold a different attitude toward me, eh? I might even trade for ya back."

Boldair stared into Ember's eye for a minute or so. The wolf cocked its head to the side and lowered its nose in submission, something Boldair had never seen Ember do before. For a moment, he considered rubbing behind the wolf's ears like Burr had, but then he thought better. As surely as he placed his hand through the gate, the wolf would try to rip his arm off.

"I'm on to ya ploy." Boldair laughed. "You *almost* had me convinced."

"Ya coming?" Burr asked from several yards away.

"Aye," Boldair said.

"Ah, good. For a second, I thought perhaps ya had changed your mind."

"No. Trust doesn't exist between Ember and myself. I'm finding myself in dat situation more and more lately."

"I understand. Any relationship can become strained, whether it's blood ties or friends. Even riders and mounts won't necessarily form a strong necessary bond. When dat occurs, it's time to look elsewhere."

Boldair nodded.

"Since wolves are pack animals, they've a tendency to include their riders as their family. This is why they're far more loyal than rams. Rams are great as long as their riders are on them. However, once the rider dismounts, rams obey their stomachs, often chewing through their ropes, and wandering off in search of food. I've known many dwarves who've lost their mounts in the wild, due to this."

Boldair laughed. "The only other thing I dislike about a ram is the horrendous odor they 'ave."

Burr laughed and nodded. "There's dat, too. But like working in the stables, ya get used to it after awhile."

"Bah! I never could. I figure ya nose probably quits working so the smell can't affect you."

"Dat's probably true. I no longer enjoy my meals because nothing smells right anymore."

The stable hall took a sharp curve to the right and opened into a large room with several larger stalls. Inside these stalls female mounts nursed their pups.

Across the room in another wide stall were three large wolves. They were approximately Ember's size but thinner, which was the tendency with the younger dire mounts. The longer they carried a rider, the more muscle they gained. Their muscular girth became wider and the wolves, stronger. Those were necessities when traveling through the rugged, snowy mountains because riders carried extra packs for supplies to go longer distances.

One young mount stood out from its two gray siblings. This wolf's fur was icy-blue. Darker blue streaks ran along both sides of its back. Its eyes were white like fresh snow. Its ears perked when it met Boldair's gaze. It wagged its tail vigorously and chuffed. Boldair was immediately attracted to this wolf.

"Dat one!" Boldair pointed and tried not to allow his excitement to resonate in his voice.

"Ahh, yes," Burr said. "Dat's the finest one in its litter. He's taken a liking to you right away. Dat be a good thing."

Burr snapped his fingers to catch a young dwarf's attention near the stall. He instructed the lad to bring the wolf for Boldair to inspect.

"What's his name?" Boldair asked.

"We leave dat to you," Burr replied.

"You've not named 'em?"

"Most of the time when we've named a mount before it's taken by a permanent rider, the new owner's displeased with the name we've given. None in dat litter are named."

Boldair scratched his bearded chin while studying the wolf. "Frost. Dat's the name he'll 'ave."

Burr smiled and a renewed wildness came to his eyes. "Dat be a good name."

"His fur reminds me of the frost dat appears on the surface of the snow after the morning fog disappears," Boldair replied.

"I'm confident the young dire mount will give you many years of devoted service, unlike Ember."

"Ember's certainly taken well to you," Boldair said.

"Aye," Burr said. "But the majority of animals are drawn to me. They feel safe in my company. I'm not entirely certain why. I'm often called an animal charmer."

The young dwarf brought Frost to Boldair. The young wolf leaned downward in a submissive stance. Boldair scratched behind Frost's ears.

"Do we 'ave a trade?" Burr asked.

Boldair nodded and laughed as Frost licked the side of his face. "Aye!"

"Get Boldair's saddle," Burr said to the lad. "And get Frost ready to ride." He glanced at Boldair. "You're leaving this morning, correct?"

"Aye," Boldair replied.

"In dat case, I'll 'ave someone ready your party's mounts," Burr said.

"Yotram's already doing dat," Boldair replied.

Burr offered his hand and Boldair shook it fiercely. "In a year or so, I invite you to return to see what Ember's offspring look like. I'm sure we'll have several litters by then."

"I look forward to dat," Boldair said. "But, if I might request, I'd like first choice in any of them dat favor Ember."

"And you shall 'ave it," Burr said.

THIRTY-NINE

B oldair rode Frost to where Dwiskter and Drucis stood with
their mounts. Forboud sat atop his ram with his wrists chained
together. Forboud eyed Boldair and paled. He peered frantically
behind Boldair.

"Where's Ember?" Forboud asked.

"I traded 'em for Frost 'ere," Boldair replied.

"Don't you think you should've consulted me first?" Forboud
brimmed with anger.

Boldair shook his head. "Why should I consult *you*? You didn't own
Ember. I did."

"You didn't spend years rearing and training him like I did with
father," Forboud said. "I'd 'ave bought ya the mount ya 'ave now and
paid you twice Ember's worth, just to keep 'em."

"Ember has proven too dangerous to trust during our travels. He
tried to kill Viorka and me. We don't need dat while we ride."

"Boldair, please reconsider," Forboud said.

"Sorry, brother. I cannot. Our trade has already exchanged." Boldair
sighed. "I understand dat Ember meant a lot to ya—"

"King or not," Forboud said, "you had *no* right to trade 'em."

"I had *every* right," Boldair said with narrowed eyes. His hands tightened into fists. "One more outburst or calling my decisions into question will ensure dat you ride gagged for the duration of our journey. Is dat understood?"

Dwiskter and Drucis exchanged shocked expressions.

Boldair leaned in his saddle toward Forboud. "Is dat clear?"

Forboud's jaws tightened. Tears of heated anger burned at the edges of his eyes. His face reddened. His hands tightened, and it was obvious Forboud was flexing and straining against the metal cuffs. In spite of his fueled temper, he bit off a quick, "*Yes.*"

Hatred echoed in Forboud's voice. His eyes narrowed with unrelenting fury. Were Forboud not a prisoner, Boldair and the others knew Forboud would've dismounted and grabbed the nearest weapon to attack Boldair. Dwiskter and Drucis slid their axes partially from their sheaths.

Having noticed the extreme tension, Yotram walked to the side of Frost and gazed at Boldair. "You can leave your brother in our prison and return for him at a later date, if you wish."

"No. I've not time to return anytime soon," Boldair replied.

Wynneffin stood outside the main gate of the stables. Boldair caught her gaze, which was a bit frostier than when he'd seen her in the library. Whatever memories he held of her beauty withered, and it saddened him. He doubted he could ever revisit the fonder memories they once shared. She was different and he couldn't deny that he'd changed, too.

Boldair said, "Thanks, Yotram, for your welcome and the drinks. Please extend my thanks to Brandrum and Kairun as well."

"Aye," Yotram said with a broad smile. "I look forward to your next visit."

"As do I," Boldair replied. "Remember my extended offer for you to venture to Nagdor. Now, if you'll excuse me, I think Wynneffin wishes to speak to me."

"Good luck with dat," Yotram whispered with a slight grin.

Two dwarves opened the gate to allow Boldair and his party to leave the stables. Boldair rode Frost to where she stood.

"Wynnie?" he said with a slight nod and a partial smile. "I didn't expect you to see us off."

"I'm not 'ere for dat purpose," she spat bitterly. "Father insisted I tell you what I saw in the Fae Stones."

"You found them?"

She nodded.

"Where?"

Wynneffin remained silent for several moments. He realized she wouldn't be there at all, except for Rigrim's orders. She glanced at a Frosthammer guard who stood nearby. His interest was on her and Boldair.

"Well?" Boldair asked.

"She covered the stones with a cloth and tried to hide them on a bookshelf."

"Ah, good, I suppose. She didn't keep them."

"Look," Wynneffin said, "I don't want to speak to you any longer than necessary, but being as father sent this guard to ensure I find and tell you, I've no choice in the matter. It's my hope dat after today, our paths never cross again."

Boldair stared stoically in an attempt to prevent her from seeing how her words affected him. They cut him to the core, but he didn't want the hurt to show. He couldn't allow her to see his pain. Not as king. Inside, he was a coiled bed of mixed emotions; partially angered, hurt, and ready to spout vehement words at her for betraying his trust. Instead, he held himself in check. "What did you see?"

"Telsia hasn't left Frosthammer," she replied.

"Where is she?"

Wynneffin shrugged. "Somewhere dark. Possibly in the tunnels beneath Frosthammer or on the floor where the three forest elves had taken Viorka."

"Thanks." Boldair nudged Frost's flank gently and the wolf turned away from her.

"So dat's it?" she said.

"It's as you asked," Boldair replied. "Or at least how you implied, right? You don't want to talk to me longer than necessary, or did I mishear dat?"

She huffed and nodded. "Those were my words, yes."

Boldair regarded her for a few moments. "Okay, then."

"You can turn off your feelings, just like dat?"

"Seems you did well before I," Boldair said. "Ya can't 'ave it both ways, Wynnie. Now, if you'll excuse me, we must get on with our journey. Although seeing you again wasn't as I hoped, I wish you ... a happy life."

Wynneffin fumed and walked in front of Frost. She grabbed the wolf's bridle and clung tightly. In a low voice, she said, "One should never leave their differences unresolved. As a new king, you've much to learn."

"You've taught me lessons dat'll last a lifetime, but those also prevent me from repeating *mistakes* I don't need to fret over."

Her eyes narrowed. "You leave without resolve, and I assure you, you'll be back in Frosthammer quicker than ya imagined. I'll see to dat."

"You dare threaten a king?" Boldair's eyes narrowed.

"Until you survive the coronation, you're not king. Isn't dat what you told me yesterday?"

Boldair sighed and shook his head. "Wynnie, I don't want any hard feelings between us. We could talk for days 'bout the situation, but where would dat take us? It won't change how our relationship was severed. You desire to craft magic. Dat's fine, but don't abuse your powers and turn them against me. We should say our goodbyes and when I leave today, know dat I won't return. Dat's the finality you didn't get when I left the first time, but it's not the same outcome this time, either."

"Then *leave*," she said harshly. "But, you'll come back. I assure you."

Wynneffin released Frost's bridle and stormed away. A cold breeze funneled through the stables and gusted around him. An impressive exit but Boldair wondered if the breeze was merely a coincidence or was it a product of her magical abilities?

After she left the stables, Yotram opened the large steel gates to allow the riders to exit Frosthammer. Although Frosthammer was frigid for a city, nothing prepared Boldair for the biting, cold winds sweeping through those gates. He'd forgotten how severe the outside temperatures were, and in retrospect, he was thankful they had not left during the middle of the night. The night beasts would've been the *least* of their concerns.

Boldair wrapped his bear hide around him, offered his thanks to Yotram once more, and led his party through the gates.

FORTY

Boldair and his party rode in silence for the better part of an hour. The whipping cold winds lashed with their whistling, banshee shrieks of coming doom. On occasion, long bluish-white icicles broke free of the jagged, icy cliffside and shattered on the rocky bottom like glass. Snowy rocks cracked and popped. Boldair watched the ledges with suspicion. They were being watched or perhaps followed.

He pulled the bearskin tighter around himself to block the harsh wind. Tiny icicles coated his beard around his nose and mouth. The rest of his beard was white from captured snow.

In spite of the cold, Boldair felt a rush of heat from the hot angered stare of his brother riding behind him. Even without looking, Boldair pictured Forboud's indignant glare, which made him uneasy. The wedge between them cut deeply without any amicable feelings left.

In ways, he didn't blame Forboud for his anger. He understood the reasons, but after Ember nearly killed Viorka, Boldair could never justify having the wolf travel in their company. Besides, he still wasn't certain what Forboud's fate should be for his disrespect and disobedience. But Boldair needed to make the decision *before* they reached Nagdor.

With Ulthor's fate still in Queen Taube's hands, sentencing

Forboud to death for his underhanded, traitorous behavior was not in Boldair's best interest. Boldair couldn't hand down such a verdict anyway. Doing so made Forboud a martyr for those still loyal to King Ulthor and Boldair would be viewed as a tyrant.

After all, Forboud was his brother. Even if Boldair chose to imprison him, Forboud's imprisonment would have to be in another city. Otherwise, Nagdor would remain in constant unrest. Regardless of what punishment Boldair decided, or if he chose to pardon his brother altogether, neither could fully trust the other again.

Boldair sighed. He had yet to have his coronation and already enemies surrounded him. Estranged family and friends were enemies he never expected. He wasn't certain if King Rigrim was an ally or not, based on their short meeting. Rigrim seemed more displeased with Wynneffin's actions and scolded her outright for her behavior in front of Boldair.

In turn, Wynneffin focused her anger and resentment on Boldair, perhaps merely magnifying her feelings from her earlier frustrations, but her last words were an outright threat. How she actually *planned* to deliver her threat remained unclear. Boldair hoped by putting distance between them, her festered anger might eventually diminish and she'd forget about him.

He doubted things between them could end so easily or in a peaceful manner, because she'd never forgiven him for his departure the first time. His apology about his behavior was sincere and heartfelt, but she remained unconvinced. What he said to her was correct. Regardless of how much more time he spent in Frosthammer trying to mend their differences, nothing fruitful could ever be gained. Her biases, as well as his own, were set. The undertones of bitterness and their lack of trust prevented them from moving forward. The best thing was to separate and move on with their lives. But her threat ... she wasn't finished and she seemed to be scheming a plot for revenge.

Boldair sighed and adjusted in the saddle. Viorka, who was curled under the bearskin behind him and asleep, straightened and sat up.

She peered through a slit in the bearskin. A yawn escaped her mouth. "We're still in the snowy mountains?"

"Aye," he whispered. "Go back to sleep."

"It's too cold to do anything else," she replied. "I certainly have no wish to *walk* in this snow and ice."

"Is all okay?" Dwiskter asked. "You've been quiet since we left Frosthammer."

Boldair shrugged.

Drucis rode up beside Boldair. "It'll get better once we're out of this cold."

"I'm glad you're so optimistic," Boldair said.

"Looking around," Drucis said, "Could ya see anything getting much worse."

Dwiskter shook his head. "Shh! Don't jinx us."

"Jinx us?" Drucis said. "Merely words of observation, friend. Fate deals whatever it wishes, *regardless* of my words. I'm no sorcerer or wizard or witch."

"Thank the gods for dat," Dwiskter said dryly. "The white skies indicate more snow and our path is increasingly more narrow. Not many travelers ever come this direction. Is this the route you took before, Boldair?"

Boldair studied his surroundings for a few moments. He nodded. "Aye. The path will serpentine downward and after that, a short line of trees. The cold will lessen, as will the snow. We're on our way out of the Frosted Peaks."

"Sorry things didn't work out between you and Wynneffin," Dwiskter said. "What'd she tell you before we left?"

"Dat Telsia was still in Frosthammer."

"How's she know dat?"

"The Fae Stones."

"She can use them?" Drucis' brows rose.

Boldair nodded.

"When did ya learn of her ability to consult them?" Drucis asked.

"Last night when I spoke with her father in his private library."

Drucis frowned. "Something's amiss."

"Whatcha mean?" Boldair asked.

"It's not normal for any dwarf to read Fae Stones," he replied. "It's *not* possible. I say dat because we dwarves are no kin to the Fae or the elves. Nowhere near one another at all. Regardless of how one learns magic or draws upon it, a dwarf should 'ave no access to the Fae magic."

"Aye, I agree," Boldair said. "But Telsia did, too."

"I know Wynneffin swore dat Telsia used magic, but I've thought long and hard over this." Drucis shook his head. "It's not possible nor does it bear any logic. We dwarves craft and consult runes to protect us against magic. But wielding it? Few ever 'ave. And certainly not *Fae* magic. Our bloodlines have never crossed with Fae or elves. Besides, even if any dwarf wished to marry an elf—"

Dwiskter spat on the ground.

Drucis nodded and pointed a stern finger. "Rightly so! No offspring could ever be birthed between the two. Our bloodline can never be tarnished by the elves or vice versa. Humans and elves, now dat be a different matter altogether. We encounter half-elves all the time, as humans 'ave no problem tarnishing other races with their substandard blood. But half human and half dwarf? 'ave ya ever seen one?"

Boldair shook his head, as did Dwiskter.

"I'm not certain I'd *want* to see one," Dwiskter said. "A combination of our traits into one being? Talk 'bout deformities."

"Aye. There's a reason for dat," Drucis said. "We're a proud race, but our creation apparently was far different than either of theirs. We cannot blend our bloods to form a half with the others. Not to say I've not ever been attracted to a female human or elf, because I 'ave. Some of their beauty is far greater than anything I've ever beheld, but more than admiration, I don't possess the desire."

Boldair frowned. "So ya don't believe it possible a dwarf could effectively use the Fae Stones to view the future or search for lost loved ones?"

"No," Drucis replied. "I know you've been fretting over a lot since we left Frosthammer, but 'ave you ever considered dat Wynneffin lied to you about *seeing* anything?"

"It's crossed my mind."

"Understand, Boldair, dat Frosthammer's an unusual city and not commonly known to the rest of Aetheaon. For a place with a river of molten steel, it's colder than a tomb. Dat river should billow heat throughout the entire city but it 'as no effect. The surrounding mountain should be like a volcano without a flake of snow gracing its peak. It's contrary to what it should be."

"Aye," Boldair said. "King Rigrim has tapped into magic, too."

"How do ya know?" Dwiskter said.

"He admitted such. The frost warhammer he wields is how the city obtained its name, and it seems to be the very heart of the city. The entire time I sat in the library, the weapon constantly released a stream of cold frost dat seeped through the floor. Everything in the city looks like it's been bitten by frost. Every Frosthammer dwarf's hair and beards all are tinted blue. They 'ave brilliant amber eyes."

Drucis nodded. "I noticed dat as well. I hope you've no intention of ever returning."

"No immediate plans," Boldair replied.

"Good. Too many things don't settle well, but I can't quite place a finger on what exactly troubles me the most," Drucis said. "How comfortable do you feel about Yotram and Brandrum?"

"I consider them friends, but not anywhere as strongly as I do about you and Dwiskter. Why?" Boldair asked.

"When you were arrested—" Drucis said softly.

"Yes! Please, tell me what happened?" Boldair's eyes widened from his curiosity. "I've no recollection of my outbursts dat they insist I did."

"Dat was no exaggeration," Dwiskter said. "You did those things."

"For what reason?"

"Yotram said something about taking you on a dragon hunt," Drucis said, "and to be honest, from his tone of voice and sly grin, it was all in jest. But something about it set you off. Yotram insisted it was one of the drinks you had while seated at the table. But, Dwiskter and I drank the same drinks. Nothing altered our states of mind."

"A dragon hunt?" Boldair asked.

Drucis nodded. "Yes, but he wasn't being serious."

"Ya see, though, I don't recall dat," Boldair said. "And you drank everything I did?"

"Aye," Dwiskter said. "Some of 'em twice!"

Boldair frowned for several moments before suddenly realizing something he'd forgotten. "Bloody Hells!"

"What?" Drucis asked.

"When I was in the library with King Rigrim, one of his servants *brought* me a drink."

"You think it was spiked with something?" Dwiskter asked.

"Quite possibly," Boldair said, nodding. "Wynneffin was hiding in the shadows and listening to my conversation with her father. She had every opportunity to do so."

"Would she actually do that?" Viorka asked from under the bearskin.

"She's quite bitter and angry at me," Boldair said. "She's set on revenge."

"Then most likely, dat's what happened," Drucis said. "But *why?*"

"The last words she spoke were more a threat than anything," Boldair said.

"And *I'm* the one shackled?" Forboud said.

"For entirely different reasons." Dwiskter turned in his saddle and frowned.

"I've done nothing wrong," Forboud said.

"You've done plenty," Drucis said. "Undermining a king is a capital offense, worthy of death."

"He's not *my* king."

"Ah, he's king. You openly committed treason," Dwiskter said. "Treason's a quick death in most cities."

"Ignore Forboud," Boldair said. "Can we get back to discussing what happened in the tavern?"

Drucis nodded. "Not much more to tell. Your outrage sparked the surrounding guards into a rage dat made them draw their weapons. Yotram, Brandrum, and Kairun are the only reason you weren't attacked and possibly killed."

"For several moments, though, they weren't in any mood to protect you," Dwiskter said.

"Really?"

Dwiskter and Drucis nodded.

"I wonder why?" Boldair said.

"I can think of several reasons," Forboud said under his breath.

"It appeared as though they no longer recognized you," Drucis said.

"Perhaps the spiked drink was also bewitched with a spell? Something dat altered your outward appearance?"

Boldair frowned. "Dat's possible, I suppose."

"Yotram must 'ave some persuasion with the other guards or maybe he has greater authority, as he talked them down."

"But did I lose consciousness?" Boldair asked.

"No, never," Dwiskter replied.

"I told you dat you were flaring mad when they dragged you into your cell," Forboud said.

"You did," Boldair said, nodding. "I wish I remembered what happened."

"Shh!" Dwiskter rose in his saddle.

"What is it?" Boldair said.

"Ya smell dat?" He scrunched his nose. "Smoke."

"Now dat you mention it, yes," Boldair said.

Drucis nodded and pointed. "There's a stream of smoke drifting through those evergreens."

"Approach with caution," Boldair said.

"Perhaps you could remove my restraints?" Forboud asked. "In case we are forced to fight?"

"I don't think any of us trust handing ya a weapon at the moment," Drucis said.

Boldair glared and placed his forefinger to his lips. Then he pointed ahead.

FORTY-ONE

Dead, frozen goblins were sprawled around the smoldering, charred sections of the firs. Seeing the carnage, Boldair hesitated any further approach. He scanned the area for what might've recently killed these goblins. The fire wasn't produced by any natural means. The scorched goblin flesh resembled the results of a wizard's magical flames, as though their bodies suffered from intense flash burns. Direct fire from a dragon would've incinerated them beyond recognition.

The goblins appeared to have been taken by surprise. Their wide eyes, frozen by death and the cold, revealed as much. Their fallen bodies lie as though they had turned to run while looking over their shoulders. Something or someone had hurled fire at them, possibly toying and antagonizing their fear. The goblins weren't grouped in an attacking formation. They'd tried to flee.

None survived the heat. If any survived their burns, the elements would've killed them in a matter of minutes.

Due to Frosted Peaks' extreme cold, a living thin-clothed body might freeze in minutes, but a dead body ... the frigid winds turned the flesh into ice in a matter of seconds. Since the trees smoldered, the fiery attack had occurred within the past half hour or less.

In a grim, soured tone, Forboud said, "So much for the goblins being driven out of Aetheaon."

Drucis laughed. "Their numbers are far less, though."

"Aye." Boldair nodded and glanced at Drucis and Dwiskter. "But the graver danger is da goblins 'ave come to the surface."

Dwiskter nodded. "The good thing is dat they're all dead. But what killed them?"

"Dat's a great question." Boldair slid off his mount.

Drucis and Dwiskter dismounted as well.

The melted, snowy path was thirty yards from where the circle of intense heat blasted the frozen, forest edge. Boldair stepped forward. The crunchy ice echoed beneath his feet. The reverberating sound, though slight, could attract the attention of whatever had scorched the area. They needed to approach the goblin corpses without being seen or heard, but the ice-crusted snow prevented it.

Boldair slid one axe from its sheath.

"Ya see something?" Drucis asked.

"Only the dead," Boldair replied.

"Maybe we should mount up and ride on?" Dwiskter said.

"Either way," Boldair said, "we still 'ave to pass through these dead goblins."

"True, but my mount's far faster than my legs," Drucis said.

Frost tilted his massive head upward and howled. A colder chill shot down Boldair's spine.

Boldair turned his head and tried to find the reason for wolf's howl. Almost invisible in the white cloudy sky was a massive dragon in flight. Its wings straightened and it glided over the mountainside outside of view. The magnificent giant beast made no sound and was mesmerizing to behold.

"Dragon," Boldair whispered and pointed. "A *snow* dragon."

"Where?" Dwiskter asked.

"It flew over the ridge and out of sight. Mount up," he replied. "We need to scurry, in case it returns."

They hurried to their mounts.

"How many goblins?" Viorka asked.

"I counted thirty-five," Dwiskter said. "Not a massive amount, but enough to have inflicted a lot of misery and damage on a small village."

"More than we'd want to fight right now," Forboud said.

"Ah, dat's what *you* think," Dwiskter said. "Me axe could take out a dozen in a few minutes."

Drucis reared back his head with a hearty laugh. "It'd be a worthy challenge."

Forboud sighed and looked down. "What brought them back?"

Boldair tapped Frost's flank gently. "Perhaps they never left. The Dwarven Alliance slaughtered thousands of them and the survivors retreated to the mountain caverns. After dat? Who knows? No stories 'ave been told of our generals sending any troops after them."

"Legends are often exaggerated," Forboud said. "Especially after Dwarven stout."

Boldair nodded his agreement.

"Something's obviously disturbed them enough to bring them to the surface," Drucis said.

"Aye." Boldair nodded. They rode past the charred trees and dead goblins. His mind returned to when he had led the troops with Taniesse along the Fae Barrier Pass between the Black Chasm and the Woodnog Forests. The Pass was a neutral zone between opposing magical forces. However, whatever creatures were hidden within the chasm constantly tried to break through the Fae magical barrier.

Strange creatures had grabbed several of his troops, pulled them into the chasm, and eviscerated them. If ever the Fae magic protecting the Pass lessened or failed, he feared what dark forces would be unleashed. The dam of magic was the only reason the Black Chasm had never reached the mystical Woodnog forests. Had Tyrann been responsible for the goblins' return to the surface?

"Keep alert," Boldair said, softly. "The dragon must've killed these goblins in one engulfing ball of flame. Dat dragon's white enough to camouflage itself in the snowy peaks, so it took them by surprise."

Dwiskter nodded. "I noticed the goblins were petrified by fear and extreme cold."

Drucis said, "There could be more than one dragon lying in wait."

A loud fierce roar pierced the air and originated from the peak where the dragon descended. Although Taniesse was Boldair's friend, he mainly interacted with her human form. He didn't know if this roar was a forewarning of its coming attack or if it rallied a cry to gather more dragons to its position.

Taniesse had made it clear. She and her siblings weren't the last dragons in Aetheaon. They were hidden from the general population. He assumed she'd meant in human appearance so they could pass through cities undetected.

"Ya heard dat, too?" Dwiskter asked.

"Aye. Let's pick up the pace," Boldair said.

"I'm with ya on dat," Drucis said. "A few dozen goblins we could handle, but I'm afraid on our best day, we're no match for an angry dragon."

They rode down the winding mountain trail. The ice and snow lessened. More trees lined the edges of the slope and the road. Boldair wondered if the snow dragons were the dragons Yotram had invited Boldair to hunt. But the Frosthammer dwarves' armor was blue and from frost dragons. They were two different species altogether, but no travelers had seen frost dragons for nearly a century.

Of course, few *survived* their encounters with snow or frost dragons and lived to tell the tale. Could the two types of dragons coexist peacefully?

They rode hard until they left the permafrost level and the terrain was greener.

"Do snow dragons spew fire?" Dwiskter asked, breaking the silence. "I mean, frost dragons don't. They spew icy breath and freeze their victims."

Boldair straightened in his saddle. "I don't rightly know."

"Cause if they don't," Dwiskter said, "dat dragon didn't kill those goblins."

Drucis' eyes widened. "Never thought of dat. Dat's worrisome. Could be a sorcerer or wizard."

"Aye." Boldair scratched his beard. "Whenever I see Taniesse again, I'll ask her."

"We might be dead before we ever see her," Forboud said.

Drucis cocked a brow and glared at Forboud. "*One* of us might be."

Forboud frowned. "Look, if ya want me dead, as seems your hopeful verdict, end me life 'ere and now! Do it! I'm fine with it. It beats being dragged through frozen mountains, dragons and wizards, and being shackled while you torment me with degrading words."

"Bah!" Drucis said. "Don't tempt me."

"Don't hold yourself back," Forboud said. "I know ya want to use dat axe. It's itching at ya. You need to shed blood."

Drucis frowned. "Nice try, but your greatest punishment's keeping ya alive. Dat's why you're needling me to end your life. But, keep talking and I'll find something to stuff in your mouth, like bitter moss. Hard to speak when your mouth's shriveled like a prune."

"Brother," Forboud said, with a tired sigh. "Please, end all this. You'll never trust me enough to allow me freedom, so execute me. I'm no use to you or Nagdor. Regardless of any actions on my part to better our relationship, nothing will rectify our situation. I'd rather die than—"

Boldair turned at Forboud's sudden silence.

"There!" Viorka jumped off Forboud's ram mount.

Forboud's eyes widened and his face scrunched. Sticking out of his mouth was a large wad of yellowish-green moss she'd shoved in his mouth.

"Long overdue!" Drucis said.

Boldair tried to hide his smile but couldn't. "Sorry, brother, but my axe could never take your life. I'll not 'ave your death on me conscience. But your fate's uncertain. We're less than a day from Meadwyrm Pass, and a few days from Nagdor. I'll 'ave made me decision by then."

FORTY-TWO

Their good fortune was the snow dragon never pursued them. A day later, and without incident, Boldair stood at a vendor table in Meadwyrm Pass in the forest to the northeast of Bridgebarrow. With anticipated amusement, he watched Drucis and Dwiskter stare at their drinks. While they'd never admit their uneasiness at drinking the fiery, potent brew, their eyes indicated their slight nervousness.

Boldair chuckled. "Ya going stare at the drinks or drink 'em?"

Dwiskter grunted and met Boldair's gaze. "I know ya said dat ya never lie, but you *embellish* your tales."

"Aye," Boldair said with a firm nod. "But not in this case."

Drucis frowned. "No? Then ya lied 'bout how harsh they be?"

Boldair shook his head. "No-o-o. No lie but also no embellishment."

Dwiskter stared at the small shot glass. "From this little amount?"

"Aye," Boldair said.

Sweat beaded Dwiskter's and Drucis' brow. They seemed to dare one another with their eyes to take the first shot.

Boldair shook his head and sighed. "We traveled 'ere in less time than ya're taking."

Drucis' hesitation didn't last long. He made quick glances to Boldair and Dwiskter, took a deep breath, and smiled. He grabbed the shot, turned it up, and downed the contents.

"Blasted!" Drucis shouted and slammed the glass on the table beside his steel helm. He wiped froth from his beard with the back of his gloved hand. His teary eyes widened. He opened his mouth to speak but only a dry hiss came from his mouth.

"Ya okay?" Dwiskter asked with slight fear in his eyes.

Drucis nodded and cleared his throat. "Dat, me friends, be a mighty potent liquid!"

"Aye!" Boldair laughed heartily. He clapped his hand against Drucis' back a couple of times. "I told ya. You'll never guess what the secret ingredient is."

Drucis coughed with tears blurring his vision. He beat his chest with his fist. His voice rasped. "Gah! The heat's getting worse. Not sure I *want* to know. Molten steel?"

"Bah-ha!" Boldair exclaimed a moment before turning up his drink. He held his breath and braced himself. Tears formed in his eyes. He beat a hearty fist against his chest-plate. He hiccuped and belched.

"Whew! You might 'ave wilted a few plants with dat burp!" Drucis pinched his nose and coughed. He rubbed his throat and flicked a hardened gaze at the barkeep. "What *is* this?"

The barkeep smiled. "Briarthorn Firespit."

Boldair winced and patted his chest. "Made from the toxic barbed vines in the forests. The ones I told you had nearly killed me."

Drucis' eyes watered. He nodded at Boldair and cleared his throat. "Aye, ya did. So what now? We've all been poisoned? Dat's what this little side trip be all about. Ahh, just what we need. A drink to end all sorrows."

Boldair shook his head and wiped away a tear. He and Drucis watched Dwiskter grab his shot glass. Dwiskter seemed to have second thoughts.

Dwiskter eyed his drink, frowned momentarily before closing his eyes, and then he gulped down the liquid. He slammed down the glass, gagged, but he forced the harsh, bitter drink down against his throat's obvious protest. He expelled heated breath and shook his head. He steadied himself against the table. "Whew! Blast it! Dat burns and makes me skin crawl."

Boldair and Drucis offered raspy howls of laughter.

The barkeep grinned. "And ... what of your unbearded companion? Shall I pour him one as well?"

Boldair glanced at Forboud. Forboud shook his head. "Nah. He doesn't 'ave the gumption."

The barkeep stared at Forboud for several quiet moments. "What crime has this dwarf committed? I mean, isn't that why his beard's been removed?"

"Most of the time," Boldair said.

"And his fate?"

"Not known at this time," Boldair replied.

Dwiskter rubbed his throat. "This is made from a toxic plant?"

The barkeep nodded.

"We've been poisoned?" Drucis rubbed his stomach. Oily sweat dripped from his reddened face. "Where's the antidote? Feels like the flames of Hell are burning from my stomach to my throat."

"We distill out the toxin," the barkeep said with a sly smile. "The heat settles in its own time. It's the fiery kick dwarves crave the most."

"Aye," Boldair said with a shrewd smile. "No lie there. I've found myself wanting another shot for some time."

The barkeep nodded. "'Tis true with a lot of travelers. Once they've gotten a taste of this, they eventually come back for more. Of course, they tend to forget how painfully harsh it is until they drink it again."

"Aye." Boldair nodded. "Still stings and burns as badly the first time."

"I imagine so." Drucis squinted. "Tomorrow I'll need to take a dump in a creek to prevent setting the forests on fire. Might need the cold water to relieve my arse, too."

The barkeep laughed.

Dwiskter plopped a gold coin on the crude booth table before the strange barkeep. "Aye, give me a second one."

A devious grin spread across the old man's face. "You sure, dwarf? Few can handle more than one."

"Dwarves can drink any human or elf under da table," Drucis said.

"Ah, but surely nothing as potent as *this*," the barkeep replied. "No human has ever drank a second, and those dwarves who've drank two never asked for a third."

Dwiskter frowned and placed his hand atop the gold coin. "Then why give away the first for free?"

"'Tis charity to weary travelers," the man replied.

"Ah, now, *is* it?" Dwiskter asked. "I be thinking it more an opportunity for you and your surrounding vendors to take advantage of inebriated customers. A new type of highwayman. Get passersby drunk and then rob 'em."

Viorka stood behind Boldair with a large hunk of boar meat she had gotten from a neighboring vendor. She chewed while she watched the dwarves drink. Her interest seemed intent on the barkeep, and Boldair assumed she did so because of how their last meeting had gone. Either the barkeep hadn't noticed her, or he'd forgotten about her stealing the orb from Sissrow when they visited Meadwyrm Pass before.

The old man's eyes narrowed. "Dare you make such an accusation against me, *your host*, in this secluded, off the beaten path, tavern?"

Drucis howled with laughter. "Tavern? *This*?"

"The whole lot of you dwarves dare to offend me? *Us*?" The old man waved his hand toward the neighboring vendor tables. "Your insults are the reasons we isolate ourselves so far from any civilization. We seldom make a profit, *scrounge* to survive with barely a roof over our heads. What crime have we done, other than freely offer a rare drink no other tavern in Aetheaon is capable of making? Nothing else compares to it! You're nothing more than wretched dwarves who spit in our faces!"

Dwiskter placed his hand on the heel of his axe. His face hardened and he held the gold coin between his thumb and forefinger. "I offered you gold for me second round."

"Moments before outright accusing us of thievery," the barkeep replied. "When your first drink was free."

"Aye," Dwiskter said with a firm nod. "But even a dwarf understands *nothing* comes for free. Everything has a price, no matter how small." He glanced at Drucis and winked. "No pun intended."

Drucis chuckled.

The barkeep's eyes darkened. "So, say you drank one and kept traveling on down the path, what price is required of thee?"

"A sword in me back to rob me?" Dwiskter said.

The old man's jaw tightened. Fury set in his dark eyes. It was almost like staring into the eyes of a venomous serpent moments before it struck.

Boldair placed his thick hand on Dwiskter's shoulder. "Easy. He never showed any ill will when I was here before."

The barkeep flicked his gaze from Dwiskter, and he eyed Boldair curiously.

"You were not king when you passed by before, either," Drucis said softly to Boldair.

"King?" The old man gasped. He gave Boldair a shrewd stare. "I see no crown."

"The coronation has yet to occur," Forboud said.

"Of what city?"

"Nagdor," Boldair replied.

The barkeep shook his head. "Ulthor's their king."

"Not ... anymore," Boldair replied.

"Interesting. So the king has fallen?"

"In ways unexpected."

"Pray tell, how?"

Boldair's face tightened. "I'll not be discussing the affairs of my kingdom with outsiders, especially not *human* ones."

"I remember you now," the barkeep said. His eyes widened with recognition and he pointed a crooked finger. Beads of sweat glistened on his bald head. "Not too long ago, you traveled to my booth, had one of these drinks while *your* fynx companion robbed one of my patrons. Ridiculous. Your companions this eve accuse *me* of being a thief and trample my hospitality. As I recall, Sissrow was nearly killed in the forest after he tried to get the orb your fynx friend had stolen. We offered our aid, but he denied us and he pursued the two of you on his own. I must assume you later murdered him, as he's never returned. He was a devoted customer, a true friend, and his absence remains a mystery. Nagdor's doomed to disarray if their new king's a murderous thief!"

"What be your name, barkeep?" Drucis asked. His bushy eyebrows rose. His black eyes shimmered.

"Cadell Prowell. Why?"

"You make treasonous remarks about our king, which is worthy of immediate death," Drucis replied in an angered whisper.

"He's *not* my king, nor am I *in* his kingdom. What I speak's the truth. Ask these vendors. We all witnessed what transpired that night. None of us drink in the presence of patrons, but *your king* drank at least two. Perhaps he doesn't remember?" He glanced at Boldair. "Do you deny killing Sissrow?"

Boldair's jaw tightened but he held the old man's gaze. His voice was gruff. "I didn't kill him."

"Is he dead?" Cadell asked.

"Aye. He is."

"How?"

"The fynx killed him."

Cadell cocked his head to the side with a mocking sneer. "See? *You*, a *king*, robbed the man and killed him. Who are the real highwaymen?"

Boldair formed fists and shook his head. "No. His death and the situation are not so easily explained."

"How's that?"

"For one, the orb we took from Sissrow was one *he* had stolen first. He was the farthest from being noble than an imprisoned, assassin thief. We took the orb because of the danger it posed, not for Damdur or Icevale or Nagdor but for all Aetheaon."

"What threat did the orb impose?" Cadell asked.

"Sissrow possessed the Dark Orb of Misthalls," Boldair replied.

Cadell's eyes widened. He salivated and swallowed hard. His voice lowered to a whisper. "The Dragon Conjuring Stone?"

"Aye, the same."

"But we've no dragons in Aetheaon."

Drucis laughed. "You've been hidden in this forest far too long."

Cadell cocked a brow while studying each dwarf's stern face. "Wait. Dragons exist?"

"They live and reign in the skies once more," Boldair replied. "The fynx and I worked with the great dragon, Taniesse. She sent us to retrieve the orb."

"You're fr-friends with a dragon?" Cadell wiped sweat from his brow.

"Aye," Boldair replied. "And we're closely aligned with Hoffnung."

"I see. And the orb? What of it?" the barkeep asked.

"Destroyed. Smashed to a thousand bits."

Regret claimed Cadell's face.

Boldair stared at him harshly. "You seem disappointed dat the orb was destroyed."

Cadell flinched slightly, and his eyes narrowed. "No. Not at all. Just taken aback, tis all."

"About the stone or the dragon?" Drucis asked.

"Both."

"It's our duty to protect Hoffnung and the great dragons," Boldair said. He pointed to the silver pendant riveted to his breastplate. "Not only am I King of Nagdor, but Drucis, Dwiskter, and I are Dragon Skull Knights."

"How does a dwarf get ... such an honor?" Cadell asked.

"We were the driving force that aided Lady Dawn to reclaim her throne," Boldair replied.

"And this one?" Cadell nodded toward Forboud.

Boldair shook his head. "Ah now, well, he cowered from the battle."

"So that's the reason for his shorn beard? Was that his shame?"

"Again," Boldair said sternly. "Nothing dat concerns ya."

Cadell's eyes set on Forboud. "Perhaps you'd like to tell me of your dilemma?"

Drucis, Dwiskter, and Boldair looked at Forboud with their hands on the heels of their axes. Forboud took a sharp breath and swallowed hard.

"I serve my brother," Forboud said, "and support him as our new king. Our kingdom's affairs are none of yours."

Cadell's shrewd stare at Forboud mellowed at a moment's notice. The fear in Forboud's eyes was obvious. He faced Boldair and his eyes subtly glanced from each dwarf's hold on their axes. Cadell bowed deeply at the waist to Boldair, and greatly exaggerated lifting his left arm in the air behind his back, which looked more theatrical than sincere. "My apologies, dear King of Nagdor. I had no knowledge you weren't a commoner. Please forgive me."

"*None* of us are commoners," Drucis said with a fierce glare. "We be warriors through and through."

"Yes. Sorry." He waved his hands pleadingly. "Dragon Skull Knights. Please, accept this gift as a token of my goodwill." He placed a large flask on the table.

Dwiskter frowned. "What's dat?"

"A flask of Briar-thorn Fire-spit. Anytime you or your party travel through our pass, all drinks are on the house."

"Acceptable terms, if you ask me." Drucis grabbed the flask with a broad smile.

Dwiskter placed his hand over Drucis' and yanked the flask from Drucis' grasp. "The terms aren't yours to accept."

"Aye," Drucis said.

"Sire?" Cadell said.

Boldair eyed Cadell harsh and long until the barkeep broke their gaze and fidgeted with his wool tunic. "Tell me why you set your *tavern*, as you call *this*, on the forest pass and not in Bridgebarrow?"

"Bridgebarrow?" Cadell scoffed. "Surely you jest?"

"No," Boldair replied. "It's a reputable little village with an ample number of travelers passing through daily. You'd make, if you pardon the quip, a king's ransom of more gold than you do 'ere along the narrow wood pass."

A sly grin spread across the Cadell's face. His eyes narrowed, and he couldn't hide his greed. "King's ransom, you say?"

"Indeed," Boldair replied. "Perhaps even more."

"All the same," Cadell said, "we prefer the tranquility of the forests and less with the bustle of traders, merchants, and competitive vendors."

"You 'ave no fear of highwaymen?" Drucis asked.

"No. Most are enticed by free drinks and move on. Not something one can do in Bridgebarrow. A free drink to a weary traveler is far different than offering a free drink in a tavern filled with greedy farmer peasants. I'd be outta business in hours."

"The more people learn of your powerful concoction, the more gold you'll make. You'd never 'ave to give them for free," Boldair said.

"You're probably right, but Bridgebarrow doesn't have the proper ingredients necessary to make our brew, and our ... distillery, it's impossible to uproot that. Besides, we've a limited clientele, barely able to keep the supply equal to the demand." He pointed to the flask Dwiskter held. "Take that, please, as my apology for misjudging you and the fynx about Sissrow. I never knew he was a thief. He always seemed such a kind fellow whenever he visited."

"Looks can be deceiving," Boldair replied.

"Quite true. I suppose it shouldn't surprise me."

"By chance did you ever meet Sissrow's father?"

Cadell shook his head. "No, I never did. He never spoke of his father. Why?"

"Long story," Boldair said.

"Beware, barkeep," Drucis said. His blue eyes sparkled in the faint light. He ran a hand along his white-knotted beard. "Boldair's known to weave long tales *before* he became king."

Boldair shot Drucis a sharp glance beneath a harsh frown. "Not this evening, I won't. We must travel onward to Nagdor. But ... to make a *long* story much shorter, Sissrow and his father were once one person unified."

Cadell eyed him curiously. "You only drank one shot of the Briarthorn, right?"

"Aye."

"'Cause it sounds like you might've already drunk the entire flask."

"No, me senses are keen. Wylard was Sissrow's father, in a sense of the word, but Sissrow was actually the product of Wylard's wish at the Well of Misfortune where he pleaded for a son. The child he received was conceived and molded by taking Wylard's bad traits and containing them in flesh. His wish became his curse and ultimately, his death."

Cadell nodded. "Seems right. The well, that is. Only a fool makes a wish there. Sissrow, however, never cheated or stole from us. Always the perfect customer. Now, about the flask. It's yours. You may enjoy it now or wherever you venture next."

Boldair took the flask from Dwiskter and set it on the vendor table before Cadell. "I appreciate your hospitality, and know I've no hard feelings against ya. But, I cannot accept your gift."

"What?" Drucis and Dwiskter looked at Boldair in shock. Each dwarf's lower lip quivered.

"It's best our wits are keen while we travel," Boldair said. "But when we return, we'll take you up on your offer for a few more rounds."

"Your Highness, *please*," Cadell said.

Boldair looked fiercely in Cadell's eyes and grinned. "As you clearly pointed out, I'm not *your* king, and while a gift's a gift, taking it beholds me to you."

Cadell's eyes widened for a moment. He shook his head. "No, it's not intended as such. I swear."

Boldair nodded with a gracious smile and gently placed a hand the Cadell's shoulder. "I believe ya. All the same, we must go."

With disappointment in Cadell's eyes and a slight degree of offended agitation, he set the flask down and shrugged. "Be safe in your travels, new king."

"Aye."

FORTY-THREE

B oldair led the way down the forest path. Drucis and Dwiskter grumbled under their breaths until the covered vendor tables were out of view. Boldair chuckled at their mild fit of anger. But his gut told him Cadell's *gift* held a darker intent.

Frost's ears perked. Something drew his interest on the right side of the path. Were they being followed?

Dwiskter's accusations had angered the barkeep, but Cadell's anger stirred more from being identified for what he and his companions were: Highwaymen.

And while Cadell insisted he never knew Sissrow was a thief, his admission was most likely a lie. Thieves protected one another. It was an unspoken code, even if they were thieves from different guilds. Being a backstabber or a snitch marked a thief and often caused other thieves to set a bounty on the tattler. Since thieves were masters of hiding and deception, the last thing a thief needed was to be hunted by one of his own. Naturally, Cadell would lie about Sissrow's true character.

A lie was a small transgression. Theft and murder were a part of some thieves' occupation, especially highwaymen. The majority weren't murderers. They took pride in purloining items without the victim noticing until the thief was gone. Killing a victim to steal someone's belongings proved the thief inadequate in his skills. No thief wanted a tarnished reputation amongst other thieves. Pride was almost as great a reward as fencing the best loot.

A branch crackled in the underbrush to the right side of the trail. Frost sniffed in the direction of the sound but didn't slow his pace. He didn't growl, either.

"Bah!" Drucis said. "What'd ya do dat for? A *whole* flask of dat stomach-kicker could've been ours."

"It'd have been our deaths," Boldair replied evenly.

Dwiskter cocked a brow and looked at Boldair. "What'd ya mean?"

"It was poison."

Forboud nodded. "My thoughts exactly. I don't see why any of you even tempted your fates by drinking the Briarthorn Firespit to start with. How could you trust their distillery process even worked? They're hidden on a dark trail far from any decent civilization. Dat should've been your first warning. No doubt the flask is as my brother has said. Filled with poison."

"Those shackles giving you a change of heart, Forboud?" Drucis glared. "*Now* ya offer counsel to Boldair?"

Forboud frowned. "I only offer what's the truth. With you and Dwiskter's insults, Cadell would've reveled in your deaths."

Dwiskter looked at Boldair. "You believe dat he'd have poisoned us?"

Boldair nodded.

"How can ya be sure?" Drucis asked.

"He switched the flasks," Boldair said.

"What! When?"

"Moments before he offered the flask to me, his hands lowered beneath the table. He lowered the flask in his right hand but when he brought his hands up, the flask he offered was in his left."

"Slight of hand?" Drucis asked in a near whisper. "Like a street magician?"

Dwiskter shook his head slightly. "Bah! Doesn't mean it was poison."

Forboud sighed. "Never let your cravings for the hard drinks override your rationality."

Dwiskter pointed a stern finger at Forboud. "Look, you keep ya trap shut or I'll find more moss to shove in ya mouth!"

Viorka leapt off the back of Boldair's saddle. "Would you all stop bickering? Your fiery belches have continued since we left the vendor tables, along with your grumbling complaints of ailing stomachs. Now, all this fighting over whether or not a flask of liquid was poison or not? If it wasn't poison, you'd be happy to contend with your insides being torn asunder? Perhaps that would be the *least* of your concerns. But what if it was poison? If it were, the lot of ya would be on the forest floor gasping your last breaths of life."

"I still 'ave me doubts, lil' cat, dat it was poison," Dwiskter said.

"You'd be willing to risk your life to find out?" she asked.

Dwiskter's lips tightened but he held his silence. His eyes indicated he was mulling over the possibilities more than before.

Drucis gave Boldair a confused expression. "Dwiskter's right. Ya could be wrong about it being poison."

"What about your loyalty to Boldair, your king?" she said. "You're arguing with him for his decision to decline the offer? He might've saved your lives."

Drucis' eyes narrowed in anger. He opened his mouth to reply, and then, he lowered his head in shame. "You're right, lil' cat. My greed for dat drink clouded me judgment."

Dwiskter sighed and looked away. "Aye, my apologies, Boldair."

Boldair shook his head. "Like she said, I was looking out for all of us. But Dwiskter was right about his earlier point, but not about the flask being filled with poison."

"What exactly was I right about?" Dwiskter asked with curiosity.

"About their plot to get patrons drunken out their wits in order to rob them. They don't fear highwaymen because they *are* highwaymen. Rather than hiding in the shadows to attack unsuspecting passersby, they lure them in for food and a powerfully strong drink. Your insinuation angered him because ya saw through their guise." Boldair ran a hand along his knotted beard. "Cadell made mention dat the poison's distilled from the brew, which made me wonder what they did with the filtered poison afterwards? He was insistent dat we take an *entire* flask. His true intentions were deeply shady and reflected in his eyes. Either to kill us, so we didn't alert others to the possibility of these traders being highwaymen, or to rob us for what we have. We dwarves have a high tolerance for the strong stuff, but I'll tell ya, dat Firespit almost rendered me unconscious the first time I drank it."

"Drat!" Drucis formed fists. "All I got was the one shot. Nothing more! More fire than jarring my senses."

"Perhaps this time dat was best for all of us," Boldair said.

Dwiskter shook his head. "Ah, perhaps. My stomach's still throbbing."

Viorka rolled her eyes and shook her head. "And you wanted an *entire* flask of it?"

"Now dat I think 'bout it, not so much anymore." Dwiskter belched low and long. "My gut's rumbling more. Might need to hide behind a shrub soon."

Drucis cackled. "Me, too! My insides want to drain. Dat wicked brew seems to 'ave unsettled everything else!"

"Aye." Dwiskter belched again and waved his hand to disperse the odor.

"Cadell seemed quite amused by your king's ransom statement," Dwiskter said.

"He did entertain dat notion, didn't he?" Forboud glanced at Boldair.

"Aye. Had we drunk from the flask, we might all be dead."

"King's ransom?" Drucis howled. "If only they knew how much poorer you are since you returned the dragons' treasures."

Boldair winced slightly. "I lost a lot, tis true, but all those gems and gold weren't mine to begin with. Now dat I'm king, the tradeoff's worthwhile. Besides, Taniesse rewarded me handsomely for leading the troops into battle and by keeping me alive."

"No king's ever poor." Forboud eyed Drucis sharply.

"I be far wealthier than I've ever been in my life," Boldair said softly. His eyes drifted into thought.

"How so, brother?" Forboud's eyes narrowed with the question.

After a few minutes, Boldair responded to Forboud's question. "Father never told you?"

"About what?"

"The gold and silver ore veins abandoned by the Dredgemen?"

Forboud's bushy eyebrows rose. "No."

"Never?" Boldair asked.

Forboud shook his head. A stunned expression froze on his face.

A gleam came to Dwiskter and Drucis' eyes.

"This be another of your tales?" Dwiskter asked.

"It must be," Forboud said, angrily. "Father *never* mentioned these rich ore veins to me."

"So he kept secrets from you, too?" Boldair asked with amusement. "You said he favored you highly? Seems he didn't trust to tell you everything."

Forboud's jaw tightened. He gritted his teeth. "Surely, you're jesting at me expense."

"No, brother," Boldair shook his head. "I wish I were. But if our father was telling the truth ... Of course, he's lied about so many things ... So, if it's not true, tis not my doing, only my speculation on the words he boasted before King Thorgum, King Staggnuns, and myself. After my coronation, I plan to send a mining exploration to survey Snowloch. Drucis, I want you and Dwiskter to accompany me."

"You plan to go?" Drucis asked.

"Aye, why wouldn't I?"

"You're the king," Forboud said.

"I am, but I'll not 'ave my ass welded to a throne. If the gold and silver are there as father said, it was deeded to him and is Nagdor's property now. I want to oversee the initial mining operations."

"It's hard to protect a traveling king," Forboud said.

Boldair frowned with curiosity. "Brother, are you having sympathies toward me now? Or is it because we're so close to home dat you want to find yourself in my good graces."

Forboud shook his head. A partial smile curled on his nearly beardless face. He raised his cuffed hands. "I've had a lot of time to think along this overly long journey."

"Cuffs chaffing ya wrists, eh?" Drucis said with a sly smile.

Forboud frowned. His held back his agitation and kept eye contact with Boldair. "Things might never be the same between us, but you still hold the throne by all rights. I can never ignore dat. Especially not when the Dwarven Alliance placed you there. If I chose to remove you, they'd kill me and destroy half our kingdom in the process. When we arrive at Nagdor, I'll openly voice my support of you before the council and the entire city. You 'ave my loyalty, and I hope dat you'll be able to one day trust me again."

Boldair studied Forboud's eyes. His voice indicated his sincerity, and his eyes never flinched. Although it was possible Forboud had undergone a change of heart, Boldair couldn't allow complete trust yet. Or ever.

Trust couldn't be rebuilt in a day's time, and perhaps not in a year or a lifetime. Boldair would simply have to study Forboud for some time to come. One's consistent actions indicated the trueness of one's heart. Their father was a master of telling lies and hiding the truth. Something Boldair couldn't ignore. Since Forboud had been under their father's training and tactics, and his direct influence, it was possible Forboud had discovered the ease of telling a lie without the slightest tell. He wanted to believe his brother's allegiance for him, but Boldair had met too many swindlers during his travels.

Forboud hadn't drunk any Briarthorn Firespit, either. He might hope Boldair was in a stupor and could disregard Forboud's behavior during their journey. Boldair chuckled slightly at the thought. He'd not ingested enough brew to alter his perceptions of Forboud.

Boldair's prolonged silence brought a look of confusion on Forboud's face. He frowned, prompting Boldair to speak.

"I appreciate dat, brother," Boldair said.

"It's not in your best interests to travel into those mines so far from the city," Forboud said. "The dangers are far too great."

"I haven't any enemies," Boldair replied.

"Aye, not yet," Dwiskter said. "Queen Taube didn't either, but Waxxon tried to kill her and he was one of her personal council. Your enemies are sometimes disguised as close friends or family." He leveled a frown at Forboud. "Jealousy causes more murders than anything else, especially amongst royalty."

"Dat be true." Boldair looked over his shoulder at the darkened forest. Frost's ears remained perked, and he slowed its pace.

"You keep looking back, brother. Do you think Cadell and his companions are following us?" Forboud asked.

"Yes," Boldair replied. "I've heard the occasional branches snap along the forest floor near this trail. Frost is on high alert, too."

Viorka nodded. "I've not said anything, but I've heard those same noises."

Forboud peered over his shoulder. "No one seems to be following us."

"We're not out of the forest yet," Boldair replied.

"If they're excellent thieves," Viorka said, "you'll not see them until *after* it's too late. But the snapping branches indicate their stealth lacks polish."

Faint light from the moon spilled through the trees, not enough to see clearly, but the right amount to make the shadows stretch into ominous, slender figures that moved as the dwarves rode.

"Any forest elves in these woods?" Drucis asked.

"No dwarf's ever reported any." Boldair studied the shadowed canopy. "Of course, they're the masters of stealth, especially at night. So, unless forest elves sought to kill travelers, no one would know of their presence. Besides, we're between two major Dwarven cities. It's unlikely. Why?"

Drucis placed his thick hand on the hilt of his axe. "Aye, 'cause eyes are watching us. I've never held such a feeling dat it not be true."

"Then keep your wits about ya," Dwiskter said. "'Tis good we *didn't* drink more."

"Aye," Boldair said.

"I hate to admit such a bold admission," Drucis said, "but I agree."

Off the path in the darker recesses under the massive trees, leaves crunched. Occasional birds fluttered, chirped, and darted past them. Boldair pulled Frost's reins slightly. The dire wolf stopped and peered in the direction where the birds fled.

"A forest elf would be silent," Viorka said. "They're stealthier than the best thieves."

"Aye," Dwiskter said in a near whisper. He slid his axe from its sheath and nodded at Drucis. Drucis pulled his axe and slid one leg over the saddle, so he could drop to the ground in a moment's notice.

"Any idea what Cadell and his companions do to the victims they rob? You think they kill 'em or do they rob 'em and send 'em on their way?" Forboud asked.

"For a dwarf, you've a lot of jitters," Drucis said. "We encountered worse in caverns than here."

Forboud rolled his eyes and held up his cuffed hands. "I'm a bit vulnerable, as you know."

"Aye," Boldair said. "My guess is they kill 'em. We've no proof. But as often as I've visited Bridgebarrow Tavern, I've never heard a tale about someone getting robbed on this pass. Dat's why dat flask probably holds poison. To kill us."

"You mind freeing my hands?" Forboud frowned at Drucis. "You'd have jitters, too, if you couldn't defend yourself."

Drucis glanced at Forboud's cuffed wrists, huffed slightly, and then looked at Boldair for an answer.

Boldair nodded. "Unshackle him. He's right. If we're soon to be attacked, we'll need all the help we can get."

Drucis' eyes narrowed. "If ya recall, he never lifted his axe in the Battle for Hoffnung."

Boldair shrugged. "All the same. If he fails to defend us, kill him first."

Forboud's eyes widened at the threat.

Drucis took a key from his belt pouch and grinned. "Gladly."

Perplexed, Forboud said, "How 'ave I become your enemy?"

Unlocking the cuffs, Drucis leveled a glare at Forboud. "Undermining the king's a great offense. None greater in my book. Dat's what ya've done most of the journey. So prove yourself by protecting Boldair, and my disapproval of you will lessen a tinge."

Forboud rubbed his wrists and nodded. A few seconds later, he reached for his beard and found stubble instead. Hurt filled his eyes.

Another branch snapped, but from the opposite side of the path.

"What was that?" Dwiskter slid from the saddle and pointed with his broadax.

Boldair stopped. "Don't know."

A spark of blue light flashed farther down the path.

"Did you see that?" Viorka asked.

Boldair nodded and whispered, "Aye. A wisp?"

Drucis shook his head. "No. Too large and too bright for a wisp."

The blue light flashed again.

"Much too large," Viorka said softly. "Shimmers with strong magic, too."

The leaves rustled in the dark canopy. The wind, although warm, brought chills to Boldair. With the breeze came the scent of musk and aged sweat.

"Be on alert," Boldair said sternly. He gripped the axe handle tightly. With his free hand, he took Frost's reins and led the massive wolf. "Let's go see."

"Brother," Forboud said. "Allow me to lead the way?"

Boldair faced Forboud and stared at him momentarily. Drucis and Dwiskter nodded their agreement.

Boldair sighed. "Fine."

"To rebuild your trust in me," Forboud said, "I must prove myself to you and the others. Right?"

Drucis elbowed Dwiskter and whispered, "Dying honorably is an unyielding trust."

Boldair stepped aside and allowed Forboud to pass. Forboud led his ram and held his axe ready to attack should something or someone emerge from the shadowed edge of the forest.

Where the winding forest path ascended and turned at a sharp rising curve, a dim blue dome of light shimmered through narrow slivers of leaves and branches. The vibrations hummed steadily with an odd, pulsating sensation, which softly shook the ground beneath their feet.

Forboud nervously looked at Boldair, swallowed hard, and led them closer to the mystical object.

Drucis and Dwiskter exchanged nervous glances with Boldair. He shrugged and returned to following Forboud.

Curiosity forced them to approach with their axes and daggers drawn. As they came closer, the light cast a bluish tint over a pile of skulls and skeleton bones.

Forboud stopped and pointed. "Look."

"Blasted," Drucis said softly. "You think these are the skeletal remains of the highwaymen's victims?"

"Could be," Dwiskter replied.

"Fresher corpses over 'ere." Boldair pointed. An arrow zipped past his head and struck a massive tree trunk with a sudden thud.

"Elves?" Forboud flicked his gaze at Dwiskter.

"No," Dwiskter replied. "Elves aren't *dat* foolish!"

"Or dat *bad* a shot!" Drucis said, readying both axes.

"Give us the Dragon Conjurer Orb," Cadell said from the shadows of the trees. "And we'll let you live."

"But a greedy barkeep t'would be," Drucis said through clenched teeth. His hand tightened around his axe.

The bluish light brightened. In the shadows of the trees, the faint outlines of three men stood behind Cadell with bows trained on the dwarves.

Boldair turned. Anger tightened his brow. "I told ya. The orb was destroyed."

"You lie," the barkeep said.

"You dare threaten the King of Nagdor?" Boldair held an axe in each hand. "I told you the orb was smashed into a thousand bits. It's useless and I certainly won't tote worthless glass shards in me pockets!"

"Then Nagdor shall be seeking a new king." Cadell pulled back the bowstring.

In the blink of an eye, Dwiskter and Drucis removed their thick shields off their backs and swung them into defensive positions, directly in front of Boldair. Arrows plinked off the shields and before the highwaymen fired again, one screamed and went silent.

Boldair frowned.

Cadell looked behind him. One archer lie dead in the underbrush. Another archer cried in pain, dropped his bow, and clamped his hand to the back of his knee. He tried to scramble forward but fell flat on the ground. His severed leg failed support him.

"*You!*" Cadell gasped. "So the King of Nagdor *still* uses the thieving little fynx to fight your battles?"

"What?" Boldair stepped forward. His brow furrowed, but Drucis and Dwiskter stopped his approach.

Viorka sprang from the thick underbrush and raked her long jagged claws across Cadell's face. He dropped his bow and flung his hands over his slashed cheek. He growled. Blood coated his fingers.

"Take him!" Boldair said.

Dwiskter rushed Cadell with the pointed spike of his axe aimed for the barkeep's throat.

Cadell dropped to his knees. He pressed the flayed flesh of his cheek to the side of his jaw and tried to hold it in place. "Stop! I'm not armed. She killed the other vendors. I'm no longer a threat."

"Ya never were," Dwiskter said in low gruff tone. He pressed the tip of the axe spike against the softness of Cadell's throat. "So we were right 'bout ya all along. You get patrons drunk, kill them, and take their loot. Tried to poison us as well, eh?"

Cadell didn't meet Dwiskter's gaze. He stared at the ground with his hand pressed against his flayed cheek.

"Tis a good scheme you had going," Boldair said, walking to the barkeep. "I'm surprised you hadn't done the same to me when I came 'ere before."

Cadell's dark eyes flicked to Boldair. "We'd have 'cept the fynx became the distraction."

"Now, you've sealed your fate. Tis no wonder you hid your tables on this forest path far from any civilizations," Boldair said.

"And you, a proposed king, set out with your fynx to steal from passersby like before. I realize dwarves have greedy eyes and hearts lusting for gold, but using a fynx to help you steal—"

Boldair holstered his axes. His wide muscled hand wrapped around Cadell's neck. With one quick motion, he heaved the man to his feet and lifted him off the ground. Cadell's feet dangled and kicked slightly. Boldair squeezed the man's throat tighter. "I 'ave you know I've never stolen from another. While I hunted treasures throughout Aetheaon, I sought treasures in ancient caves and ruins. I never robbed anyone. I found three large dragon lairs filled with gems, jewelry, and gold and silver coins. These dragons were believed to be long dead. Their treasures made me richer than all the Dwarven Kings combined for a time. But when Taniesse revealed who she and her two sisters were, I returned their treasures.

I detest any thief, and for you to insinuate I'm one is quite an insult."

Cadell struggled to breathe but couldn't. His mouth moved, but only strange, gurgling sounds sputtered out.

"More than dat, I abhor a murderous swindler. As for the fynx, she's a mind of her own. She could've filleted your throat instead of your face in less time than ya could sneeze, which is a suitable punishment, don'cha think?"

Cadell gasped for air and tugged against Boldair's hand with both of his. But there was no loosening Boldair's tight grip. Veins swelled on the barkeep's forehead, and his eyes widened.

Boldair glared at Cadell. "Now, what to do with you?"

Viorka stepped closer. Her humanoid figure was slender. Her excessively long claws extended to sharp tips. The backs of her hands and arms were covered with fur as was her delicate face. The claws and fur prevented her from blending into a crowd unnoticed. Her emerald eyes peered like a cat. She placed her sharp claws to the back of Cadell's neck.

His body stiffened.

"Like the King of Nagdor told you, the orb's gone. If it were intact, he'd have no need to roam the countryside when he could conjure a dragon and fly. He'd have no reason to ride a dire mount, now would he?" She pressed her claw harder until she broke the skin. A thin line of blood trickled.

Boldair flicked his gaze from Cadell's nervous eyes and looked at Viorka. For a moment, he didn't recognize her. The wildness of a hungered beast had taken over. She looked like a massive cat ready to pounce its prey.

Slowly, Boldair lowered Cadell and lessened his grip. Cadell gulped several deep breaths, sputtered garbled words, and fought to stand.

"What of your fate now?" Boldair said.

"Please spare me, Your Highness," Cadell replied.

"Oh, it's Your Highness now?" Drucis said. "Earlier, as I recall, you stated dat he wasn't *your* king."

"Clearly, I was wrong. My apologies. I was brash."

"Judging by those corpses, he's killed several dozen travelers recently," Viorka said. "Probably hundreds have been murdered over the years at his party's hands. You release him and he'll continue doing this. Put him to death and you'll spare the lives of his future victims."

"Never known you to resort to violence so readily," Drucis said with a broad grin. "I'm beginning to like you more."

"One does what's necessary," she replied. Her eyes flickered and glowed like glistening gems, which made it difficult for Boldair to look away.

"You missed the battle." Boldair released Cadell. The barkeep didn't attempt to flee. He fell to his hands and knees and gasped desperately for air.

"Hoffnung?" she asked.

"Aye."

She shook her head. "I was there. Don't forget how well I blend into my surroundings."

"I cannot kill Cadell in the forests," Boldair said. "It's not proper without a trial."

"He tried to kill you," Forboud said.

Viorka jabbed her slender, needle-tipped claws into the side of Cadell's throat without any hesitation. The man looked up in horror. He clutched a tight hand to the wound. Blood spurted between his fingers with each heartbeat. He opened his mouth to speak, perhaps to curse, but nothing escaped his lips except the gurgling sound of blood. Within minutes, Cadell was dead.

Boldair cocked his head to the side and eyed the Fynx. She had never been so darkly violent in her decisions, even though she was correct. "You killed him?"

She shrugged and wiped her bloody claws on soft moss. "He'd have slowed our journey, and undoubtedly caused more problems along the way. A token of appreciation would be nice."

"For *what*?" Boldair asked.

"Saving your life."

"What? We had things under control."

"Three archers had their arrows trained on you. Close up, you could've killed them since they wear cloth, but they held a vantage point. I took 'em out," she said with a wide grin.

"No arrow they fired could've pierced our shields," Drucis said with a firm brow. "Their arrows were blunt. You gave an element of surprise, which was necessary and much obliged."

"Don't embolden her!" Boldair said.

"So I shouldn't have gotten involved? Is that what you're implying?" Her voice sounded like a fragile girl. She looked hurt and peered down. "I thought we were friends, and I feared you were in a deadly situation, so ... I helped the best I could. I suppose you being king has changed that?"

"No, not at all. We ... we're friends," Boldair said. "Ya did good, lil cat. You caught me off guard is all."

"When we were here before, this man and those around him had been determined to *protect* Sissrow. I wondered about their true intentions, then," Viorka said.

"Aye," Boldair replied. "Cadell implied Sissrow was a trustworthy individual."

"Perhaps Sissrow was one of them?" Forboud asked.

"Could be, brother," Boldair exhaled a gruff sigh.

Viorka leveled a stern frown. "Cadell said Sissrow was the *perfect vendor*. Perhaps a slip of the tongue?"

Drucis' eyes widened. He pointed a stern finger. "Dat he did!"

Boldair shook his head. "Ah, well, it's best we head on. The worst part 'bout their deaths ... Their firespit brew died with them."

All four dwarves lowered their heads sadly and pounded solemn fists to their chests.

"*Dat's* truly a loss," Dwiskter said.

"What about their corpses?" Drucis asked.

"We leave 'em for the crows and worms," Dwiskter said. "The same way they left their victims."

Boldair faced the shimmering blue light at the edge of the sloped path. "What do ya make of this, Viorka?"

She took several timid steps closer. "It wasn't here the last time we passed through."

"I know. Tis why I asked."

"I don't know." She came closer but paused outside its edge.

Dwiskter took his axe and sliced away the low, leafy branches partially concealing it. The discus radiated a faint, blue light. On closer inspection, glyphs weaved together in a unique pattern and pulsed bright energy at the circle's center.

"Can any of ya interpret these glyphs?" Boldair asked.

"No." Forboud shook his head. The others shook their heads as well.

"I've never seen anything like this," Boldair said. "I've been all through Aetheaon."

"Aye." Drucis studied the bluish glyph. He took his axe and brought it overhead. "We could smash it."

"No!" Boldair gripped Drucis' elbow.

"Why *not*?"

Boldair shook his head. "Haste brings death. I almost learned dat the hard way when I visited these forests before." Boldair placed the tip of his boot on the platform. Whatever magic controlled the disc could quite possibly be far worse than the poisonous barbed plants.

"Ya sure?" Drucis said.

"No," Dwiskter said. "Let us inspect it."

"A king must be unafraid to lead," Boldair said.

"A king must be *alive* to lead," Drucis said.

Forboud nodded. "I agree with ya."

Boldair placed his foot on the platform but nothing altered. He allowed a partial, nervous grin and shrugged before stepping fully on the blue disc. He took a couple more steps.

"What's it feel like?" Forboud said. His brow furrowed with a mixture of concern and partial fear. "Does it hurt?"

"No. No pain," Boldair shivered. "Lots of energy though. Makes the back of my neck tingle."

Viorka stepped on the disc. Her fur stood on end. She giggled. "Tickles!"

"Ah, come now," Drucis said, joining them. "Aye, tis strange energy it is. Wonder why it's here and who's responsible?"

Dwiskter frowned. He placed a timid step on the platform. He tapped his steel boot twice before walking beside them. "Sorcery?"

The bluish gleam brightened around them. Their images looked like apparitions caught between two realms.

"Could be," Boldair said.

"Then you should get off!" Forboud shouted.

The light intensified around the dwarves and Viorka.

Boldair laughed and shook his head. "Ah, brother, you worry too much!"

A moment later, the blue light shone brightly around them. They all vanished on the platform and left Forboud alone on the forest path. The disc darkened.

FORTY-FOUR

The Meadwyrm Pass faded slowly from view. Surprised, Boldair attempted to step off the glowing disc, but his feet held steadfast. Forboud rushed off the path with fear in his eyes. He seemed to be wanting to help them. Consumed by fear, Forboud mouthed Boldair's name in a silent scream, and reached his hand toward the platform.

In the blink of a wisp, Boldair's stomach plummeted. The sensation was similar to the time he dove off a high bank into the cool waters of Shade River. Except in this case, he fell continuously in complete darkness. He didn't know if Viorka, Drucis, and Dwiskter were still with him.

Even though he lofted downward like a bird's lost feather, every muscle in his body tensed. He braced for the inevitable landing he expected to occur.

"Ya can't fall forever, can ya?" he asked aloud.

No reply came.

If his companions replied, he didn't hear them. He figured at the least, Drucis and Dwiskter would be shouting obscenities at whatever had taken them from the forest.

Whenever and wherever Boldair finally landed, he was uncertain. He awoke on a cold stone floor. He slowly opened one eye. When his vision cleared, Viorka was staring at him. She lie prostrate nearby, and apparently had awoke at the same time.

"Where are we?" Boldair asked. He pressed his hands against the broken, stone floor. Before pushing himself up, he scanned the floor and walls beyond Viorka, in case they were in a hostile place.

No sunlight beamed, and there were no lit sconces. Instead, luminous mushrooms, nestled in the cracks and crevices, cast dim light along the walls and rocky ceiling. For several moments, the walls seemed to have glowing eyes.

Viorka rolled, sat up, and rubbed her head. "I don't know. I was going to ask you."

"What kind of Hellhole is this!" Drucis said in a gruff whisper. He walked to Boldair and offered his hand.

"Thanks." Boldair craned his neck, popped it, and winced. "No idea, but I've a feeling we're a long way from Nagdor."

"Aye." Dwiskter combed his beard with his hand.

Boldair glanced at Drucis and sighed. "I'm afraid your luck has shriveled."

Drucis frowned. "How's dat?"

"There be no taverns here," Boldair said with a slight grin. "No taverns ... no stout."

"You don't think I know dat?" Drucis held a glum expression. "Hell at its finest. Or worst? Bah!"

Dwiskter chuckled. "We need to find out where *here* is."

"Aye." Boldair nodded. "Magic brought us to whatever this place is. But for what reason?"

Viorka shook her head. "Which was clearly our fault."

"How's dat?" Drucis asked.

She shrugged. "It was sheer foolishness to step on that disc."

"She's right," Dwiskter said.

"Bah!" Drucis said. "She was right there with us."

"Nothing'll change dat now." Boldair pulled his heavy axe from the right sheath. "Our travels now are on foot. We've no food. Nothing to drink. And no idea which direction we should take."

"It appears we're in a cavern," Dwiskter said. "One dat's drier than a bone. We need to find an underground stream and follow it to find our way out."

"Few caverns ever lack water," Drucis said.

Viorka shivered. "As cold as it is, any water should be ice."

Dwiskter sighed and his breath fluffed like a white cloud. "Aye, I agree with ya, little cat."

Boldair nodded, and looked both directions. He sniffed the air and scrunched his nose. "The smell of death's in the air."

Viorka frowned. "My sense of smell is far greater than yours. I don't smell anything rancid. All I smell is musty, stale air and earth."

Boldair glanced at her. "Aye. Those who 'ave died here, died long ago. If I had me guess, we're in an ancient burial chamber."

"Ya think dat's where we are?" Dwiskter asked. "In a tomb or mausoleum?"

Boldair shrugged.

"Where are the vaults?" Drucis looked around.

"Nearby," Boldair said. "But it's a gamble which direction we take. We're in the middle of a tunnel."

Drucis scratched his bearded chin and pondered. "Either direction has equal chance of leading to nowhere."

"Or to an exit," Boldair said.

Frustrated, Dwiskter said, "I'd be satisfied knowing *where* we are."

"Aye, me too," Boldair replied. "I wonder how long dat magical disc was in the forest?"

"Perhaps it was a snare to capture you," Drucis said.

Boldair shook his head. "For dat to be true, the summoner would've had to know I was in Meadwyrm Pass."

"You think coincidence?" Dwiskter asked.

"I don't know. For once I should've heeded my brother's advice," Boldair replied.

"What about your brother?" Dwiskter asked.

"Aye," Drucis said. "We left him behind."

"He was fearful we faded," Boldair said. "No telling what'll become of him."

Dwiskter's eyes widened. "Forboud could return to Nagdor and claim the throne. All he need do is tell the council dat you're dead and since your father's in prison, the throne's rightfully his."

Boldair's jaw tightened.

"He's yellow-bellied and underhanded enough to do it," Drucis said.

Boldair shook his head. "Although Forboud might attempt such deceit, he doesn't possess the crown. Without the crown, the Dwarven Alliance will reject his ascent and hold him in contempt."

"You 'ave the crown?" Drucis asked. "It's not in your saddle pack?"

"No. I 'ave it with me," Boldair replied. "It's tucked behind my axe sheaths. When King Staggnuns handed it to me, I vowed to never keep it outside of me grasp."

"Dat's good!" Dwiskter said with a broad grin.

"Ever since my brother's outrage in Hoffnung for leaving our father behind, my trust in him diminished," Boldair said. "I never said anything. But he rummaged through my saddle pack several times when he didn't know I was watching."

"He was trying to find it?" Viorka asked.

"I believe so." He chuckled and pointed. "Now, I say dat we go this way."

FORTY-FIVE

With his axe drawn, Boldair led them down the narrowing tunnel. Viorka followed with Drucis and Dwiskter immediately behind her. The air became colder, even though the path didn't rise or descend.

"Should this path gets narrower," Boldair said, "we turn back."

Drucis laughed. "Aye, this tunnel wasn't hewn by dwarves. Dat much is certain."

"Then by whom?" Viorka asked.

"No idea," Drucis said. "But whomever did, they took enough time to mine the pockets of ore from the walls. The path's getting smaller."

"Perhaps we're going the wrong direction," Boldair said.

A deep growl rumbled ahead of them. The short growl turned into a sudden cry of pain, followed by a harsh hiss.

"Did you hear that?" Viorka's emerald eyes widened.

"Aye. What was *dat*?" Drucis asked.

"I'm not certain," Boldair replied. "The sound isn't from a small creature. I can't tell what the beast is."

"Shouldn't we go see?" Viorka asked.

Boldair placed his hand against the rocky wall. Water dripped.

"Seems we've moved away from the vaults of the dead. There's water here."

Viorka scrunched her nose and covered it with her furry hand. "Now, *that's* rancid."

"Aye," Boldair replied. "The smell's getting worse but in a different way."

"Blood, excrement, and rotten carcasses," she said, gagging.

"Whew!" Drucis covered his mouth and nose. "Smells like a sun-scorched battlefield weeks *after* the battle's ended."

The large animal dispelled a weakening growl, and oddly, the sound pleaded for rescue.

"Should we keep going, Boldair?" Drucis asked. "Or would you prefer to turn back?"

Boldair huffed and tightened his hand around the axe heel. "Something's being tortured. Until we know what it is, I cannot justify turning around. Plus, I'd like to know what's at the end of this narrow passage."

"Then lead the way," Dwiskter said, and he pulled his second axe.

The ceiling lowered. Boldair stooped in order to keep walking. His boot struck a metal object, which clicked slightly. At his feet was a pickax and a kobold's skeleton. Its dry, leathery skin hung loosely on its bones. Small chunks of silver spilled from its pack. Boldair pointed. "Dat explains why the tunnel's so crudely carved."

"It's been dead a long time," Viorka said.

"Agreed," Boldair said. "Dat doesn't mean more aren't nearby."

"This one was fleeing right before it died." Dwiskter knelt beside its corpse.

"Kobolds might not be our biggest worry," Boldair said. "The good thing is the tunnel opens into another room."

"Please." Drucis placed a gentle hand on Boldair's shoulder and stepped past. "I'll enter first."

Boldair sighed with regret, squeezed against the wall, and allowed Drucis to pass. One thrill Boldair savored was discovering new places. As king, he realized those days were few.

After Drucis cleared the small opening, Boldair followed through and stood. He stepped aside for Viorka and Dwiskter to join them. He marveled at the height of the lofty, cavern ceiling. With perfect symmetry, the large round stones with rough oval bumps stood in long lines. A narrow walkway wound through them. Delicately carved, each of these gray stones was larger than the dwarves.

"Such majestic detail and precision." Boldair ran his hand against the bumpy side of the closest stone. "What artist carved these? Unusual texture."

"Turn around slowly and leave quietly," Viorka whispered.

"Why?" Boldair asked.

"These are dragon eggs," she said softly.

Boldair stepped back. His mouth dropped in awe. "Indeed, they are. I was so fascinated by their beauty. I thought these were carved stones." He ran his hand along the bumpy surface and grinned.

"There's at least a hundred of 'em," Drucis said. "Maybe more. We can't see past them, so dat's a crude estimate. No dragon lays dat many for one nest."

"We're in a den of dragons," Dwiskter said. "We be no match for one angry mother dragon. Even less should there be more than one."

The pain-filled cry echoed on the other side of the eggs.

"Come on." Boldair walked through the meandering line of dragon eggs. "Let's see what's making dat noise."

"No," Drucis said. "We should leave."

"Not without seeing what's happening." His foot slid in a small pool of a thick sticky substance. He raised his boot and grimaced. The viscous pink and greenish goo stretched between his foot and the floor.

"Ugh." Viorka covered her nose. "What's that?"

Boldair leaned against an egg and wiped the bottom of his boot on the rough cavern floor. He winced. "Whatever it is, it has a powerfully rotten odor."

"Look." Dwiskter pointed.

The broken shell of a freshly hatched egg lie on the path. A goo trail stretched from the dragon egg where it had slithered away. The top section of the egg was large enough for a dwarf to crawl inside and hide.

Boldair scanned the area around them. "Where's the dragon? It must be nearby."

"Perhaps dat's what made the earlier noises?" Drucis asked.

"Maybe," Boldair replied.

"And if so, the mother dragon won't be thrilled to find us here," Dwiskter said.

"Keep alert," Boldair said. "As large as her eggs are, she'll be one Hell of a dragon."

Several gruff growls and tiny roars erupted on the other side of dragon eggs. Boldair stepped between the eggs as quietly as possible. When he reached the last row of eggs, he stopped and raised his hand for the others to slow their pace. He peered around the egg and anger overtook him.

"Bloody Hells," he whispered.

"What?" Drucis asked.

He nodded. "Take a look."

Drucis glanced in the direction Boldair indicated and a growl rattled in his throat. "I'll not stand for dis!"

"Wait." Boldair reached to grab Drucis' shoulder but missed. "We don't know how many are here."

"Doesn't matter at this point," Drucis said. "I'm angry enough to take on a small battalion."

"I'm with ya." Dwiskter pulled his second axe.

"You there!" Drucis yelled. "Stop what you're doing!"

Two armored dwarves turned in surprise. One was tugging the baby dragon—which was the size of a large horse—by a thick chain attached to the dragon's muzzle. The dragon pulled, tugged, and tried to break free. The second guard flailed it with a long whip. Several welts swelled on the infant dragon's rear flank. It emitted small, agonizing whimpers of pain.

This newborn dragon was wingless and resembled a massive serpent with legs. Its claws were thick and sharp and cut into the stoney cavern floor. Although small, it was incredibly strong. If it possessed wings, these two dwarves wouldn't have been able to control it. This dragon wasn't like Taniesse and her sisters. It was a drake. Although wingless, its venomous bite could kill any elf, dwarf, or human in a matter of minutes.

"Who let you in here?" one dwarf asked. He released the dragon's reins and reached for his short sword. His amber eyes glowed. His short beard was black with a bluish tint.

Frosthammer guards? Boldair shook his head. Surely, the transporter disc hadn't returned them to Frosthammer.

Boldair stepped forward with both axes in hand. "We sorta arrived unannounced and against our wishes. Pardon our intrusion, but I must insist dat you not torture the young drake any longer. It's in your best interests."

The other dwarf held a whip in one hand and a sharp serrated dagger in the other. "Mind your business, intruder. You didn't answer his question. Who let you in here?"

"No one."

"Then how'd you get here?"

"Dat puzzles us more than it does you," Boldair said.

Dwiskter and Drucis nodded.

Viorka flexed her paws and exposed her long sharp claws.

"There's no way you got past our guards," the first dwarf said. He walked toward them, but never allowed his eyes to move from Viorka. He didn't fear her. He seemed more interested in her possible attack. The anger in his voice matched the glowing rage in his eyes. "Even if ya got past them, you'd have never gotten through the massive gate."

"I spoke the truth. We've no idea how we got 'ere," Boldair replied.

"Are you saying dat you simply *appeared* in our cavern?"

"Aye," Boldair said, nodding. "Exactly like dat."

The dwarf laughed and looked briefly at his comrade. "Whipped in 'ere like magic, eh, Cerphid? Ya believe him?"

Cerphid shook his head. "No, Lukrean, I don't. They must've entered the tunnel by the Sepulchers of Twilight. But dat entrance is buried under a massive landslide of heavy snow and ice."

Viorka leaned forward and laughed heartily. The madness of her cackles caused Boldair, Drucis, and Dwiskter to turn their attention to her instead of the two dwarves. After her laughter subsided, her eyes narrowed. She lowered her clawed hands to her sides, ready to sprint toward them.

"What do ya find so funny, cat?" Lukrean asked.

"How else would *you* explain our arrival, if not by magic?" she asked. "Or are you so daft?"

The two dwarves frowned. "Hurling insults will get your little tongue cut out."

"You don't think before you speak, do you?" she asked. "I could split both your tongues from your mouths before either of you could stop me. Don't make threats you've no ability to carry out."

The statement jolted Lukrean. The anger in his eyes subsided. He regarded her claws with a bit of fear.

Her emerald eyes narrowed. Any former sign of amusement she displayed vanished. "You admitted we couldn't have gotten past your guarded gate and the only other entrance is buried ... so how else, other than magic, could we gain entrance into this dragon nest?"

The two dwarves exchanged confused glances.

Boldair studied them for a moment. "By your appearance and dragon-scale armor, you're Frosthammer guards."

Confused, Cerphid said, "Aye. How'd you know dat?"

"We departed Frosthammer over a day ago, but we never expected to return. Especially, not so soon or like this."

"And yet, here you are," Lukrean said.

"Much to our displeasure, if ya don't mind my saying," Boldair said. "So we're in Frosthammer?"

"Yes," Lukrean said. "Trespassing in this area warrants your immediate death."

"Before you get hasty," Boldair said.

"I dare him to come at us," Viorka said.

Boldair tried to stop his smile but failed. "Perhaps you could send word to King Rigrim dat the King of Nagdor has returned."

Lukrean lowered his weapon. He frowned at Boldair for several long seconds. "You know King Rigrim?"

"Aye, and he knows me. So before it's your heads placed on pikes for threatening an allied king, you might reconsider your words," Boldair said.

"He gave you access to our drake breeding grounds?" Cerphid asked.

"No. What I said is the truth. I've no idea how we got in this chamber. We were on our way to Nagdor. We stepped on a glowing disc in the forest and were teleported here. It places us days behind our return home. But, after witnessing your mistreatment of this young drake, I'm apt to say our return gives me insight to your kingdom's wickedness. I knew Rigrim held dark secrets, but I never imagined something so cruel. Is this how you get the scales for your armor and the bones and teeth dat you decorate your buildings and taverns with?"

"You dare slander King Rigrim?" Lukrean asked.

"No slander and no accusations. Only my deductive observation," Boldair replied.

"You might be king in Nagdor," Cerphid said, "but Rigrim's our king. You've no right to dictate rule over us. Doing so is enough reason for us to kill you where you stand."

Viorka took a nimble step forward. Cerphid and Lukrean stepped back.

"Then by all means," Drucis said, "come forward and—"

Boldair chuckled. "You're no match for us. I've no doubt in Viorka's quickness to slit your throats. Allow us passage to see King Rigrim and no blood will be shed between us. You get to live another day."

"You hurl insults and threats at us and *think* we'll step aside? You're trespassers and as such, King Rigrim won't hesitate to reward us for killing you."

"What reward comes from your own deaths?" Viorka asked.

"We might be trespassing, but not at our own doing," Boldair said.

"Lukrean and Cerphid, he speaks the truth! I'm the reason for their return."

Boldair, Dwiskter, and Drucis turned in the direction of the familiar voice.

Wynneffin and six of her guards stepped from the shadows. Her narrow gaze bore into Boldair's confused stare. "Drop your weapons, King of Nagdor, or it'll be the deaths of you and your friends."

FORTY-SIX

"You!" Fury rose in Boldair's voice. "You used magic to summon us back here?"

"Yes," Wynneffin replied.

"Why can't ya understand I no longer hold any affection for you? Not after what ya've done and well, using magic to force our return," Boldair said.

Hurt and anger stirred in her eyes. The hardness of her jawline indicated she wasn't past her scorn. Her words were sharp and cold. "I understand perfectly."

Viorka whispered, "If you wish, I can disarm her."

Boldair shook his head.

Wynneffin flicked her gaze at Viorka for a moment before regarding Boldair once more. Her stance held defiance, even though she looked like she wanted to say something.

"Then why use sorcery when you know I never wanted to return," Boldair said through his teeth. "Ya can't let it go, can ya?"

Cerphrid and Lukrean exchanged puzzled looks.

"You two know one another?" Lukrean asked. Confused, he lowered his weapon, as did the guards standing beside Wynneffin.

"Unfortunately, I've had the displeasure," Boldair said.

"The displeasure was all *mine*," she spat back.

Drucis grinned at Lukrean and shrugged. "Lovers' quarrel."

Boldair glared at him. "*Ya* keep outta this!"

Drucis's grin shrank and he nodded.

Boldair returned his attention to Wynneffin. "I wanna know why you'd interfere with my return to Nagdor? My business in Frosthammer was finished. For good, I had hoped."

"Don't make this about you," she replied.

"Then *what* should I make this about?"

"I brought ya back because of a more important problem dat doesn't concern what we once had. So if you hold what a true king possesses, set aside your distaste for me and help us with the real issue."

"And what's dat?"

"The dead are rising," she said. "They're undead wanderers. And they're nearly impossible to destroy."

The news sent a cold chill down his back. "Where?"

"On the lower floors, where I went with you to find Viorka." She narrowed her eyes at Viorka. "Who seems to have no gratitude for me aiding her safe return."

Viorka sneered. "You've caused more ill-fated consequences for Boldair than you *ever* aided in my rescue. Or have you forgotten so quickly?"

Wynneffin took a deep breath and held it. Her face reddened. Boldair realized she was several seconds from allowing her anger to overtake her.

Boldair waved his hands to calm the situation between both sides. "Aren't Frosthammer's dead tossed into the River of Steel?"

She nodded. "Most are. Some dwarves died under unusual manners in the mining pits. By the time they're found, they're already undead, possessed with an urge to kill. You can't reason with them."

"How can I help?" Boldair asked.

"You've dealt with this before. You know who's responsible."

Boldair nodded and sheathed his axe. "Aye. The Plague-bringer."

"Then *please* assist us? I'm not asking for myself. I'm asking for Frosthammer." Wynneffin lowered her dagger and tucked it in its sheath. Her eyes softened.

He read the pleading in them, which was even greater than her pleading tone. For her, saying *please* was more difficult than asking anything else.

Boldair sighed. Swallowing her pride was difficult, and yet, she did so. As much as he wanted to be angry for her actions, the truth she expressed couldn't be ignored. Frosthammer's population could be in jeopardy. This wasn't about her or him.

Finding and destroying the Plague-bringer benefited all of Aetheaon. The more he thought about it, the more he wondered why they had all departed in different directions after Queen Taube regained her throne. They had essentially won a major battle, but in the celebrated victory, they ignored the greatest danger. No kingdom was safe until the Plague-bringer was defeated.

"If you don't wish to aid us," she said, "I'll send you to Nagdor immediately. I swear to never bother you again."

Boldair crossed his arms. "Before I agree to aid your cause, I need some answers first."

"What answers do you seek?"

"You never hesitated to summon me and my two best warriors when your father has a vast army at his disposal. Why hasn't King Rigrim done *anything* about the undead? He has thousands of troops at his command."

Wynneffin turned to her guards. Waving her hand dismissively, she said, "Leave us."

The Frosthammer guards nodded, turned on their heels, and walked away.

Once they were were out of sight, Wynneffin said, "Father doesn't believe me or any of the guards I've sent to consult with him concerning this epidemic. He dismisses it as a minor problem. But he has since posted guards to patrol the mining and construction areas."

"You believe it's much worse?"

She nodded.

"Why?"

Her eyes grew distant for several moments. A slight tinge of fear flickered before she focused on him. "The last few found in the lower levels were not undead dwarves."

Boldair frowned. "What were they?"

"I should say they weren't *normal* undead dwarves," she replied. "They were ... mummified, and somehow brought back to life. The conditions their bodies were in, they should never have been able to move. Their flesh was harder than stone."

"Where would those come from?" Drucis asked.

"The Sepulchers of Twilight dat lie on the other side of the entrance where you emerged," Wynneffin said. "Dat's the only bodies mummified to my knowledge. Ours aren't."

"So you planned to 'ave us teleported into the narrow passageway?" Boldair asked. "Dat's why you were nearby when we approached Lukrean and Cerphrid?"

"Yes."

"If we'd 'ave gone the other direction, instead of this way?"

She allowed herself a half-grin. "You'd have seen firsthand what our miners chopped to pieces in the lower levels."

Boldair shook his head and his jaw tightened. "Ya know, every time I'm close to forgetting the reasons for my anger toward you, you make certain to rekindle dat anger."

"I'm sorry." She shook her head. "The reason I'm in the drake hatchery with my personal guards is so we could make certain you were safe. We were preparing to enter the passage to find you."

His narrowed eyes studied her.

"It's the truth, Boldair," she said. "I swear it."

"Why not close off the tunnel dat leads to the sepulchers?"

"We plan to," she replied. "But first I wanted to get your assessment."

Boldair chuckled. "What's to assess? If you 'ave undead stumbling out of the sepulchers and invading your city, you blast the tunnel until enough rock and debris prevents another undead from getting through."

Wynneffin sighed. "I realize dat, but those tombs hold the history of a former civilization dat occupied Frosted Peaks before my father founded Frosthammer. They're known as the Twilight Stone-shapers. Often, histories of past cities are the keys to future cities' survival. We need to study and learn what we can from those before us. I expect tomes and scrolls line the insides of some sarcophagi. Blasting to collapse the only remaining opening could prove costly in losing precious knowledge."

"Dat's true," Dwiskter said.

"Aye," Boldair said, nodding. "Such knowledge should be gathered and placed in your father's royal library. What 'ave you learned about the previous settlements?"

"From the appearance of the undead corpses, they're our Dwarven predecessors. The resemblances cannot be denied, but they were more primitive. Dat's why I want to examine the sepulchers to learn all we can from them. You rob tombs, so I thought you'd know more about the histories of past civilizations."

"I don't *rob* tombs," Boldair said. "You cannot rob the dead. They 'ave no need for trinkets and treasure after they're buried."

"Dat's my point. The greatest treasures in the tombs are the tablets, tomes, and scrolls dat contain valuable history, which is all the same to me," Wynneffin said. "Accompany and help me explore. Anything you consider treasure, other than written tomes and scrolls, is yours for the taking, as payment for your troubles."

Drucis and Dwiskter's exchanged excited glances.

Boldair sighed. "I don't know, Wynnie."

"Are ya mad?" Drucis asked. "We could loot a fortune."

"Gold and silver hold no value when I beheld how Frosthammer's guards are treating these baby drakes," Boldair replied.

"What do you mean?" she asked.

"One of your guards whipped a newly hatched drake hard enough to leave welts on it. You called this a hatchery. Tell me how you possess these eggs? And why your guards tortured the newly hatched one?" Boldair asked. "Are you slaughtering these drakes to use their scales for your armor?"

"No." Wynneffin shook her head and frowned with concern. "A guard actually struck a baby drake?"

"Aye," Boldair said. "We all witnessed it."

Drucis and Dwiskter nodded. Anger filled their eyes.

Boldair pointed to the Dragon Skull pendant on his armor plate. "Ya see this? Lady Dawn knighted me, Drucis, and Dwiskter into the

Dragon Skull Knights. We're the first dwarves *ever* to be initiated into dat Order. I'm friends with three dragons, and as such, I never tolerate mistreatment of any dragon or their lesser relatives. So tell me what's going on? How'd you come to possess so many eggs? And what are you doing with the babies?"

Wynneffin's eyes grew colder. "Tell me which guard struck the dragon. His punishment will be harsh, I assure you. The whips are only to be used for their sound to frighten them, never to harm them."

"Instilling fear into a dragon dat has yet imprinted is harmful in itself."

"I agree," she replied. "None of these drakes are ever to be harmed. I'd never allow it."

"Then explain where you got these eggs and how your entire army and guards wear armor made from the scales of these drakes or from dragons," Boldair said. "I've seen the sconces, the chandeliers, and other ornaments carved from dragon bones throughout the taverns and shops. Dat's a lot of scales and bones, which means shiploads of dead dragons and drakes, especially if every floor of Frosthammer displays them."

Wynneffin sighed. "Come with me."

FORTY-SEVEN

Boldair frowned. His gaze was fierce.

Wynneffin's face reddened. She waved him and the dwarves to follow her.

"What kind of drakes are these?" Boldair asked.

"Rime drakes," she replied.

"How'd you obtain hundreds of their eggs?" Boldair asked.

"They're entrusted to our care," she replied.

"By whom?"

"The drakes."

"Really?" he asked.

"Yes."

"I find dat odd."

"Why?"

"Your father invited me to go dragon hunting," Boldair said. "He didn't indicate any friendly coexistence with them. But, he never mention drakes, either. He was specific in saying *dragons*. Even he knows the difference."

"I bet he grinned when he said it, too?"

Boldair shrugged. "Sorta."

"Dat's because he enjoys seeing the terror on Dwarven warriors' faces any chance he gets," she said with a forced grin. "Let's just say dat it's far worse should he ever entertain visiting elves. Most are so paralyzed by fear dat when they leave Frosthammer, they never return."

"Is dat so?" Boldair asked.

Wynneffin smiled and nodded.

"Sounds more like a jester than a king," Drucis said with a harsh laugh.

"Don't mock my father," she said.

"Mock him? I like him already! Dat's the same thing I'd do!" Drucis laughed harder. Tears moistened his eyes.

Dwiskter wailed with laughter. "Yes, Drucis, you'd definitely do dat."

Wynneffin laughed and shook her head. "Do you realize how many suitors I've lost because of those *supposed hunts*? If any dwarf was serious in his effort to ask for my hand in marriage, they abandoned the idea after agreeing to hunt with my father."

"He made it difficult for ya?" Boldair asked.

"Always," she replied.

"The way he talked about ya, he's quite proud of your toughness and zeal," Boldair said.

"Perhaps." Wynneffin motioned the guards to hoist the chain winches and pull open the massive door. "But actually complementing me isn't something he does. Regardless of my skills or how I've performed while dueling, he points out my mistakes in spite of my victories."

"So he only invited me to hunt dragons to discourage me from asking for your hand in marriage?"

She shrugged. "*Dat's* not a matter needful of discussion anymore, now is it?"

The coldness of her words pricked his heart no less harsh than a frozen spike. In spite of her sarcasm, her eyes held pain and disappointment. He found himself wanting to console her, but with greater issues at hand, now wasn't the time. He knew it, and he figured she did, too.

The metal gears groaned and pulled the massive steel door upward. Two giant, serpent-like heads rose from the floor. The creatures stood and showed their full height, but like the hatchling, these full grown drakes didn't have wings. They chuffed. Small clouds of ice crystals puffed from their mouths and their long forked tongues licked their lips. They eagerly expected food.

Their narrow, serpent eyes appeared colder than their breath. Much like a viper or a dragon, their mesmerizing eyes were seductive in their gaze. They could probably entice victims to sacrifice themselves should they stare too long.

The drakes fastened their gazes on Boldair, Drucis, and Dwiskter, but apparently hadn't noticed Viorka scrunched behind Boldair. Their pupils narrowed. They took deep breaths to get the dwarves' scent. A harsh gargling rumbled in their throats, and Boldair feared the sound came from their hungry stomachs.

Dwiskter, Drucis, and Viorka froze. They immediately held their breath.

Licking their massive chops, the two drakes craned their necks while inspecting their new guests.

"Uh-uh." Wynneffin shook her head. "Look at me."

The drakes blinked and looked away from Boldair and turned their attention to Wynneffin. She smiled and walked closer to them. She extended her hand and the smaller one leaned its massive head down to her. She patted the underside of its scaly chin.

"By the gods," Boldair whispered. "Why are these imprisoned in there?"

"Imprisoned? No." She shook her head. "It's not a prison, Boldair. Dat chamber's where the two eldest Frost Drakes live. They're free to leave, if they ever choose. But they realize dat we need them, and they need us. We have a mutual need for one another."

"Need them? For what exactly?" Dwiskter slowly ran his hand along his beard. His eyes stared intently at the dragons.

"The heat off the River of Steel would prevent our survival by making the air too hot for us to breath at the higher levels of the city. Without these drakes cooling the river's barriers at both ends of its flow, the molten steel would rise and spill over the barriers, effectively killing us."

"There are more of them?"

Wynneffin nodded. "Two more are on the other end of the river."

"I see. What do they *need* from you?" Boldair asked.

"Protection from the Frost Dragons dat live in the Frosted Peaks. Those dragons have sought to kill them throughout time," Wynneffin said.

"The Frost Dragons kill drakes?" Dwiskter asked while still studying the two drakes with great interest.

"Yes. Dragons have a greater advantage since they have wings," Wynneffin replied.

"Why would dragons kill them?" Viorka asked.

Her small voice immediately caught the attention of the two drakes. They looked from Wynneffin, twisted their long necks, and slinked closer to Boldair, apparently trying to locate Viorka.

Boldair took a deep breath and swallowed hard. Despite Wynneffin's obvious control over the scaly drakes, the worst thing he could do was show fear.

"No!" Wynneffin said, snapping the drake's attention to her. Its head lofted upward and slowly moved to her soothing hand. Without looking at Viorka, Wynneffin said, "Drakes and dragons compete for their food. Since both cannot survive long outside the frozen environment of the Frosted Peaks, they must fight for whatever prey exists. Drakes are weaker, so the dragons often prey on the drakes. Not for food necessarily, but as a sign of dominance."

"So they share the same territory?" Boldair asked.

She nodded. "Yes. Dragons actually have a better range for finding food since they fly over the ridges and peaks with ease. Drakes must resort to ambushing smaller animals between the ridges where they can corner them. Humans dat raise sheep have killed more drakes since they cannot fly."

"I never thought about human herders," Boldair said.

Wynneffin forced a slight smile and rubbed the drake's scales. "Have you known a time when humans have ever befriended drakes or dragons?"

"Actually, I know several humans who hold dragons sacred," Boldair replied. "One former king, his living queen, and Lady Dawn, to name a few. Might as well say the entire City of Hoffnung reveres dragons."

"How about other kingdoms?"

He shrugged.

She said, "Most kings view them as sport, a prized trophy to mount in the city's square to show a king's power."

"Frosthammer boasts the same," Boldair said coldly. "With your dragon-scale or drake-scale you're wearing, I'm surprised these two massive beasts don't take offense and kill you and your guards where you stand."

"Dat will never happen," she said. "They know the truth and therefore, they'll never turn on us."

Boldair studied the closest drake's eyes. Each time Wynneffin spoke, the drakes' eyes glowed with obvious affection, as though mesmerized by the sound of her voice. Was her magic keeping these massive beasts in check?

Drucis frowned. "What do ya feed 'em?"

"Sheep," Wynneffin replied.

"Sheep?" Drucis shook his head in wonder. "Dat's a *lot* of sheep."

"It's their food staple and another reason why they're safer with us than along the mountainsides where herders can kill them. In the past, disgruntled farmers have hired wizards or small armies to rid themselves of the great dragons. The majority of humans deem all types of dragons to be the same thing." She shook her head. "Wizards have limited power against the greater dragons. Most wizards kill drakes, because it's easier. They drag its head to the village as *proof* of the kill. Farmers don't know the difference based on the head alone and are in such a state of relief dat they pay the wizard anyway. While some, like myself, behold them in spectacular beauty and reverence, others view them as hostile pests. They had ruled the sky for generations, until they vanished almost within a day. Without dragons flying in the sky, the drakes perished faster."

Boldair was fascinated by the two drakes. Both were captivated by Wynneffin and remained submissive to her. He'd never witnessed such a strong creature, which was mightier than Rigrim's best fifty warriors, being controlled by one person. He remained suspicious. Wynneffin must've bewitched these drakes to keep them docile. With the proper words, she could command these two drakes to rip him and his comrades to shreds.

"They're loyal to a fault," Boldair said with a smile.

"Shouldn't they be, since we're protecting them?" she asked.

He shrugged. "This doesn't explain the scale armor or how you 'ave a den of hatching eggs."

"In time," she replied.

"If what you said about the undead's true, we might not 'ave a lot of time."

Wynneffin placed her thumb and forefinger into her mouth and shrilled a loud whistle. She motioned to a guard at the bend of the chamber. The guard nodded and unlocked a small cage. He led several sheep from the pen and headed to where Wynneffin stood.

"We should leave the drakes alone during their feeding," she said. "It gets a bit ... messy. Come and I'll show you more."

FORTY-EIGHT

Boldair walked in near silence. Wynneffin exited the massive chamber where the two drakes resided. Guards lowered the door, but not before the sheep bleated in terror. Their cries ended in seconds but the pelts being torn apart and bones snapping caused the dwarves to wince. Viorka shivered.

Was Wynneffin's sudden willingness to reveal Frosthammer's mysteries sincere or was her magical control over the drakes a subtle threat of her power? He recalled the power to summon a dragon through the magical Orb he'd taken from Sissrow. Wizards and mages could enchant items to lure control over others and great beasts, but Wynneffin didn't seem to possess such an object.

She walked along a narrow path at the outer edge of the hatchery. The path was almost hidden in the shadows. Like the other recesses in the tunnel where Boldair and his companions had arrived, large luminous mushrooms—some taller than the dwarves—lit the cavern. No flaming sconces offered heat or light. Midway across the hatchery, they came to a metal door guarded by two Frosthammer dwarves.

"We need entrance," Wynneffin said.

The guards glanced at Boldair momentarily before nodding. One unlocked the door and pulled it open. After they entered, the guards closed the door.

This cavern room was lit by large torches and oil lanterns. Rows of rock tables—each approximately one hundred yards in length—lined the large room. Seamstresses were seated every ten yards from one another on both sides of these tables. Piles of dragon-scales were stacked between each seamstress. These scales were different than the drakes'.

These were icy blue dragon-scales and what the guards and Wynneffin wore.

"As you can see, these aren't drake scales," she said.

"I'm aware, but they *are* dragon-scales. Where—"

"You'll see where we found these." Wynneffin walked between two long tables toward the gated door on the opposite side of the room. None of the seamstresses looked up from their work.

A dwarf pushed open the door from the other side and backed through. He pulled a two-wheeled wagon with several bundled stacks of scales. After he passed, Wynneffin held the door and motioned Boldair and the others to pass through.

On the other side of the door, they stood at the ledge overlooking a deep, circular gorge below. A smooth pathway outlined the edge of the pit and spiraled all the way to the bottom. Flaming torches lit the pathway.

"What is this place?" Boldair asked.

"At the bottom are piles of dragon remains," Wynneffin replied. "Scales, much like bone, don't deteriorate quickly, especially in the cold depths of a cavern. This is where we've gotten dragon-scales to make our armor and the bones you inquired about as ornaments in various taverns and other decor."

"Why are so many dragons' remains at the bottom?" Viorka asked.

Wynneffin shrugged. "We assume this was a dragon burial ground. A place they came to die with their ancestors." She pointed to a narrow crevice at the edge of the cavern's domed ceiling. "They must've crawled through there."

"How'd you know you'd find their remains at the bottom of the pit?" Viorka asked.

Wynneffin smiled. "My dear, dat's how far *down* we've excavated. At one time, their scales and bone were level with where we stand."

Boldair's eyes widened.

Drucis and Dwiskter exchanged astonished looks.

"Dat's a lot of dragon carcasses," Drucis said.

"I never imagined so many had flown the skies," Boldair said. "It's sad to know their numbers have dwindled."

"Actually, the number we've excavated are not dat many," Wynneffin replied. "Still, it'd be a shame to let them rot."

"How many have you unearthed?" Boldair asked.

"Fifty-seven so far," she said.

"Dat's all?"

She nodded. "There's probably three times dat number by the time we reach the bottom. Eldest dragons are huge beasts. One's thick hide and massive bones take up a lot of space. Do you realize how many suits of dragon armor can be made from a single dragon alone?"

Boldair shook his head. "No idea."

"Since these dragons died without suffering injury from weapons or sorcery, fifty to seventy chest-plates and leggings can be fashioned from one dragon. Depending on the length of a great dragon's neck, about as many shields can be made."

"Fifty to seventy?" Drucis asked.

Wynneffin nodded. "The scales from an elder dragon dat size are quite large. If the seamstress is frugal and precise with her cuttings, she can make a lot of armor. I never lied about dragons being spared. We never killed any of them."

"I see dat. It's good dat you're using the dragon carcasses though," Boldair said.

"Why?"

"The Plague-bringer, Mors, brought a dead dragon's skeleton to life. We witnessed it."

"When?" she asked, stunned.

"The Battle of Hoffnung. Mors resurrected the bones of a Frost Dragon. The dragons' remains in this deep pit would look like real dragons if resurrected. It'd be impossible to tell the difference."

"Their corpses were well preserved."

"Any idea why they're so well preserved?" Drucis asked.

Wynneffin shrugged. "Probably the frigid climate inside Frosthammer. It could be because these are Frost Dragons, too. Their resistant to freezing. The armor keeps us warm, even when we venture outside into the Frosted Peaks."

"Don't brag," Boldair said with a sly grin. "I'm envious. Even the heaviest bear pelts fail to keep me warm while riding through the Frosted Peaks."

"Aye," Dwiskter said. "Tis why I crave hard stout on those long, cold rides. Gotta 'ave something to warm me insides."

"For the troubles I've caused in bringing you back to Frosthammer," Wynneffin said, "I'll make certain each of you get undershirts and under-leggings made from Frost Dragon skin. You'll be amazed at the warmth such a thin layer of their skin adds. They don't chaff, either."

Boldair shook his head. "While I greatly appreciate your offer, I must decline. Our dragon allies would not view us favorably for wearing it."

Wynneffin frowned. "I see."

"So tell us about the drake eggs?" Boldair asked. "You've well over a hundred dat will hatch. As large as the elder drakes are, you cannot possibly house and feed dat many inside Frosthammer."

"I know," she replied. "We're attempting to find a place where to release them when they're old enough to fend for themselves. A place where no farmers will try to kill them."

Viorka shook her head slowly, deep in thought. "You have four elder drakes?"

Wynneffin nodded. "Yes."

"There's no way four drakes produced a clutch of eggs as large as you have in the hatchery," Viorka said. "How'd you acquire so many?"

A flicker of anger flashed in Wynneffin's eyes. "We have younger breeding pairs of drakes."

"How many pairs?" Viorka asked. "May we see them?"

Wynneffin shook her head. "Dat's not advisable."

"Why?" Viorka spoke with an almost defiant, demanding tone.

"The younger drakes are far more aggressive than the elders," Wynneffin said. "I cannot control them as easily."

Boldair regarded the information with curiosity, but didn't ask further questions. He wondered why Wynneffin had withheld the information and why Viorka's questions obviously angered Wynneffin. Was Wynneffin withholding something she feared them witnessing?

"Anything else you wish to know?" Wynneffin said sternly.

"No," Viorka said. "I'm satisfied. Boldair?"

Boldair shook his head. "I've nothing more. Show us the Sepulchers of Twilight and let us assay the situation better."

Wynneffin nodded but stared firmly into Viorka's eyes. A daring smile curled on Viorka's lips. Wynneffin turned away.

"If you will," Wynneffin said, "let's return to the hatchery first."

FORTY-NINE

Before Boldair and his companions returned to the narrow cavern passageway, Wynneffin gathered eight heavily armored guards to accompany them.

"Keep your guard up," Boldair whispered to Drucis and Dwiskter.

"Ya think she's up to no good?" Drucis asked.

Boldair shrugged. "Not sure. Just because she's shown us the drakes doesn't mean she won't turn on us later."

"You don't trust her?" Dwiskter asked.

"More than I did when we parted," Boldair replied. "I wish I fully trusted her, but for now, I can't. She's withholding darker secrets. Besides, we're outnumbered and those passageways ahead are narrow. Quite easy for her soldiers to run a short sword through our backs."

Wynneffin nodded at Boldair in passing and led the way to the narrow tunnel with her guards pressed close behind her. She placed her steel helm on her head.

Boldair shook his head. He, Dwiskter, and Drucis had left their helms with their mounts, which was a worrisome regret. He didn't know the glowing disc would transport them or he'd have never stepped on the platform in the first place.

"I'll send my troops ahead, in case more undead have arisen," Wynneffin said. "Once we're through the tunnel and in the crypts, we'll 'ave room to spread out."

"Aye, good," Boldair said, somewhat relieved. Had she insisted he and his group go first, he'd have known his suspicions were accurate.

Drucis stepped between Boldair and Wynneffin's last guard. He waited until after the guard left the narrow tunnel and entered the room filled with crypts.

"Well?" Boldair asked.

"One second," Drucis said, pulling his axe.

Dwiskter stepped between Boldair and Drucis and drew his axes.

Drucis gave a firm nod and walked through the carved doorway into the crypts. He cautiously peered to each side to make certain Wynneffin's guards weren't ready to attack them. The guards stood near the center of the large room. They were mesmerized and silent. They weren't concerned with Boldair.

Boldair scanned the walls from the floor to a ceiling with no end in sight. Glowing mushrooms in the recesses between each sepulcher kept the room dim.

He regretted not having an herbalist in his party. Those mushrooms and the grave soil providing nutrients were no doubt quite valuable to a wizard or sorcerer. He leaned to Viorka and whispered, "Can you gather some of the mushrooms and dirt to carry with us?"

She nodded.

Boldair returned his attention to the walls of stacked, sealed sepulchers. "By the gods! There must be a legion of dead entombed here."

Wynneffin walked to him and nodded. "See? Dat's why it'd be disastrous to totally close off this area."

Boldair nodded. "We could spend an elf's lifetime excavating and never examine what's hidden inside."

"I know. But a brief search might be enough to discover whether or not a wealth of knowledge is buried with the dead," Wynneffin said.

Dwiskter said, "They might've been too primitive to have a written language."

"Dat's true," Wynneffin replied.

"But the architecture," Boldair said in awe. "Delicate artwork and detail is more similar to elves than human or Dwarven."

She nodded.

"I don't see any undead," Dwiskter said.

"Nor I," Drucis said.

"Are you certain the undead roamed out of here?" Boldair asked.

"I know no other place," Wynneffin replied. "I can't see how the Plague-bringer would know about these tombs."

"He's a dark sorcerer," Boldair said. "Being a necromancer, he must 'ave some connection to where the dead are buried, especially massive graves like this."

A guard rushed to them.

"What is it, Filgam?" she asked.

"Voices on the East side of the sepulchers," he replied.

"Did you see anyone?"

Filgam shook his head. "No, I thought it best we go as a group."

Wynneffin nodded. She glanced at Boldair. "What do ya think?"

"The undead do not speak," Boldair said. "We should investigate. Should Mors be here, his power's unlike any wizard you've ever encountered."

"In what way?" she asked.

"He carries bags of carrion beetles, flies, and other insects. They spread his diseases to claim more undead followers," Boldair said. "Should he toss a bag at us, flee. We probably can't kill the insects before they infect us."

Wynneffin motioned all her guards to her. When they gathered around, she said, "Proceed silently. We need to know if Mors is here—" She looked at Boldair, not certain what to say.

"If he's here," Boldair whispered, "we exit and blast the tunnel."

"What?" Wynneffin asked, perplexed.

"Wynnie, we 'ave no choice. None of us carry range weapons," Boldair said. "If we had an Elven archer or two, we could attack. Without range, we're no match against his magic. We'll all become undead. Believe me, there's no undoing the infection."

Wynneffin chewed her lower lip while she thought. She nodded.

"Do as Boldair suggests. If the Plague-bringer's inside the Sepulchers of Twilight, don't make a sound. Retreat for Frosthammer's safety." She shook her head. "I've never longed to befriend elves any more than I do now."

Boldair looked around and sudden fear twisted his stomach. "Where's Viorka?"

FIFTY

Boldair gazed in disbelief at the wall of stacked sepulchers adjacent to the chamber entrance. By his estimate, several thousand sepulchers formed the first wall. Behind the wall were hundreds of similar walls with aisles between them. Over centuries, some sepulchers had broken loose and crashed to the floor. By a quick, rough estimate, he figured a half million or more tombs occupied these connecting chambers.

Fires flickered in the sconces lining the lower walls. With the amount of thought and detail the former civilization used, the sepulchers couldn't have been a primitive society. Their knowledge to preserve their dead was more advanced than current civilizations. What secrets were buried inside the sepulchers with the corpses?

Several fire pits, which should've been buried underneath layers of dust and cobwebs from nonuse, blazed high and hot. Six individuals dressed in black hooded robes stood with their backs to Boldair and his company. Wynneffin's eyes widened with curiosity. She exchanged glances with Boldair.

Boldair imagined his facial expressions reflected her sudden shock, which wasn't her normal expression or his. The six hooded individuals chanted softly. They repeated the same words over and over in a constant hum.

"What are they doing?" Wynneffin asked.

Boldair shook his head and shrugged. "More importantly, how'd they get 'ere?"

She bit her lower lip but said nothing.

Boldair assumed these priests or monks were summoning Mors. What better place to teleport a necromancer to? Mors' black carriage and hellish beast of a horse were nowhere to be seen.

With a tinge of fear tightening his gut, he worried the Plague-bringer had already been here and left these necromancers behind to raise the mummified remains in the sepulchers. Resurrecting a half million undead with bodies hard as stone could prove unstoppable. Fire couldn't harm them and the sharpest axes would dull and be ineffective. Frosthammer's inhabitants would become diseased and join the mummified undead, further increasing the army's number. Mors' undead army would be too large for any kingdom to defeat.

The Plague-bringer could rule the entire continent of Aetheaon without opposition, which was an odd accomplishment. What purpose did it serve to rule over a world of undead humans, dwarves, and elves? They obeyed whatever the Plague-bringer instructed, but he'd have no intellectual intimacy with any of them. What good was it to be a king over a continent of undead races?

Or could it be the Plague-bringer hated the living so much that he'd rather destroy all humanity in their realm?

The black robed chanters raised their hands before them over a crudely hewn altar set against the mountainous wall of stacked crypts. Their ominous chants were in a language Boldair didn't recognize. Plumes of black spiraled from the ground. The earth shook.

"Stop them!" Dwiskter shouted. He drew his axes and ran toward the robed summoners. "They're summoning the Plague-bringer! The black carriage is materializing in front of them."

"What?" Panic furrowed Wynneffin's brow. She looked at Boldair.

Boldair nodded. "He's seen it before. He knows."

Drucis pulled his axes and darted across the rough cavern floor. Boldair did the same.

Wynneffin commanded her guards to kill the summoners. The wheels of the black carriage became visible within the swirling, black smoke.

Boldair rushed the closest summoner and swung his double-edge axe over his head with his keen focus on the back of the summoner's head. He brought down the heavy blade, but the summoner glided to the side. Boldair swung and missed.

"Bloody Hell!"

How had this practitioner seen him? The hood covered his head and his back was to Boldair. Even if the summoner heard Boldair's footsteps, he couldn't have known where Boldair aimed the axe. The summoner moved at the last second with the steel axe less than an inch from splitting flesh. Somehow, the summoner moved faster than Boldair anticipated. He didn't have time to adjust his attack.

The unyielding power of his downward strike pivoted him forward, off-balance, and Boldair scrambled to keep his footing on the rough, uneven cavern floor. His steel boots scraped the rock until he struck stone and tripped. He hit the floor hard on his side. The air dispelled from his lungs and pain rattled throughout his body.

Boldair grunted and winced. Helplessly, he watched the summoner's crimson red eyes glow like a demon rising from the flames of Hell. Bluish waves of fire flowed from this unusual summoner's fingertips. They weren't fighting anything human, Elven, or Dwarven. These *were* demons. Not anything like the occasional, traveling ones he'd encountered in taverns where they hoped to blend in with other races.

These demon summoners were vile-natured creatures. They were devoted to inflicting harm and desired to destroy all the races in Aetheaon or any continent. This one's eyes spewed unspoken hatred for the living. Was this why Mors sought to slaughter all kingdoms and resurrect them as undead minions? Afterwards, he could easily open the pits of Hell and free the chained demons to roam the realm unchallenged by priests, paladins, and demon-hunters. Everything pure in nature would be destroyed forever.

Blue flames spread and encircled the summoner's hands. The runes on Boldair's axe glowed. Their power wasn't enough to block the fire's blast when the demon unfurled them. His shield could possibly thwart the magical fire, but it was still strapped to his back.

He rocked side to side and tried to roll over. The weight of his armor trapped him. His lungs ached and his side stung. He coughed and winced.

"Blasted!" he shouted, unable to twist over to free his plated shield.

The zagged, blue flames shot from the summoner's fingertips and spread outward in a broad swath before narrowing their aim directly at him.

Tears heated his eyes. He met Wynneffin's frightened gaze. She bit her lower lip and a look of genuine sadness filled her eyes. She flung a dagger, but the dagger wouldn't strike the summoner before the flames consumed Boldair.

Boldair closed his eyes, ready to accept death as an uncrowned king. He never thought his fate would be such, and in those final seconds, his anger toward Wynneffin ignited. She'd teleported him and his companions to Frosthammer. Otherwise, he'd be riding through Nagdor's gates by now. But his slight rage wasn't enough to strengthen his resolve to push himself to his feet. His bruised side ached too much.

Metal scraped the cavern floor and chiseled a groove several inches deep. Boldair opened his eyes. Dwiskter and Drucis stood side-by-side and thrust their combined weight behind their shields. The wave of blue flames hurled upward and extinguished.

Dwiskter and Drucis each offered a hand to Boldair. Boldair clasped his fingers tightly around theirs. They yanked Boldair to his feet. Boldair winced and growled in pain.

Leaning against his axe, Boldair was disappointed Wynneffin's dagger failed to strike the summoner. The summoner turned and cast a blue fireball at her. She rolled. The blast of fire struck a crypt behind her. The rock split and a chunk of the vault fell with a loud thud and shattered.

Three summoners kept their attention on the swirling circle of magic. They continued their pursuit to bring Mors and his black carriage into the Sepulchers of Twilight. The black smoke plumes lessened, instead of growing darker. Their power was weakening since their focused circle was broken.

Wynneffin's guards attracted two summoners toward them. But her guards were unable to land any blows with their short swords.

Wynneffin pushed herself to her feet.

"Wynnie!" Boldair shouted. "Watch out!"

The summoner cast a second blue ball of flame at her. Before she could react, the flame stuck her chest, lifted her off the ground, and slammed her against the broken sepulcher.

Despite his pain, Boldair pushed off the handle of his double-edged broad axe and scrambled for her. Dwiskter and Drucis rushed the summoner with their shields in front of them. The summoner faced them with two huge balls of fire engulfing his fists. His crimson eyes glowed like boiling blood. His face creased with a wicked grin. Deep laughter rolled from his mouth with mockery. He raised his hands ready to cast.

Viorka leapt off the side of the sepulcher wall over thirty feet above. She extended her long sharp claws during her descent and thrust them into the back of the demon's neck. The long tips of her nails protruded through his throat. His laughter ended and his fiery flames died in an instant. The demon staggered, attempting to reach around to yank Viorka off. She pulled her right claws free and rammed them through the side of his throat.

Dark blood spilled from his mouth. He sputtered and gurgled.

After he dropped to his knees, Dwiskter said, "Move!"

Viorka withdrew her claws and kicked off the summoner's shoulders.

Dwiskter swung his axe in one swift arc and separated the demon's head from its shoulders. The wet plop of its head struck the cavern floor and rolled past the three demons summoning the Plague-bringer. Their abated concentration turned to immediate fear.

The Plague-bringer—sitting on his carriage, moments from fully materializing— angrily shouted, "No!"

Seeing the crimson glow of the Plague-bringer's eyes left no question. Mors was not only a necromancer, he was a demon. Fury tightened Mors' tattooed brow and brightened his eyes. His hands tightened on the reins of his hellish horse. Spittle dripped from his sharp, yellow teeth. "Kill them and then resurrect them! Bring their undead bodies to me at the edge of Woodnog Swamp near Fae Barrier Pass!"

Drucis decapitated another demon summoner before it turned to attack.

After the two demons died, the image of the Plague-bringer faded, and then vanished completely.

Boldair knelt beside Wynneffin and ignored the pain pinching his ribcage. She sat slumped with her back against the wall. He carefully slid her helmet off her head. Blood trickled from her nose and down the sides of her mouth. He took her hand in his and squeezed.

"Wynnie," he whispered. He dared a glance at the dwarves fighting the four summoners without any success. He patted her cheek. "Wynnie!"

She didn't respond. He yanked off his plated glove and pressed two fingers to the side of her neck. Her pulse was strong, so she was alive. *When* she'd awaken, he didn't know. *If* she awakened ...

Boldair stood. Saddled with pain and a sudden fear Wynneffin might've sacrificed her life to spare his, he pulled free his other double-edged axe. He twirled each axe in his thick hands, and growled through clenched teeth.

Although he'd openly admitted to Forboud he'd never had much experience with hand-to-hand combat, he was too angry to allow himself to doubt his fighting skills. He was impressed to see these demons dodge each axe and sword attack from his companions and Wynneffin's soldiers. The summoners glided effortlessly and even with attacks coming from multiple sides, they suffered no minor cuts at all. Not an axe or short sword touched them. Their reactions indicated their ability to predict which direction and the timing of each weapon's thrust, so they fought unscathed.

Dwiskter and Drucis were better trained than Boldair, but he refused to be a spectator. He walked slowly and advanced from the closest summoner's blindside that was entangled between two Frosthammer soldiers. It was time to end this invasion before the summoners gained an upper hand and managed to kill them.

FIFTY-ONE

Ignoring his injuries, Boldair rushed the summoner. He approached without any battlecry, which was difficult with the increasing fury inside him.

The demon within Boldair's sights somehow kept dodging the blades of the two Frosthammer soldiers, and slowly wore them down. It moved so swiftly, at times, its appearance was more a blur than a steady image.

To Boldair's advantage, the demon ducked and darted past the dwarves' blades and the occasional swing of their heavy shields, but kept its back to Boldair. Boldair plowed forward. The two Frosthammer soldiers noticed his approach, and slightly backed away from the demon. When it noticed their retreat, it spun a one-hundred-eighty turn, but not fast enough.

Its eyes widened a moment before Boldair pummeled the demon's head with the flat side of his axe. The impact smacked the demon hard enough to send it spiraling through the air. It dropped hard and sprawled on the floor, barely moving. Boldair pressed the edge of his blade against the softness of its throat and forced it to open its eyes and it gasped.

"Fool!" it sputtered. Blue flames flickered on its fingertips.

A guard brought down his short sword in one swift motion and cut off the demon's right hand. It howled in pain, cursed, and writhed. Black blood spilled from its wrist and its urge to cast spells was buried by its pain.

Boldair pressed the pointed tip of the axe head against the demon's throat. "Why's the Plague-bringer going to Woodnog?"

The demon sneered and laughed. "He's already there."

"Why?"

"Why else? Destroying Woodnog unleashes our kindred from the Black Chasm. Mors' plague will consume the living and he'll rule Aetheaon. Only a selected few he'll allow to live, provided their allegiance to him is true."

Boldair frowned. "Tyrann rules the Black Chasm. Not Mors."

"Aetheaon shall belong to Mors. Tyrann will bow to him or die, as will you and your comrades on this day."

"*Not* this day." Boldair pressed the sharp spike through the demon's throat and twisted. "Not *ever*."

The demon's legs twitched and thrashed. When its body no longer moved, Boldair yanked the axe spike free. He nodded to a Frosthammer soldier. He almost grinned with triumph but a cold blast struck the center of his back. He was tossed against the soldier with enough force that both were hurled halfway across the room.

Boldair's axes hit the rock floor and skidded. He and the other dwarf landed hard on their sides and faced one another.

"What was dat?" Boldair asked.

The soldier shrugged. "No idea."

Boldair groaned and pushed himself up. Two Frosthammer dwarves lie facedown on the cavern floor. Neither moved. Blood spilled into circles around their heads. Boldair winced. Most likely, they were dead.

He extended his hand to the dwarf beside him and helped him sit.

"How bad are ya?" Boldair asked.

He shrugged. "I can manage."

Boldair pointed at an altar. It was partially deteriorated, but was high enough to block any magical blasts the summoners could cast. "Can you make it there?"

The dwarf nodded.

"You go first, and I'll try to protect us with my shield," Boldair said. He slid his shield off his back and around until he was able to adjust his left arm in place. He nodded. "Go, now!"

The dwarf crawled until he reached the long side of the sepulcher. Boldair held his shield steadily until they reached the crypt and slinked out of sight.

Another demon howled and fell silent. Drucis laughed. "Ya can't dance and dodge forever."

Boldair risked peering around the side of the crypt to check on Dwiskter and Viorka. Both were trying to get closer to a demon, but neither were having any luck.

Boldair took a deep breath and held his ribs. His armor prevented him from checking his injury. He gritted his teeth. Pressing his back against the crypt, he pushed himself into a slight crouch.

A leathery hand grabbed for his shoulder. The sudden movement forced him to turn. From the crypt an undead creature attempted to pull itself over the side, but its hardened, mummified flesh prevented its joints from bending easily. Mobility was nearly impossible.

Boldair yanked his shoulder out of reach. The undead's hand gripped the air, opened and closed, and blindly tried to grab anything. Boldair hurried to one of his axes. He returned and chopped off the undead corpse's head. The body spasmed.

He returned his attention to where the black carriage had partially materialized. With four summoners dead, and the other two sparring to stay alive, the magical portal no longer existed. Tired and aching, he heaved his heavy axe on his shoulder and walked to where Drucis and Dwiskter tried, unsuccessfully, to strike the summoners with deathblows.

"What? You've returned without inviting us to share in the sport?"

Boldair turned. Yotram smiled broadly. Brandrum and Kairun stood beside Yotram.

Kairun laughed. "You look worse for wear, king."

"Aye, I imagine so."

"We're fresh for battle," Kairun said.

"As am I!" a voice thundered not too far behind them.

They all turned, stunned. King Rigrim stood, dressed in full armor.

He held the Frosthammer in his thick, muscled hands. His amber eyes glowed like fire through the slits of his winged helm.

"Everyone stand back!" he shouted.

Drucis, Dwiskter, and Viorka retreated from the two summoners. Once they were out of Rigrim's line of sight, Rigrim brought the warhammer overhead and slammed it on the cavern floor.

The rocks split apart. Cracks splintered across the floor like icy spider webs. Ice crept from the head of the warhammer straight at the two summoners. They were too stunned to move or contemplate casting any spells. Their eyes fastened on the path of ice. Ice formed around their feet, up their legs, and down their arms. Only the demons' heads remained unfrozen.

King Rigrim marched to them. Fury blazed in his glowing eyes. The demons' eyes widened with greater fear than a demon should ever display. Their jaws shivered from the layers of ice cocooning their bodies and their obvious fear of King Rigrim.

"I sensed demons lurking in Frosthammer," Rigrim said. "Since you're demons, your death will be painfully slow. The ice freezes your flesh to the core. If you were human, you'd already be dead."

The demons opened their mouths to speak, but icy crystals were all that came out.

"Tell me why you're here, and I'll end your life quicker," Rigrim said.

"To re-re-resurrect an army," one demon said.

"Who sent you?"

"M-m-mors," the demon replied.

Rigrim's brow furrowed, and he glanced at Boldair.

Boldair said, "Mors is the Plague-bringer. He's a necromancer, as are these two. But Mors' power is far greater. Had they brought the corpses in these sealed tombs back to life ... Frosthammer would've been destroyed in a matter of days."

Rigrim's jaw tightened. His lips curled in anger. In a swift swing of his warhammer, he shattered the demons' bodies into small frozen bits of frozen flesh. Their heads fell atop the frozen mounds of demon flesh. For several seconds, they blinked. Confusion tightened their brows.

Rigrim set the head of the Frosthammer on the cavern floor and faced Boldair. "I thought you left Frosthammer."

"Aye," Boldair said, nodding. "I had."

"What brought you back so soon?"

"I brought him back." Wynneffin staggered toward them. She rubbed her temples.

"Wynnie!" Boldair said with a broad smile. "You're okay!" He walked to her and braced against her side. She didn't protest and graciously leaned against him. He groaned in pain.

"I'll survive," she said with a half grin.

"Did King Boldair come at his own freewill?" Rigrim asked. "Or—"

Wynneffin shook her head. "I used a bit of deceit and his curiosity lured him back."

"I see," Rigrim said through tight lips. He shook his head with disappointment. "Why the deception?"

Wynneffin sighed. "Father, he knows far more about Mors than I or anyone else in Frosthammer. I sought his help."

"Why didn't you consult me first?" Rigrim asked.

"I've tried before."

"When?"

"Numerous times. You've shrugged it off each time, as if the undeads' presence wasn't a threat. With Boldair's help, we stopped these summoner demons."

"Summoners?" Rigrim asked.

She nodded. "Yes. They were performing a ritual to pull the Plague-bringer inside this chamber. We interrupted it in time, or matters would've become far worse."

Boldair nodded. "Yes, they'd formed a portal. Mors was moments from materializing. He's the reason Glacier Ridge ceases to exist."

"What?" Rigrim asked with a stern expression. His amber eyes flickered. "What happened to Glacier Ridge? Last I heard, Riese was the overseer."

"He was," Drucis said. "But the Plague-bringer appeared in Glacier Ridge. He released pestilence on the town, and I lost me brothers. Damn near lost me own life."

"How do we find Mors?" Rigrim asked. "Is there any way to predict where he might appear next?"

"Usually, no," Boldair said. "But this time, we know where he awaits."

"Where?" Rigrim asked.

Boldair grinned. "Woodnog."

"The Elven city," Rigrim said with bitterness in his tone.

"They're my allies," Boldair said.

Rigrim's brow rose. "Allies? Elves? How could you ever completely trust them?"

Boldair pointed to the Dragon Skull Pendant on his chest. "I fought side-by-side with them at the Battle of Hoffnung. To defeat Mors, we'll need the aid of every race, even if we must set aside our scorn and differences."

Rigrim sighed and a rumbling, low growl came with it. He thought for several moments before nodding his agreement. "It's been ages since I've emerged from our mountain city. I've been a hermit so long dat I've lost touch with the outside world. Have things changed so much?"

"They 'ave," Boldair replied.

"Then it's time." Rigrim placed his hand atop Boldair's shoulder. "Dat my army aids all of Aetheaon by finding and destroying the Plague-bringer."

"Dat would be an incredible army of power," Boldair said.

"Mors must be stopped," Rigrim said. "He tried to invade Frosthammer. Such cannot be ignored. Besides, if you and my daughter set aside your differences for a joint cause, I can ally with other cities and races for a greater purpose."

Wynneffin and Boldair exchanged glances. With her pressed against him, he stared in her eyes. They smiled at one another.

Rigrim laughed. "See? Dat's what I thought. Perhaps our kingdoms will one day join after all."

Boldair almost protested. He and Wynnie had not verbally settled on any proposal and only aided one another to survive.

"Now, Wynnie," Rigrim said. "Since you hastily brought Boldair and his companions to Frosthammer without their consent, you're to accompany his party and scout ahead to Woodnog. It'll take the passing of at least two full moons before my armies are equipped to join the battle. Once you arrive at Woodnog, inform them dat help is on its way."

"Two full moons?" Boldair said. "Mors might be gone by then or have already attacked the city."

Rigrim chuckled. "He'd have to raise an army capable of attacking elves, who are rangers and archers with magic and nature on their side. He'd be a fool to attack with a meager army."

Boldair nodded.

Rigrim faced his guards. "Yotram, Brandrum, and Kairun, accompany Boldair and Wynnie to Woodnog."

They nodded. "Aye."

Boldair sighed.

"Is there a problem?" Rigrim asked.

"Word needs to be sent to Nagdor. I've yet to be coronated. My brother's probably traveling to the city alone. He might tell them I'm dead so he can take the throne. Send word dat I'm alive and I want my best warriors in route to Woodnog."

Rigrim smiled. "Dat I can do. I assure you dat your brother won't protest, and if he does, he'll sorely regret it."

"Send messages to Icevale and Damdur, too. They'll aid our cause."

"Consider it done. The two of you should see a medic before you leave Frosthammer."

"A medic?" Boldair asked.

Rigrim nodded. "You two took a battering."

"Nothing more than I can handle," Boldair said.

Wynneffin nodded. "A headache, father, is all."

"All the same, see a medic," Rigrim said. He grinned at Boldair. "We captured Telsia but the bad news is dat she's not in prison."

"She escaped?" Boldair asked.

"No," Rigrim replied. "She drank a potion before the guards reached her. She died immediately. She poisoned herself."

Sadness filled Wynneffin's eyes. She shook her head and looked away.

"I'm sorry, Wynnie," Boldair said with genuine concern. After the words escaped his lips, he realized his heart ached because of Wynneffin's loss. Even the death of estranged friends hurt.

She shrugged. "It's for the best, isn't it? At least you don't need to worry about her stealing your treasures."

"Her death isn't for the best," Boldair said. "Surely you don't think dat's how I feel. If she could've been taken alive, dat benefited us far more."

Wynnie smiled. "She betrayed both of us, Boldair. I'm sorry I had not seen dat earlier on."

"I'm sorry I overreacted." Boldair took her hand in his.

"The both of ya!" Drucis waved his hand at them as he turned and walked away. "Get a room!"

The dwarves burst into laughter.

Rigrim laughed along with them. "No, they need to see a medic. Preparations need to be made. Woodnog's quite a journey. You'll need mounts, too."

Boldair nodded and looked at Wynneffin. "Aye, your father's right. Let's see what the damage is."

"Perhaps dat's it," Drucis said. "You both got hit in the head too hard. Turned their brains and words to mush. As for me, I prefer stout to mush me brains. Who's for a tankard?"

Dwiskter and the others cheered.

FIFTY-TWO

Since Frost had been left with Forboud after Boldair and his party stepped on the teleport disc and ended up in Frosthammer, Boldair rode Ember along the Lost Pass.

Surprisingly, when Boldair returned to the stables, the dire wolf greeted Boldair with a chuff and wagged his tail with vigor. The wolf licked Boldair's cheek when he came closer. Somehow, Ember had taken a change of heart, possibly due to Burr's brief training. Boldair hoped the wolf's radical new behavior wasn't a ruse.

When Boldair had seen Ember in the stable, his heart sank. A part of him loved the obstinate wolf. He couldn't deny Ember was worthy of being a king's mount. The wolf's temperament was equal to the stubbornness of almost any mule or dwarf. Boldair couldn't fault the wolf for its disdained independence, but he understood keeping the wolf as his mount meant to be on guard for occasional, sudden outbursts.

Burr, the stable-master, didn't offer any argument when Boldair asked to buy the wolf, especially after Ember had tried to maul Burr after he'd snapped the whip one too many times while giving Ember commands.

With his arm in a sling, Burr said he loved the wolf's beauty, but he'd never seen one as strong-willed and ill-tempered as Ember. Burr expressed he'd rather not risk life or limb by keeping the wolf inside the stables. Before the sudden attack, Ember had bred two white furred wolves, and Burr hoped to get a few pups with Ember's unique color.

Boldair chuckled. Perhaps Ember's newfound affection for Boldair was because the wolf *wanted* to ride the steep, cold trails more than being housed inside a stinking stable.

The harsh wind carried sharp, ice shards and sliced snow-snake patterns across the frozen pathway. Boldair covered his face to prevent his eyes and skin from getting cut.

Viorka rearranged her position. She curled beneath the draped bear hide that wrapped her and Boldair. She'd spoken little since Wynneffin joined their group. Boldair thought she seemed jealous. He'd never given any indication he and Wynneffin would reconcile. Since the journey to Woodnog was quite long, perhaps Viorka suspected he and Wynnie would patch their differences. The little cat chose to let her objections be known by her silence.

Wynneffin rode alongside him with Drucis and Dwiskter on their new ram mounts behind them. Wynneffin's soldiers rode in pairs behind them with their shields and weapons ready. At total, they were a dozen strong, which were good odds against traveling caravans or high-waymen, but not if they encountered the Plague-bringer and his minions near cemeteries.

Due to the whipping, freezing wind, none in Boldair's party said much. Their silence caused Boldair to evaluate the length of the treacherously long ride they needed to endure in order to reach Woodnog. Two more days of riding through the Frosted Peaks lie ahead before they reached a warmer climate. Two days in the subzero temperatures seemed an eternity. He sighed.

"Ahoy!" a voice shouted in the wind.

Boldair and the others glanced over their shoulders but saw no one. They searched the cliff sides and then directly overhead. A huge ship glided on the breeze several feet above their heads.

"Do my eyes deceive me?" Drucis rubbed them and looked again. He shook his head. "Nah, I'm past what I drank last night. Probably need a few more tankards *now* though."

"Ice'ik!" Boldair shouted in surprise. He hailed the captain with his right hand.

"Bloody Hell!" Dwiskter said.

"Lay anchor!" Ice'ik shouted. A hearty dwarf tossed an anchor, which dragged along the trail ahead of Boldair and his company.

The anchor uprooted several large trees before finally catching the edge of a heavy boulder with enough weight to stop the ship from flying any farther.

Two dwarves on the deck turned the winch attached to the long anchor chain. Turning the winch steadily lowered the airship until its keel rested on the Lost Pass.

"Where ya headed?" Ice'ik asked from over the ship's rail.

"Woodnog," Boldair replied.

"Woodnog?" Ice'ik frowned. "I thought you were going to Nagdor!"

"Changed agenda," Boldair said.

Ice'ik rubbed his bearded chin. "I see. Hmm. Sounds adventurous. Would you like to fly to Woodnog with us as our official maiden voyage?"

"To get out of this painful cold quicker? You bet. Provided you have room for us and our mounts," Boldair replied.

Ice'ik laughed heartily. "More than plenty of room. Mind you, now, the cost of the flight is dat each of ya have to contribute with the labor. Are ya up to dat?"

They nodded.

"Even the king?"

"Aye!" Boldair said with a fierce grin.

"And a princess!" Wynneffin shouted.

Ice'ik frowned and squinted. "Wynneffin?"

She smiled. "Aye!"

With a confused grin, Ice'ik said, "How unexpected. Ya not afraid to dirty those maiden hand, eh?"

"Not at all," she replied.

"Good. Once the bow door touches the ground, all of ya ride up the ramp."

Boldair studied the ship with curiosity. "Ya never said dat you were building a ship dat could fly."

Ice'ik howled with laughter. "Ya never asked, did ya? What'd ya think? Dat we were going to melt ice and float our way out to sea? There's not enough ice to get us to the closest sea." Ice'ik said with a sly grin. "I'm daft from time to time, but I'm *not* crazy."

"But how?" Boldair asked.

Ice'ik pointed to the oblong balloon floating over the sails. "We tapped into a flow of odd gas. When trapped inside small wineskins, the skins float. Being an engineer, my mind clicked with this grand idea of making a ship dat could float over the land instead of 'aving to sail across the sea. Fabulous idea, eh?"

Boldair nodded. "Indeed!"

Wynneffin grinned and shook her head.

"Ya find dat funny, Princess?" Ice'ik asked.

"No," she replied. "But it answers a lot of questions about your sanity. You're not crazy. You're a genius."

"I'll settle for crazy genius," Ice'ik replied with a wink.

She laughed.

The bow door creaked open. When the top settled on the frozen path, Boldair rode Ember up the steep ramp. The wolf's curiosity and slight fear surprised Boldair. The dire wolf took timid steps walking into the hull.

After a quarter hour, all the mounts were tethered inside feed stalls built by Ice'ik and his team. Ice'ik seemed to have thought about all the possible needs his potential passengers might have.

They lifted anchor. Two crew members changed the direction of the ship's sails. The flying ship rose, turned, but instead of following the frozen path, they flew over the mountain ridge.

Boldair stood beside Wynneffin at the edge of the railing. The world beneath them expanded. The mountains and trees became smaller as the floating ship gained altitude.

Viorka stepped beside Boldair and climbed on the rail, swung her legs over, and sat.

Boldair clutched the railing tightly until his knuckles whitened. "Don't do dat!"

"What?"

"You could fall." He shook his head. "Aren't ya afraid of getting dizzy and falling?"

"Nonsense," she replied. "I'm a fynx. Heights don't bother me, and besides, I have claws. My claws are slightly embedded in the wood."

"Well, unless ya are capable of sprouting wings, it's a daring thing you're doing," Boldair said.

"Look at dat." Wynneffin pointed and her voice rose in awe.

Boldair looked to where she pointed. The white mountainside and ice covered trees changed into lighter whites and then various shades of green as they crossed the descending slope.

The wind whistled harshly and caused the dwarves' thickly knotted beards to ruffle like the sails.

Boldair shook his head in wonder, having never seen Aetheaon from overhead. He had ridden on Taniesse's back a few times, but she'd never flown much higher than the treetops. The changing terrain below was stunning, but nothing compared to what they noticed before they left the Frosted Peaks.

Roars captured their attention. Then they spotted the magnificent Frost Dragons soaring over the peaks. The dragons almost seemed to be escorting the ship from the Frosted Peaks. And perhaps they were, because the moment the ship left the frozen mountains and drifted over massive green conifers, these dragons lofted and suspended themselves in place for several moments before diving and turning back. The scaled giants glided in unmatched beauty.

Boldair sighed. Tears burned his eyes.

Wynneffin cautiously placed her hand atop his, perhaps fearful he'd yank it away and embarrass her, but Boldair liked her hand resting there. She faced him. "What's troubling you?"

His jaw tightened, and his cheeks reddened. "Look at all dat beauty for as far as we can see."

"Glorious," she said softly.

"Aye. All the more reason to not allow the Plague-bringer to defeat us. If he destroys the City of Woodnog, his power increases, and being dat Woodnog is beside the Black Chasm, those two cities combined can't be stopped."

"We won't allow it to 'appen," Wynneffin said.

"You bet we won't," Dwiskter said with a growl rolling in his voice. "I'd 'ave stopped him on the Hoffnung Docks had he not vanished."

Ice'ik rolled a large barrel to the center of the deck, hammered a spigot into its side, and motioned everyone. "The ship successfully left the Frosted Peaks and we're all alive. Let's celebrate!"

Boldair frowned. "You didn't expect to get this far?"

Ice'ik shrugged. "Bah! Who knew? Eh? It's not called a maiden voyage for nothing. Never had a chance to test the kinks, either. So drink up!"

A crew member brought a crate of tankards and set them beside the barrel.

The dwarves cheered.

Ice'ik laughed. "Drink plenty. I've dozens of barrels below deck dat we might need to empty soon."

"Why's dat?" Boldair asked.

Ice'ik rubbed his eyes for several moments. His face flushed with embarrassment, and he laughed with slight nervousness. "We might've already had a problem and don't know dat it can be rectified."

"What sort of problem?" Drucis wiped the froth off his beard and mouth.

"Dat gas in the balloon," he replied, pointing.

"Yeah?" Boldair and Drucis asked in harmony.

"An odd thing occurred dat I had no foresight in expecting."

"What's dat?" Wynneffin asked.

"Seems dat now we're in warmer air ... we keep rising. It wasn't like dat in the frigid air. But now, we keep climbing," Ice'ik said. "Don't know how to lower it."

"Ya can't get us down?" Boldair asked.

Ice'ik pointed at the tankard. "Don't get all rigid on me, King of Nagdor. Down a tankard or two while I try to figure this out."

Dwiskter studied the large air-tank above the sails. He pointed. "Were the ropes tied around the balloon that tightly?"

Ice'ik shook his head and frowned. "The balloon's swelling."

Dwiskter nodded. "If ya don't stop its growing size, it's going to rupture. And if it does, I don't care how good your sails are, we'll crash."

Ice'ik motioned a dwarf at the top of one highest mast. "Release some of the gas from the balloon. But don't release all of it!"

The dwarf did as commanded. After several minutes, the balloon shrank and the ship steadily lowered.

Boldair sighed with relief. "I think I'll get a tankard or *three*."

Ice'ik laughed nervously. "How was I supposed to know dat would happen? No one else has fashioned such a ship to my knowledge. Some inventions cost lives before they become successful."

"Might I take back my *genius* complement?" Wynneffin asked.

Ice'ik's face withered. "We're not dead."

"*Yet*." Drucis stood and waited to fill his tankard again.

"All's going fine," Boldair said. "Let's not give our captain and host grief. Thanks for your hospitality, Ice'ik, and for giving us a quicker route to Woodnog."

———

One day in flight passed rather quickly. The airship didn't suffer any further mishaps. The most frightening ordeal, which was even greater than the possibility of the balloon rupturing was when the ship flew within sight of the Black Chasm.

The purplish-black veil prevented anyone from seeing what was beneath this unusual atmosphere. It wasn't composed of clouds, but lightning and thunder were present nonetheless. The most worrisome thing was not knowing what lie beneath the rolling cloud-like wall, which seemed an entity in itself. Again Boldair recalled the strange long tendrils that had reached out of the chasm, grabbed soldiers, and killed them within seconds. What other ominous horrors existed below?

Apparently, Ice'ik was disturbed by the swirling black mass and fearful for the airship to pass through. At his order, the ship diverted southwest to fly outside its range.

Boldair and his companions couldn't take their eyes off the chasm. He continued wondering what forces lie in wait. He couldn't shake the sensation of being watched. He held no doubt that if the ship flew into the chasm's territory, something horrible would attack. Twice, black wings poked through the clouds and then disappeared.

Less than an hour later, Ice'ik and his crew released more gas from the giant balloon and lowered the ship slowly over the swampy territory of Woodnog, which was directly south of the great City of Woodnog. Upon descent, Ice'ik and his crew lowered thick rope ladders. Because of the forked trees, they couldn't land on the ground. To unload their mounts, some trees needed to be cut.

After the ladders rolled out and touched the soggy ground, Boldair and the others noticed several horsemen approaching on the miry road. As close as these horsemen were, Ice'ik couldn't possibly get the ship to rise before these riders reached them. If they were Elven archers, rising wouldn't matter. They'd easily puncture the balloon with a hail of arrows. Repairing the balloon would not be an easy venture.

Boldair and Wynneffin exchanged puzzled glances. Dwiskter and Drucis pulled their weapons and stepped to the airship's rail.

Boldair's eyes widened with sudden recognition. He knew two of the riders: Roble and Lehrling. Boldair turned toward the others. "Allies, my friends."

"Allies?" Dwiskter frowned and squinted to better see.

"Aye, Sir Roble and Sir Lehrling. Fellow Dragon Skull Knights," Boldair said. He waved his hand widely overhead. "Let's go greet them!"

FIFTY-THREE

Boldair, Wynneffin, Drucis, Dwiskter, and Viorka hurried down the rope ladder while Ice'ik instructed his crew to trim back the branches of several trees, so they could land the airship.

Boldair grinned and hurried to greet Roble and Lehrling. Shawndirea, in faery form, sat on Roble's shoulder.

"What brings you to this discarded muddy excuse of a road?" Boldair asked.

"We've scoured the Woodnog swamps for days. I could ask the same question of you." Roble offered his hand to Boldair. Boldair shook it eagerly.

Shawndirea looked at the airship with sheer fascination. "A flying ship?"

"Ice'ik's invention. Got us 'ere in less than a day from the Frosted Peaks," Boldair replied. "Why are ya here? Have ya come to help defeat the Plague-bringer?"

Roble nodded. His gaze was even. "That's why you're here?"

"Aye." Boldair nodded. "King Rigrim's gathering his troops and preparing to dispatch them to join the war."

"King Rigrim?" Shawndirea asked. "Of Frosthammer?"

"Aye."

"The city still exists?" she asked.

Wynneffin nodded. "It does."

"She's Rigrim's daughter," Boldair said.

"I see," Shawndirea replied. "For generations we believed your Dwarven race was no more."

"As have the other kingdoms in Aetheaon, I'm sure," Wynneffin replied.

"So you learned of the Plague-bringer from Boldair?" she asked.

"In part," Wynneffin replied. "But, we've encountered undead wandering the lowest levels of our city. Boldair and his party, along with some of my guards, helped destroy the summoning demons attempting to teleport Mors into The Sepulchers of Twilight. A few million are buried there."

"Millions?" Lehrling scratched his short beard.

"If it weren't for Boldair's aid," Wynneffin said, "Frosthammer would've been destroyed and our numbers would've joined the undead armies."

"I'm afraid that threat hasn't lessened," a voice said from the darkly shadowed swamp trees. He stepped forward with a gnarled staff. A silver crystal, a black crystal, and a ruby-red crystal were fashioned into an orb clutched inside the tight gnarled roots of the staff.

"Zauber?" Roble asked in surprise.

Zauber offered a slight bow and a haunted grin. "I traced Mors' emergence somewhere near the outskirts of the City of Woodnog."

"Since Woodnog's shrouded by magic, he can't enter the city, can he?" Roble asked.

"To those unfamiliar with magic, the city's always hidden," the wizard replied. "To someone with death and darkness and the ability to raise a fleet of undead ... Mors won't have trouble locating Woodnog's hidden gates."

Galloping horses approached from the Barrier Pass between Woodnog's forests and the Black Chasm. Roble and Lehrling drew their swords. Boldair and the dwarves readied their axes.

"Allies, my friends." Zauber raised his hand. A blue raven landed on his hand. Zauber brought the raven closer and stroked its feathers. "I've sent word to all the Dragon Skull Knights and the kings of the other kingdoms, in hopes we can destroy Mors once and for all."

When the three horses came into sight, the riders were Lady Dawn, Sir Caen, and Odlon. Surprise registered on their faces when they noticed the airship and the party of dwarves. They studied the ship with intense interest.

Zauber smiled. "Right on time."

Boldair frowned. "How is it dat you knew Mors was coming to Woodnog before the lot of us knew? Magic's one thing, but predicting the future ... bah! No wizard can do dat! And yet, here you are."

Zauber smiled. "You're right, young king. I cannot predict the future but I've an ally who can. She's the one who showed me the pestilence Aetheaon will suffer should we fail to stop Mors in Woodnog. If he shatters the magical veil of Fae Barrier Pass, the Black Chasm will consume everything the elves hold sacred. After that, the swamps of Woodnog will give up their dead at Mors' command. Most likely, his massive army will travel south and destroy Oculoth before resurrecting them into undead soldiers. Nothing shall stop his reign if he succeeds."

"We're the last hope before worse things befall Aetheaon?" Roble asked.

Zauber's eyes narrowed. "Yes."

"That's quite a burden to carry," Roble said.

Intrigued, Zauber rubbed his chin and approached Roble. "There's something ... different about you, Overlander. You're veiled by protective magic, but not the faery's. Not the magic of any Fae. Be careful what magic you draw upon for protection." His eyes flicked to Shawndirea. She glanced away. "You know what the magic it is, don't you?"

"Yes," she replied. "I've offered the same warning."

"As have I," Lehrling said, somewhat frustrated. "Like any human from the Overlands, he's too stubborn to heed our advice."

"Overlander," Zauber said, "while dark magic can protect you, it comes at a price. Sometimes a greater price than you're willing to pay."

"I know," Roble replied.

Zauber looked amused. "Do you now? Tell me where you received this protection."

"We don't have time for the full details," Roble replied.

"Actually, we do. Because if there's one thing we cannot afford, it's for a bumbling fool to give Mors forewarning of our arrival. If I can sense this strange dark magic enchanting you, so can he. I insist you tell us where you got this blessing and whom it was that gave it to you!"

Boldair rolled a log from the edge of the muddy pathway. "This sounds like it shall take some time. Might as well sit. Ice'ik, ya 'ave another barrel of stout you could spare? I'll pay ya for it."

Ice'ik nodded.

"Drinks all around," Boldair said.

The dwarves cheered, but Lady Dawn, Caen, and the others were less celebratory. Boldair shook his head and grinned at Roble and Shawndirea, "Every dwarf knows dat tales are much *better* with several tankards of stout. Now, Overlander, tell the tale. Your audience awaits."

THE END

Read Roble's tale in Shadowfae (Aetheaon Chronicles: Book Four).

About the Author

Leonard D. Hilley II grew up a quiet, shy kid with an inquisitive mind. Learning to read at an early age, he fell in love with books. He read every book he could get his hands on and stacks of dark comics about ghosts, monsters, and creepy things that stalk the night.

Like a lot of boys, he caught beetles, wooly bears, butterflies, and had an ant farm. When he was ten, his interests in science increased even more after seeing a local college professor's insect collection. Soon, he set out on his quest to build his own collection. He learned to rear butterflies and moths to obtain perfect specimens. He learned botany, gardening, and set his goal to become an entomologist.

At eleven, he watched the original Star Wars on the big screen. His imagination soared. Soon after, he discovered Roger Zelazny's Chronicles of Amber. Six months later, he had written the first draft of a novel. A novel he discarded, but the characters stuck with him. Years later, these characters came to life in Shawndirea, which Hilley intended to be a prequel novella for Devils Den. The characters, however, refused to be ignored and took the opportunity to unveil Aetheaon in their first epic fantasy. Lady Squire was quick to follow.

Shawndirea was Hilley's farewell to butterfly collecting, and those who have read the novel understand why. He has taken Ray Bradbury's advice to heart: "Follow the characters." He does. He follows, listens, and take notes—often never knowing where they're going to take him, but he's never been disappointed in the results.

Hilley earned a B.S. in Biology and an MFA in Creative Writing to combine his love of science and writing.

Sci-fi Titles: Predators of Darkness: Aftermath, Beyond the Darkness, The Game of Pawns, Death's Valley, The Deimos Virus.

Epic Fantasy: Shawndirea (Aetheaon Chronicles: Book One), Lady Squire (Aetheaon Chronicles: Book Two), Frosthammer (Aetheaon Chronicles: Book Three), Shadowfae (Aetheaon Chronicles: Book Four), and Devils Den.

UF/PR: Succubus: Shadows of the Beast (Nocturnal Trinity Series: Book One), Raven (Nocturnal Trinity Series: Book Two), A Touch of the Familiar

YA UF/Paranormal: Forrest Wollinsky Vampire Hunter; Forrest Wollinsky: Blood Mists of London; Forrest Wollinsky: Predestined Crossroads.

www.ingramcontent.com/pod-product-compliance
Lightning Source LLC
Chambersburg PA
CBHW060225030726
47499CB00004B/1197